BLADE BREAKER

ALSO BY VICTORIA AVEYARD

Realm Breaker

Red Queen
Glass Sword
King's Cage
War Storm
Broken Throne: A Red Queen Collection
Red Queen: The Official Coloring Book

Digital Novellas
Queen Song
Steel Scars

Novella Collection
Cruel Crown

BLADE BREAKER

VICTORIA AVEYARD

An Imprint of HarperCollins*Publishers*

HarperTeen is an imprint of HarperCollins Publishers.

Blade Breaker
Copyright © 2022 by Victoria Aveyard
Map art by Francesca Baraldi
Map © & ™ 2022 Victoria Aveyard. All rights reserved.
All rights reserved. Printed in the United States of America. No part of this book may be used or reproduced in any manner whatsoever without written permission except in the case of brief quotations embodied in critical articles and reviews. For information address HarperCollins Children's Books, a division of HarperCollins Publishers, 195 Broadway, New York, NY 10007.
www.epicreads.com

Library of Congress Control Number: 2022931760
ISBN 978-0-06-287266-1 — ISBN 978-0-06-325344-5 (special ed)

Typography by Jenna Stempel-Lobell
22 23 24 25 26   PC/LSCH   10 9 8 7 6 5 4 3 2
❖
First Edition

To those who bend but never break

BLADE BREAKER

1

NO CHOICE BUT DEATH
Corayne

The voice echoed as if down a long passage, distant and fading, difficult to make out. But it shuddered within her, a sound as much as a feeling. She felt it in her spine, her ribs, every bone. Her own heartbeat pounded in time with the terrible voice. It spoke no words she knew, but still, Corayne understood its anger.

His anger.

Dimly, Corayne wondered if this was death, or simply another dream.

The roar of What Waits called to her through the darkness, clinging even as warm hands pulled her back to the light.

Corayne sat up, blinking, gasping for breath, the world rushing back around her. She found herself sitting in water up to her chest. It rippled, a dirty mirror reflecting the oasis town.

The Nezri oasis had been beautiful once, filled with green

palms and cool shade. The sand dunes were a golden band around the horizon. The kingdom of Ibal stretched in every direction, with the red cliffs of the Marjeja to the south, the waves of the Aljer and the Long Sea to the north. Nezri was a pilgrim town, built around sacred waters and a temple to Lasreen, its buildings white and green-tiled, its streets wide enough for the desert caravans.

Now those wide streets were choked with corpses, coiled serpent bodies, and broken soldiers. Corayne fought back a wave of revulsion but continued to look, her eyes passing through the debris. She searched for the Spindle, a golden thread spitting a torrent of water and monsters.

But nothing stood in its place. Not even an echo.

No memory of what existed a moment before. Only the broken columns and shattered causeway remained in testament to the kraken. And, Corayne realized, the bloody ruin of a tentacle, cut neatly from the monster as it was forced back into its own realm. It lay among the puddles like a fallen old tree.

She swallowed hard and nearly gagged. The water tasted of rot and death and the Spindle, gone but for a fading echo like a ringing in her ears. She tasted blood too. The blood of Gallish soldiers, the blood of sea serpents from another realm. And, of course, her own. So much blood Corayne felt she might drown in it.

But I am a pirate's daughter, she thought, heart pounding. Her mother, the bronzed and beautiful Meliz an-Amarat, grinned in her mind's eye.

We do not drown.

"Corayne—" a voice said, shockingly gentle.

She looked up to find Andry standing over her. The blood was on him too, smeared across his tunic and the familiar blue star.

A jolt of panic shot through Corayne as she searched his face, his limbs, looking for some terrible wound. She remembered Andry fighting hard, a knight as much as any of the soldiers he slew. After a moment, she knew the blood was not his own. Sighing, she felt some tightness lift from her shoulders.

"Corayne," Andry said again, his hand working into hers.

Without thought, she tightened her grip on his fingers, and forced herself to stand on shaking legs. His eyes shone with concern.

"I'm fine," Corayne bit out, feeling the opposite.

Even as she caught her balance, her mind spun, the last few moments washing over her. *The Spindle, the serpents, the kraken. Valtik's spell, Dom's rage. My own blood on the edge of the sword.* She sucked down another gasp of air, trying to center herself.

Andry kept his hand on her shoulder, ready to catch her should she fall.

Corayne would not.

She straightened her spine. Her gaze flew to the Spindleblade, submerged in half a foot of corrupted water, gleaming with shadow and sunlight. The current moved over the sword until the steel itself seemed to dance. The old language of a realm long lost ran the length of the sword, etched into the metal. Corayne couldn't read the letters, nor pronounce the words. As always, their meaning lay just beyond her grasp.

Then her hand plunged into the water, closing on the hilt of the Spindleblade. The sword splashed free, cold and dripping. Her heart faltered. There was no blood on the sword, not anymore. But she could still see it. The kraken, the serpents. And the Gallish soldiers, dead by her own hand. Mortal lives ended, cut in half like the Spindle.

She tried not to think of the men she'd killed. Their faces came anyway, haunting in her memory.

"How many?" she said, her voice trailing off. Corayne didn't expect Andry to understand the broken musings of her mind.

But pain crossed his face, a pain she knew. He looked beyond her, to the bodies in green and gold. He shut his eyes and bowed his head, hiding his face from the desert sun.

"I don't know," he replied. "I will not count."

I have never seen a heart break before, Corayne thought, watching Andry Trelland. He wore no wounds, but she knew he bled within. Once he was a squire of Galland who dreamed of becoming a knight. *And now he is a killer of them, a killer of his own dreams.*

For once, words failed Corayne an-Amarat, and she turned away to stand alone.

Her eyes roved over their surroundings, taking in the destruction fanning out from the center of the town. The oasis felt eerily quiet after the battle. Corayne almost expected some echo to remain, the cry of a kraken or a serpent's hiss.

She could hear the old witch Valtik as she wandered through the limestone ruins, humming to herself, skipping like a child. Corayne watched her bend a few times, collecting fangs from the serpent corpses. There were already a few teeth braided into her long gray hair. She was her strange, bewildering self again, just an old woman puttering around. But Corayne knew better. Only moments ago the Jydi woman and her rhymes had driven the kraken back, clearing a path for Corayne and the Spindleblade. There was deep power in the witch, but if Valtik cared or even remembered, she did not show it.

Either way, Corayne was glad to have her.

The Ibalet sun continued to rise, hot against Corayne's back. And then suddenly cool, as a long shadow fell over her.

She looked up, her face falling.

Domacridhan, immortal prince of Iona, was red from eyebrows to toes, painted in swaths of blood. His once-fine tunic and cloak were ruined, torn and stained. His pale skin looked rusted, his golden hair gone to fire. Only his eyes remained clear, white and emerald green, burning like the sun above him. His greatsword all but dangled from his fist, threatening to fall.

He heaved a rattling breath.

"Are you well, Corayne?" Dom said, his voice grinding and strangled.

Corayne balked. "Are *you*?"

A muscle flexed in his jaw.

"I must make myself clean," he murmured, bending to the water. Red clouds bloomed from his skin.

It will take more than that, Corayne wanted to say. *For all of us. All of us.*

Corayne jolted, a sudden shock of panic arcing through her. Her eyes darted, searching the town for the rest of the Companions, heart in her teeth. *Charlie, Sigil, Sorasa.* She did not hear or see them, and fear churned in her gut. *So many lost today. Gods, don't let us lose them too.* As much as her own sins weighed in her mind, their lives weighed more.

Before Corayne could call out, yell their names across the oasis, a man groaned.

She snapped to the sound, Andry and Dom flanking her like guards.

Corayne exhaled when she saw the Gallish soldier.

He was wounded, crawling through the water now steadily draining into the sand. His green cloak weighed him down, slowing his progress as he slithered forward, pawing through the mud. Blood bubbled from his lips, his only words a gurgle.

Lasreen comes for him, Corayne thought, naming the death goddess. *And she is not the only one.*

Sorasa Sarn abandoned her shadows, stepping into the light with the grace of a dancer and the focus of a falcon. She was not as bloody as Dom, but her tattooed hands and bronze dagger dripped scarlet. Her eyes fixed on the soldier's back, never wavering as she followed him.

"Still alive, Sigil?" she said, calling out to the bounty hunter. Her manner was easy even as she stalked a dying man across the town center.

A hearty laugh and a scuffle of feet answered from a nearby rooftop. Sigil's broad frame appeared, wrestling with a Gallish soldier in broken armor. He raised a knife, but Sigil caught his wrist with a grin.

"The iron bones of the Countless will never be broken," she laughed, snapping his hold. The knife fell and she hoisted him over her shoulder. He wailed in opposition, fists beating against her leather armor. "You cannot say the same."

It was not far to fall, only two stories, but the water was shallow. He broke his neck with a wet crack.

Corayne did not flinch. She'd seen far worse today. Slowly, she blew out a breath, steadying herself.

As if summoned, Charlie stepped out into the street. His eyes fell on the body, his face devoid of emotion.

"Into the hands of mighty Syrek go you, son of Galland, son of war," the fallen priest said, bending over the body.

He brushed his ink-stained fingers through the water, touching the soldier's unseeing eyes. Corayne realized Charlie was giving him as close to a godly burial as he could offer.

When Charlie stood again, his face was blank and pale, his long hair free from its usual braid.

Alive. All of them.

All of us.

Relief surged through Corayne's body, swiftly followed by exhaustion. She flagged a little, her knees going weak.

Andry moved quickly, bracing his hands against her shoulders.

"It's all right," he said softly.

His touch was almost electrifying, hot and cold all at once. She jumped away and shook her head.

"I will not mourn them," she muttered sharply. "I will not mourn men who would have killed us. You shouldn't mourn them either."

Andry's face tightened, his lips threatening a scowl. Corayne had never seen anger on Andry Trelland, not like this. Even the shadow of it stung.

"I cannot do that, Corayne," he bit out, turning away.

Corayne followed his gaze, a flush of shame crossing her cheeks. Andry looked back to Charlie, now making his way through the dead, blessing the Gallish corpses. Then his eyes went to the soldier crawling through the muck.

The Amhara stalked him still.

"Gods damn you, show some mercy, Sorasa," the squire barked. "Give him an ending."

The assassin did not break her gaze. She was trained too well to take her eyes off an enemy, even one so wounded. "You may do as you like, Trelland. I won't stop you."

Andry's throat bobbed, his brown skin bare above the collar of his tunic. His fingers grazed the sword at his side.

"Don't," Corayne said, grabbing his bicep. The flesh felt hard beneath her fingers, tight as wound rope. "Don't give this man mercy if it means losing another piece of yourself."

Andry did not answer, but his brow furrowed and his face grew grim. Gently, he shrugged Corayne away and drew his sword.

"Andry—" she began, moving to stop him.

Then a ripple went through the water and something splashed, its skin coiling and scaly.

Corayne froze, heart pounding.

The serpent was alone, but still deadly.

Sorasa stopped in her prowl, drawing up short. She watched with her glowing tiger eyes as it unhinged its jaw and took the soldier's head in its mouth. Corayne could not help but be darkly fascinated, her lips parting as the serpent ended the soldier.

It was Dom who finished them both, his greatsword cutting through scale and skin.

He leveled a glare at Sorasa but she only shrugged, waving him off with a swipe of one red hand.

Corayne turned away, shaking her head at the two of them.

Andry was already gone, his footsteps squelching through the wet sand.

While Sorasa and Sigil searched the oasis for survivors, the rest of them waited on the outskirts of the town, where stone road gave over to sand. Corayne sat on a windblown rock, thanking the gods for the blissful shade of a few palm trees. Somehow she was grateful for the heat too. It felt cleansing.

The others were silent, the only sound the two horses pawing the ground. Andry kept to the sand mares, brushing them down, tending to them as best he could with what little he had. Corayne knew by now it was his way of coping, to lose himself in a task he knew. A task from his old life.

She winced, eyeing the squire and the mares. There were only two horses left, and only one of them still had a saddle.

"The Spindle fought hard," Dom muttered, following her gaze.

"But we're alive, and the Spindle is closed," Corayne answered. Her lips pulled into a tight smile. "We can do this. We can *keep* doing this."

Slowly Dom nodded, but his face remained grim. "There will be more portals to close. More enemies and monsters to fight."

There was fear in the immortal. It flashed behind his eyes,

drawn up from some memory. Corayne wondered if it was her own father Dom thought of, his body broken before the temple. Or something else, something deep in the centuries, from the time beyond mortal reckoning.

"Taristan will not be defeated so easily," Dom murmured.

"Neither will What Waits." Just mentioning the hellish god put a chill in Corayne's skin, even against the desert heat. "But we'll fight them. We have to. There is *no* other choice."

The immortal nodded forcefully. "No choice for us, or for the realm."

It was past noon, the sun high, by the time Sigil and Sorasa rejoined them. The bounty hunter cleaned her ax as they walked, the assassin her dagger.

The oasis was empty of all enemies.

The Companions were the last ones living.

Charlie followed the women, half-bent, massaging his lower back. *Too many bodies to bless,* Corayne knew, glancing away. She refused to think of them. Instead she glared into the hard sheen of the desert, at the miles of sand. Then she looked north. The Aljer was close, a gleaming ribbon where the great gulf opened into the Long Sea. It was lightning in her blood.

What next? she wondered, feeling equal parts thrill and fear.

She eyed their number, sizing them up. Dom had washed as best he could, and slicked back his wet hair from his face. He'd exchanged his ruined shirt for what he could find in the abandoned homes and shops. He looked like a patchwork of different places, with an Ibalet tunic and embroidered vest over his old breeches. His boots and cloak of Iona remained, scrubbed with sand. Though the cloak was half ruined, the antlers were still there, embroidered at its edges. A little piece of home he refused to give up.

Corayne wished for her own tattered blue cloak, long since lost. It used to smell of oranges and olive groves, and something deeper, a memory she could no longer name.

"The danger has passed, Corayne," Dom said, watching the village like a dog hunting for a scent. Or listening for trouble. He found neither.

Indeed, the waters of Meer, the realm beyond the Spindle, had drained back into the sand or burned away beneath the fierce sun of Ibal. Only puddles remained in the shade, too shallow for serpents to hide in. The lucky ones were already gone, following the short-lived river downhill to the sea. The rest cooked in the streets, their slick skin cracked and drying.

As for the soldiers, Sorasa and Sigil had already put any enemies to their final rest.

Corayne pursed her lips at Dom. Her chest still felt tight. Her heart still ached.

"Not for long," she answered, feeling the truth of it in her belly. "This is far from over."

Her words echoed over the outskirts, a heavy curtain to hang over them all.

"I wonder what happened to the villagers," Andry mused, grasping for something to say.

"Would you like my honest opinion?" Sorasa answered, striding into the palm trees.

"No," he was all too quick to reply.

Though he was a young man, Charlie groaned like an old crone as he rejoined them. His red, burned face peered out of his hood.

"Well," he said, glancing between the carnage and the ferocious sun above, "I would prefer not to stay here any longer."

Sorasa leaned back against a palm tree with a smirk. Her teeth flashed white against bronze skin. She pointed back to the oasis with her dagger.

"But we just finished cleaning up," she replied.

Next to her, Sigil folded her great arms, her ax stowed away on her back. She nodded in agreement, pushing a lock of raven hair out of her eyes. A burst of sunlight filtered through the trees, dappling her copper skin, making her black eyes gleam.

"We should rest a while," Sigil said. "There's no danger in ghosts."

Charlie quirked a grin. "The iron bones of the Countless can't break, but can they get tired?"

"Never," the bounty hunter snapped back, flexing.

Corayne fought the urge to scoff. Instead she drew herself up, sitting straighter in the shade. To her surprise, all eyes flew to her. Even Valtik, counting serpent fangs, looked up from her work.

The combined weight of their eyes fell heavy on already-weary shoulders. Corayne tried to think of her mother, of her voice upon the deck. Unyielding, unafraid.

"We should keep moving," she said.

Dom's low rumble answered. "Do you have a destination, Corayne?"

Immortal as he was, one of the ancient Elders, he seemed exhausted.

Corayne's confidence faltered and she picked at her stained sleeve. "Somewhere without a massacre," she finally offered. "Word *will* get back to Erida and Taristan. We must keep moving."

A chuckle escaped Sorasa's lips. "Word from *who*? Dead men don't carry news, and there's only dead men behind us."

Red and white flashed behind Corayne's eyes, a memory as much as a physical presence. She swallowed, fighting back the dreams that plagued her more and more. They were no longer a mystery. *What Waits*, she knew. *Can he see me now? Does he watch us? Is he following me wherever I go—and will Taristan follow too?* The questions overwhelmed her, their paths too fearsome to follow.

"Even so." Corayne forced her voice to turn to steel, channeling a bit of her mother's strength. "I'd like to use whatever head start we have to get away from this place."

"Only one gone." Valtik's voice was a scratch of nails on ice, her eyes a vibrant and impossible blue. She shoved fangs into the pouch at her waist. "We must keep on."

Despite the Jydi witch's constant and insufferable rhyming, Corayne felt a smile rise to her lips.

"At least you aren't entirely useless," she said warmly, dipping her head to the old woman. "That kraken would be terrorizing the Long Sea by now if not for you, Valtik."

A murmur of agreement went through the others, except for Andry. His eyes trailed over the witch, but they were far away. *Still with the Gallish bodies*, Corayne knew. She wanted to tear the sadness right out of his chest.

"Care to explain exactly *what* you did to the sea monster of another realm?" Sorasa said, angling a dark eyebrow. Her dagger slid home in its sheath.

Valtik didn't reply, happily rearranging her braids, plaited with fangs and old lavender.

"Suppose krakens hate her rhyming too," Sigil replied, chuckling through a crooked smile.

Charlie smirked in the shade. "We should recruit a bard next. Really round out this band of fools and sing the rest of Taristan's monsters back home."

If only it were so simple, Corayne wanted to say, knowing it was not. But even so, hope fluttered in her chest, weak but still alive.

"We might be a band of fools," she said, half for herself, "but we closed a Spindle."

Her hands balled into fists and she stood, legs strong beneath her. Determination replaced her fear.

"And we can do it again," she said. "As Valtik said, we must keep on. I say we go. Head north to the Long Sea, hug the coast until we reach a village."

Sorasa opened her mouth to argue, but Dom cut her off, rising to his feet at Corayne's side. His eyes were on the southern horizon, finding the red line of the Marjeja and the once-flooded plain of gold.

Corayne turned to smile up at him, but stopped short at the sight of his face.

Sorasa saw the fear in him too. She flew to his side, shading her eyes to match his stare. After a long moment of searching, she gave up and turned back to the immortal, glaring up at his stone-blank face.

"What is it?" she bit out, breath ragged through her teeth.

Sigil's hand went to her ax and Andry roused from his dreamlike sorrow, whirling from the horses. Charlie cursed down at his feet.

"Dom?" A swoop of terror dropped in Corayne's stomach as she abandoned her shade. She eyed the horizon too but found the glare of sun and sand unbearable.

At last the immortal sucked in a gasp of air.

"Forty riders on dark horses. Their faces are covered, their robes black, made for the heat."

Sorasa kicked at the sand, hissing to herself.

"They carry a flag. Royal blue and gold. And—silver too."

With a will, Corayne racked her memory, trying to remember what those colors meant.

The assassin knew.

"Outriders of the court," she snapped, looking for all the world like she might breath fire. There was fear too, hiding behind her frustration. Corayne saw it glimmer in her tiger eyes. "Hunters for the King of Ibal."

Corayne bit her lip. "Will they help us?"

Sorasa's hollow laugh was brutal. "They're more likely to sell you to Erida, or use you as some bargaining chip. You're the most valuable thing in in all the Ward, Corayne. And the King of Ibal is not a fool with his treasure."

"What if they aren't after Corayne?" Charlie piped in, his face drawn in thought.

Sorasa's eyes narrowed, some doubt clouding her face. Whatever words she wanted to say died in her throat.

"I will take Corayne and the blade," Dom said heavily, turning from the horizon. Before Corayne could protest, she found herself in the saddle of a sand mare. Dom mounted up on the only other horse, ignoring the lack of saddle. The Elder did not need one.

Corayne sputtered, fighting the reins being pressed into her hands. To her surprise, Andry appeared at her knee, tightening the girth of the saddle. His fingers closed on her ankle, forcing her foot into a stirrup.

"Andry—stop it. Dom!" she protested, kicking her boot free. She made to slide off the mare's back, but Andry held her firmly in place, his lips set in a grim, unyielding line.

"We're not abandoning you," Corayne said, half wild.

The Elder grabbed for the bridle of Corayne's horse as he tugged his own mare's mane, forcing both mounts along. "We have no choice."

"You have no choice but to wait, Elder." Sorasa remained still, but her voice carried fiercely. She put her back to the horizon. Over her shoulder, the dark riders appeared out of the gleaming line where plain met sky. "The outriders of the king have no equal on sand or road. You might outlast them for a day, maybe. But even *you* will be run down, and an ocean of blood spilled for nothing."

Dom snarled as if he might run her through. "The coast is less than a day's ride, Sarn."

"And then what? You wish to face the king's navy instead?" Sorasa scoffed.

Corayne could not help but agree. The Ibalet fleets were unmatched.

"You don't even know which direction to go," Sorasa added, casting a hand at the distant bay and Long Sea beyond. "But be my guest."

It was Andry who growled, the anger in him taking Corayne aback.

"So it's no choice but death, then?" he said, brow set with fury. Even in battle she had never seen him so enraged—and so hopeless. "For Corayne, for the Ward?"

Sorasa barely batted an eye, crossing her arms over her chest. There was dried blood under her fingernails, gone to rust.

"No one said anything about them killing *you*, Squire," she answered wearily. "Me, I'm a marked Amhara. Might not fare so well."

"Uh, wanted fugitive here!" Charlie piped in, raising a finger.

Sorasa's braid snapped like a whip as she turned her head, sneering at the Madrentine forger. "The Ibalet king hardly gives a shit about some errant priest with nice penmanship."

He recoiled into his robes. "Gods willing."

"Then *you* go," Corayne offered, trying to dismount again. Andry remained firm, blocking her way. "Run. It's us they want."

The assassin waved away the offer with her usual smirk, as good as any mask.

"I'll take my chances with the outriders. You'll certainly need me too," she added, gesturing to Dom still glowering in the saddle. "I don't expect this one to be negotiating anytime soon."

Corayne set her teeth, feeling the familiar sting of frustration. "Sorasa."

You must run, she wanted to say.

Next to her, Dom slid from his horse. His face was stone, unreadable.

"Sorasa," he growled. "Take her and go."

The assassin's mask slipped, if only for a moment. She blinked furiously, a flush rising in her cheeks. Beneath her steady confidence, Corayne saw doubt. Doubt and fear.

But Sorasa turned away, her expression clearing like a slate wiped clean. She refused the waiting horse with a wave of one bloodstained hand and faced the horizon again. The riders were nearly upon them, the pounding hooves of forty horses thundering over the sand.

"Too late," the assassin muttered.

Dom bowed his head, looking as he had in Ascal, a hole in his ribs, bleeding out his life as they ran for the gates.

But even in Galland, we could run. We had a chance. Corayne felt herself slump in the saddle. She was suddenly glad for Andry's closeness. Only his hand on her ankle kept her steady. The squire did not let go, nor did he look at the approaching outriders. They could hear their voices now, yelling in Ibalet, calling out orders.

"You think he won't feel it?"

Andry's voice was soft, nearly inaudible.

She glanced down at him, noting the set of his shoulders, the tightness of his fingers. Slowly, Andry raised his eyes to hers, letting her read him as easily as she would one of her maps.

"You think he won't feel the Spindle is gone?" Andry murmured.

Despite the outriders bearing down, Taristan filled Corayne's vision. He bled to life in front of her, blotting Andry out, until there was only her uncle's white face and black stare, a red gleam moving behind his eyes. She turned away before he could swallow her whole.

Her eyes trailed back to the village, her gaze weaving among the ruins. Back to where the Spindle once burned. Even as the outriders closed in, their voices growing louder, Corayne felt herself drift further away.

"I hope not," she whispered, praying to every god she knew.

But if I can feel its echo—and its absence—
I'm certain he does too.
And so does What Waits.

2

BETWEEN QUEEN AND DEMON
Erida

The flaming brazier crashed against the wall, spilling hot embers across the stone floor of the small receiving chamber. The edge of an old rug caught fire. Queen Erida of Galland didn't hesitate to stamp it out, even as the same fire roared inside her. Her face burned, pale cheeks red with anger.

Her crown lay discarded on a low table, only a simple band of gold, plain but for its gleam. She had no use for opulent gems or ridiculous finery in a cold castle at the edge of a battlefield, in the middle of a war, in the eye of a Spindlerotten hurricane.

Across the chamber, Taristan's chest rose and fell, his bare hands unburned as he threw another bronze bowl of hot coals. It looked as easy as tossing a rag doll, though Erida knew the brazier must be twice her weight. He was too strong, too powerful. He felt neither the heaviness nor the pain.

Thank the gods, he did not feel the poison either.

Not after Castle Vergon and the last Spindle cut. The portal still glittered behind Erida's eyes, a thread of gold near invisible, so important and yet so easy to overlook. The door to another realm, and another link in the chain of her empire.

Taristan's shadow loomed behind him, guttering with the torches and embers, leaping like a monster on the wall. His ceremonial armor was gone, leaving only the deep red of his tunic and white skin beneath. He did not seem smaller without iron and gilt.

Erida wished she could loose that shadow onto the Ward, send it out into the night, seeking whatever road her cousin Lord Konegin now raced down. Her anger flared brighter, the flames fed by thought of her treasonous kin.

I do not want Taristan to kill him, she thought, *but to drag him back here, broken and defeated, so we may kill him ourselves, in front of all the court, and end his insurrection before it can begin.*

She pictured her royal cousin and his entourage, their horses thundering through the darkness. They had only a small head start on her own riders, but the sky was clouded, the moon and stars veiled. It was a pitch-black night on a shifting border. And her own men were weary from the day's battle, their horses still recovering. Not like Konegin, his son, and their loyal few.

"They planned for this," Erida muttered, fuming. "He meant to kill Taristan, my husband, their own prince, and take the throne from us. But Konegin is cunning, and he knew to plan for failure too."

Her fists curled and she wished she could throw a brazier as well. Rip down the tapestries. Tear at the walls. Do something to unleash the anger inside herself, instead of letting it sit and fester.

Konegin sneered at her in her mind, teeth flashing beneath a blond beard, his eyes like blue daggers, his face like her dead father's. She wanted to wrap her hands around his wretched throat and squeeze.

Red Ronin flinched at the embers on the floor, twitching the edges of his scarlet robe away lest it burn too. He glanced at the single door, oak and iron, leading back to the feasting chamber. The stone hall was long empty, cleared of the court.

Erida tried not to imagine her lords and generals whispering about the attempted poisoning. *Most will remain loyal. But some—enough—might not. Some want Konegin to wear my crown, even as they stand by my side.*

"My concern is for the desert Spindle—" Ronin began, but Taristan fixed him with a black stare, and his voice died in his throat.

"Gone. You said as much," Taristan growled. He shifted to pacing the floor, boots heavy on the rugs. "That bastard brat," he added, nearly laughing. "Who knew a seventeen-year-old girl could be more of a nuisance than her golden father?"

Despite the circumstances, Erida felt a twitch at the corner of her lips. "The same has been said of me."

Then Taristan really did laugh, his chuckle like the drag of steel on stone. But it did not reach his eyes, black with that red shadow shifting in the firelight. The demon was always in him, but never so much as now. Erida could almost feel His hatred, His hunger, as Taristan stomped back and forth across the chamber.

"The door to Meer is closed, its monsters driven back," Ronin muttered, his hands twitching in his sleeves. Like Taristan he began to pace, running a path between door and window. He looked sharply between prince and queen. "We can only hope enough creatures of Meer have been released already, and that they continue to plague the waters."

"Indeed, krakens and sea serpents will do a great deal to hinder the fleets of the Ward, especially the Ibalet navy," Erida answered. "I wonder how many of their war galleys are already at the bottom of the Long Sea?"

The loss of the Spindle, devastating as it was, did not press against her mind so firmly. The events of the evening haunted her still, too close to ignore. Better than anyone, Erida knew the dangers of a hungry court.

While Taristan prowled in front of her, the shadow pulling with him, Konegin galloped through her mind.

"You haven't forgotten that my cousin tried to murder you an hour ago?" she said, her voice sharp.

"I still taste poison, Erida," Taristan answered, whipcrack fast. She glanced at his mouth, thin lips pulled into a sneer. "No, I have not forgotten."

Ronin waved a dismissive white hand. "A small man with a small mind. He failed and fled."

"He will have half the kingdom rise against us if given the chance," she snapped, her teeth bared. She wanted to squeeze the wizard's weak throat too.

To her immense frustration, Taristan only shrugged. The veins along his neck stood out, like moon-white scars. "So don't give it."

"You know so little of kingdoms and courts, Taristan." Erida heaved a weary sigh. *If only his demon lord would gift him some common sense.* "Invincible as you may be, strong as you are, you are nothing without my crown. If I lose my throne to that wretched, scheming troll—"

At that Taristan stopped his pacing, coming to a halt in front of her. He stared down, his black eyes seeming to swallow the world.

Still that red sheen gleamed.

"You will not, I promise you," Taristan growled.

Erida wanted to believe him.

"Then listen to me. Both of you," she said, snapping her fingers between prince and wizard. Her words spilled, blood from a gushing wound. "He must be tried for his crimes. Treason, sedition, attempted murder of his prince, my consort. And then he must be executed in front of every eye, every person who might sway to his cause. The court, my lords, the army, they must be given no reason to doubt my authority. I—*we*—must be absolute if we are to continue our war of conquest, and claim the Ward."

Taristan took another step forward, until she could feel the wicked heat rolling from his body. His jaw tightened.

"Shall I hunt him for you?"

Erida nearly smacked the suggestion aside. She did not fear for Taristan's well-being—he was far stronger than almost anyone in the Ward. But he was not invincible. The scars on his face, still refusing to heal, were proof of that. Whatever Corayne did left deep marks on otherwise-flawless skin. More than that, it was foolish to think that the prince consort himself would ride out into the wilderness, into a land that was not his, to find his own potential usurper. But worst of all—the idea of him going made her afraid. *I do not want him to leave me*, she knew, difficult as it was to admit. Erida tried to smack that away too, turning her mind and her body from Taristan to fix her gaze on the single door in the small chamber.

On the other side was the empty feasting hall. The castle around them bristled with whispering courtiers, the fields with an encamped army. *How many will Konegin lure to his side? How many will run to his flag instead of mine?*

Taristan did not step back, still staring. His gaze ran over her face, searching her eyes, waiting for her to speak. Waiting for her *command*.

The thought was enticing, deliciously so. To have a prince of Old Cor, a conqueror, a warrior born and blooded, hanging upon her approval. It was intoxicating, even to the Queen. She felt a bolt of tension draw between them, like a line pulled taut. For a second, Erida wished the chittering rat Ronin were far away, but the wizard remained, simpering in the corner, his red eyes darting between queen and demon.

"You cannot be spared, Taristan," she finally said, hoping he did not hear the tremble in her voice.

Ronin raised a finger, stepping forward. Whatever cord ran between queen and consort, the wizard neatly cut it in two.

"On that we agree, Your Majesty," he said. "One Spindle is lost. Another must be gained, and quickly."

Erida turned away. *I will not war for attention, especially with that rat of a wizard.* Her lip curled with distaste as a curtain of exhaustion fell over her. *I began this day on one battlefield, and now I stand on another entirely.* She certainly felt like a soldier, fighting with wits and intelligence instead of a sword. *A sword is far more simple*. She ached to undo the lacings of her underclothes, tightly pulled behind the folds of her gown.

But she was a queen. She did not have the luxury of weariness.

Erida drew herself straight again and planted her hands on her hips. "The Spindle is not the only thing you lost today. We walk a knife-edge," she sneered, again cursing her husband's political ignorance. "Taristan of Old Cor can crush skulls in his fist, but he cannot inspire allegiance."

She glanced up to find Taristan staring, his black eyes boring into hers.

"And for that matter, neither can I," she bit out, her teeth gnashing together. One hand fisted in her skirts, wringing the fabric between her fingers. Her throat bobbed, the words coming out too quickly to stop. "No matter what I do, no matter how much glory or gold I bring these awful, viperous courtiers, they do not love me the way they should. The way they would a man on my throne."

Taristan looked on through it all, a strange look crossing his face. His lips twitched.

"What must I do to win them?"

His question shocked her, and Erida felt her eyes widen. *Perhaps not so ignorant.*

"Win a castle," she answered sharply, gesturing to the window. It was shuttered, but they both knew the warring border lay beyond. The rich, weak lands of Madrence, waiting to be taken. "Win the battlefield. Win every mile into Madrence, until you and I plant the Gallish flag in the middle of their lovely capital, and claim all we see for the Lion." The green-and-gold snapped in her mind, raised high among the glittering towers of Partepalas. "Bring my lords victory, and we will *make* them love us for it."

As they loved my father and grandfather, and every Gallish conqueror before who lives in our paintings and stories and songs.

I can join them, she thought. *Not in death, but in glory.*

Already she felt the warmth of it. It wasn't the cloying heat of Taristan, but the gentle, familiar embrace of a parent returning home. Her father was more than four years gone, her mother alongside him. Konrad and Alisandra, taken by illness, felled by too common a fate. Erida cursed their ending, unbecoming of a king and queen. Still, she missed their arms, their voices, their steady protection.

Taristan looked on quietly, his gaze like a brush of fingers against her cheek. She set her jaw to a fierce edge and blinked away the memories before they could take hold. Before her husband could see their weight.

I cannot give over to sorrow, she knew. *Their memory should be a current pushing me forward, not an anchor.*

"Win, and win quickly," Erida bit out, tossing back her head. Her ash-brown hair coiled against her pale cheeks, finally coming loose from the intricate braid that had survived the morning's bloodshed. "We must have victory before any allies rouse to defend this land. Siscaria will already be on the move, maybe even Calidon or the Tyri fleets. We must hope Ibal is preoccupied with monsters in the Long Sea. If Galland conquers Madrence quickly, with you and me at the head of her army, the road to empire becomes much, much smoother for all of us."

That road stretched out before her, long but straightforward.

The legions of Galland would continue to march, cutting a line down the valley of the Rose River. There were castles along the border, fortresses to defend small towns and lush farmlands, but nothing to stop the might of Erida's armies. The first true test would come at Rouleine, the city at the joining of the Rose and the Alsor. *And when Rouleine falls, the capital is only days away, a jewel waiting to be claimed.*

"I'll have Lord Thornwall take stock of the armies," she added, thinking aloud. A list spun in her mind, things to be accomplished as quickly as possible. "By first light we'll know how many men, if any, deserted with Konegin."

Taristan blew out a frustrated breath. "Certainly your cousin does not hold so much sway, Erida," he said, almost placating.

"My cousin is a *man* with king's blood in his veins," she snapped, near to spitting. The injustice of it all still stung like a salted wound. "That holds enough sway for too many in my kingdom, let alone my own court."

His reply was steady, unyielding as his black-eyed stare. "It holds no sway with me."

Erida held his gaze, sapphire crashing against jet. Any retort died on her lips. Of course her prince consort would take her side. After all, his power in Galland came from her, as his power of the flesh came from his demon lord. But there was something beneath, unspoken.

An admission she could not yet understand. But she certainly wanted to try.

"We cannot forget our master, Taristan." Ronin's voice was nails on glass.

Erida clenched her teeth, turning her eyes on the red wizard as he moved between them, a scarlet wall. She did not need to see his horrible white face to know what message lived between his words. *Our master is What Waits. Not the Queen of Galland.*

And while she thought herself equal, if not superior, to all who walked the Ward, even Erida knew her measure against the demon king of hellish Asunder. Though her spine remained as steel, she felt a tremor in her skin.

"Gifts have been given, and payment must be made," Ronin pressed on, gesturing to Taristan's body.

He is strong as an immortal now. Stronger, even, Erida thought.

At Castle Vergon, he crushed diamonds in his fist, testament to his new strength.

In Nezri, the Spindle gave him the monsters of Meer, a force to terrorize his enemies in the Long Sea. *That Spindle is lost, but the monsters remain, patrolling the deep.*

And then there was the gift given at the temple, where Taristan drew a corpse army forth and killed his own brother. *Flesh cut and then made whole again, wounds wiped away*. Erida remembered their first meeting, when Taristan sliced his palm and bled before her throne, only for the skin to knit back together. Healed before her very eyes.

What comes next? she wondered, thinking on What Waits and the hellish realm He ruled beyond their own. But those were not thoughts she could entertain long. A god or a devil, who blessed and cursed in equal measure. But thus far—only blessings.

The Prince of Old Cor furrowed his brow, lowering his head so red locks of rough-cut hair fell into his eyes. He leaned over the wizard, using his greater height and bulk to much advantage. But Ronin knew his own measure too. He did not quail, his quivering hands finally still.

"Have you another Spindle, Wizard?" Taristan said through sharp, white teeth. His voice guttered like the embers on the floor. "Have you another place to send me?"

Ronin's eyes flickered. "I have a few leads. Strange doings, whispers from the archives. Whispers from Him."

A corner of Taristan's mouth twitched. "So nothing of use yet."

"I've led you to three Spindles, my prince," the wizard said proudly, though he bowed his white-blond head. Then he glanced back up, his red-rimmed eyes alight. "Don't forget, I'm Spindle-touched as you are, gifted by realms beyond our own."

"Gifted like me?" Taristan flexed a fist, his message clear.

Ronin bowed lower. "What Waits makes servants of us all."

Erida eyed the wizard's exposed neck, the gap of flesh like fresh snow.

Taristan caught her gaze; then he bowed too, a dip of his head. "And serve we shall," he said, gesturing for Ronin to rise. "Your service is best performed in the dust and pages, Wizard. I've a Spindle to replace."

Ronin nodded. "And two to protect."

At least that is easy.

"I convinced Lord Thornwall to leave a thousand men at Castle Vergon, dug into the hill below the ruins," Erida said, examining her ring of state. She let the emerald catch the light, the jewel glowing green. When she looked back up, both the wizard and the prince were staring, brows raised.

She allowed herself a small, satisfied smile and a shrug. "As a rear guard," she said, as if it were the most obvious thing in the world. "To defend our march forward, and protect against any vengeful Madrentines who might wish to slip past us and threaten Galland."

Even Ronin looked impressed.

"And," she added, "to stop any teenage nuisances from making trouble. The Spindle is safe, and not even Corayne or her miscreant guardians can do anything about it."

Taristan tipped his head. "What about your soldiers? What happens when some Gallish knight wanders into the ruins and finds himself in the Dazzling Realm?"

Erida shrugged again, donning her courtly smile. "The Vergon ruins are unstable, born of an earthquake. It isn't safe for them, and their captains have been told as much."

"Very good," Ronin said, genuine for once. "The Spindle remains. With every passing moment, it tears at the foundations of the Ward itself."

Taristan's grin was quick, crackling with energy. "We still have the temple too, in the foothills, all but forgotten."

The wizard nodded, pink spots rising on his cheeks. He seemed renewed, either by their improving fortunes or his master's will. "Defended by an army of corpses, the broken soldiers of the Ashlands."

"Is that not enough?"

Erida's question hung in the air.

"Two Spindles left open, left eating at the Ward?" She imagined the Spindles like insects gnawing at the roots of the world. Wearing through with acid and teeth. "Is it only a matter of time now?"

Ronin's responding laughter set her hair on end. He shook his head, despairing of the queen. "If it worked that way, What Waits would no longer be waiting. We need more. *He* needs more."

"Then *find* more," Taristan said, pacing again. He could not stay still for long. Erida wondered if that was his own nature, or the product of his gifts, jolting inside his skin like lightning in a bottle. "If I cannot hunt Konegin, perhaps I can travel back into the desert. Return to a known place of crossing. Reopen the way to Meer."

Again the Queen felt that confusing jab of terror at the thought of Taristan traveling so far from her side. Luckily, a retort was easy to reach for. Her wits did not fail her.

"Normally I would agree, but hundreds of Gallish soldiers now lie dead in the sands of Ibal," Erida said, matter-of-fact. Their endings did not bother her. Too many soldiers served her command. It would do no good to weep for them all. "And the Ibalet king is no fool. He will know of my trespassing army and be ready for more. I cannot give another kingdom cause for war, especially not one so powerful. Not yet, not while we have Madrence within reach."

The window was shuttered, the night beyond pitch-black. But in her mind she could still see the river valley, the sentinel line of castles, the forest hiding the Madrentine army. *The way forward.*

"Strong as Galland may be," she breathed, "I am not stupid enough to fight a war on two fronts."

Taristan opened his mouth to reply, but Ronin cut him off with a wave.

"Nezri is beyond reach now," the wizard said. "On this we agree."

"She's still there," Taristan snarled. The ragged scars beneath his eye stood out furiously.

Before she knew what she was doing, Erida felt his body beneath her fingers, her palms pressed against his shoulders. She blinked fiercely.

"You won't catch her, if she's even still alive."

He did not push her away, but he dropped her gaze.

"Perhaps the Spindle took her with it. Perhaps the danger of Corayne an-Amarat has passed," she added, sounding desperate even to her own ears. *Wishful thinking. The girl is Corblood, with an immortal at her side and perhaps a witch too. Gods only know who else.*

"We both know that isn't true." Every word from Taristan's lips cut like a knife, slicing her foolish hope down to size.

But Erida did not shrink with it. She straightened up instead, her hands still curled on his shoulders, against solid muscle and bone.

"And we both know the way forward," she hissed.

After a long moment, Taristan nodded, setting his mouth into a grim line.

"Wizard, find me a Spindle," he said, the full force of command in his voice.

He sounds like a king, Erida thought.

"Find me another place to destroy." He stepped from her grasp, all movement. "I'll lead the charge tomorrow, Erida. And lay victory at your feet."

Air whistled past her teeth as she drew in a sharp breath. *Will it be enough?* she wondered. *Will we succeed before Konegin ruins all we've worked for, all we've done? All I have already sacrificed—my independence, perhaps my throne.*

The red sheen was unmistakable, a crescent in Taristan's eyes. *And maybe my soul too.*

The prince cocked his head. "Do you doubt me?"

"No," Erida shot back, almost too quickly. Heat bloomed in her cheeks and she turned, trying to hide her rising flush. If Ronin and Taristan noticed, they said nothing.

She fussed with her skirts, smoothing them down. "At worst, if we cannot inspire loyalty, cannot win the hearts and minds of my court—we will buy them."

Taristan's dry manner returned. It was like pouring a bucket of ice water over the Queen's head. "Even you aren't rich enough for that."

She went to the door, putting a hand to the iron pull. On the other side, the Lionguard lay in wait, eager to protect their young queen.

"You opened a portal to the Dazzling Realm, Prince Taristan," she said, wrenching the door ajar. Cold air flowed in from the rest of the dreary castle. "I have all the wealth we will ever need."

And something else, too.

She remembered the diamonds in his fist, big as eggs, then

crushed to fine, starry powder. She remembered the Spindle and the glimpse of beyond, into Irridas. It was like a realm frozen, not with ice, but with jewels and precious stones.

And she remembered what moved within it: a glittering storm, now loose upon the Ward.

3

IN THE SHADOW OF THE FALCON
Sorasa

Sorasa remembered the first night she spent alone in the desert.

She was seven years old, young even by Guild standing, but already four years into her training.

Older acolytes took her from her bed, as they did the other twelve children of her year. A few of them wept or screamed as they were bundled up, hoods drawn over their heads and their wrists bound together. Sorasa remained silent. She knew better already. While they tied her hands, she remembered her lessons. She clenched her fists, flexing her small muscles so that the bonds might not be so tight later on. When two acolytes carried her out like a rag doll, their fingers digging into her bony shoulders, she listened. They spoke to each other in low voices, complaining of the night's assignment.

Ride the sevens into the sand until midnight and leave them there. See which ones make it back alive.

They joked as the young girl's heart sank.

It is three strokes to midnight now, Sorasa knew, counting in her head. *Only a few minutes since they put out the bunk-room lanterns. Near three hours' ride into the desert.*

In what direction, she tried to gauge.

The hood made things difficult, but not impossible. Her acolytes threw her on the back of a sand mare and turned left outside the gates of the citadel. *South. Hard south.*

The wailing of the other children soon died away, as the acolytes bore them in varying directions. Soon there were only her acolytes and their mares, moving swiftly beneath a sky she could not see. She breathed slowly, gauging the pace of the horses. To her relief, the acolytes were not pushing a gallop, but an easy canter.

Beneath the hood, she prayed to every god. Most of all to Lasreen. To Death herself.

I will not meet you yet.

Two days later, Sorasa Sarn stumbled toward a mirage, half-dead, her small hands reaching through open air. When they brushed harsh stone, and then wood, she smiled, her lips cracking. It was no mirage, but the citadel gates.

The young girl had passed another test.

Sorasa wished things were so easy now. What she would give to be abandoned in the Great Sands with nothing except her wits and the stars. Instead she found herself chained to an infuriating pack of misfits, with the King of Ibal's own hunters bearing down.

One thing had not changed, though.

Lord Mercury still waits for me.

She shivered at the thought of him, of what he would do if he caught her back in these lands.

The sun was bright now, the desert sky a clear, pressing blue. Pounding hooves kicked up sand, shimmering the air. The outriders' voices fell away as they drew near, replaced by flint-eyed stares and the snap of leather reins on horseflesh.

The Companions pulled together, closing ranks. Even Sorasa stepped back into the palm trees, her fingers twitching as a fresh rush of energy coursed through her veins. Corayne slid from her horse, Andry and Dom flanking her on either side, their swords in hand. Charlie slunk into their midst, his hood thrown back to show his red face and disheveled brown hair. For once, Valtik did not disappear, but she didn't move from her perch on a rock either. Sorasa doubted she noticed the approaching riders at all.

Only Sigil stood firm, unmoving, her broad form a silhouette against the storm closing in. Her ax turned in her hand. Its wicked edge caught the sun. With a grin, she wiped the last drop of old blood away.

"So nice of them to wait their turn," the bounty hunter grumbled.

Sorasa scoffed low in her throat. "The King of Ibal is nothing if not polite."

Dom's eye was true. Sorasa saw forty riders on forty horses, one of them bearing the flag of Ibal. *Worse than the flag of Ibal*, Sorasa realized, squinting at the standard against the sky.

All thoughts of Lord Mercury melted away.

At first glance, the flag looked like the Ibalet sigil—an elegant golden dragon on deep royal blue. But Sorasa saw the silver in the wings, the smaller body, the sharper eyes picked out in flashing metal and blue jewels. Not a dragon, but a falcon. There was a sword in its talons, distinctly curved. *Outriders,* Sorasa had called them to the others. But any son or daughter of Ibal knew their symbol, and knew their name.

"Who are they?" Corayne hissed, grabbing Sorasa by the arm.

Sorasa only grit her teeth. *"Marj-Saqirat,"* she forced out. Ahead of her, Sigil's shoulders tightened. "The Crown's Falcons. Guardians sworn to the King of Ibal."

Like the Lionguard of Queen Erida, or the Temur emperor's Born Shields, the Falcons were handpicked warriors. Their skills were matched only by their devotion to the Ibalet throne. Even with the Elder on their side, Sorasa knew they had little chance of fighting them off. Most Falcons were trained from childhood, recruited at a young age, as Sorasa had been long ago.

We are not so different. I learned to kill for the Amhara Guild. They learned to kill for a crown.

The Falcons circled the Companions like wolves running down prey. Their bright-eyed sand mares kept rigid formation, trained to perfection. Their flanks gleamed ebony, chestnut, and gold, their saddles worked into the shape of dark wings. The Falcons wore black robes—the loose outer layer trapped the desert heat, keeping their clothing and skin cool beneath. Their heads were wrapped in similar fabric, marked only by braids of gold, silver, and royal blue thread. No helmets, no armor. It would only slow them down in the desert. But each bore a brace of daggers, their fine leather belts crossed at the chest, with a sword lashed to each saddle. The blades were like Sorasa's own, bronzed steel, but far more beautiful in their crafting.

The sand kicked up in a small whirlwind, hanging in the air even as the horses stopped short. They faced inward, their riders intent and alert. But the Falcons did not move to attack. Their swords remained sheathed, their mouths shut.

To Sorasa's surprise, she saw no king among them, though the Falcons were charged to defend him always. Every man upon a sand mare was young and lean, forming a wall of keen eyes and still hands. Sorasa searched their faces for another leader, hunting for the telltale flicker of authority. Beneath their head coverings, Sorasa noted bronze skin, black eyes, and strong brows. These were men of the Ibalet coast and the Ziron River, the rich cities. Most were sons of wealthy lords, diplomats, generals, scholars. Given to the king, no doubt, pledged in hopes of gaining more favor.

Not like me at all, Sorasa realized. *Taken from a wrecked slave ship, saved from death or chains.*

A few riders stared back at her, not meeting her gaze. But they eyed her clothing, her Amhara dagger. Her tattooed hands and neck. Symbols of who she was once, and where she came from.

She watched them harden, black eyes turning to jet, foreheads furrowing with grim disgust. Guardians of the king held no love for assassins. *One might even call us natural enemies*, Sorasa thought. Her heart thumped in her chest, her pulse rising from its steady rhythm.

At her side, Dom shifted, his emerald gaze passing over her, a question in his eyes. *He can hear my heartbeat*, Sorasa knew, battling a swell of shame. She gritted her teeth, trying to calm her own heartbeat. *He can hear my fear.*

Forty Falcons will not hesitate to kill someone like me, even if I am no longer Amhara. Her jaw tightened in frustration. *Even if I'm trying to save the realm from total destruction.*

Then Dom opened his mouth and chased all her fears away, replacing them with embarrassment.

"We are the Companions, the Ward's last hope," he shouted, his greatsword drawn. The massive blade still looked idiotic to Sorasa's eye. She winced as his proud voice boomed into the desert. "You will not stand in our way."

A cloud of amusement crossed some of the Falcons, their eyes crinkling.

Sorasa wanted to smack the immortal. *Does he realize how ridiculous he sounds?*

"My apologies, but I do not know who the Companions are," a voice answered from the line of riders.

Sorasa's eyes flew to him, their leader. Nothing distinguished him from the rest, but he raised a hand, pulling the coverings on his face away. He was roughly handsome, wearing his forty or so years well. He had a strong, curved nose and a neat black beard flecked with gray. She noted the laugh lines around his mouth, carved deep by a life of smiles. *Odd, for a Falcon. Odder still for a Falcon without a king to defend.*

The fool Elder was undeterred. He shifted to stand in front of Corayne, guarding her from view. "I am Domacridhan, a prince of Iona—"

Sorasa's elbow found his ribs. They felt like granite. "Let me do the talking, you stupid troll," she growled under her breath.

To his credit, Dom took the insult in stride, his usual scowl barely a flash on his lips. *Either he's getting used to me or he knows better than to argue surrounded by forty soldiers.*

Charlie hissed somewhere behind them, fear lacing his words. "Then you'd better *start* talking, Sorasa. I'm not just going to stand here and wait to be killed."

"If they meant to kill us, you would already be dead, Priest," Sigil answered, lazily stroking her ax.

Sorasa ignored them both, her eyes on the leader. She studied his face, trying to read his manner to no avail.

"The Falcons are sworn to protect Amdiras an-Amsir, King of Ibal, Grand Lord of the Fleets, the Protector of the Shirans, the Prince of Salt." She rattled off the many titles of their king with ease. Her voice sharpened. "But I do not see him here. What wind blows the Falcons so far from their king?"

A muscle ticked in the commander's cheek. He held her gaze, his lips pulling into a frown. The smile lines disappeared. "What contract sends an Amhara to slaughter an entire town?"

"You think that was me?" Sorasa half laughed, putting a hand to her chest. "I'm flattered, but you know that isn't the Amhara way. Gallish soldiers, on the other hand . . ." Her voice hardened, teeth on edge. "They flatten cities for the love of their queen."

The commander did not answer, his frown still pulled.

Sorasa pointed back to Nezri with her chin, her jaw tightening. "Go on, send one of your pigeons into town. Check the bodies. Check the *armor*. You'll find lions all over the oasis. And mind the sea serpents. I'm not sure we killed them all," Sorasa added.

The commander did not flinch. Did not scoff or laugh or dismiss her. He did not even blink.

Corayne shifted behind the cage of Dom and Andry's protection. She waved them back before they could stop her and stepped out into the blazing light, raising a hand to shade her eyes. Her palm was still an open wound, red with blood.

The pirate's daughter looked over the Falcons, studying them as she would a map or a wax seal.

"That news doesn't seem to shock you, sir," Corayne said sharply.

Sorasa could not name the feeling in her chest, but she thought it might be pride.

"You were told what to expect here," Corayne pushed on, taking another step forward. Sand shifted around her scuffed boots.

The Falcons turned their eyes to her. She unsettled them. The Spindleblade on her back gave Corayne a strange silhouette, full of contradictions. A teenage girl was no warrior, but she wore a warrior's sword and stood straight as any king.

"Monsters of another realm." Her voice strengthened. "A Spindle torn."

The Falcons were soldiers first, regarded for their physical prowess and loyalty. Not their political skill or subtle nature. Without his face coverings, it was easy to see the commander's eyes. The reflection of truth.

"And a young woman who can save the world. Or end it," the commander finished.

In spite of all they had done and all they had yet to do, a bit of relief stole into Sorasa Sarn. *Whatever they're here for, it isn't death. At least not for Corayne.*

The feeling did not last long.

The commander spurred his horse, trotting into the circle. Still a safe distance from Corayne, but enough to put Dom and Andry on edge. Both moved to her side again, firm as ever. This time, she didn't wave them back.

"I will be taking custody of Corayne an-Amarat," said the commander.

Inwardly, Sorasa groaned.

Dom's sword rose, furious with sunlight. "You may try."

The commander was undeterred and unmoving, content to remain in the saddle. *He has us outnumbered, even with Dom. He has no cause to fear us.*

Sorasa did not move her hands, but her mind flew to her daggers and sword, grasping for options and opportunity. She found none.

Corayne raised her chin, tipping her golden skin to the sunlight. She looked less like her uncle in the desert, but her black eyes remained, deeper than any cloak, consuming as the night. She fixed the commander with a penetrating glare.

"You know my name, sir," she snarled. "It's only fair you share yours."

Again Sorasa felt that unfamiliar flare of pride.

The commander blinked, drawing himself up in the saddle, like a bird ruffling its feathers. He paused for a long moment, looking over Corayne again, eyeing her sword, her worn boots, the flecks of blood and muck all over her clothing. Then he took in her strange Companions, united behind her, but as disparate from each other as wolves and eagles.

She half expected Dom to say something bold and foolish again, but for once he kept his immortal mouth shut.

"I am Hazid lin-Lira, Commander of the *Marj-Saqirat*."

Sorasa kept her face blank, but her jaw tightened. *The commander of the Crown's Falcons, their leader, the King of Ibal's closest bodyguard. Sent for us—for Corayne.*

"The rest of you are, of course, welcome to accompany her," lin-Lira added, glancing through their strange number again.

Sorasa almost laughed at the absurdity. "And if we refuse?"

Lin-Lira knotted his reins in his fists. "I have orders to follow, Amhara."

Corayne did not quail. She glared up at the Ibalet commander, fierce as ever. "Accompany me where, exactly?"

In unison, the Falcons saluted, each one drawing a circle on his brow, then a crescent on his chest, looping from shoulder to shoulder. The sun and moon. The sign of Lasreen.

The sign of—

"To Their Peerless Highness, Lasreen's Chosen," lin-Lira said, his voice catching oddly. "The Heir of Ibal."

Sand mares were given, fully tacked, drawn from the back of the Falcons' number. No caravan or cavalry rode into the Great Sands without spare horses, and there were more than enough to go around. *At least no one has to share with Valtik*, Sorasa thought, finding a small mercy in their otherwise-cursed existence. *Or Charlie, for that matter.* The fallen priest bounced like a sack of potatoes in the saddle, and Sorasa winced for the poor sand mare set to bear him across the desert, wherever the Falcons might lead.

Sorasa noticed that Corayne's fierce attitude seem to melt when Andry helped her into the saddle again. His years as a squire made him quick and skilled, and he tended to her like he would a glorious Gallish knight. Corayne watched him in silence, her lips pursed into a thin line, and Sorasa could almost see the words fighting to escape her throat.

Let your fear guide you, Sorasa wanted to say, but kept quiet. It was time to take her own advice. She feared the Falcons, feared the Heir, feared what any member of the Ibalet court might do to an Amhara killer. But that fear was small compared to what loomed over them—and what lay behind.

Her horse's coat gleamed, black as oil, its mane long to protect against flies and the sun's fierce rays. She worked a hand into it, tightening her grip, letting the feel of the horse ground her.

One Spindle is closed. How many others remained, how many others Taristan knew of, she could not say. Sorasa doubted even Valtik knew, but now was no time to ask.

The Falcons kept their swords sheathed, but Sorasa still felt like a prisoner. They formed up in a column, with the Companions in their middle. Sigil and Sorasa rode ahead of Corayne while Andry and Dom flanked her, with Valtik and Charlie clustered behind.

Snapping his reins, lin-Lira set his Falcons surging forward, and their sand mares with them.

All Sorasa could do—all any of them could do—was follow.

The king's bodyguards were silent escorts, herding them southeast as the sun began its descent across the sky. Lin-Lira set a good pace, fast but not grueling.

Dom kept close to Corayne, a nervous mother hen, his eyes never leaving her back, ready to catch her should she fall. His nannying put Sorasa somewhat at ease, letting her fall into the familiar rhythm of a sand mare's smooth gait.

Sigil's voice broke through the steady tattoo of hoofbeats, indecipherable at first. The language of the Temurijon was rare in the south, and Sorasa had to concentrate to understand. She glanced left, to the bounty hunter riding alongside her.

Sigil leaned toward Sorasa, repeating herself, the words slower and easier to translate. Her native language was an easy shield against everyone around them.

"What will they do with Corayne?" Sigil hissed. "What does the Heir of Ibal want with a pirate's daughter?"

"We all know she's more than that," Sorasa answered, her own Temur shaky at best.

She glanced ahead, through the charging mass of horses kicking up sand in a grim line. Lin-Lira rode at the column's head, bent low over his mare's neck.

"I don't fear for Corayne, not yet," Sorasa added. "The Falcons seem straightforward enough—but why does the commander ride for the Heir? And not the king he was sworn to protect?"

Sigil frowned. "Too many questions, too few answers. I miss the days of good, simple contracts," she said. "Grab, drag, and collect. Instead I'm burning my face off in your godsforsaken desert, and I still stink of kraken."

Sorasa's skin prickled at the prospect of traveling through the Great Sands, dragging the rest of their band with her.

"We can lose them," Sigil said suddenly, her voice sharper.

"Lose them where?" Sorasa growled back.

Sigil shrugged her broad shoulders, gesturing with her chin.

The desert stretched in almost every direction, with only the barren red cliffs of the Marjeja or the cruel salt waves of the Long Sea to break the sand. While the horses were well cared for and good steeds, they had no saddlebags. Even if they could somehow escape the Falcons, they would do so with no food, no freshwater, and no aid for weeks.

"What are they whispering?" Dom rumbled behind them, glancing to Corayne.

"I don't speak Temur," Corayne answered, annoyed.

Sigil ignored them. "They let us keep our weapons. My ax, Dom's sword. We can cut a hole in these birds and be gone."

Sorasa wished that were true. She shook her head, tightening her grip on the mare's mane. "Forget the Falcons. We are in the claws of the Dragon now."

By the way the bounty hunter scowled, falling back in the saddle, Sorasa could tell it was not the end of her argument. Sigil wouldn't submit, even under the worst of odds. The Temur were skilled tacticians, taught to fight to the bitter, glorious end, and it usually meant victory.

Not today, Sorasa knew.

But perhaps tomorrow.

They rode through the night. It was well into autumn, with the spring blooms of Ibal long dead, but Sorasa still caught the herbal tang of juniper trees, clinging to water somewhere. Sorasa's muscles ached, stiffened by the dropping temperature and the long hours of riding without rest. Lin-Lira finally whistled a halt after dawn, when the heat returned and the sun began its climb. Both Corayne and Charlie nearly fell from their horses, stumbling to the sand on weak legs. They exchanged small smiles.

"At least I'm not the only one," Charlie chuckled, fighting to his feet with Andry's help.

Corayne rose on her own, dusting off her knees and flexing her fingers, clawed from hours gripping her reins. Dom stayed glued to her side, unbent by their travels. He glared in every direction, as if his eyes alone could send the Falcons running.

The Falcons dismounted as one, following lin-Lira's example, and drew their horses into the shadows of a sand dune. Within minutes they strung up a rope paddock to enclose the sand mares. Sorasa watched as the rest of the camp went up in seemingly the blink of an eye, the Falcons working in swift unison. They unraveled sheets from their packs, some big as a ship's sail, tying them off and nailing their pegs into the sand. The one-sided tents were simple but effective, creating a blanket of shade. The Falcons knew how to cross the Great Sands without dying. They would sleep through the worst of the heat and continue to travel through the cool hours of night.

Sorasa kept her gaze on lin-Lira, who kept his gaze on Corayne, his dark eyes like twin spears. He watched her not as a predator, but as a scholar trying to work out an equation. His eyes never left her, not even flickering to Dom, her massive nursemaid in bloodstained clothes.

After loosing her horse into the paddock, Sorasa rejoined them, taking shelter in Dom's shadow.

"What a sight we are," Sorasa muttered for the hundredth time.

Dom loomed, storm-faced, standing over Corayne like an unbent tree.

Corayne sneered up at him as she laid out her bedroll and cloak. "Are you going to do that all day?"

Dom somehow drew himself up another inch or two. "As long as we are surrounded by enemies, you won't leave my sight."

"You can see for miles, Elder. Give her room to breathe, at least," Sorasa said, shooing him off with a sweep of her hands.

Andry nodded along with Dom. "We should set a watch of our own," he said firmly, sitting down on his cloak. He drew up his long legs, balancing his arms on his knees. "I can go first."

"Then me," Sigil boomed, laying her ax down on Corayne's other side.

Charlie snored in reply, wrapped up in his cloak like a sweet roll.

"I'll finish, I suppose," Dom offered, still standing. The others nodded, but Sorasa knew the Elder would not sleep at all. He would keep watch through the long, burning hours.

She wished she could do the same, but she felt the creep of exhaustion in her limbs, working its way to her head. Again she glanced to lin-Lira, still staring their way. This time, Corayne saw him too. Her lips pulled into a frown.

"He does not know why he's been sent to get you, or what the Heir wants," Sorasa muttered, bending to speak at Corayne's ear. "It will be no use to question him now."

"I'm too tired to try, anyway," Corayne whispered back. Her eyelids drooped as she spread out her cloak, preparing a bed.

"I doubt that," Sorasa said. "Your curiosity is endless as the horizon."

Corayne flushed with pleasure and pulled her cloak up to her chin.

Sorasa wanted to do the same, and sleep away the heat of the day. Instead she eyed the sandy slope above the camp. Six Falcons looked down from the shadow of the sand dune, watching every single one of them. Their eyes burned into her body.

Sigil glared up at the Falcons' watchmen, refusing to blink. The Temur woman's frustration was so palpable it seemed to smoke the air.

"Every step we take with them takes us further from ending this," she said hotly.

Sorasa sighed with weariness. "And how exactly do we end this?"

"The next Spindle," Sigil said with an obvious shrug.

"And where is that?" Sorasa countered.

Her scowl deepened and she pointed her chin away from the tents. "Ask the witch."

At the edge of the circle of shade, Valtik drew whorls in the hot sand with her bare toes, singing softly in unintelligible Jydi.

"What is she saying?" Sigil asked, tipping her head to one side.

Sorasa waved a hand. "I never want to know."

"He called the Heir *Lasreen's Chosen*." Sigil hissed the name of the goddess, not from disrespect, but fear.

"Born royal, and made the voice of a goddess," Sorasa replied, matter-of-fact. The assassin set to making up her own place, some yards away but still within the cool boundaries of the shade.

Of course, Corayne perked up on her makeshift bed. She fought her own exhaustion, still very much awake and listening. "What does *that* mean?"

"Lasreen is the goddess of many things," Sorasa sighed, rolling out her own cloak with practiced precision. "To Ibal, she is most sacred of the godly pantheon. Both sun and moon. The giver of Life."

"She's also the goddess of death," Sigil muttered, folding her muscular forearms. As if she could defend her body from Lasreen herself. But there was no wall the goddess could not climb, no fortress she could not overthrow. There was no escape from Blessed Lasreen.

Even the realm itself might not escape her hand.

Sorasa scoffed. "I'm very aware. Life and death are two sides of the same coin."

"So we're being dragged off to a death-worshipping cult," Dom rumbled, his emerald eyes going black.

"Lasreen's Chosen honors life as much as death, light as much as darkness," Sorasa answered.

"Will the Heir try to kill us?" Corayne asked around a wide yawn. Despite the hood she wore all day long, she sported a blush of red across her cheeks and nose.

Frowning, Sorasa shook her head. "Like I said, we'd be dead already, Corayne. And you should sleep. You may still have the energy for your relentless questions, but I do not."

At her side, Andry chuckled into his hand. Even Dom's lips twitched, threatening to pull out of his usual scowl.

Corayne drew herself up straighter, blinking fiercely. "Before you came to Lemarta, before you and Dom found me—I arranged buyers for everything my mother smuggled or stole. One of the last shipments I sent was a crate of Jydi furs. Bound for the royal court of Ibal. I thought it was odd, a desert king buying wolf pelts, but he paid well, so I didn't question it. But now . . ." Her eyes sparked with realization. "The King of Ibal has been in the Mountains of the Blessed for months, and he intends to stay there for a long time."

A chill stole through Sorasa, the desert air cooling on her skin. She tried to think, sifting through snippets of memory. Only a few months old, but now those days seemed far away.

"I heard rumors the royal family left the court citadel at Qaliram early, but . . ."

Corayne nodded along. "You thought nothing of it. Just royals with their strange fancies. I thought the same."

"Zimore is far to the south, over many weeks of harsh terrain," Sigil cursed, naming the summer palace in the southern mountains. She got to her feet, pacing, her heavy boots making furrows in the ground. Again, she glared at the watchmen in the dunes. "Past the Sands, the headwaters of the Ziron, then up into the mountains themselves—"

Sorasa gritted her teeth, her frustration cresting. "Thank you, Sigil. I've been there."

Corayne opened her mouth for another inevitable interrogation, but Sorasa glared her off. She remembered the palace, if barely.

One of my first contracts. I never even breached its walls. I didn't need to. He was only a bumbling boy who liked to chase sheep in the hills. *The kill was quick and easy, and perhaps inevitable. There were so many cliffs, a danger to any intrepid prince.*

"Royals are strange," Andry offered, shrugging his lean shoulders. "Like Corayne said, they have passing fancies."

Corayne shrugged back at him, her arms wrapped around her knees. The Spindleblade lay sheathed at her side, half wrapped in her cloak. For once, she looked her age. Small, unassuming. A girl among wolves. After Nezri, after the kraken and the closing of the Spindle, Sorasa knew better.

The assassin set her teeth, her mind racing. "In season, Zimore is a sanctuary from Ibal's blazing summers. Every year the Ibalet royals sail south along the river, leaving their shaded citadels and perfumed lagoons for the mountains. But the winters are brutal. Feet of snow. Windstorms in the hills. Even spring and fall are dangerous." *Not even the most brainless royal brat would go to Zimore on a whim. Let alone the King of Ibal.* "It's no place for an aging king and the many branches of his blessed tree."

But with the Spindles torn, with Taristan of Old Cor seeking to ruin the realm to rule it, Sorasa wondered, *Did the king know something was amiss before I did? Before Corayne? Before even Dom?*

"But they left months ago, before this all started," Andry said, his dark brows furrowed in confusion. After days in the desert, he wore a fresh crop of freckles like black stars in a warm brown sky.

"And when exactly did *this* start?" Sorasa answered, cutting a glance at the Elder hulking over them.

Dom met her gaze, silent, his lips pressed to nothing. He was never difficult to read, too removed from emotion to know how to hide it. Sorasa saw doubt in him, clear as the empty blue sky.

"When the sword was stolen," Corayne offered. "Somehow my uncle made it past the immortal guards of Iona and into their vaults. He took a Spindleblade for his own, and set to tear the world apart."

The assassin did not drop her stare, tiger eyes meeting emerald gone to black. After a long moment, Dom relented, unsticking his tongue.

"It began thirty-six years ago," he muttered, and Corayne whirled to face him. "When a pair of Corblood twins were born, their mother dying to give them life. Two boys, two paths. And only one fate the Monarch could foresee."

For once, Corayne was silent, her breath ragged through her teeth.

But the question she could not ask was obvious.

Sorasa asked it for her.

"What fate was that?"

Dom's eyelids fluttered and he shifted, putting the scars on his face into harsh relief.

"The breaking of the realm," he said. "The ending of the world."

On the ground, Corayne drew a sharp breath. Sorasa almost did the same, her heartbeat pounding again. *The road to this day is thirty-six years long*, she thought, feeling anger and fear twist together.

"I do not know your monarch, Elder. And I never wish to meet her," she bit out, near to hissing.

To her surprise, Dom only dropped his gaze. His shame was clear to see.

Some yards away, Valtik's haunting lullaby rose, swirling like smoke, carrying up into the heavens. Usually, her rantings were an annoyance at best. Now they shuddered through Sorasa, and the Elder too.

"I don't think your monarch was the only one to see this," Sorasa breathed, her thoughts going back to the mountains, to a palace made for summer.

Something trembled down her spine. A terror she had not felt since childhood, when the acolytes had left her alone in the sands, with nothing but bound hands and bare feet.

But even then, she'd known which direction to run.

Now there is nowhere to go, and yet I keep walking forward.

Into what, I do not know. And neither does anyone else.

4

WHATEVER GOD WILL LISTEN
Andry

Somehow, Andry felt relief among the Falcons. The cord wound around his heart seemed to release a little, day by day, even as they rode farther into the desert.

"The road suits you," Corayne said as they made camp on the third morning. Dawn broke behind her, edging her silhouette in red. Her eyes were gentle, her face open. Andry felt her gaze like a touch.

He dipped his head, hiding the flush of warmth across his face. "I'm used to it," he answered, chewing his words. "If I close my eyes, I can pretend."

She blinked, puzzled for once. "Pretend what?"

"That none of this ever happened," he said in a low voice. He swallowed around a sudden lump in his throat. "That I'm home in Ascal, in the barracks. That I'm a squire again, with none of this behind me."

The smell and sound of horse filled his senses, the jingle of tack, the heavy breath of a nearby rider. Without the desert and the endless horizon, the Falcon warriors in their black robes, or Corayne at his side, her silhouette familiar even beneath her hood—without his eyes open, it could just be home. Training with the other squires, moving through their riding lessons in the palace training yard, or racing the green farmlands outside the Ascal walls. Back then his only worries were his mother's worsening cough and Lemon's taunts. Nothing compared to the burdens he carried now, the fears he held for his mother, for himself, for Corayne—*for the realm*. He tried not to feel the sword at his belt. He tried to ignore the heat on his skin, born of a fiercer sun.

He tried not to remember.

And for a long, blissful moment, he did not.

But the faces returned, rising behind his eyes. Gallish soldiers all, their green tunics stained scarlet, their lives ended by his own hand. Again and again, his sword sank into their flesh, until the steel went red and he tasted their blood in his mouth.

He stared at his hands, knotted on the reins. The leather wound through his brown fingers. If he squinted, he could still see the blood. Their blood.

When he looked back to Corayne, her face pulled with regret.

"You did it for the Ward," she said forcefully, throwing down her pack. "To save yourself. To save me. To save your *mother*."

But he remembered the soldiers at the end of his blade. It was too much to bear. He wished he could drop the burden of their bodies, let them slip from his shoulders like a heavy pack. Instead they hung on, fingers cold and clawed, weighing every inch forward.

The sun rose red against the horizon, painting the desert in flaming shades of copper. Its warmth held his face, almost pleasant after riding all night. His sand mare idled next to him, waiting to be turned out. She was bred to endure.

Not like me, he thought.

"Andry."

Corayne's voice was sharp and close. He jumped.

She was still in front of him, standing only a foot away, her eyes blazing up into his own.

"Stop torturing yourself," she said, taking his shoulders in her hands. "You were every inch a knight out there. You might not want to remember, but I do. You should be proud—"

Andry's stomach twisted. Reluctantly, he stepped out of her grasp, putting some distance between them.

"I take no pride in what I did, Corayne." His voice faltered. "And I won't justify it either. I know what's at stake, the monsters we face, but I won't let it turn me into a monster too."

She drew in a sharp breath. Her black eyes darkened somehow, growing deeper. "Am I a monster, then? Are we all?"

Andry nearly swore in frustration. "That's not what I mean."

"Then say what you mean," she said coolly, folding her arms.

The squire could only shrug. His tongue stuck in his mouth, and while a dozen words rose in his throat, none felt right.

"I guess I don't really know," Andry finally murmured, lifting his saddlebags.

Corayne seemed to deflate. "Fine," she said, her voice too

sharp. Then she shook her head, her braid coming loose after the night's ride. When she raised her face again, her eyes were soft. "I'm sorry. I'm tired," she mumbled. "We're all tired."

Despite the circumstances, Andry almost laughed. He shouldered his pack, his teakettle clanking within. "Agreed."

This morning's camp was at a small oasis, barely more than a stand of shrubs, wet rocks around a pool, and a narrow well. But after three days crossing the Great Sands, Andry could taste the extra moisture in the air. He led his grateful sand mare over with the rest of the horses, leaving Corayne behind.

Instead of setting their shades, the Falcons refilled their myriad of waterskins at the well, as did Sorasa and Sigil. The horses were eager to drink too, crowding the pool. Andry let his horse nose in among the other mounts, picking through the stones to the shallow freshwater.

Andry's legs ached beneath him, despite his long years of training. Army marches and quick races were nothing compared to their thunderous days across the desert. Even his trek with Cortael and the Companions had not been so arduous.

Maybe it should've been. A few harder days, a few more nights without rest. Maybe then we would've arrived at the temple in time, and stopped this before it could even begin.

Andry hissed under his breath and shook his head, as if he could banish such thoughts. But like the faces, they never left.

He drew back from the rocky pool, his own waterskin and teakettle filled with water. Others crowded in to fill his space, but one Falcon hung back. He stared at Andry, his robes dusty from the ride.

Andry stared back, giving a small nod of acknowledgment.

Quickly, the Falcon removed his protective headdress of wound cloth and gold braid. His bronze face and mahogany eyes were soft. He was young, unbearded, only a few years older than Andry himself. Though the Falcons often threw insults and glares at Sorasa, Andry saw none of that now.

Instead he saw curiosity.

The Falcon looked the squire over, his gaze snaring on Andry's hands, then his face and curling black hair, now growing out of his close-cropped squire's style. After long years in the north, surrounded by pale skin and fair heads, Andry knew why. He fought back a weary sigh, feeling the sharp edge of annoyance.

"You're Gallish?" the Falcon asked, eyeing Andry's tunic. The blue star on the squire's chest had certainly seen better days and cleaner moments.

"Yes," he replied, matter-of-fact, squaring his shoulders. He was keenly aware of the dried blood on his clothes, and the disheveled state of his appearance. "But my mother is of Kasa."

The Falcon's swooping black eyebrows rose. Like Commander lin-Lira, he had angular features—sharp cheekbones and a long, regal nose.

Ibal and Kasa did not share a border, separated by the small, proud kingdoms of Sardos and Niron. Their lands were not enemies, but certainly rivals, alike in their great histories and even greater riches.

The Falcon half smiled, impressed. "I was not certain, but you ride like a knight."

Heat spread across the squire's cheeks, not from the sun, but from pride.

The Falcon took in Andry's silence, his face falling. "A good knight, I mean," he added quickly. "I hope you take no offense."

"Of course not," Andry said without thought.

The Falcon smiled again, coming around Andry's horse to face him. They were of the same height and build. Lean, young men, trained to fight, loyal to their kingdoms.

"Most of the Gallish hunch in the saddle like a sack of barley shoved in armor," the Falcon said, grinning. "But you move with the horse."

In spite of himself, Andry felt a small laugh in his throat. For the first time, he remembered Sir Grandel as he was alive. A bit too big for his armor, a bit slower than the younger knights. The memory lifted his heart instead of dragging it down. The corners of Andry's lips pulled, wanting to smile.

"Thank you," the squire said, and he meant it. He looked over the Ibalet warrior again. The young man wore no sword, but a long dagger hung from his belt, the sheath pattered in gold and copper. "I've heard great tales of the Falcons. They say you rival the Lionguard."

The Falcon blew out a scoff, putting his hands on his hips. "I prefer the Born Shields," he said, referring to the storied guardians of the Temur emperor.

At that, a raw-faced Sigil popped up from among the horses, towering over their flanks. Her eyes crackled like kindling.

"You and your chittering birds aren't worth their horses," she sneered, eyeing the young Falcon like he was mud on her boots. She put a fist to her heart, near to spitting. "The iron bones of the Countless will never be broken."

"Sigil," Andry warned, trying to head off a fight before it could start.

Somewhere among the horses, Andry heard Charlie's laughter. The fugitive priest bumbled off, a waterskin in hand. He only incensed Sigil more, and the bounty hunter's glare deepened.

The young Falcon joined in Charlie's laughter.

"Let it be, my friend," he said, touching Andry lightly on the shoulder, guiding him away from the pool.

The dune shade fell over them, Sigil fuming in their wake.

"The Temur thinks we took her freedom. We can leave her some pride if she needs it so badly." The Falcon frowned against the rising sun. "And she is not our prisoner, nor are you. Everyone but the girl may go as they please."

The girl. Andry's chest tightened, his teeth grinding together.

"Everyone but the girl is expendable, Falcon," Sigil called after them. "Her blood can save the realm, if your commander would only let it."

Huffing, she stalked off, stopping only to grab Corayne away from the oasis pool. Corayne allowed herself to be dragged, scowling with every step.

The squire knew where they were going, and that Sorasa would soon join. Corayne's fighting lessons had begun again, now that they were no longer half dead with exhaustion. He did not envy Corayne. Sorasa and Sigil were talented teachers, and far from gentle.

"Are all Temur women like that?" the Falcon muttered, his eyes still following Sigil's form.

Andry tried not to smirk at the Falcon's clear fascination, if not infatuation.

"I wouldn't know," the squire replied. *I've never met any.* "But she isn't wrong."

He looked from Sigil to Corayne, her shoulders squared, the Spindleblade sheathed across her back. When they stopped walking, content with some flat ground, she laid it gently in the dirt. Her fingers brushed the sword for a lingering moment.

Does she remember the Spindle cut beneath its edge? Does she think of the blood it spilled?

Andry shuddered despite the growing heat, feeling his skin prickle beneath his cloak. He felt the weight of the dead so keenly, the bodies lying heavy across his shoulders.

Does Corayne? Can she?

His mouth went dry.

Will the sword make her a monster, as it did her uncle?

"Corayne an-Amarat is the key to saving us all," he said forcefully, for the Falcon as much as himself. "Whether you believe it or not."

The Falcon rocked back on his heels, cracking a half smile. "She's certainly the key to something." And then he leaned close, tapping two fingers over Andry's heart.

Another searing bloom of heat crossed Andry's cheeks. *Am I eternally sunburned or eternally embarrassed?*

"Sir—" the squire sputtered out, only to have the Falcon hold up a quieting hand.

"We've only been riding together for three days, but it's clear to see where your heart lies," he said, his face softening, his voice devoid of judgment. "Keep her close."

With that Andry could not argue. "Always."

"And keep an eye on the Amhara viper." The Falcon sharpened again. "She'll poison you all if it means saving her own wretched scales."

Andry followed the Falcon's stare, finding Sorasa Sarn's lean silhouette. She busied herself repositioning Corayne's raised fists, improving her defenses. Killer though she might be, an assassin with more blood on her hands than Andry could fathom, he felt only gratitude toward her. He remembered the canyon, how Sorasa leapt into the saddle, risking Gallish arrows and stampeding horses to save Corayne from being crushed. He remembered when Sorasa returned to the court at Ascal in the nick of time, saving them all from Erida's betrayal and Taristan's hunger.

"I do not agree," Andry forced out, meeting the Falcon's eye with all the steel he could muster.

The Falcon opened his mouth to argue, but thought better of it and bowed his head instead. "Very well, Squire," he said, stepping back. "I wish you a good day's rest."

Grateful, Andry dipped his brow. "And you, Falcon."

The squire strode over the sand, feeling the heat of it even through his boots. Though exhaustion ate at his edges, he wandered toward the lesson, which had gained a small audience.

Corayne stood between Sorasa and Sigil, red-faced. From exertion or embarrassment, Andry couldn't tell, but she pushed through. *As she always does.*

A few Falcons watched from a respectful distance, silent and observant.

Andry drew up alongside Dom, who glowered beneath his cloak. The hood hid his scars, but not his darting green eyes. They followed every move Corayne made.

Andry followed her too.

There were no blades today, at least. Corayne had tiny nicks all over her hands from blade training, and they were healing slowly after so many nights riding the desert. *She'll have bruises now too*, he thought, flinching as she dodged a punch only to have Sorasa trip her to the ground.

"I find it difficult to watch as well," Dom muttered out of the corner of his mouth.

Andry could only nod.

Corayne rose alone, planting her feet as she was taught, shifting her weight properly. As a squire and a future knight, Andry was trained to fight in armor and on horseback, with fine swords and shields. His teachers were old soldiers, very far from an Amhara assassin and a bounty hunter of the Temurijon. Corayne might never wield a longsword or lead a cavalry charge, but she was certainly learning to scrap in a back alley.

And learning well.

"She needs this," Andry said. This time, Corayne dodged Sorasa's lashing foot, jumping instead of falling. But she lost her balance and ended up on the ground again, Sorasa at her neck.

Dom's lip curled. "She has us."

"And I hope she always will."

He glanced sidelong at Dom. *We are surrounded by death, and still he doesn't understand it*, Andry thought, gritting his teeth in frustration. *He doesn't accept it.*

The squire dropped his voice. "But you and I know how quickly that can change."

After a long, hard moment, Dom met his eye, his brow furrowed into a single grim line.

"I am an immortal of the Vedera, a son of Glorian Lost. I do not think of death the way you mortals do, and I will not fear it either," he growled.

It was a poor mask.

Andry's natural instinct was to swallow his retort, to bury rough words. To find a gentler way. But the road had ways of changing a person, especially the road they were walking now.

"I've seen too many of you so-called immortals die," Andry said, unblinking. "Once, I wondered if you Elders could even bleed. Now I've seen enough of your blood to last a lifetime."

Dom shifted, uncomfortable. One hand touched his side, where a dagger once stabbed through his rib cage.

"I do not need to be reminded of such things, Squire."

"I think you do. We *all* do," Andry forced out. Again Corayne hit the ground, and again he winced with her. This time, Sigil pulled her up and dusted her off. "We need Corayne to save the realm, and we need her to be capable enough to do it when—*if*—we can no longer stand beside her."

With a sigh, Dom lowered his hood. Even in the dune shade, his golden hair gleamed and his scars stood out, red and ruinous. He looked back to Corayne, to Sorasa, to Sigil, to the horizon that was both a shield and a threat.

"By the gods of Glorian, I pray that day never comes," he said.

Andry blew out a slow breath. "By the gods of the Ward, so do I."

The squire did not consider himself religious, like many of his compatriots back in Ascal, who dedicated their swords and shields to mighty Syrek. Nor even like his mother, who prayed every morning at her hearth, calling to the cleansing fires of Fyriad the Redeemer. But still he hoped one of the gods of the pantheon would hear them, and the gods of Glorian too. Whatever god there was to listen, across the many infinite realms. *We certainly need you.*

"I bid you both to sleep," Valtik said, suddenly so close she might have popped out of the sand. Her wrinkled white face leered beneath her gray braids, woven with fangs and fresh jasmine. Where she'd found such a flower in the desert, Andry did not know.

"Away, Witch," Dom muttered, drawing up his hood again.

She barely reacted, her lightning-blue eyes locked on Andry. "Sleep," she said again. "Look forward, forget the creatures of the deep."

It was not the sea serpents of Meer or even the kraken that plagued Andry's mind, but he nodded anyway, if only to keep the witch moving along.

"I will, *Gaeda*," he said, using the Jydi word for *grandmother*. One of a few Corayne had taught him.

He looked past the dunes, up into the desert sky. The pink wash of sunrise had given over to searing blue. Every second ticked against them, and Andry felt it keenly, as he felt a cloak of exhaustion settle on his shoulders.

"The Falcons may not want to kill us, but they're certainly slowing us down," he muttered.

Dom growled in agreement.

At the edge of the rudimentary training circle, the onlooking Falcons whispered back and forth. One of them cracked a cruel smile, his sharp eyes darting over Sorasa.

Andry tensed, his jaw tightening, as he remembered the other Falcon's warning.

They kept talking, louder now. Still in their own language, but the hateful tone was clear even to Andry. Sorasa didn't react, gathering her gear.

Corayne didn't share such restraint. She snapped back in Ibalet, the words as harsh and hard as her black-eyed stare.

The Falcons only roared with laughter, watching her pace across the sand to join Andry and Dom.

"You speak our tongue well!" the tallest one shouted at her, raising a finger to his brow in salute. "Has the snake been teaching you that too?"

"I only teach her what is useful," Sorasa answered, crossing the sand without so much as a glance. "Speaking with you is not useful."

Then it was Corayne's and Sigil's turn to laugh, smothering their grins with battered hands. The Falcons lost their keen smiles, all three of their faces dropping into scowls. The tall one took a step forward, his black brow furrowed into a grim line.

"The Heir only wants the girl," he said loudly, his voice meant to carry. He took measured steps, eager to put himself in Sorasa's path. "We should cut the snake's head off and leave her to rot."

Dom's lip curled and he shifted, planting himself between Sorasa and the Falcon's cold eyes.

"You are very welcome to try, boy," the Elder said, staring down at the Falcon. "Would you like to meet that goddess of yours?"

To the Falcon's credit, he did not flinch or show fear, even as death itself loomed over him.

"You must be getting slow," the Falcon called around Dom's form. "I didn't know Amhara needed bodyguards."

Sorasa's response was faster than her whip.

"We Amhara have many weapons, not all of them blades." She spun as she carried on, walking backward. This time, she smiled as wide as she could, her tiger eyes malicious with joy. "Sleep well, Falcon," she called, blowing him a kiss.

The Falcon recoiled as he would from a disgusting insect.

"Relax, Elder," Sorasa added, turning back around. "These birds are all song."

Sigil moved to flank Dom, a half smile across her bronze face. She swept a lock of black hair out of her eyes, rolling her broad, muscular shoulders.

"Are we scrapping, sparrows?" she said, raising her chin. "I love a good fight before bed."

Andry's heartbeat quickened. He wanted to go, to move them all along, but he stayed rooted to the sand beneath his boots. If his friends were in danger, he wanted to be ready. *Not like the temple. Here I can stand my ground.*

Instead Corayne caught him beneath the arm, pulling him along.

"C'mon, let them be," she said, urging him back to camp. "Even the Falcons aren't brave enough to take on Sigil and Dom alone."

"They may be stupid enough," Sorasa said from his opposite side.

"You should be careful, Sorasa," Corayne muttered. She looked around the camp, at the dozens of Falcon soldiers taking up their posts or sleeping. "They really do want you dead."

Andry nodded, fixing Sorasa with a firm look. "Don't go anywhere alone."

She stared at them both, stone-faced. "Your concern is insulting," she said, waving them away.

Corayne and Andry returned to their cloaks and saddlebags, eager for sleep. It wasn't the most comfortable place Andry had ever slept, but he certainly didn't mind. His limbs seemed to melt into the sand as he lay back, shutting his eyes to the clear blue sky.

She was almost too close, one hand only inches from his own, their fingers near to brushing. He needed only shift to touch her, to take her hand and squeeze. Their disagreement earlier still stung, twisting his insides.

Tell her it's going to be all right. Tell her we can do this. Even if you don't believe in it, believe in her.

Andry looked out through slitted eyes, only to find Corayne already fast asleep, her face slack, her lips parted. The wind stirred over her, blowing a single strand of black hair over her cheek. It took all his restraint as a courtly squire not to push it away. Even looking at her felt like a step too far.

He tore his gaze away, his eyes passing over the camp.

At the base of the dune, the Falcons knelt in the sand, a figure in a brown cloak among them. After a long moment, Andry realized it was Charlie.

He was kneeling too, his hands raised toward the sun. With his hood lowered, he looked younger. There were splotches of sunburn across his cheeks, and his brown braid trailed past his shoulder blades, freshly woven. It was almost easy to forget that the fugitive priest was only a few years older than Andry. He had lived so much life already.

His lips moved, and though Andry could not hear his voice, it was easy to guess.

Charlie was praying, and the Falcons prayed with him.

To which god, Andry did not know.

It will not hurt to try them all, he thought, shutting his eyes again. With a deep breath, he began the names.

Syrek. Meira. Lasreen. Fyriad . . .

5

THE ICE ALWAYS WINS
Ridha

The princess of Iona took a liking to Dyrian's bear, and little else in Kovalinn. Autumn in the fjord was like deepest winter in Calidon, and snow fell almost every day, blanketing the immortal enclave in white. It glittered in the morning sun, a beautiful hindrance. Ice choked the fjord, and Ridha spent many days breaking it apart with the other Vedera, keeping the water clear for ships. So did Dyrian's bear, who took to prancing along the shattered edge, bashing at the ice floes with his massive paws. But more ice bloomed overnight, spreading with the cold.

Kesar joined Ridha today, a long, spiked ax in hand like the rest of them. Her topaz cheeks flushed in the cold; the rest of her body swaddled in leather and fur. Despite her centuries in the north, Kesar was of Salahae, far south in Kasa, and the deserts of Glorian before it. Though she'd spent long years in the cold, her years in the sun were longer still.

"You have no love for this weather," Ridha said, watching her work. They all stood on planks built out over the water, supported docks to allow ice-breaking without any risk of dropping into the fjord.

Today Kesar's black-and-gray locks were pulled back, tucked into a fur hat. She stabbed her ax into the ice, and a long fissure cracked through the white like a bolt of lightning.

"Observant, Princess," Kesar replied, smiling.

Ridha drove her own poleax into the ice. She leaned against it, peering at the older Veder. "Then why remain here?"

"In Glorian, I was a soldier. In Salahae, I was a teacher. In Kovalinn, I am right hand to the Monarch. Why would I leave?" Kesar said, shrugging.

Ridha could only nod.

The great hall of Kovalinn loomed over them, set high into the cliffs, alongside a half-frozen waterfall spilling into the fjord. Its walls and long, angled rooftops gleamed with snow.

"What about you?" Kesar gestured to Ridha, waving a hand over the princess's own furs. "You have no reason to remain here. We expected you to be gone a week ago, off to rouse more enclaves to war. Or can you send, as your mother did?"

Ridha snarled in frustration. "No, I have none of the power my mother wields, but what I lack in magic, I make up for in sense. Would that I could send, and raise the immortal armies of the Ward."

"So why stay?" Kesar said again, pressing closer.

Ridha drew back her broad shoulders. "I will not ride away from a fight I pulled you into."

"I suspected as much," Kesar said with a smirk, returning to her ice-breaking. "So did Dyrian."

Grimacing, Ridha did the same, wrenching her ax from the fjord's frozen grip. She tightened her grasp, raising the poleax high before driving it into the ice with all her considerable strength. It shattered beneath her, cracks spreading in every direction. It wasn't the same as training, preparing for the war to come, but the exertion pleased Ridha all the same.

She glanced back up at Kovalinn, and the long, zigzagging road up the cliff face that led to the enclave. A few horses and Vedera moved along it, passing back and forth between the hall and the fjord docks below. Ridha's keen eyes saw them all with hawk's precision. Like the clans of the Jyd, the Kovalinn enclave was home to Vedera from all across the world, each varying in appearance and origin.

One of them stood out, perched on the ramparts crowning the walls. She was as still as the bears carved into her gates, and just as fearsome. Ridha noted her pale white skin, red hair, and steely disposition. Her manner had not changed since Ridha first came to the enclave and begged her son to fight.

"His mother does not like me," she growled, lowering her eyes from the Lady of Kovalinn.

"Lucky the Monarch has a mind of his own, far sharper than his years might suggest." Kesar added, "And Lady Eyda doesn't like anyone."

"She's a cousin of my mother's," Ridha said. "Distant, but still family."

Kesar only laughed. "Most of the older generations are by now, bound either by blood or our shared destiny in this realm. If you were expecting a warm welcome from one such as Eyda, you were mistaken."

"Clearly." The Lady of Kovalinn still stood the walls, staring out into the long, craggy jaws of the fjord, toward the Glorysea. "She seems to be made of stone."

"She is Glorianborn." Kesar's joyful air faded a little, and a grim shadow Ridha recognized passed over her face. "We are graver than you children of the Ward."

Ridha tasted bitterness on her own tongue. *The light of different stars*, she thought, remembering her mother and how she used to glare at the sky, as if she could will the stars of Glorian to replace the stars of the Ward.

"I know that more than most," the princess muttered, cracking an ice floe to pieces. They scattered across the frigid waters, white against iron gray.

"Do not hold it against her, Princess." Kesar dropped her voice. "Eyda did not cross to Allward by choice."

In the great hall, Eyda stood taller than the rest, her long red hair plaited into two braids, with a circlet of hammered iron on her brow. Her gown was chain mail; a fine white fox fur draped around her shoulders. Every piece of her screamed warrior queen, but nothing so much as the scars. The ones on her knuckles were ancient, from brawling. But the other, the pearly white line across her throat? Ridha saw it in her mind.

Not the work of a blade. But a rope.

Her eyes widened and Kesar nodded gravely.

"She was forced into Allward as punishment. The old king of

Glorian gave her a choice between death and exile, and this is what she chose." She raised her hands, gesturing to the fjord, and the lands beyond it. "Whatever joy she found in this mortal realm died with Dyrian's father."

That was a tale Ridha knew.

Dragonflame and ruin, she remembered. It was three centuries ago, and still she could smell the air choked with ash even miles away from the battlefield. The beast had been mountainous, ancient, its jeweled hide stronger than steel. Now its bones were dust, its shadow gone from the realm, like all the other Spindleborn monsters upon the Ward. So many Vedera had not returned, including Domacridhan's parents. They had died bringing down the last dragon left upon the Ward, and so had the old Monarch of Kovalinn.

"Three hundred years since the enclaves came together and fought what the Ward could not defeat," Ridha said, the weight of it sinking in.

Kesar nodded. "Until now."

"Until now," Ridha answered.

"How many will not return from this battlefield?" Kesar murmured.

Ridha steeled herself. "Everyone, if the battle is not fought at all."

Fear had become familiar to the Vederan princess in the short months since the slaughter at the temple. It grew in Domacridhan's absence, blooming like roses in a garden. She had heard nothing of him since he rode from Iona, dead but for his still-beating heart. He could be truly dead now, for all she knew. *Leaving only me to stand between the Ward and What Waits.* She heaved a rattling breath, trying to ignore the ache in her bones. Not from the cold, not from the ax, not even from her hours in the training yard, practicing in full armor. It was her mother who had made this wound. The cowardice of Isibel, Monarch of Iona.

The ash branch still lay across her knees, the sword she would not wield forgotten in her gray halls. Ridha cursed her mother. *Perhaps she'll hear me*, she thought, thinking of her mother's power, and the far reach it gave her.

"I see the anger in you, Princess," Kesar said softly, hesitant. Tentative as a traveler walking across broken ice.

Ridha sighed, her chest rising and falling beneath her furs. "There is gratitude in me too," she murmured. "So much it is almost overwhelming. To you, to Dyrian, even to the cold Lady of Kovalinn. For ignoring my mother. For refusing to leave the Ward to its dark fate. For all of you who refuse to surrender." The air froze on her teeth. "I will not surrender either."

She looked south down the fjord, toward Calidon and Iona. She could not see the only homeland she'd ever known, but she felt it still, miles across the freezing sea, through mountains and glens.

Then her gaze sharpened, her eyes fixing on something much closer than Iona.

Dark shapes took form on that distant horizon, spots at first but quickly solidifying into something familiar. Ridha squinted her immortal eyes, looking down the miles.

Longships bearing white flags, sailing under a symbol of peace.

"Mortals," she said aloud, pointing with her ax.

"The first have arrived," Kesar said, clapping Ridha on the

shoulder. "Leave the ax," Kesar added, tossing hers away. She glanced at the fjord and the choking pieces of ice. Even shattered, they clustered together, floating on the frigid water.

Ridha did as instructed, abandoning her ax to the other Vedera chopping at the frozen landscape. She set off with Kesar, silent, waiting for some explanation. With a click of her teeth, Kesar summoned the bear to follow. It gave a friendly roar and tromped along, ice shaking from its paws.

Behind them, the longships continued their journey toward Kovalinn.

Kesar pressed her lips, stepping off the dock to join the long, winding path up to the enclave. "The ice always wins," she muttered, glaring at the fjord.

As with the other mortal kingdoms, Ridha knew little and cared even less about the politics of the Jyd. They had no monarchy, she knew that much, with no king or queen she could call upon for the full might of raider country. Instead there were a dozen different clans, all ranging in size and strength, that controlled different regions of the bitter northlands. The Jydi were a strong people, fearsome to the other mortal kingdoms, but disjointed, each clan separate from the others.

The mortals were of Yrla, a settlement across the mountains, at the spearpoint of another fjord. They'd brought four longships, now docked at the bottom of the cliff.

The long hall of the enclave waited, bursting with Vedera eager to see the Jydi. The doors yawned wide, spilling the orange light of sunset across the stone floor.

Dyrian held his seat, his back straight against the carved wood. His feet dangled, his legs still too short to reach the floor. Like his mother, he had red hair and pale skin, a starburst of freckles across his cheeks. To the Jydi, he looked like a young boy, but the Vedera knew better. His wolf-gray eyes were sharp, and he held a smiling ax across his knees. The pine branch was long discarded. His enclave was at war.

Kesar and the snoring bear held his right side, while Lady Eyda stood as always, a statue behind her son. Ridha sat at Dyrian's left, befitting her status as a princess and child of a ruling monarch, though she looked nothing like it. She'd abandoned her fur coat for her green steel armor, eager to look as much a warrior as the Jydi. Both pit fires were lit, filling the long hall with warmth. She basked in it, the numbing grip of the ice finally melting away.

A dozen mortals entered the hall, their shadows stretching long across the floor. They walked between the pit fires, approaching Dyrian's throne. Light from the flames played over them, shifting their faces with every step. Ridha surmised that the rest of their number were outside in the gateyard, or still down with their ships. She guessed at least a hundred Jydi folk had come to Kovalinn.

For what reason, no one said, but Ridha was no fool.

Dyrian was unbothered by the Jydi raiders, fierce in every inch, but Ridha eyed their weapons. Of all the mortals upon the Ward, only the Jydi ever attempted to war with the Vedera, and she had not forgotten it. They bore axes and long knives, and two even carried cruel, hooked spears. These were not farmers. These were raiders.

Half were fair-skinned and blond or red-haired, if not shorn bald. But one of the men was once of the Temurijon, wearing their distinct plated leather armor beneath a cloak of wolf pelts. He had short black hair, angular dark eyes, high-boned cheeks, and bronze skin. Two women were from the kingdoms of the Long Sea, perhaps Tyriot, with curly hair the color of mahogany, their faces olive-toned. Only one had gray hair, his braids woven with herbs. He alone wore no furs, only a thick wool dress that covered his boots, with a long chain of iron looping from shoulder to shoulder. All were tattooed in Jydi whorls, the backs of their bare hands marked with distinctive knots.

Their leader, a small, pale woman with a longbow and an anvil jaw, even had a wolf tattooed on the shorn half of her scalp. The rest of her hair was plaited into a long blond braid, set with chain and carved bone. Though she was smaller than the other raiders, they clearly deferred to her, letting her walk ahead. When she came closer, Ridha realized she had one green eye and one blue, the shared colors of the Jyd.

"Welcome, friends," Dyrian said, standing from his seat. "I am Dyrian, Monarch of Kovalinn, of the Vedera of Glorian Lost."

The raiders did not bow. A few eyed the bear, snoring at Dyrian's right hand.

"I am Lenna, Chief of the Yrla," rasped their leader, her voice deeper than expected. She spoke in Paramount, her words heavily accented by the Jydi language. This far north, she clearly had little use for the common tongue of the Long Sea.

Dyrian dipped his head in greeting. "It has been many years since mortals of the Jyd entered my hall."

"The chief of my chief came here, long ago," Lenna said. She squinted at the Monarch. "He met a boy king. You are *still* a boy."

"I am," Dyrian answered. "My people do not age as yours do."

"I can see."

Lenna noted the Vedera gathered around the throne and throughout the hall. Her gaze passed over Ridha, hanging for a moment. The princess of Iona did not move, but curled her hands on the arms of her seat, the silver ring on her thumb scraping against wood. Ridha was a warrior trained, with centuries on the Yrla chief, not to mention twice her size. But she saw the challenge in Lenna's sharp stare.

"Thank you for coming," Kesar said, moving to stand with Dyrian. "I know our kinds have not always been friends, but we need each other now."

Grinning, Lenna showed a pair of gold incisors. They gleamed, catching the light of the pit fires. "We fight everyone, not just you, Elder."

The Jydi were not politicians. They did not need to bluster or boast. It was simply true. They were known for their raiding throughout the Glorysea and even as far south as the Tyri Straits. Port cities dreaded their longships as much as any storm.

Ridha felt her legs moving before she even knew she was out of her seat. In three long strides, she stood nose to nose with Lenna. Or, rather, nose to neck.

"And now we must fight together," Ridha said, looking down at the chief.

The raiders did not quail, and Lenna only smiled wider. "That's why we have come."

"Good." Ridha breathed an inward sigh of relief. *At least they're straightforward.* "Allward will need you. All of you."

"And more will come," Lenna answered, her voice deepening. In spite of her smile, Ridha saw the understanding in her. Things were far worse than they seemed. "But Yrla came first."

"Yrla came first," Ridha echoed, nodding in gratitude. "History will remember that. I promise."

Lenna wagged a finger inked like a snake. "Put us in a song, not a book."

Ridha could only nod again. *If there is anyone left to sing*, she thought.

"The Queen of Galland is on the march," Kesar said to the hall, her words carrying. "She is waging war against the world, and Prince Taristan of Old Cor—"

"Yes, yes, the Spindle man," Lenna said, cutting her off. She waved her hand in a circle, gesturing for Kesar to move on. She seemed almost bored by the ending of the world. "He will bring a great evil to the realm—we know this already. And that silly queen," she scoffed, rolling her blue and green eyes. Behind her, a few of the raiders laughed. "Too much power. It rots, and we will rot with them."

The Vedera stood silent, perplexed by Lenna's boldness. Ridha only found it intriguing.

"You know Erida of Galland?" she asked.

Behind their chief, the raiders laughed among themselves. Lenna's gold teeth flashed as she joined them.

"A little, I tried to wed her," she said, shrugging.

"You could have saved us all a great deal of trouble," Ridha sighed. *Such a union would be impossible, of course. Rulers need heirs.* The princess of Iona knew that far too well, and rued the day her turn would come to provide the next monarch of her enclave. "I'm sorry she said no."

"I am not," Lenna answered bluntly, meeting Ridha's gaze. She stared, unblinking, the full weight of her focus boring into her.

Ridha did not mind her attention in the slightest, and stared back.

It was Dyrian who broke them apart, striding between chief and princess. He was nearly Lenna's height, and judging by his mother, he had a great deal left to grow. At his throne, the bear yawned. After a week in Kovalinn, Ridha found him harmless, but the raiders drew back, wary of his massive jaws.

Only Lenna did not flinch.

"We will go south to Ghald, all of us," Dyrian said. "And see what clans answer the call to fight."

"Many will. Blodin, Hjorn, Gryma, Agsyrl, the Snowlands." Lenna rattled off pieces of the Jyd, listing the many clans from the barren tundra to the eastern coast. Ridha didn't know half of them. "We have not raided this year. We are ready."

Ridha remembered those poor farmers in the Castlewood and their empty-headed plot. *Raiders aren't raiding*, they'd said, though they had no idea why.

"How did you know to stop raiding?" she asked, still holding Lenna's eye.

The chief shifted, turning aside. She gestured for one of the raiders to take her place. "Witch."

The man without armor stepped forward, long fingers arranging his braids. He seemed delighted to address the Vedera.

"The south thinks we are stupid, simple, unwell," he said, leering around at them. "But we see more than they do." The old witch rattled a pouch at his belt before spilling its contents across the floor. "So the bones tell."

Ridha's toes curled in her boots as all types of animal bones spilled over the stonework. Vertebrae, ribs, femurs. Rabbits, rats, birds. Most were boiled clean, but a few seemed *fresh*.

The witch gaped at the skeletons on the floor, showing cracked and yellowed teeth.

"A storm comes," he hissed before drawing a ragged, shallow breath. It whistled strangely.

Dyrian furrowed his red brow. "Yes, it does."

"No—*here, now,*" the witch muttered, fumbling for words. He pointed to the bones, his finger trembling. Behind him, the raiders tightened in warning, even fearless Lenna. Many hands went to many weapons.

The witch rounded on his chief. "Sound the drums."

"What storm is coming?" Dyrian demanded.

Ridha watched the chief, trying to understand. But the woman only loosed her bow and ran for the great doors at the end of the hall. Without thinking, Ridha matched her steps, until she found herself hurtling out into the cold air and dying sunlight. The others followed, thundering in their wake, both raider and Vedera. The bone witch wailed somewhere back in the hall, crying out in Jydi. Ridha could not understand but heard his terror all the same. It echoed in every mortal around her, their beating hearts suddenly louder than any war drum.

She passed Lenna, lunging up the steps to the ramparts above the Kovalinn gate. The fjord stretched out in front of her, reflecting the streaking rays of the sun as it dipped behind the eastern mountain range. It flashed orange and red, a bloody mirror between perilous cliffs. First she looked to the slopes. *An avalanche?* she wondered, searching for any sign of cold, white death. *Has the ice closed in?* But the waters remained as they were hours ago, clear enough for ships.

"What is it?" she demanded, as if the frosty air would answer.

Chief Lenna fell in alongside her, her bow already raised, an arrow to the string. Her piercing eyes stared, not at the fjord or the mountains, but at a sky brindled with fiery clouds.

"*Dryskja!*" Lenna yelled, her arrow pointed up.

Below, the raiders howled a battle cry and clanged their blades, thumping their feet against the packed earth of the gateyard. The Jydi roar echoed down the fjord, rattling between the mountains until Ridha felt it in her teeth.

The princess knew little of true fear. Until now. It felt like a knife in her stomach, a wound leaching away her resolve. "'*Dryskja*'?" she asked, a scream caught in her throat.

Lenna shot an arrow without blinking. It climbed a hundred yards into the sky, disappearing into a cloud. Ridha followed its path, her Vederan eyes narrowed. Her blood ran cold.

A shadow moved in the sky, behind the clouds, too swift to be a storm, too dark to be anything else.

In the heavens, something roared, loud and deep enough to

shake the wooden wall beneath Ridha's feet. The princess of Iona nearly fell, her legs going numb.

Beside her, Lenna dared not take her eyes off the sky as she nocked another arrow. The shadow swooped overhead, closer now but still not out of the cloud bank.

"Dragon," she snarled.

6

DEATH'S MIRROR
Corayne

At first, Corayne thought it was a mirage. It would not be the first she saw after two weeks in the dunes, a hazy image of the sea or a camel caravan. But they were still miles from the coast, and there were no trade routes through this part of the Great Sands. There were no villages to visit, no goods to collect or sell in this part of the Ward. Nothing but golden sand and jeweled sky.

And now the tent, a perfect midnight blue, planted below the horizon like a night-blooming flower. Corayne squinted through the slanting shadows of dusk, trying to make it out. She wasn't the only one. Dom stood in the saddle, his Elder eyes fixed ahead, with Sorasa alongside him. He muttered something to her and she tightened her jaw, her black-rimmed eyes going wide.

"What is it?" Corayne asked, but the thunder of hooves swallowed up her voice.

She didn't mind. It was the wrong question anyway.

Who is it?

The answer came, obvious even to a pirate's daughter on the wrong side of the sea.

The Heir of Ibal.

As they rode closer, Corayne realized that *tent* wasn't the right word. She did not know what to call it, this stretch of canvas the size of a small village. It looked like many tents raised together, connected by intricate passages like alleys. Each was the same shade of beautiful blue, the color of Ibal's flag, the slanted roofs embroidered with silver moons and golden suns. A flashing dragon perched on the highest point of the tents, its wings spread wide, its long tail curling around the tent peak. The setting sun flashed off its bared teeth. All of it was hammered gold.

As the Falcons slowed their horses, Corayne leaned in the saddle, angling toward Andry. Despite their argument, he still rode at her side, and Corayne was glad for it. Even if his words still stung.

Am I a monster too? she still wondered, feeling the sword against her legs. *Is that how he sees me?*

"Who carries a solid gold dragon into the desert?" she muttered, grasping for something to say. Her eyes traced the dragon leering over the tents.

Andry's grin flashed, white teeth in a brown face. At the sight of his smile, some tightness in her chest unwound. She blew out a sigh of relief.

"Well, the King of Ibal is rich beyond measure," he said.

"Gold are his hands, gold is his treasure," Corayne finished the old children's rhyme. "Gold are his fleets patrolling every inch of the Strait," she added with a grumble, thinking of the tolls every ship must pay to cross the Long Sea.

What I would pay to cross it now, she thought. The pang of sorrow took her by surprise, and she had to lower her face.

"Corayne?" Andry prodded, his voice gentle.

But she shook her head, turning away. She was grateful when her sand mare came to a halt, and she slid from the saddle. When her boots hit the ground, her legs weren't quite as weak as the days before.

And the Spindleblade was not as heavy.

The tent city beckoned like open jaws, the sky above streaked pink and purple with the sunset. A few early stars gleamed. In another life, Corayne would have found the sight beautiful. Now dread replaced the all too familiar exhaustion, the heat of the sun giving over to cold fear.

Dom and Andry flanked her, as always, with Sigil and Charlie behind. Sorasa led, her gait easy to match, her head turning back and forth like a hawk looking for prey. Valtik plodded behind them, the old woman just as pale as she had been when they landed in Almasad. Not like the rest of them. Even Dom's Elder skin had a pink tinge, while Sigil's and Sorasa's faces had darkened in the sun.

Mine too, Corayne knew, though she had not seen her own face since—she could not even remember. But the prickling pain had receded from her cheeks, her sunburn at last giving over to tanned skin. *Perhaps I look more like my mother*, she thought, her heart giving a tiny leap. Years of sailing had left Meliz the color of finely made bronze. *And less like my father. Less like Taristan.*

Even his name was a dark cloud. It settled over her, heavier than the sword on her back.

But worse than his name was the presence behind her uncle. What Waits was always waiting, curled in the corners of her mind, her nightmares of Him only a heartbeat away. Only her exhaustion kept him largely at bay, thanks to their grueling pace across the desert and her daily training. Sorasa and Sigil were a better lullaby than any Corayne had ever known.

The Falcons marched them to the largest tent in the makeshift outpost. Guards protected the open flap, wearing scale-patterned bronze armor beneath deep blue cloaks. Each held a steel-tipped spear twice his height. Unlike the Falcons, they wore helmets forged to look like dragon skulls. They obscured their faces, turning each guard into a grim monster.

The Companions passed into the massive tent without a word, a mouth of cool air and dark shadows swallowing them up. Most of the Falcons remained outside, but for Commander lin-Lira, who fell in beside Sorasa.

Falcon and Amhara, side by side.

When Corayne's eyes adjusted to the dim light, she could see that the tent was subdivided into rooms on either side, with the center forming a long hall. There was a round table in the middle, surrounded by chairs, but no one sat. The only figures in the room clustered at the far end, standing around a polished bronze mirror. It illuminated the room better than any candle, catching the pink light of sunset from a slit cut in the tent high above.

Someone knelt before the mirror, staring at its surface. *No, into it*, Corayne realized. *At the light itself.*

"Lasreen's Chosen," Charlie whispered under his breath, his usually calm voice oddly sharp. He put a hand to Corayne's arm, pulling her close as they walked.

"Every god in the pantheon has their hand upon the realm," he whispered. Charlie was not tall, and it was easy to bend their heads together. "One who can see their will and speak their words. Meira's Tidewatcher. Syrek's Own Sword." He ticked them off on his free hand. "The Heir is Lasreen's Chosen, both royal and holy."

Meliz an-Amarat had never been one for religion or prayer, even for Meira, goddess of the sea she loved so much. And Corayne followed suit. She knew trade routes and tax law better than the godly pantheon and its many intricate weavings.

She dropped her voice, leaning into Charlie.

"They can speak for a goddess?" Corayne muttered, glancing at the Heir again. The mirror gleamed. Even after all Corayne had seen, it felt difficult to believe.

"They can say whatever they like," Charlie said, scoffing in reply. Bitterness laced his voice, and his warm brown eyes seemed to cool. He lowered his hood, exposing his sunburned faced and deepening scowl. "The gods speak through all of us, not just the so-called chosen."

Suddenly it was not so difficult to imagine why Charlie was a priest fallen, his order left behind. But he kissed his fingers and touched his brow. The fallen priest was still holier than the rest of them put together.

And holier still was Lasreen's Chosen, both dedicant and heir to the Ibalet throne. A royal servant to the goddess of life and death.

Corayne swallowed hard, trying to see the Heir's reflection in the mirror, but their visage was distorted in the dying light, mottled by the hammered and warped surface. Still, Corayne could make out that black, curling hair, unbound with no crown to mark their station, though their clothes were the finest Corayne had seen since Ascal. Blue woven with silver and gold thread, a long silk coat over an even longer tunic, both light enough for the desert heat.

The dragon guards flanked the mirror and their charge, stoic and inscrutable behind their helms. They were silent, as were the dark-eyed handmaidens seated nearby, both in identical dark blue dresses. Another guard stood over the kneeling royal, his scaled armor gleaming, but his head was bare, his fanged helmed beneath one arm.

He rounded on the approaching Companions with a glare like living fire, black eyes bright in the dim hall. Like the Heir, he had ebony hair, wound back in a single braid, its tail held with a circle of blue lapis.

He looked down a long, elegant nose, one side of his mouth curling with distaste.

"You took your time, Commander," he said, his gaze flickering to lin-Lira.

The leader of the Falcons dipped his brow, touching his forehead in a small salute. "Our guests were not accustomed to our . . . *pace*," he answered, choosing his words carefully.

Still, he drew a barely veiled snarl from Sigil.

"I've not ridden so slowly since childhood," she grumbled under her breath. Thankfully, the bounty hunter fell silent as the Heir stood, rising from the carpeted ground.

The Heir had the same coloring as the dragon guard, and

the same piercing glare. *They must be siblings*, Corayne thought, glancing between them. Both were furious in their bearing, not beautiful but striking, like living statues of bronze and jet. Gold glimmered on the Heir's fingers, wrists, and neck. They wore no jewels, but countless chains thin as thread, all bright as the mirror.

Corayne knew others like the Heir, those who were neither man nor woman, or somewhere in between. Remembering her manners, Corayne dipped into a shaky bow, the best she could muster for an Ibalet royal.

"I saw your coming. I felt your presence in the shifting of the wind, in the disturbance of the sacred Shiran," the Heir said, their voice firm. For a moment, their gaze passed over them all, taking in each Companion from head to toe. Then their coal-black eyes settled, staring directly into Corayne's own.

"Corayne an-Amarat."

The Heir of Ibal raised their chin.

Never had Corayne's own name felt like a blow. She clenched her jaw, trying to look as fearsome as the rest of the Companions.

Sorasa stepped forward, arms crossed over her lean frame. At the Heir's side, their brother's hand strayed to his sword hilt. Like the Falcons, he noted her tattoos and her dagger, clear hallmarks of an Amhara assassin.

"Funny," Sorasa replied, shrugging. "We must have missed the welcome party, Isadere."

"Address my sibling by their rightful title or not at all, snake," the dragon soldier barked. His fingers closed and he drew the first inches of his sword from its sheath, showing naked, flashing steel.

To Corayne's right, Dom went for his own sword, faster than

the mortals could fathom. He did not draw, but the giant Elder was menacing enough, and even the Heir's brother fell back on his heels.

Sorasa's eyelids barely fluttered. "You see the irony of that statement, don't you, Sibrez?" She took another step. "And what title should I address you by? Royal Bastard?"

For a moment, Corayne thought Sibrez would draw on the Amhara. Until the Heir stepped between them, lips pursed. Isadere glared but said nothing. Instead they waved off their brother with a flap of their brown hands, their fingers long and elegant. Smooth. Unblemished by work or war.

Sibrez bowed, releasing his sword, though a muscle trembled in his cheek.

Isadere's attention snapped back to Corayne, their eyes locking together.

"You have Corblood in your veins," Isadere said, circling. Their feet were bare on the rich carpets, making no noise at all. The tent was shockingly quiet compared to the thunder of hooves across the desert.

Corayne bit her lip. Even though the proof of it lay behind them in the oasis, in the Spindleblade itself, she still felt uneasy with the knowledge of her father's bloodline. With strangers, and in her own heart.

"Only half," she forced out.

Each step brought Isadere closer, until they were only a yard away. Corayne smelled the perfumed oil they wore, jasmine and sandalwood. *Imported from Rhashir*, she knew, thinking of the long journey a priceless little bottle made before the oil came to rest on a royal's wrist.

"But it is the Corblood that drives you, pushes you forward into the unknown," Isadere said, their eyes wide and penetrating. Corayne tried not to fidget under their examination. "That's what I learned in my lessons anyway. That the descendants of Old Cor are restless, children of different stars, wayward and always searching for a home they will never find." The Heir looked to Dom next, angling their head. He did not move. "They say the same of the Elders too. I see Glorian in your eyes, Immortal."

Dom pulled a miraculous face somewhere between a smile and a grimace. "I am Wardborn, Your Highness. My eyes have never seen Glorian."

The Heir smiled, showing too many teeth. Like a shark. "But it lives in you," they said, shrugging. "Same as the goddess lives in me.

"Lasreen's light tells me many things—riddles, mostly," Isadere continued, spreading their hands wide. Their long sleeves trailed, the threads glittering like stars in a royal blue sky. "Confusing until they are already past, and then the line can be traced backward. But on one thing, the goddess is infinitely clear."

They held up a finger banded with gold. Behind them, the last rays of sunset glowed in the mirror. "The realm is in grave danger. The Ward is ready to fall."

Corayne ground her teeth together. *Is this what we wasted so much time on? Another royal who loves nothing more than the sound of their own voice telling us what we already know?*

"Yes, we're aware," Corayne bit out. At her side, Andry nudged her in the ribs. His own face was a mask, still and unreadable. The squire was more accustomed to royal nonsense than any of them.

Commander lin-Lira put a hand to his heart and bowed, drawing Isadere's attention. Their gaze softened.

"Galland is growing bold," he said, standing straight again. "Two hundred soldiers marched across our land, all to protect an abomination that would kill us and sink our fleets."

Ibal is the greatest sea power in the Ward. A threat to their navy is a threat to their entire kingdom, Corayne knew. And so did Galland.

"So it's true. The Spindle torn," Isadere breathed, biting their lip. "I must admit, I prayed it would not come to be. Prayed my readings were incorrect. But alas, the mirror does not lie, and here we stand."

Corayne eyed the bronze disc behind Isadere. Its hammered face seemed unremarkable, inscrutable. Hardly a source of prophecy.

Sibrez bared his teeth. "What remains of the monsters?"

With a hearty chuckle, Sigil clapped a closed fist to her leather cuirass. "Nothing but their bones," she preened. "You're welcome."

Sibrez inclined his head. "Well done, Temur."

Lin-Lira pushed on. "Queen Erida has not only broken our sovereignty, but she marches on Madrence in force."

"That is hardly news." Isadere flapped their hands. In the corners of the tent, the handmaidens set to lighting candles. The shadows around the hall lifted. "Galland squabbles with Madrence every decade."

"They march down the Rose, heading for Rouleine," lin-Lira continued, his voice deep with meaning.

Corayne knew little of gods and priests, but she knew maps. She knew the Ward. She saw the Queen's route in her mind, and her heartbeat quickened as she stifled a gasp, looking to Andry. He stared back, brow furrowed. She did not need to read his mind to see her own harried thoughts mirrored in his eyes. If Erida's armies were marching south along the Rose River, heading for the Madrentine city of Rouleine, they were truly at war. Her conquest—and Taristan's—had begun.

"I despise northern politics," Isadere muttered. "So barbaric."

Ever the squire, palace raised and court born, Andry stepped forward and swept into a practiced bow, bending at the waist.

"If I may, Your Highness?" he said, looking up to them in deference.

Isadere eyed him as they would a peculiar plant. "Yes?"

Andry straightened, a hand on his chest. "I am Gallish born, raised in Erida's court. There have been skirmishes along the border for generations, but no real army has ever moved in either direction, not for a hundred years. If what he says is true, then Queen Erida is well and truly at war in the north. And she's doing it with a monster at her side."

"The no-name she married?" Isadere scoffed, looking back to Sibrez. Their noble visages broke as they shared scornful smirks. "The all-mighty Queen of Galland, married to some jumped-up Cor nobody. I admit, even that escaped Lasreen's fortunes. But who am I to judge the whims of another heart?"

Corayne set her jaw. Resolute, she pulled aside her cloak and freed the Spindleblade, drawing the full length of steel from its sheath. Isadere's eyes danced along the blade, taking in the sword and its strange markings. So did the rest of the attendants, even the helmeted guardians, their eyes dotted with candlelight. Sibrez and lin-Lira examined the sword from a distance, fascinated by the ancient weapon. Corayne felt the full weight of the hall press down, the attention of every person trained on her.

The last time I stood before a royal, she tried to kill me. At least Isadere hasn't tried to do that . . . yet.

"That nobody is my uncle, Taristan of Old Cor, and the only other person alive who can open a Spindle," Corayne said. She tried to sound as strong as the steel in her grasp. *We failed to rally Galland to our side. We cannot fail again.* "He did it here, in your own lands. Tore open a portal to Meer, and sent monsters spewing into the sea. By my hand it was closed, saving your fleets from destruction." The sword felt right in her hand, not an anchor pulling her down, but a crutch holding her up. She leaned against it, letting its strength fill her. "And he's going to do it again, as soon as he can. No matter the cost to Allward."

After a long moment, Isadere raised their gaze from the blade. Their face tightened and they looked back to their mirror. But the light was gone, and the candles glowed poorly in its face. Whatever they wanted to see did not appear.

"Do you know where he might go next?" Isadere asked, and Corayne felt a wretched flare of hope. "To another Spindle?"

Before Corayne could answer, Charlie spoke up. He wore a playful smirk. "Should we ask your mirror?"

Isadere raised their chin. "The mirror shows what the goddess wills. It does not bend to mortal whims."

"So it only shows you what you need . . . after you need it?" Charlie needled. He clearly enjoyed this.

Corayne winced, fighting the urge to step on Charlie's foot.

The Heir flushed and scowled. They shifted, planting their body between Charlie and the sacred circle of bronze, as if it were a child to be protected. "I'll not hear blasphemy."

"You may cover your ears," Charlie answered, before Sigil clapped a hand over his mouth.

"I think Ibal is the only country you *aren't* wanted in," the bounty hunter grumbled, tugging him back into her chest. Despite Sigil's unyielding grip, Charlie rolled his eyes. "Are you trying to change that?"

"Would it kill you all to behave?" Corayne hissed through gritted teeth, managing to glare from Sorasa to Dom to Charlie.

She stepped sideways, hiding the muzzled Charlie from Isadere's view. *We are not here to debate religion.*

"You're right, Your Highness," she said, her fingers worrying the grip of the Spindleblade. The leather was starting to feel familiar, wearing to her own hand instead of her father's. She tried not to think on what that meant. "The Ward is in grave danger, and you've known this for a long time."

Isadere's chin dipped only an inch, but that was enough.

The hope in Corayne, the unkillable, foolish hope she tried too hard to ignore, continued to grow.

"So has your father, right?" she prodded, weighing Isadere's reaction.

The Heir's face darkened, the shark's smile turning into a shark's scowl. For a second Corayne worried, afraid she had overstepped.

Then Isadere shared a knowing look with their brother.

"Indeed he has," Sibrez answered. His voice trembled with frustration.

"So he fled," Corayne said. The threads wound together in her mind. "To the summer palace, high in the mountains."

Together the royal siblings paled, looking away. Shame crossed them like a storm. It passed over lin-Lira too, his callused hand curling into a fist.

"And you, your Falcons . . ." Corayne turned to the commander, reading his body language. "You refused to go with him. Your king, your own blood, your duty." He shifted under her scrutiny, and somehow Corayne felt like the elder of the two, though lin-Lira had decades on her.

"You crossed the crown to save the Ward," she murmured.

Though she'd spent many days under his command, at the mercy of lin-Lira and his soldiers, she felt like she was seeing him for the first time. The smile lines at the edge of his mouth, the spattering of gray in his beard. The kindness behind his eyes. The *fear* pulling at his edges. Suddenly he did not seem so intimidating, not compared to the ragged Companions his men herded out of the desert. *Killers, all of us now.* Corayne remembered the blood on her own hands. *Even me.*

Isadere laid a calming hand on lin-Lira's shoulder. They were not as young as Corayne first thought: lines of age showed on their own fierce face. As with lin-Lira, Corayne saw the doubt in them, the fear.

"There will be no crown to save if the Ward falls," Isadere breathed, their fingers lingering a little too long. Then they snapped their hand away, squaring their shoulders to Corayne, the Companions, and the Spindleblade.

The candlelight burned in their eyes. Though the flames were warm and golden, Corayne could not help but feel that cloying red heat, the embers of What Waits. They burned now, somewhere across the Ward, begging to ignite.

Isadere gestured to the table, bidding them to sit. "Tell me everything."

The handmaidens replaced the candles twice before Corayne finished her tale, with choice additions from both Dom and Andry. While most sat around the table, Sorasa paced in easy rhythm. Charlie remained stubbornly silent, wary of Sigil's monstrous hands. Though they spoke well into the night, Isadere's guardians followed Sorasa at a distance, never breaking stride, tireless in their watch on the Amhara. Corayne learned they were called the *Ela-Diryn*: the Blessed's Dragons. Like the Falcons protected the King of Ibal, so were these warriors sworn to defend Lasreen's Chosen. They would die on their own swords if Isadere told them the goddess wished it.

It was a fierce power to hold.

The Heir listened, thoughtful and silent.

But Erida listened too, and we all know where that got us.

"And then the Spindle was gone, forced shut," Corayne said, looking at the gash on her palm. It was healing well, despite long days gripping the reins of a horse. The Spindleblade was a thousand years old at least, but sharp as the day it was made. It cut clean. She still felt the bite of it, cold steel against flesh. "The waters receded back into the sand, leaving only the bodies and an empty oasis. We went to the outskirts to regroup. That's where the Falcons found us."

"Commander?" Isadere said, speaking for the first time in hours.

At the flap of the tent, lin-Lira nodded. "That is the truth of it," he sighed, nodding along.

Sigil leaned forward on her elbows, a lock of black hair falling into one eye. "Now here we are, your prisoners."

"For the final time, you are not prisoners—" lin-Lira huffed, only for Sigil to cut him off.

"Then are we free to leave?" she snapped, eyes on the Heir.

"Yes," Isadere answered neatly, without hesitation. "Eventually."

A low hiss escaped Sigil's mouth, weaving through gritted teeth. Corayne felt the same frustration but kicked her leg under the table to keep her quiet. A Temur caged was a disaster waiting to happen, a storm begging to break.

"What does Lasreen's Chosen ask of us?" Corayne said, forming the words carefully. Isadere straightened in their seat, clearly delighted by the title.

"Information," Isadere said. "Direction. Time."

Dom seemed mountainous in the low chair, his body like a pile of rocks. One hand lay on the table, still but for a single tapping finger. "Time for what?"

"To prepare, Elder." Isadere gestured to the flap of the tent and out into the desert. "If Erida of Galland is to make war on the entire realm, then we must make ready for it. I'll send envoys to Erida and to my father—"

Again, Sigil sneered. "You don't have time for diplomacy."

Corayne felt her own patience wear through. She stood quickly, rising over the table, wishing she could show them what they'd seen in Nezri. What she saw in her scattered dreams. *Red hands, white faces, something moving behind the shadows, something hungry and growing.*

"Didn't you hear what we just said?" she forced out, her face going hot.

The seconds dripped by, made worse by the silence of the tent.

"Erida sent soldiers into Ibal. Taristan ripped open a Spindle in your own lands, to target your own navy and cut you off." Corayne sliced a finger across the table. She wished for a map, if only to shove it in Isadere's face and make them *see*. "They're trying to weaken their strongest opponent before you even know you are at war!"

She expected Isadere to argue, or for their brother Sibrez to demand respect again. But neither of the royal siblings did anything, unmoving in their seats. Isadere lowered their eyes, blowing out a low breath.

"I am not the King of Ibal," they murmured, their words tinged with regret. "I cannot command his fleets or his armies."

Corayne winced. "Then what are we even doing here?"

"I am not the king," Isadere said again, louder this time. Their gaze sharpened. "But I *am* Lasreen's Chosen. I speak for a goddess, and the goddess tells me to help you. The goddess has shown the way."

Somewhere near the bronze mirror, at the other end of the hall, Sorasa stopped her pacing. The two Dragons following her halted too, spears still in hand.

"The Ibalet navy would be a welcome start," Sorasa growled.

Isadere laughed coldly. "You've spent these long hours in silence, Amhara. I admit, I feared you might put a knife in my neck." They turned in their seat to look at Sorasa fully. They were of the same descent, children of Ibal. But they were as separate from each other as dragon and tiger. "Or are there no more contracts for me?"

"There are many, Your Highness." Sorasa loosed her usual smirk. "But I'm a little preoccupied with the end of the world. I'll collect later."

Amhara Fallen, Amhara Broken. Corayne remembered Valtik's words. Sorasa was Amhara no longer, exiled from the guild these people hated so much. But she still wore the dagger proudly and took on the title even when it marked her to everyone in sight.

"I'll be waiting," Sibrez answered, an open threat. Sorasa grinned through it, her teeth bared. Isadere was not the only one with a shark's lethal smile.

The Heir turned back, looking up to Corayne standing over them. "You have strange friends, Corayne an-Amarat."

Friends. The word landed oddly among them, most of all in Corayne. Of course she considered Andry a friend, and Dom. They were as close to her as Kastio, as her mother's crew. She trusted them; she cared for them. But Sorasa? An assassin with no loyalty to anyone or anything?

Her heart thumped. *She came back to save us at the palace. She reached for me in the canyon. When Dom could not see the danger, she did. She knew, and she risked her life to save mine.* Corayne remembered the Amhara pulling her through open air, her body missing the rock by inches.

And Valtik? The old woman was asleep in her chair, her cheek flat to the table, looking for all the world like a drunk too deep in the ale. She was a nuisance at best, unsettling at her worst. Rattling her bones and rhymes, telling them nothing and everything all at once. *The old witch stood between the kraken and the rest of us, holding it back just enough. We'd be dead without her, the Ward already lost.* In her pocket, Corayne still held the sticks, the Jydi charm from the boat a lifetime ago. Taristan's blood was still there, dried black.

Charlie, who complained every step of the way. Who taught her how to make Tyri seals and letters of passage. Who joked through the aches of the road, who made her feel a little less alone.

Sigil, boorish and overproud, risking their lives with every boast. Who had betrayed and then un-betrayed them all. Who stood watch every night.

Friends?

Isadere's voice broke through her thoughts.

"I cannot offer you the navy, but I can offer you a ship."

Around the table, the Companions exchanged excited glances, Corayne included. She licked her lips, daring to hope, trying to fight the true smile rising on her face.

"My own, anchored offshore," Isadere said, nodding their head in the vague direction of the coast. *Some miles yet*, Corayne knew, *but not far. Not after how far we've come.* "The ship is well provisioned and crewed, able to take you across the Long Sea."

Corayne's shoulders dropped. "To where, we don't know," she muttered, sounding as small as she suddenly felt. Around the table, the others gave no suggestions.

But Isadere settled back in their seat, glittering hands folded on the table. "The goddess knows."

Too many eyes snapped to the Heir.

Charlie sucked in a sharp breath. "What shadows has your mirror shown?" he said, his voice wobbling. "What path do you think you saw?"

Isadere turned in their seat, looking back to the bronze mirror now dull and empty. A corner of their cheek lifted in a smile.

"You tell me," they murmured. "I saw the first snows of winter, and a white wolf running with the wind."

"A white wolf?" Dom wrinkled his nose, confused. Corayne felt the same.

But at her side, Andry leaned forward, hands braced against the table. His eyes lit with realization.

"You're talking about the Prince of Trec," he said, matching Isadere's smile. "Oscovko. That's his symbol."

A grin split Isadere's face. "Perhaps he will be the ally you need, while Ibal rises from her sleep?"

"The Prince of Trec is a drunk and a bully, content to skirmish with Jydi raiders, nothing more," Sorasa sneered, shrugging her shoulders. "He won't stand against Taristan and Erida's army."

"Oscovko was one of Erida's most promising suitors," Andry shot back. "He holds a grudge against her, that's for certain. It might be enough to sway him."

Trec held no coastline for her mother to pillage, and Corayne knew little of it beyond simple geography. A northern country, small but proud, content to control its iron mines, steel forges, and little else.

She blinked, trying to fit the pieces together. "We don't need him to fight Erida's army," she murmured, blowing out a low breath. "We need him so we can close the next Spindle."

Her heart quailed at the prospect, still weary from the last Spindle torn.

"And where might that be?" Sorasa grumbled, glancing between Corayne and Isadere's mirror. "Any hints?"

"Of that, the mirror is unclear," Isadere answered, their grin fading.

The assassin hissed like the snake tattooed on her neck. "Of course it is."

Corayne turned in her seat. "Valtik?" she said, looking to the old woman, who was now snoring gently. "Any ideas?"

Sigil flicked the Jydi witch on the shoulder, rousing her. Valtik blinked, sitting up, her eyes that same disarming blue, now the brightest thing in the room. They even put the flickering candles to shame.

"Ideas, Valtik," Corayne said again, flustered. "For where the next Spindle might be? Where Taristan is going next?"

"He leaves roses behind," the witch answered, half giggling. She began braiding and unbraiding the strands of her hair, shedding dried sprigs of jasmine and old lavender. "Roses, dying on the vine."

Corayne gritted her teeth. "Yes, we know he's at the Rose River."

"Or she could literally mean roses," Charlie offered, shrugging. "They're the mark of the old empire, the Cors."

My own blood, Corayne thought. She remembered the roses in Erida's court, the poor servants cutting flowers all night long for a monstrous wedding. Red as the figures in her dreams, red as the blood on her sword, red as the gown Erida wore that night, when she pledged to help them save the Ward, and then threw them to the wolves.

We cannot bother with roses now. We need answers.

"What do the bones tell, *Gaeda*?" she prodded, moving to take Valtik by the shoulder. With the other hand, Corayne reached for the witch's pouch and the tiny skeletons rattling inside.

Isadere drew in a sharp breath. They stood up from the table, their nostrils flared. "I'll not have Jydi bone magic in my presence," they spat, their eyes shadowed with disgust. "Not before Lasreen."

Corayne opened her mouth to question Isadere's violent reaction, but Valtik laughed again, cutting her off. "You see all and nothing," she crowed, putting her bag of bones away. "An heir like your king."

"How dare you, Witch?" Isadere seethed. Behind them, the mirror remained dim and empty, a simple circle of bronze now. "You question the will of the goddess?"

To Corayne's surprise, Charlie moved between them, his ink-stained hands outstretched.

"She questions nothing, Your Highness," he said, his tone taking on a placating air. "Her beliefs are your own, at the root of all things. She serves the gods as you do, in her own way."

Isadere's eyes flicked over him, taking him in again. Their gaze lingered on his fingers.

"And which gods did you serve once, Priest?" they murmured.

Charlie straightened, raising his chin. "I serve them still."

"Very well," Isadere answered, sinking back into their chair.

Corayne gritted her teeth, weighing Valtik's bone magic against Isadere's help. It was a difficult scale to balance. Thankfully, the witch was in no mood to make it tip. She gave Corayne a single glance with her unnerving eyes before standing from the table and puttering off toward the desert. The guards did not bar her way, and she disappeared into the night, leaving the faint scent of winter in her wake.

At the edge of the hall, Sorasa began to pace again, shaking her head.

So what now? Corayne wondered, hope sputtering in her chest. *We are lost without a heading, a ship beyond sight of shore.* She tried to think, racking her brain for anything that might be of use.

"We don't know where the next Spindle is, that's obvious." The admission felt like defeat, but she pushed through it, pacing around the table. Again she wished for a map. Or a quill and some parchment. Something she could hold in her hands, to help her think. "What do we know?"

"Erida and Taristan are strong enough to take Madrence by force, and quickly. Before any kingdoms can rally to Madrence's side. They know it, or they wouldn't be marching on Rouleine," Andry offered, his voice low. Corayne saw the weariness wash over him, finally catching up after their long ride through the desert.

Sorasa nodded over him. "That hasn't happened in a century. And Taristan is with Erida. Either he's following the path to another Spindle, or conquering Madrence is more important to his cause."

Corayne took it all in, tallying the information like lists in her old ledger. The map of Allward rose in her mind, familiar as her mother's own face. She saw the perilous border between Galland and Madrence, drawn along the Rose River, dotted with a soldier line of castles to protect either side. Then the Rose met the Alsor, the two rivers coming together before running on to the sea. At their joining stood Rouleine, the first great city in Erida's way. Not as grand as the Madrentine capital, Partepalas, but certainly a prize for any conqueror.

At his seat, Dom ran a hand over his scars. Corayne winced, thinking of the skeleton soldiers and their knives.

"No, Taristan still hunts the Spindles as we do," he said. His lip curled with disgust. "Searching for clues in old legends, listening to the whispers of that red rat of a priest."

Isadere narrowed their eyes. "Has he torn any more Spindles since you saw him last? Drawn out . . . *worse* things?"

With a sigh, Dom rolled back his shoulders, chasing away some ache. Even immortals felt pain. "We don't know."

"There's still time," Charlie breathed. He drummed his fingers on the table.

Sigil looked at him sidelong, scoffing. "And how do you know that?"

The priest shrugged, settling back in his chair. He interlaced his hands over his belly, like a man satisfied with a good meal. "The Spindles hold up the realms. We aren't dead yet, so that's something."

"That's something," Sigil echoed, shaking her head.

We aren't dead yet. Corayne almost laughed, and the many long days of travel and toil seemed to crash all at once, a terrible wave. The sea serpents, the horses, the oasis town filled with nothing but ghosts now. *We aren't dead yet*, she thought. *Weave that into a tapestry, for it seems to be the core thread of this journey.*

"We do know where a Spindle is."

Andry's voice was a bell, clear and ringing through the tent. His eyes met Corayne's, brown on black, earth on stone. She furrowed her brow, trying to think, trying to figure out what she had forgotten, drowning in her memories. The Spindleblade was still in its sheath, leaning against her chair. Now it felt like a stone, trying to push her into the ground. Trying to bury her.

Her lips formed the question, but Andry answered before she could ask.

His face tightened with regret, his mouth drawn into a wince. Pain laced his voice, as if there were a knife in his body, twisting slowly.

He opened his mouth, his teeth gritted, his jaw tight. The words were agony to him.

"The temple," he forced out, and Dom drew a searing breath.

Faster than anyone thought possible, the Elder jumped up from the table and stalked out of the tent, the doorway flapping as if caught in a strong wind. Sorasa stopped in her pacing, her expression blank, her tiger eyes wide as she stared after him.

Corayne blinked. The world tipped beneath her feet and she nearly stumbled.

Isadere tilted their head in confusion, as did their brother.

"The temple . . . ?" Sigil began, perplexed.

She was not there. She does not know.

And while Corayne knew the story, knew who died upon the killing field, knew whose blood fed the forest in the foothills, she did not truly understand. *I was not there either. I did not see my father die, or any of the others. I cannot know its weight.*

Andry bowed beneath it, lowering his head, chin nearly resting on his chest.

"We must go back," he whispered, his voice catching.

Corayne felt his shoulder beneath her hand before she knew what she was doing, his body firm and warm beneath her fingers. It was all she could do to comfort him. *If there were another way . . .* , she wondered, already knowing the answer.

Her eyes trailed from Andry's head to the mirror at the back of the tent. The moon had risen, filtering through the hole in the sloped roof. It glowed on the mirror's bronze surface. For a moment, Corayne thought she saw a face, cold and white.

"We must go back," she echoed.

7
NOT EVEN GHOSTS
Domacridhan

It's all right to miss him. It's all right to feel this hole.

Andry Trelland said as much some weeks ago, by the river and the willow trees, when the nightmares grew too horrible for even Dom to bear. It certainly felt like a hole now, growing wider with every passing second. First it swallowed his heart. The rest of him would soon follow.

The immortal Veder glared up at a night sky furious with stars. A hundred pinpricks of light in the endless dark. They winked to life one by one, returning with every sunset. In that moment, Domacridhan of Iona hated the stars, for they could not die.

Not like the rest of them. Not like every person, mortal or immortal, who Dom held dear. All of them were either gone or close to it, dancing along the knife-edge of obliteration. It was a strange thing to grasp—that everyone and everything he knew could end.

Corayne was hunted by the two most dangerous people in the realm, her face and name plastered across the Ward. Not to mention she was the only thing standing between Allward and the apocalypse. A precarious position for anyone to be in, let alone a young mortal. Andry was a fugitive right alongside her, and too noble for his own good. He might step in front of a sword at any moment. And Ridha, his beloved cousin, was gods-knew-where, riding the Ward in search of allies who might never come.

He cursed her mother's cowardice, but missed her in the same painful breath. If only the Monarch of Iona stood with them now, her power and the power of the other immortal enclaves alongside them. He feared for her too, for everyone at home in Tíarma, for everyone inside the Heir's tent. Even Valtik, muttering her way among the sand dunes. Only Sorasa Sarn was spared his worries. Dom doubted even the ending of the world could kill her. She would find a way out of it, somehow, no matter the cost to anyone else.

It was difficult to breathe, as if he'd spent the last few days running across the sand instead of riding. Dom's chest went tight, and the wound at his side, though healed over, stung like a fresh injury. The scars were worse, hot and itching. He felt the creatures of Asunder again, their bone fingers and broken blades tearing at his skin.

In the nightmares, he did not escape them. In the nightmares, they pulled him down and down and down, until the sky was little more than a circle above him, the rest of the world black and red. He could hear Cortael screaming. He could smell his blood. Even awake, he sensed them both, the memory too sharp.

And now we must return.

The stars wheeled for minutes and centuries, endless overhead. Even in Iona, there were never so many stars. Dom searched them, looking for an answer.

The many thousands of lights did not reply.

But Domacridhan of Iona was not alone.

"Some say the stars are every realm in existence, their lights a call and an invitation."

Dom did not move as the figure appeared beside him. He was of the same height, black-skinned with a crown of braided black hair. And immortal, a son of Glorian as much as Dom was.

Dom's teeth parted in shock and he sucked in a ragged breath.

The immortal wore no armor, but instead long purple robes, with fine bracelets on his elegant wrists. They were intertwined panthers, worked in jet and onyx, their eyes set with emeralds. Dom knew what they meant, and which enclave they belonged to.

"I knew the court of Ibal kept close council with the Vedera of the south, but I did not expect to find one here. Let alone a prince of Barasa. What news do you carry, Sem?" Dom said, speaking in Vederan. The old language of his people felt good on his tongue.

He bent at the waist, bowing to the immortal prince.

The other Veder did the same.

"Prince Domacridhan of Iona. My enclave has not treated with your own since before you were born into the Ward." His face caught the torchlight, and Dom saw a proud, angular nose and high-cut cheekbones. His eyes were narrowed, as if caught in a perpetual smile. They were disarmingly kind.

A son of Monarch Shan, Dom knew. Barasa was the southernmost enclave in the known lands of Allward, nestled deep in the Forest of Rainbows. As Iona raised the emblem of the stag, Barasa bore the panther.

"I'm sorry we meet under such circumstances," Dom said with a glance to the tents. He tried to think as Corayne would, to figure out why a Vederan prince followed the mortal Heir of Ibal. "Surely you heard what was said within?"

"We Vedera are always listening, as I'm sure your mortals have discovered," Sem answered, chortling low in his throat. "Rest assured, I will pass on your tidings to my father, and the rest of the southern enclaves, but . . ."

Dom gritted his teeth and curled a fist.

"They will not listen?" he muttered. He tried not to think of Iona, of Isibel and her advisors staring through him as he begged for their aid. "Just like my aunt."

The dim light did not hinder Sem's ability to see. His eyes ticked over Dom's face, noting the clear frustration.

"Your aunt told them already," Sem said, sighing. "Barasa received a sending some months ago, as did Hizir and Salahae."

A cold hand clenched around Dom's heart. *A sending.* He turned the word over in his mind, knowing its weight. *She wouldn't use her magic to help me, but she would use it to stand in my way.* Dom scowled, a bitter taste filling his mouth. *Barasa, Hizir, and Salahae.* Immortal enclaves of the southern continent, shrouded by deserts and jungle. Distant, too far for Ridha to reach. It had been easy for her mother to get to them first.

"The sending was frail, her magic weakened by many miles," Sem offered, his tone placating.

Dom's hot temper won out, and he faced the desert, hands braced on his hips.

"When she refused to fight, I thought her cowardice would not pass the walls of Iona," he growled. "The situation is more dire than she realizes, and whatever she told you—"

"Did she speak falsely?" Sem prodded.

"No," Dom answered. Even now, he could not lie. "But she is wrong. If we do not fight, the Ward will fall."

Sem pursed his lips together, his expression unreadable. "She thinks this Taristan of Old Cor will open a way home. To Glorian."

Dom nearly cursed at the name of their realm. "That is not a price any of us should be willing to pay. The risk is too great, for the Ward—and every other realm."

To his surprise, Sem offered the smallest nod. Then he looked to the stars again, his black eyes reflecting the infinite points of light. "I thank you for your bravery, Domacridhan. We Vedera are gifted in many things, but in this, you truly excel."

"I am not brave." Dom ran a hand over his face, feeling his scars. The skin was hard and puckered. He would never be the same as he was before the temple. And history was about to repeat itself. "I am angry, saddened, frustrated—all things but brave."

"I disagree," Sem said plainly.

Dom only shrugged. He sized up the immortal prince again, noting the strong set of his shoulders beneath his robes, and the cords of muscle in his arms. Sem bore no weapons Dom could see, but he was clearly no stranger to them.

"We could use another immortal to protect Corayne," he said in a low voice.

Sem raised his brow. The panthers on his wrists glimmered. "Or I could ride for the closest enclave this very night and share what I've learned with Hizir."

Something stung in Dom's heart. He swallowed around a sudden lump in his throat. This time, when he thought of the slaughter at the temple, he remembered Nour of Hizir, a quiet warrior dead upon the marble steps. One of many Vedera fallen, from all corners of the Ward. *Surely Hizir will rise to avenge their fallen?*

"We could use that too," he said thickly. "Will the Heir miss you?"

The prince of Barasa shook his head, casting a glance back at the tent. "Isadere of Ibal will thank me for doing this work for them. I assume they'll send word to the mortal kingdoms as well as the enclaves." He dropped his voice, leaning close, like the stars themselves were listening. "A strangeness is spreading across the land. My father sent me north as his envoy, to find another side of this story, and it is my duty to pass on what I've learned here tonight. The Monarch of Iona cannot be the only singer in this song."

Dom dared to smile, the night air cold on his teeth. "You believe us, don't you?"

Sem gave him a firm squeeze on the shoulder. "I don't know what else could draw such a band together, besides the ending of the world," he said.

No words had ever been so true.

"Farewell, Domacridhan. May we meet once more."

"More than once, I hope." Dom raised a hand as Sem drew back. The prince mirrored him. "Ecthaid be with you."

Sem bowed low this time, echoing the old goodbye to honor the gods of Glorian. "And Baleir with you."

The joy of Sem's tidings did not last long, and Dom's brooding returned. He could not fathom facing the temple again, army or no army. He did not want to stand upon that cursed ground and see flowers growing in Cortael's blood.

He cursed in Vederan, kicking at the sand.

"I thought an immortal prince of Iona would have better manners."

Dom nearly snarled. Fighting Sarn would be a welcome distraction from his wallowing. But Byllskos was a sharp memory too, made of tossing horns, the taste of poison, and a faint scent of oranges.

He turned to watch a shadow materialize into the too-familiar figure of the Amhara. She still wore the desert on her, dusty all over. It suited her. This was her home, after all.

"I suppose I was mistaken," she said, running a hand down her long black braid.

When she stopped not a yard from his side, he growled in annoyance.

"Leave me, Sarn."

"I'm doing you a favor, Elder." She shrugged into her traveling cloak, drawing it against the cold of the desert night. "Or would you prefer Corayne and the squire come out here to coddle you?"

Dom kicked the ground again, sending a rock skittering. It felt childish, but he was too upset to mind. "No, I suppose not."

He felt her stare as easily as he heard her heartbeat: a level, steady drum. Sarn did not blink, watching him with those odd copper eyes of hers. They seemed filled with torchlight, though no torches burned.

"Put the pain away," Sarn muttered. "Put the memory away. You don't need it."

So easy for someone like you, he wanted to snap back. The anger felt good, better than sorrow or pain.

"Is that what they taught you in your guild?" he replied, looking her over.

Even after weeks in the saddle, crossing the ferocious sands of Ibal, she seemed dangerous as ever. Dust and sweat did not dull the gleam of her steel, in her daggers or in her heart.

But now something odd crossed her face. Sarn turned to the horizon, searching the near invisible edge where land met sky.

"It was the first lesson I ever learned."

The perfect, slow rhythm of her heartbeat quickened, though nothing changed around them. Not even the wind stirred across the dunes. All was silent, unmoving.

"You are afraid, Sorasa Sarn," Dom said slowly. "Why?"

"Are you drunk, Elder?" Her thoughtful manner dropped away. She turned, rounding on him with her usual distaste. "We're trying to stop the end of the world, and all but *failing*."

Dom squared to her, fists clenched. *I am not as blind as you think, Amhara.*

"Something scares you about your homeland. You've had your hackles up since we set foot on these shores. And if I am to protect this quest, protect *Corayne*, I must know *why*."

Sarn took a menacing step toward him. Dom towered over her, but somehow she managed to seem just as tall.

"It isn't relevant to the quest or Corayne," she snapped. "It's my head and no one else's."

Something twisted inside him. Sorasa Sarn was an assassin made, a taker of lives. And that sword cut both ways, apparently. Judging by the sharpness of her eyes and the hard set of her jaw, it was all she would say. Domacridhan did not know much of mortals, but he knew this of Sarn, at least.

"Why must you Amhara always bargain in heads?" he muttered, thinking of their agreement made back in Tyriot. His own life sacrificed for her payment, when the Ward was saved and the task finished.

To Dom's surprise, the corner of her mouth lifted. It was only the edge of a smile, but the edge was enough.

Her heartbeat slowed again.

"The Heir of Ibal might be a religious zealot, but they will be useful," she said, gracelessly changing the subject.

"I thought you also worshipped their goddess?"

The assassin was a continuous puzzle, with infinite pieces he could not even begin to fathom.

Sarn shrugged. "Lasreen rules life and death—I would be a fool not to," she said. "But the goddess does not live in mortal flesh, no matter what Isadere says, or what they think they see in an empty mirror."

The sliver of a smile disappeared as she looked back to the tent, and the people within.

"My own gods are silent," Dom muttered back.

He looked to the stars again. Now he hated that they were the stars of the Ward, and not the stars of Glorian. Stars he had never seen.

His voice dropped. "They are separated from us, until my people return home to our realm."

"I suppose your old companions are with them now," Sarn offered in a stilted manner. She had no talent for comforting anyone, least of all Domacridhan. "The ones who fell."

Dom shook his head.

"To fall in the Ward is to fall forever."

Suddenly the stars did not look so bright and the moon seemed dim too. As if a shadow had settled over everything.

"A death here is absolute," he murmured.

Her eyes went round, her brow furrowing. "Not even ghosts?"

"Not even ghosts, Sarn."

Belief was a powerful thing, and he saw it in Sarn, as it was in Isadere and Charlie. Godly mortals, who leaned upon their holy pantheon in whatever way they felt was right. Sorasa Sarn, murderer as she was, believed there was something after this life. For herself, for the others, even for the people she killed. Somehow an assassin with no morals and no direction had something guiding her way. *Not like me*, he thought. It was strange to be jealous of a mortal, let alone one he hated so much.

Sarn's voice drew him out of his thoughts, ripping him back to the task at hand.

"Corayne is already at work charting a course with Isadere's captain," she said, heading for the tent again. "I should help them map the way north."

At the tent flap, the Ibalet guards in their dragon armor drew up, their grips tightening on their spears. Dom eyed them, then caught up to Sarn, taking her by the arm.

"You should be careful around these Ibalet guards," he hissed. "They would rather kill you than look at you."

And they've said as much, to your face and behind raised hands. Some of them talk of it night and day, thinking no one can hear them. It angered him even to think of the Falcons, ready to cut Sarn's throat. Even if he understood their revulsion. Even if he wanted to do the same once.

"I'm quite aware of their hatred," Sarn answered neatly. She sounded amused, or even proud. "It is more than warranted. As is their fear."

Dom pulled a face. "Don't be rash, Sarn. Keep your guard up."

"I haven't dropped my guard since the moment I saw you, Elder."

Again he thought of Byllskos and the Tyri port, the city half ruined by one Amhara's skill.

Sarn watched him think, then tipped her head. Her eyes flitted over him and he shifted, uncomfortable under her scrutiny.

"Can you even *be* drunk?"

The preposterous question set him off balance. He stumbled, grasping for a proper answer.

"It is possible," he finally said, remembering the halls of Iona, and celebrations long past.

Again the corner of her mouth lifted. She stalked away, gesturing for him to follow.

"I think I'd like to see that."

* * *

Dom returned to find Corayne deep in her plotting, a map laid out beneath her hands. She had never looked so at home as she did now, her eyes alight as she scratched out notes or danced her fingers along a mountain range. For a moment, Dom saw her as she must have been. Before he and Sarn found her. Before the entire realm landed on her shoulders. That person had vanished so quickly, receding into who Corayne was now. Harder, sharper, worn by luck and fate.

Commander lin-Lira and Sibrez were gone, replaced by the captain of Isadere's ship. He studied the map with Corayne. The Heir remained at the edge of the candlelight, occasionally glancing to the mirror full of moonlight.

Valtik had not returned, and Charlie was gone, too, probably snoring somewhere. Andry looked like he wanted to be asleep, but sat valiantly in his chair, his eyes half-lidded. Sigil poked around the hall, a glass of wine in hand as she examined the rich furnishings, picking at everything from the chairs to the rugs underfoot.

Dom went back to the table reluctantly, his eyes falling on a familiar point on the map. Unmarked, but he knew the place all the same. The foothills, the branching of the river. A quiet forest, quiet no longer. His breath pulled between his teeth.

"The temple poses two dangers," Dom forced out, his voice harder than before.

At the table, Corayne raised her eyes.

"First, Taristan's army, the Ashlanders," he continued, each word more difficult than the last. The memory seared his mind. *Drawn out from the ruined realm.* "Either they are still there, guarding the Spindle, or they are with Taristan in Madrence."

"Either way, not good," Corayne muttered.

Dom nodded. "The second danger is that the temple sits in the foothills of the Mountains of the Ward, in the kingdom of Galland." He swallowed around the lump in his throat. "A kingdom hunting us all."

To his surprise, Corayne smiled.

"So we go around," she said, drawing her hand down the long line of mountains splitting the northern continent in two. "We cross the Long Sea." Her finger traced the path over the waves, from the Ibalet coast to a city across the water. "Make port near Trisad, cross through Ahmsare to the Dahlian Gates, and ride north along the mountains. Let them be a wall between us and Galland." She walked her fingers along their route, marking the way. "And then we're in Trec, on Galland's own doorstep. Running with the white wolf. With any luck, Oscovko will be with us, his army too."

Her cheeks were pink, not with exertion, but with glee. The map was her home, her purpose. Something she could do. *Besides open and close Spindle portals.*

She looked from Dom to Sorasa, a lip in her teeth.

Dom had not seen much of that part of the world, though he knew the map of the Ward as well as any other immortal. He looked at the mountains again, inked on the worn parchment. They seemed small like this, the journey not so far. Still, he estimated it would take many long weeks. If nothing got in the way.

"The enclave of Syrene is near," he said, pointing to an unmarked place on the map. Of course mortals would not know it anymore. The rams of Syrene were secluded, high in the mountains, and had not dwelled among mortals for many centuries. "Perhaps the Vedera there will help us in our journey."

"We don't have time for family reunions, Elder," Sorasa spat, all but knocking him aside.

He pulled his finger from the parchment as if burned, putting distance between them.

Sarn only lowered her eyes to the map. "This is a long road, and we must make all haste to walk it. But it is the right road," she added after a moment. "The only road I see, to take us into Galland without being caught. And perhaps find an ally too."

Her eyes flickered to Isadere, who nodded gravely.

Corayne all but beamed, proud of herself. "Thank you, Sorasa."

"Don't thank me—thank your mother," Sarn fired back, now tracing the route herself. "She may not have taught you how to fight, but she certainly taught you how to *think*."

Dom did not consider himself well versed in mortal emotion, but even he could see the shadow crossing Corayne's face. *Is it sadness or frustration? Does she miss her mother? Does she hate all mention of her?* He did not know.

"Very well." Isadere clapped their hands together, and the maidens jumped to attention. "We will do all we can to provision you for the journey."

In unison, the handmaidens swept from the hall of the tent into the adjoining rooms. Dom could hear other servants through the thin fabric walls, already scraping together food and supplies.

"The sand mares?" Sorasa asked, raising an eyebrow.

Dom braced himself for a denial. The sand mares were fine horses, fast and strong enough for the long journey ahead. But the road behind taught him to expect obstacles at every turn, if not outright failure.

To his relief, Isadere nodded. "The horses are yours to take north."

With that, Sarn straightened and inclined her head. It was as close to a bow as Dom had ever seen from the Amhara. Behind her, Sigil's eyebrows practically disappeared into her forehead. Clearly, she'd never seen Sarn bow either. Dom doubted anyone in the world had.

"My thanks," Sarn said, without bite or lie.

Isadere scowled, showing their teeth. "I want none of your gratitude, Amhara," they snapped, turning away as if they could not bear to look at such a creature. Isadere faced Corayne instead. They raised their proudly sculpted face, throwing their features in sharp relief against the golden candlelight.

"Sleep through the heat. You leave for the coast at dusk."

8

THE LIFE OF ONE MAN
Erida

Taristan promised to lay victory at her feet, and so he did, every single day.

Erida's army rolled over everything in its path, the Lion raised at the head of twenty thousand men. The green flag of Galland flapped high in the cooling winds of autumn. The Rose River flowed at their side, holding the eastern flank as her grand army marched south through the countryside.

The Queen was glad to be out in the air, free of the wheelhouse that held her ladies. The massive carriage lumbered at the back of the column, with the baggage train. Though her knights urged her to remain within the safety of its walls, she refused.

Erida was done with cages.

She wore her usual deep green cloak trimmed in gold, so long it covered the flanks of her horse. Beneath, her ceremonial golden armor flashed, light enough to be worn for hours without difficulty. It would hardly turn a blade, but Erida would never see the wrong end of a sword.

They left the Castlewood behind, and their line of fortresses. The kingdom of Madrence fell over them in an invisible curtain. They crossed the border in daylight, without opposition. There was only a stone to mark the line, its markings worn smooth by time and weather. The river still flowed; the autumn forest still stood, green and golden, as if the trees themselves welcomed the Lion. The road beneath their horses' hooves did not change. Dirt was still dirt.

Erida expected to feel different in another kingdom, weaker somehow. Instead, the new land only emboldened her. She was a ruling queen, destined for empire. This would be her first kill, her first conquest.

The fortress city of Rouleine loomed to the south, at the confluence of the Rose and the Alsor. The city walls were strong, but Erida was stronger.

The enemy army massed along the far bank of the Rose, following their progress. They were too weak to meet her army in battle, but they nipped at their edges as a scavenger would at a great herd. It only slowed the Gallish army down, enough for another force to cross the river and dig in, carving trenches and makeshift palisades overnight.

The Lion devoured all of them.

Erida did not know how many Madrentines lay dead. She did not bother to count the corpses of her enemies. And while hundreds of Gallish soldiers were lost, more came to replace them, called up from every corner of her wide kingdom. Conquest was in her blood, and the blood of all Galland. Nobles who resisted her first summons to war rode hard now, bringing their retinues of knights, men-at-arms, and stumbling peasants. All were eager to share in the spoils of war.

And in my glory.

Taristan was beyond her sight, marching at the head of the column, accompanied by a cluster of her own Lionguard. It had been so every day since Lotha, at Erida's behest. It earned him the respect of nobles too cowardly to ride with the vanguard, but also kept him away from such vipers.

And away from me, Erida thought, unsettled by how his absence bothered her.

It was so much to measure, but Erida had long years of practice at court. She was the Queen of Lions, and her nobles certainly lived up to the name. She felt like she stood in the lions' den now, a whip in hand. But even the tamer of lions could be overwhelmed, if outnumbered.

For now the lions were sated, fat and happy. Gorging themselves on broken men and barrels of wine. It would be the same tonight, in a siege camp instead of a castle.

Rouleine was small compared to Ascal, a village next to Erida's great capital. It stood at the crest of the hill, walled by stone and two rivers, leaving only one direction of assault. The city was well made and well placed, good enough to hold the Madrentine border for generations. But no longer. Twenty thousand souls lived behind the walls and in the surrounding farmlands. Erida could match a soldier to each if she wanted to.

The Madrentine villages were empty now, quiet as they rode through. The buildings were but husks, doors and windows hanging open. The peasant soldiers picked through anything left behind, looking for better boots or an onion to gnaw on. Any lingering livestock were driven to the baggage train at the end of the column, to join the army's own supply herd. But little else remained.

Even from miles away, Erida heard the bells calling the farmers to safety.

"Funny, it's the bells that will be their ending," she said aloud.

On the horse next to her, Lady Harrsing cocked her head.

"How so, Your Highness?" she said.

The old woman held a saddle better than ladies half her age. She wore a sky-blue cloak, her silver hair braided away from her face. At court, she wore enough jewels to remind everyone of her wealth. Not so on the road, when jewels would only weigh her down. Bella Harrsing knew better than to peacock herself in the middle of a war march. Not like some of the others, who wore gilded armor or brocade, as if this were a ballroom and not a battlefield.

"The bells call the peasants and commons inside the walls, so the gates can be shut and the city protected," the Queen said. The bells pealed without any kind of harmony, tolling from many towers. "If they would only leave the gates open, we could march on in without any bloodshed at all."

Harrsing laughed openly. "Even the Madrentines would not surrender a city without a fight. Their king may be wine-blind, but he isn't stupid."

"On the contrary, he is incredibly stupid." Erida tightened her grip on her reins, the leather soft and worn to her fingers. The autumn chill was less in the Madrentine lands, and she did not need her gloves in daylight. "I have twenty thousand men at my command, with more coming. King Robart would do well to ride out of his fine palace and kneel before me this very day."

A smirk twisted Harrsing's thin mouth. "You're starting to sound like that husband of yours."

Warmth crept over Erida's cheeks.

"Or is he starting to sound like me?" she wondered aloud, giving Harrsing something else to chew on.

"That's one way to look at it," Bella said with a sigh.

Other nobles rode with them, knotted behind the Queen. Erida glanced back, watching them as they marched south in a parade of fine horseflesh and gleaming armor. There were many lords and a few ruling ladies, commanders and generals of thousands of men ahead and behind. She knew every face. Their names, their families, their own intricate alliances, and, most importantly, their loyalty to Erida of Galland.

Bella followed her gaze. "What are you thinking, Your Majesty?"

"Too many things," Erida answered, pursing her lips. She dropped her voice a little. "Who knelt at my coronation, pledging to serve a fifteen-year-old queen? Who rode to the Madrentine front when I called the first muster, summoning legion and personal army alike? Who waited? Who whispers? Who spies for my vile cousin Konegin, still hiding somewhere, safe even as I hunt for him? Who will put him on the throne if I fall, and who will send me to that lethal ending himself?"

On her horse, Bella paled. "So heavy a burden on such young shoulders," she muttered.

Erida could only shrug, as if buckling beneath the weight. She shook her head. "And who looks on Taristan with fear? Or jealousy? Who will ruin all we seek to build?"

To that, Bella had no answer, and Erida did not expect one. The aging woman was too deft a courtier. She knew when she was well out of her depth.

Erida cleared her throat. "Thornwall, what's the latest report?"

Lord Thornwall reined his horse, and the stallion trotted to the Queen, joining her side. The commander looked taller on horseback, but most men did. Unlike the other lords, he did not wear armor for the march. He did not need to play at war. He commanded the entire army, and spent too much time riding the length of the column, meeting with his scouts and lieutenants, to bother with full plate.

Thornwall nodded at the Queen, his red beard fierce against his green tunic. There was a lion embroidered on his breast, surrounded by curling vines and thorns to mark his own great family.

"Scouts say the Madrentine army across the river is three thousand strong. Maybe," he said.

Two squires rode at his side, their tunics matching Thornwall's. Erida tried to remember their names, once so easy to recall. One had ugly yellow hair, the other a kind expression. She did know one thing—who they used to squire for, before Thornwall took them on.

Their tunics used to be bright red and silver, a falcon across their chests.

The Norths, Erida thought, all warmth receding from her face. *Sir Edgar and Sir Raymon. Lionguard knights sworn to serve.*

They lay dead in the foothills, their bones swallowed up by mud. Her loyal guardians were Taristan's first victory.

But for one, still alive. Her lip curled, remembering Andry Trelland. A noble son of Ascal, a squire raised for knighthood. *And a traitor to his kingdom,* Erida thought, seething as she remembered her last glimpse of him. Escaping through a door, the great hall destroyed behind him, with Corayne of Old Cor and her Spindleblade ahead.

Thornwall kept on blathering, and she blinked, forgetting the squires and their dead knights.

"But more soldiers arrive every day, in dribs and drabs," the commander said, rocking with the motion of his horse. The road suited him better than the council chamber did: his cheeks were filled with color, his gray eyes bright. "There are rumors Prince Orleon is with the army across the river, leading a hundred armored knights and twice as many men-at-arms."

Erida smirked. "I think he's figured out I'm not going to marry him," she said, laughing with Harrsing. The crown prince of Madrence was one of her many disappointed suitors, kept dangling on a hook for as long as possible.

The Queen had met the prince only once, at the wedding of Konegin's daughter to some Siscarian duke. He was tall and fair, a minstrel's version of a prince. But dull, without any wit or ambition. Most of their conversation had revolved around his collection of miniature ponies, which he kept in the garden of his father's palace of Partepalas.

"If he's captured, give him quarter," Erida said, her laughter trailing away. Her voice turned hard. "He'll fetch a fine ransom from his king."

On her other side, Harrsing hemmed low in her throat. "Perhaps. Everyone knows Robart is wildly jealous of his golden heir, a foolish thing for any father to be."

"I care little for their family squabbles," Erida sighed, still watching Thornwall. "What of the *other* scouts?" One dark eyebrow arched with meaning.

Thornwall shook his head. He pulled at his red beard, frustrated. "No sign of Konegin. It's as if he disappeared into the hills."

"Or was hidden," Erida mused, watching his face, noting every pull and tick of his muscles.

Her commander dropped his gaze, focusing on the mane of his horse. "It's certainly a possibility."

Is that shame I see in your eyes, Otto Thornwall? Or a secret?

"Thank you, Lord Thornwall," she said aloud, reaching across the space between them. With a practiced smile, she squeezed his forearm, no small gesture from a ruling queen. "I'm glad to have you at my side."

Still. The implication hung in the air, clear as words on a page. Thornwall read them easily. They both knew of whom she spoke. Lord Derrick had disappeared with Konegin that night at Lotha, sneaking out of the castle in the early hours of the morning. Another member of her own Crown Council, another traitor from the smallest circle she kept. That left only Thornwall, Harrsing, and aging Lord Ardath back in Ascal, the old man too weak to make war on the world.

I cannot afford another betrayal.

The siege had already begun by the time Rouleine came into view. It lay across the top of a hill like a fallen giant, church spires and towers rising behind stone walls and a marshy moat. Though the border was only a few miles away, anyone with eyes could tell the city was not Gallish. The walls were shorter, the towers less stout and strong. The rooftops were red tile, most of the buildings white or pale yellow. Flowers burst from window boxes, and burgundy flags, embroidered with the silver horse of Madrence, flapped in the wind. Rouleine was too quiet, too pretty, and nowhere near proud. Not Gallish at all.

The Rose and the Alsor joined behind the city, flowing south to the Madrentine capital and the Auroran Ocean. The two rivers were better defense than the city wall, itself only thirty feet high, but thick enough to withstand most armies. While Rouleine was a market city, well positioned on the old Cor road that once linked this part of the empire, it was also a defender of the border, the gateway to the rest of Madrence. Even in peace, Rouleine maintained a sizable city garrison, and there was a great stone keep directly on the confluence of the rivers, should the walls be broken. Erida could see its towers and ramparts, the stone like a storm cloud over the bright city.

The bells had long ceased their ringing. Everyone knew the Lion roared at the gate.

Ten thousand men surrounded the city already. They filled

the empty hilltop beyond the marsh, busy with the business side of war. Organizing the camp, digging ditches, lighting cook fires, raising tents, building a palisade wall and stake yard of their own, should Orleon's men attempt a surprise attack. They cleared the outskirts of the city, the few structures and streets beyond the protection of the city walls. A cacophony of hammers and axes replaced the bells. Trees fell, their trunks and branches cut apart for fuel or wood planks. Or battering rams.

A thousand Gallish soldiers massed at the edge of the moat, beyond the range of the Madrentine archers bristling on the ramparts. Their rows were organized, imposing, a sight to strike fear into even the bravest of warriors. These men were not Jydi raiders, disjointed and chaotic, but Gallish legions. They waited, as planned, for the Queen and her commanders. She knew a red cloak would be with them, surrounded by guards in golden armor. It took everything in the Queen not to tear through the camp with all the urgency she felt.

Erida wished she had a trebuchet rolling alongside her, instead of a moving court of fools and vipers. But the siege engines were slow, and they would not arrive for hours yet. They would not have the catapults ready until morning at least, and then the true assault would begin.

Somehow, already, the camp stank and the road beneath her horse had turned to mud, the few old stones like islands in a thick sea.

The Cor road cut the camp in two, leading straight to the moat bridge and city gates. *Yesterday, this road saw only commons and country nobles*, she thought, riding straight for the soldiers massed at the edge of the marsh. *Now it greets a queen and a Cor prince.*

The soldiers parted for the queen, their number swinging like a gate yawning open. She spotted his red cloak first, the unmistakable shade of imperial scarlet. Taristan stood on the bridge, the wide thoroughfare arching over the marsh below. Even in silhouette, he seemed a king.

No, Erida thought. *Not a king. An emperor.*

Arrows broke at his feet, inches away.

Taristan never flinched, but Erida certainly did. Her heart rose in her throat.

If that stoic, stupid fool ends up dead because of some archer with passing skill . . . , she thought, gritting her teeth. Then she remembered. *No, he is invulnerable,* she reminded herself for the hundredth time, the thousandth time. *What Waits has blessed him, and will keep him safe.*

Though Taristan's hellish god made her shiver, He also brought her some comfort too. What Waits was better than any shield, and he made her husband near to a god himself.

Her horse kept pace beneath her but was otherwise quiet. The gelding was a well-trained war horse, used to the smell of blood and sound of battle. The camp offered little distraction.

I am growing used to it too, Erida thought, counting the days since she left Ascal. *Two weeks since Lotha. Two weeks since my weasel cousin scurried away into some infernal hole.*

Ronin stood as close as he dared to the archers' range. Clearly he was not immune to harm as Taristan was, and the sight of the red rat trembling some feet behind her husband brought a smile to Erida's face. *If only one arrow might arc a little farther, drawn by a slightly more lethal hand than the ones on the wall.* What complications his death might bring, she did not know. It was the only thing that kept Erida from removing him herself. The priest of What Waits had not tracked down another Spindle, but he formed some bridge between her consort and the Torn King of Asunder. Severing it would certainly not be wise.

Her legs wobbled only a little when she dismounted, a Lionguard knight at her side, all but breathing down her neck. Thornwall slid down with her, and they marched forward together, Erida and her commander, to join the prince of Old Cor.

Soldiers bowed or bent. These were skilled men of the legions, not peasants pressed into service by their lords. Erida basked in their attention, knowing the strength of a thousand well-trained men. Even Ronin inclined his head, his watery, red-rimmed eyes terrible as ever, his face like a glowing white moon beneath his hood.

Taristan did not move, his focus fixed on the gates, and the city cowering behind its walls. The Spindleblade hung at his side, the ancient sword brilliant even sheathed. He kept one hand upon the hilt, rubies and amethysts winking through his fingers.

Erida saw Taristan every morning before the march and every night at whatever castle they stopped at next, but this was different. Today they stood before their first real enemy. And her nobles were watching, waiting for any sign of fracture between the Queen and her consort.

Turn, idiot, she thought, willing him to see her. To kneel.

When she stopped alongside him, her toes only inches from the arrow range, he did just that.

In a single motion, he squared to face her and lowered, one hand sweeping back his cloak. The other hand was blazing hot in her own, his fingers rough but gentle, as he pressed his fevered brow to her knuckles. She shuddered at his touch, surprised by the display. Taristan had bowed to her before, acknowledged her place as his queen, but never like this. One knee to the ground, his head bent like a priest at an altar.

She stared down at him, her face a porcelain mask, but her sapphire eyes went wide. She hoped the nobles could not see her confusion. She was certainly glad they could not hear her pounding heartbeat.

Taristan's black eyes met her own, his expression stony as ever. She read nothing in him, but he held her gaze for a long moment, longer than she expected. And then that red sheen moved in the shadows of his dark eyes, barely a glimmer, but more than enough.

The Prince of Old Cor rose to his feet, still grasping her fingers.

"Your Majesty," he said, his voice as rough as his hands.

"Your Highness," she answered, allowing herself to be led from the bridge and the arrows. He seemed eager to push her away from danger, small as it was.

The simpering priest shuffled over the moment they were off the bridge, his white-blond hair falling into his eyes. Erida weighed the cost of stepping on the hem of his robes and letting him fall on his face.

"I require a word with you both," he said, bobbing his head in a poor excuse for a bow.

Erida offered him her worst smile. "Hello, Ronin."

He matched it, his thin lips pulled over uneven teeth. It was like watching a fish try to fly.

"At once, if you please."

Taristan stood between them but said nothing, glowering in his usual way. He kept his body turned sideways, refusing to put Rouleine at his back. No matter his title, no matter his blood or his destiny, Erida knew Taristan was a survivor first, born of hardship and long, rough years upon the Ward.

Thornwall cleared his throat. "I suggest it wait until we offer terms," he said, eyeing the city gates. Then he bent forward, careful to offer Taristan a proper bow. "Your Highness."

"Lord Thornwall," Taristan answered stiffly. To Erida's pleasant surprise, he dipped his head in return. Though Taristan sneered at seemingly all requirements of court or any kind of simple etiquette, he seemed to be learning in spite of himself. "You think they'll accept terms?"

Erida shrugged, adjusting her cloak so it fell neatly about her shoulders. The clasps, two roaring lions, gleamed golden in the sunlight.

"It is tradition to make such a show of things, even if it is useless."

A look of utter confusion crossed Taristan's face. "It's tradition for the monarch to pretend to negotiate before a battle she is certain to win?"

She smiled wryly. "I suppose there is nothing traditional about this war of ours."

To say the least.

Taristan pressed his lips into the grim line she now recognized as his smile.

On the walls, the archers drew back behind their ramparts, and the gentle patter of wasted arrows on the bridge died away. Then there was a rough, scraping noise at the gate, and the shriek of iron chain as the portcullis drew up.

Someone is coming.

Erida whirled to the sound, her heart leaping in her chest. She wished for more armor, or a sword at her side. Something to mark her as the conqueror she was to become, someone older and more fearsome than who she was now.

The Lionguard reacted as trained, six of them drawing their swords. Four behind, one on either side of Erida and Taristan. After so many years of rule, she barely noticed them anymore. The glare of sun on golden armor was far too familiar.

"This is a waste of time," Taristan growled under his breath, so low only Erida could hear him.

She shot him a look of frustration. Even if he was right, she wanted to enjoy this moment. And no bad-tempered prince of Old Cor was going to stop her.

The truce flag appeared, shoved through the narrow gap between the thick, wooden gates.

Half white, half red.

Half peace, half war.

Any person who walked beneath a truce flag could not be harmed until negotiations were ended, for better or worse. It was less defense than a white flag of peace, but enough to dare the bridge, and one thousand Gallish soldiers.

The herald was freckled, overtall, with a neck like a swan and thinning orange hair. Beneath his tunic, burgundy and silver for Madrence, he wore loose chain mail, too short at the wrists. It was clearly not his own.

Taristan saw it too.

"That man's never worn armor in all his life," he growled under his breath.

"Madrence is a soft country filled with soft people," Erida answered. She eyed the herald as he crossed the bridge, two soldiers in tow. "Too weak to rule. Unworthy of command. I will relieve them of it, and shoulder the burden they are not strong enough to bear."

The herald stopped at the highest point of the bridge, halfway between the gate and the waiting army. His throat bobbing as he found his voice.

"Your Majesty, Queen Erida of Galland." The herald bowed, a picture of respect. "And Your Highness, Prince Taristan of Old Cor," he added, bowing again to Taristan.

He only sneered, disgusted.

The herald swallowed again, and met Erida's eye with a sterner manner. "You are trespassing in the kingdom of Madrence."

Taristan made a show of looking over his shoulder, his eyes sweeping across the massive army at their back.

"You're an observant man, sir," he called across the bridge. Then to Erida, and Erida alone, he whispered low, "May I kill him?"

She gritted her teeth, fighting another wave of annoyance. "He carries a truce flag. It would be poor form."

"Under whose judgment?" Taristan's eyes flashed, both black and red, man and beast. Even through her cloak and beautiful armor, she could feel the angry heat of him.

Erida bit her lip. Again, he was not wrong to wonder. *We intend to conquer the world. Why must we answer to anyone?*

Thornwall spoke up, stepping forward.

"The Queen of Galland declares a war of conquest upon Madrence," he said, his voice booming. Erida had never heard him speak with such force, not in the council chamber at least. This was Lord Thornwall at war, where he truly belonged. "Kneel, pledge loyalty to Her Majesty, and be spared her wrath."

The herald's jaw dropped open. "A war of conquest is no cause. You have no right to this kingdom!"

Erida drew herself up, chin raised, her voice cold and sharp. "I claim it in the name of my line, my heirs, who will be born the blood of Old Cor."

There was more scuffling at the gate. Before the sputtering herald could form some semblance of a reply, a golden-haired man burst out onto the bridge, six knights trailing behind him. One of them held another truce flag. They stomped across the bridge like spoiled children.

Taristan tightened at the sight of the newcomer, his grip on his sword unyielding. His breath turned strangely ragged, as if he could barely contain the rage burning inside him.

Why, Erida had no idea. If anything, she found the sight of the

Madrentine prince cause for amusement, not anger.

The herald scrambled to catch up with his prince, half shouting as he ran. "I present Orleon Levard, Crown Prince of Madrence, son of His Serene Majesty, King Robart of Madrence—"

The prince waved him off, a look of disgust marring his otherwise-handsome face.

"I see no heir beside you, Queen," he shouted, a lock of blond hair falling into his blue eyes.

Maidens the realm over would have traded their youth to be so close to such a man, a beautiful crown prince. Erida wanted to shove him in the marsh.

Orleon's eyes passed from the Queen to her consort, roving over Taristan like he was an insect to be stepped on. "I only see a mongrel *dog* you found in some ditch, with no proof of blood but his own hollow word."

"Jealousy does not become you, Orleon," Erida snapped, neatly stepping between the princes, lest Taristan's temper get the better of him. Not for Orleon's sake, but for the sake of the conquest. "Surrender in your father's name. If you even have the power to do so."

Orleon flushed, furious. "The realm will rise against you. Even Galland can not do as it pleases. Our allies in Siscaria—"

"Are weaker than you are," Erida said, cutting him off. "Their eyes face behind, to an empire fallen. I look ahead, at what must be rebuilt." She shrugged, making a show of her indifference. It only incensed Orleon more, precisely as intended. "In fact, they'll probably join me, if only for the chance to see the old empire reborn."

Orleon trembled with rage, his face matching his burgundy

surcoat. He had no skill in hiding his emotions, and Erida knew exactly why.

He is a man. His emotions are not considered a burden or a weakness. Not like mine, which I must keep hidden, so men might feel a little less threatened and a little more strong.

Her fingers curled until she felt her own nails dig into her palms. Part of her wanted to claw Orleon's red face right off and give him a mask to wear all the time, as she had to.

The prince raised a hand, and Erida half expected him to strike her. Instead he fixed his hair back into place and adjusted the collar of his tunic, drawing up the fine silk edged in silver. His pale blue eyes flashed over her again.

"I hope the Countless ride across your throats," he growled, leaning forward.

Behind her, Taristan stirred. She did not have to look to know he still had a hand on the Spindleblade, his infernal eyes locked on the besieged prince.

"Orleon, the only throat you should be worrying about is your own," Erida warned. "Surrender the city. I'll even allow you to ride out and bring my terms to your father."

"Your terms are no terms at all," he said, dismayed. Something broke in his face, his gaze wavering. "Kneel or be slaughtered?"

Erida smiled. *He realizes there is no hope of victory. He sees the path before him, and it only runs in one direction.*

"It seems a simple choice to me," she answered.

Orleon fumed, his lips pursing. Then he drew his head back. Erida scowled as his spittle landed inches from her boots.

"I preferred the arrows," Erida muttered.

Taristan moved beside her, deliberate, a prowling cat, his focus trained on princely prey. But still he remained silent, his lips pressed almost to nothing. If he opened his mouth, Erida feared he might devour Orleon whole.

Orleon did not see the danger in her consort. He did not know Taristan as she did, even in these short months that now seemed to eclipse the rest of her days.

The prince of Madrence grinned cruelly. "Have you removed his tongue as well as his balls?"

Erida knew the question before Taristan even asked.

"May I kill him?" he whispered.

The truce flags hung over them, full of warning. Again Erida wondered. The truce right was an age-old agreement, one of the core tenets of war.

Taristan waited, patient as a snake in its hole. The red sheen was in his eyes again, barely more than a glimmer, but enough. What Waits watched through her consort's eyes. And yet Taristan held back. She could see his restraint in every corded muscle, in the slow pulse thrumming at his neck. And in his eyes too, holding off the red presence. Keeping it—keeping Him—at bay.

Until her own decision was made.

Erida inhaled, lips parted, as if she could taste the power in the air. *Her* power. She blinked, holding Taristan's gaze. Her fingers twitched, and she could almost feel a leash in her hand, begging to be let go.

The Queen looked back to Orleon.

"Yes."

The Spindleblade loosed from its sheath and the Lionguard

closed in, shielding Erida from the bloodshed. Her heartbeat thundered in her ears, somehow louder than the clash of steel and iron. Breathless, she peered through the gaps in golden armor, wide-eyed as Taristan carved his way through the Madrentine soldiers. They were no match for Taristan, even without his many dark blessings. He was a ruthless killer, lethal and sure. She watched as he dodged their swords and found the weak points in their armor, felling each with a few careful jabs. The herald's body collapsed in a pile, the truce flag splayed across lifeless legs. His head rolled off the bridge and into the marsh.

Erida had seen men die before. Executions, accidents at tournaments, her own parents wasting away in their beds. She was not unfamiliar with blood. She felt no roiling in her stomach, no light-headedness. It was surprisingly easy to watch her consort massacre his way across the bridge, even as the archers returned to their assault. They only managed to stick their own; the bodies pincushioned where they lay.

Prince Orleon of Madrence was no soldier of a city garrison. He was as well trained as any noble son, familiar with blade and armor. And eager to prove himself somewhere other than the training circle or the tourney ground. His sword rose high, silver at the hilt, rich garnets winking between his fingers.

He was only a little older than Erida—twenty-three years old, if she remembered correctly. The silver horse charged across his breast, flashing in the midday sun as he parried a blow, his blade meeting Taristan's. They glared at each other over crossed swords, their faces only inches apart.

Orleon grimaced, buckling under the strain of holding Taristan at bay. An arrow buried itself in Taristan's shoulder, but he hardly noticed, and Orleon paled, sputtering in confusion.

It took only a sweep of the Spindleblade to sever the royal line of Madrence.

Red bloomed in the marsh beneath the bridge as the sword continued to swing.

Even in death, the herald did his job. He was a warning to his own city, testament of the massacre to come.

9
THE DAZZLING REALM
Ridha

Her sword had not seen blood in decades. She had not truly fought since the raiders tried Iona a century ago. Though her mind and body were as skillful as any upon the Ward, Ridha froze atop the walls. She stared at the bleeding sky, terror coursing through her veins. This was not a wolf or a bear or even an army set against her.

This was a dragon. It roared again, and Ridha shuddered. The sound echoed off the cliffs of the fjord, surrounding them.

Down the wall, a Veder quailed. "Are there two of them?"

Ridha's mouth went dry. "One is more than enough to kill us all," she said, her low voice swallowed by another snarl across the sky.

Lenna shouted down from the Kovalinn walls, barking orders in Jydi. Her folk moved in unison, with archers climbing up to their chief, arrows bristling at their sides. Dyrian quailed. On his throne, he seemed imperious as any monarch, despite his young age. Not so anymore. He went white as the snow, mouth moving without sound, as the same fear Ridha felt took over his small frame.

It was Lady Eyda who shouted orders instead, every inch a warrior queen in chain mail and fox fur. She raised a sword, pointing at the open gate. The carved bears stared back, locked in an endless snarl. Dyrian's sleepy, lumbering pet looked like a cub next to them. He bellowed in fear, sniffing the air. He smelled the danger too.

"To the fjord!" Eyda's voice boomed over the chaos in the gateyard. Between the Vedera of Kovalinn and Lenna's clan, hundreds of bodies jostled together. "Leave the hall. We must make for water!"

"Yrla, to the fjord!" Lenna cried, turning to face her own below. She yelled in both Jydi and Paramount, so all could understand. Her raiders responded with a howl, thumping their chests in agreement. "Archers, stay! Keep the dragon with us!"

Eyda gave a short nod. "Bring up bows and arrows!" she roared, and her people rushed to obey.

Ridha's stomach swooped, and she was nearly sick over the edge of the wall. She leaned, heavy, against the wooden rampart. Fear was a tiresome thing.

Whirling, Lenna touched her shoulder, barely a brush of her tattooed fingers against Ridha's tunic.

"Breathe," she said, gesturing for Ridha to inhale. The immortal did so, sucking down a bracing gasp of air. It helped, if only a little. "And run."

Bone met bone as Ridha's teeth gnashed together and she pushed herself to stand.

"I am a princess of Iona, daughter of the Monarch, blood of Glorian Lost." Someone pressed a bow into her hand and she took it, rising to her full menacing height. Her green armor settled over her figure, fitted to her form. She felt the warrior she was trained to be. Her fear remained, tight as a rope around her throat, but she would not let it control her. "I will not run."

Lenna's mouth pulled into a half-crazy grin, her gold teeth winking with the brilliant sunset. The sight filled Ridha with a strange warmth, though she had no time to think about it.

She racked her brain, trying to remember how her mother and the others had killed the last dragon three hundred years ago. There were many stories, most of them more concerned with sorrow than strategy. Useless tales of noble sacrifice. That dragon had been as big as a thunderhead, gray in color, ten thousand years old at least. It made its den in the highest peaks of Calidon, along the coast, where the ocean met blistering peaks of stone. They thought it survived off whales. But it grew too hungry, or simply too cruel. So the Vedera of Iona and Kovalinn battled the monster on the northern shores of Calidon, at the edge of the Glorysea. *It was spring, raining,* she remembered. *The storm helped quell the dragon's fire, and allowed the army to get close enough.* Ridha snatched an arrow from the quiver at her feet, one of dozens rushed up to the walls. She hissed out a breath, drawing her bow. *They did something to its wings, forced it to land.*

The shadow swooped through a cloud. A long tail lashed

through the air, the first visible part of its body. Like the gold in Lenna's mouth, the tail reflected the blazing sunset, its scales flashing so brightly it hurt her eyes.

Ridha squinted, her Vederan gaze sharp even from such a distance.

"The hide," she murmured. Her memories took shape, the stories her mother used to tell her returning. "The hide is made of jewels," she said, louder, shouting down the wall. "You won't penetrate the hide with arrows or anything else. You must aim for the wings!"

Lenna didn't argue. She snarled another command in Jydi, translating for her own folk.

Most scrambled to leave the high cliffs of the enclave, pressing through the gate and onto the steep, winding way down to the fjord. Lady Eyda and Dyrian led them, urging both peoples toward safety. Ridha peered over the wall, down the nearly sheer face of the mountain Kovalinn perched on. Her stomach swooped again. Heights did not bother her. Still, she did not enjoy the prospect of a dragon chasing her down the mountainside.

"I was not there in Calidon, when the last dragon fell," Kesar said, falling in alongside Ridha. She still wore her courtly garb, a soft tunic. Hardly ready for battle.

Ridha was glad for her own armor. "Nor was I."

Near a hundred Vedera mirrored Kesar, finding space among the raider folk, their own longbows at the ready, each one carrying as many arrows as they could. Any mistrust or discomfort melted away.

A common enemy unites like nothing else.

The light was dying, the last rays of the sun drawing back over the western mountains like fingers releasing their grip. The snow on the slopes lost its gleam, fading from pink to graying purple. Ridha shivered as Kovalinn began its descent into cold darkness. Night would only aid the dragon, and doom the rest.

"I never thought you were lying about the Spindles, but even so, I had my doubts," Kesar said, lacing the collar of her tunic to cover the topaz skin of her exposed throat. She never took her eyes off the sky, and the danger in it. "Not anymore."

Ridha felt as if the air had been pressed from her lungs.

"Taristan," she growled, her fear giving over to rage. Suddenly she wanted the dragon to show itself so that she might have somewhere to turn her fury.

Kesar curled her lip, just as angry. She pulled back her locks, tying them together with a leather cord. "The Prince of Old Cor unleashed this monster upon the Ward, and left another Spindle torn open." She shook her head. "To which realm, I don't remember."

Ridha was a future monarch, and her schooling had gone far beyond the training yard. Her mother's advisor Cieran had painstakingly taught her Spindle lore when she was a child. Most of her time was spent dodging his lessons, but she remembered what he managed to teach.

"It's called Irridas," she hissed, thinking of the pages in some book older than the Ward. The drawings blurred in her memory, but she could never forget the spiky landscape of craggy gemstones, and great, scarlet eyes leering up at her. It was a world of unimaginable riches and insatiable dragons to guard it. "The Dazzling Realm."

Shadows gathered in the darkening sky, making the dragon harder to spot. It roared, closer now, and every bow followed the noise, tracing a black shape across the deep blue heaven. One or two arrows fired, arcing away into nothing.

The raiders should escape with the others, Ridha thought, eyeing Lenna at her side. *Mortals are so quick to die.*

As if reading her mind, Lenna met her gaze, her jaw set hard, a muscle feathering in her pale cheek. Her bow was smaller than Ridha's, meant for hunting rabbits and wolves. *It will never bring down a dragon*, Ridha wanted to tell her, but held her tongue. Truly, she doubted any of their bows would.

"Be strong," Lenna said, clapping a fist to her chest, slapping the leather as her raiders had before. Her eyes gleamed, mad as her smile. "The Yrla are with you. And Yrla fight."

Ridha straightened her spine. "So do we."

Blackness bled across the sky, chasing off the last purple and blue. Torches crackled to life, a poor defense against the pressing dark, but enough for the raiders to see by. A wind blew down the fjord, shuddering through the pines and snow. The archers, mortal and immortal, waited without sound, as if they all held the same fearful breath. Below, the others echoed off the rocks, Eyda's shouts of encouragement swallowed up by the thunder of boots over stone. And behind Kovalinn, farther up into the mountains, wolves howled, a dozen packs singing out the same warning.

The dragon answered, appearing at the mouth of the fjord. It dropped out of the cloud bank, blotting out the newborn stars, a black mass of wings and claws, its eyes like a pair of flaming coals. They gleamed red, even at a distance. A ferocious, dancing light played between its teeth, begging to be loosed from lethal jaws. Its wings beat louder than any sound in the fjord, even the harried thump of Ridha's own heart.

"The wings!" she tried to shout, but her voice died in her throat.

Lenna did it for her, calling out orders down the wall. The raiders trained their bows on the monster. It picked up speed as it began its run down the fjord, growing larger with every passing second. Kesar called commands in Vederan. *Hold until it is nearly upon us. Save your arrows until you can wait no more, and tear those wings to shreds.*

Loosing another breath, Ridha reached for the arrows at her feet and pulled three from the nearest quiver. She set them between her fingers and put them to the bowstring, drawing all at once. Her pulse rammed a chaotic rhythm, but she schooled her breathing, settling into her archer's stance. Her muscles went taut. They knew what to do, even as fear paralyzed her mind.

This time, when the dragon roared, she felt the furious heat of its breath across her face. It blew back her hair, black strands coming loose from her long braid. The torches guttered but still burned, stubborn as the rest of them. A few of the archers quailed, breaking stance, but none abandoned the walls. They refused to cower, even the mortal raiders.

Ridha wished for her mother, for Domacridhan, for every warrior within the walls of Iona. And she cursed them too, hating them for leaving her here alone. *If Domacridhan is even still alive.* But that was a thread she could not afford to pull on, not now, while her own death careened down the fjord.

The arrows flew from her bow when the right moment came, the dragon close enough to devour them all. It passed overhead, wings spread so wide Ridha thought they might scrape both sides of the fjord. Its hide reflected the torchlight, countless precious stones winking red and black, ruby and onyx. Sweat trickled down Ridha's neck, born of terror and the sudden, relentless heat of the dragon. Arrows sprang from every bow, aiming for the wing membrane, the only piece of its body not covered in jewels. Maybe a dozen hit home. They looked like needles in the dragon's skin, small and useless.

Lenna let out a crow of excitement before firing another arrow.

The dragon banked hard, maneuvering out of their range in half a second, its wings beating tirelessly to climb straight into the sky again. It let out a snarl, either in pain or annoyance. Ridha hoped the former, putting three more arrows to the string.

"Again!" she heard herself shout. Her bow twanged, her arrows disappearing into the night. "It's testing us!"

"Not for long," Kesar ground out. "The creature will turn us to ash as soon as it realizes we're no match."

Ridha took her eyes off the dragon for only a moment, though every warrior instinct she had screamed otherwise. She glanced over the wall again, down the steep path, to the edge of the fjord. Raider folk and the Vedera clustered near the waterfall, the cliffs at their back. Even in the dim light, Ridha picked out Eyda and Dyrian among them, with their bear lumbering along.

"The others have reached the fjord," she said, wrenching back. Kesar nodded grimly. "So must we."

Three hundred years ago, my mother and her warriors brought down a dragon. Hundreds of Vedera, armed to the teeth, prepared to fight and die to kill a Spindleborn monster. She looked over the walls around them, taking in the raider folk and the immortal archers both. They were certainly not the army Isibel of Iona had led to battle. *But they could be so much worse.*

The dragon wheeled in the sky, circling beyond the range of even the finest Vederan archer. Ridha knew the gods of Glorian could not hear their prayers in this realm, but perhaps the gods of the Ward did. The clouds were blowing away, and the bright face of the moon peeked over the mountains, illuminating white slopes and dragon hide. Moonlight flashed through the jewels like sunlight on fish scales.

"We need to get to water," Ridha murmured, eying the river flowing through the gateyard. It plunged off the cliff to the fjord below. The icy waters would not be an escape, but they were certainly a shield. And a weapon, too, if they were lucky.

To her surprise, Lenna bumped her shoulder. She turned to see the smaller woman staring up at her with livid eyes. The blue and green were entrancing in the moonlight.

"The Yrla do not run," the chief said through her gleaming teeth.

Ridha had half a mind to leave her on the walls, but raider folk were nothing to sneer at. They were good fighters, some of the best in the Ward. And the Jydi and the Vedera would certainly need each other to survive the long night of the dragon.

"It isn't running," she snapped, letting her frustration show. "We'll be fighting every step of the way. And in case you haven't noticed, Kovalinn is made of wood." Indeed, only the foundations of the wall and the buildings were stone. The rest was pinewood, massive logs cut from the thick forests of the Jyd. *Would that it were steelpine*, Ridha thought, *and we could simply weather the flames*. "It's a mercy we aren't on fire already."

Lenna bucked her chin, as if trying to frighten an animal away. "Run away, Elder," she said. "And leave Yrla the glory."

As a princess of Iona, Ridha was not accustomed to being ordered around by anyone but her mother. Especially not a mortal woman of the raider folk, who seemed better suited to a cave than a monarch's throne room.

Ridha drew up to her full height, her armor reflecting the moon. She towered over Lenna, fixing her with the full weight of her immortal gaze.

"Move your raiders or I'll move you," she said, lowering her bow.

Lenna's lip curled and Ridha braced for another brave but foolish display. Instead the dragon swooped low again, this time its four legs trailing, claws extended.

Chief and princess ducked together, firing off arrows as best they could. With a scream, two figures were dragged off the wall, one raider and one Veder. Their bodies launched into the air, hurtling through the cold sky to disappear against the mountainside. The raiders could not hear it, but Ridha flinched at the crack of bone on rock. Triumphant, the dragon roared its warning to the rest of them, in a scream to split iron.

"Yrla, to the ground!" Lenna shouted in Paramount, and then in Jydi, slinging her bow over her shoulder. Kesar followed, barking the same orders down the line of Vedera.

As one, they abandoned the walls of Kovalinn, leaping into the snowy gateyard to begin the dizzying run down to the fjord. Another blast of heat chased them down, and for a second Ridha feared the dragon itself was upon them. But it was only the great hall, a fireball tearing through its roof. Flames licked up, eating the pine building from the inside, as the dragon hovered over the collapsing roof, spitting fire, its wings stirring up a ferocious, scalding wind to feed the blaze. The many rooms branching off the hall caught too, and then the many houses, the barracks, the stables and storerooms—until the entire great enclave of Kovalinn was an inferno. Bears burned across the clifftop, the carved wood charring to embers.

Ridha skidded on the slick pathway but kept her balance. Vedera were quick and agile. The terrain would offer no trouble, even with the waterfall throwing icy mist over the stone. Some immortal archers leapt from path to path, climbing down the zigzagging way as if it were a ladder instead of a road. Ridha could not blame them. No one was immortal before a dragon's flame. She would not ask them to hang back to protect the raiders, not if it meant sacrificing their own lives.

Her legs slowed.

But isn't that the point of all this? To fight for everyone in the Ward, and not just ourselves? Isn't that the only way we win?

Her boots skidded as she hung back, letting the rest of the immortals surge past, with the raiders fighting to keep up.

"Princess!" she heard Kesar call, but the dragon's roar swallowed up anything else. Ridha dodged with all her Vederan swiftness, moving against the crowd streaming down the cliffside.

She spotted a blond braid and a wolf tattoo at their rear, holding the gate, refusing to leave anyone behind. Raiders streamed by her, smoke clinging to their furs, their eyes alight with pure terror.

Ridha took up the other side of the gate, holding position. Carved bears snarled over her head. She almost laughed at them. The gates would be ash by morning, the great bears of Kovalinn dust in a frozen wind.

Across the gate, Lenna offered the smallest nod of thanks. It was better than flowers heaped at Ridha's feet. She replied with a nod of her own and glared into the fiery belly of the enclave, smoke and flame blowing with every beat of the dragon's wings.

Two more raiders limped out of the destruction, coughing and choking. Lenna demanded something in Jydi, words Ridha could not understand. The reply was clearly not to her liking, and the chief paled, swallowing hard.

"There are more inside," Lenna shouted across the din.

Ridha's stomach twisted. She counted a hundred Vedera upon the walls, with twenty more mortal archers. Near that many were below now, fighting down the cliff bank before the dragon turned its wrath on them. The princess looked through the gates again. Smoke and flame had turned the enclave into an apocalypse, and she wondered if this was what Infyrna, the Burning Realm, looked like. *Or Asunder itself, the kingdom of What Waits. The hell coming for us all.*

Smoke stung her eyes and Ridha squinted, searching for any

stragglers in the flames. Wood cracked and splintered, sending up a burst of embers. Ash began to fall in a blanket of wretched gray.

Lenna looked too, a hand raised to cut the glare of the fire. Another roar like a tear of metal sounded overhead. With a heaving breath, the chief abandoned the gate and plunged back into the burning enclave.

It took less than a second for Ridha to follow, the steel of her armor absorbing the heat, going hot against her skin.

The enclave smoldered, wooden beams and thatched roofs collapsing all around them. Lenna cupped her hands and shouted, calling for whoever might be left behind, but the hellish landscape swallowed up her voice. Not even Ridha could hear her. It was a foolish endeavor, no better than suicide. Again Ridha squinted into the fire, hunting for any sign of survivors. But she saw nothing, not even a shadow in the flames.

"We must go," she screamed, grabbing Lenna by the collar, her lips nearly brushing the chief's ear. "Or this will be your ending."

Not mine, Ridha told herself, even as corrosive fear wore through her body, eating at her strength. *I am a princess of Iona. I will not die this way.*

Lenna shoved her off, teeth bared like an animal. She looked as fearsome as the dragon itself.

"Leave me," she said, drawing a shortsword. The blade was wide and heavy, the tip pointed at Ridha. "I'll die with them."

"Die *for* them." Swinging her arm, Ridha disarmed the raider chief with a simple maneuver she'd learned long ago. Lenna blanched, raising her fists to strike, but Ridha only tossed the sword into a snowbank. "The ones still living are the ones who need you to survive."

Lenna sneered; then her gaze shifted, locking over Ridha's shoulder, back toward the inferno.

"*They* need us too," Lenna hissed.

Three figures tumbled out of the blaze, their faces ashen, with rags or furs over their mouths. One fell to his knees, wheezing, before Lenna grabbed him by the arms and hauled him up, urging him toward the gate. Ridha took another, a tall woman with burned clothes and a wounded leg. They blinked at each other.

"Your Highness," the woman muttered, and Ridha realized with a jolt that the woman was not raider, but Veder. Her own people.

They all were.

"To the gate," she forced out, as shame crashed over her.

The third Veder was not harmed, and he helped the others to the gates, smoke blowing at their backs. The snow melted in the heat, turning the gateyard to mud. Ridha held firm to the other immortal, using all her skill to keep from falling, while sweat poured down her face and neck. *All those centuries in the training yard*, she thought, cursing, *and I'm spent in a few moments*. Weariness clawed at her limbs, threatening to pull her backward into the dragon's jaws.

"Almost there!" she heard Lenna shout, and Ridha gave a mighty lunge toward the gate.

A tail swung like a battering ram, stirring the air inches from Ridha's face. The Veder under her arm disappeared, swept from her grasp by the dragon's pendulum of a tail. She caught a glimpse of the immortal's face, her jaw wide in a soundless scream, as the dragon slammed her body into the gates. The sheer force smashed the carved bears and the walls apart, splintering the wooden palisade. The doors fell together, cracked in half, as the rest collapsed in a heap of burning rubble. Lenna shrieked as the embers rose in a spiral, burning against the starlight.

Ridha fell to her knees, staring at the flames where the gate used to be. Her fingers trailed through the melting snow and she closed her fist, holding on to the cold. The ice bit under her fingernails.

It might be the last thing I ever feel.

She stood rooted to the ground, numb, as another sweep of the dragon's tail cut through the gateyard. Lenna leapt out of the way, landing face-first in the snow, but the other wounded Veder was not so lucky. The dragon's tail launched him up and over the crumbling wall, the Veder howling as he plunged over the edge of the cliff.

"Move, Elder!"

This time it was Lenna screaming in her ear, close enough that Ridha could smell her hair. Smoke, blood, burning pine—and something sweeter beneath. *Wildflowers.* The chief hauled Ridha to her feet as best she could, forcing the princess to find her bearings. While the dragon rounded the enclave, its shrieks echoing off the mountains, Lenna ran to where the gate once stood, trying to clear a path through the burning ruins. The third Veder joined her, shouldering aside broken planks and logs.

Ridha flexed her hands, willing the feeling to return to her body. Her breath came in short, stinging gasps, the smoke threatening to suffocate them all. *I will not die this way*, she thought, throwing herself at the rubble. Her bare hands bled and burned as they worked, furious and desperate. Ridha winced, but every splinter pushed aside was one more gasp at life.

Lenna did not falter, mortal as she was. Tears ran down her face, from pain or the smoke or both, but she fought on, throwing aside debris.

"There's a path. At the bottom of the fjord, behind the waterfall," the chief forced out, stifling a cry as sparks rained down on them. Her coat caught flame and she shook it off, leaving it to burn. "The Yrla know the way."

So will Eyda, Ridha thought, relieved. *At least the Ward will not die with us. There is hope still, small as it may be.*

"Here," the other Veder said, getting his shoulder under one of the larger logs. Panting, he pushed with all his strength, dislodging a cascade of logs and planks. They rolled apart, spitting embers, and Lenna kicked through the shattered remains of the carved gates. Ridha nearly wept, her throat burning like the enclave.

The cliff road waited, the fjord beyond it, a knife of moonlight between the raging curls of smoke.

They made for the gap in the rubble, stumbling together, covered in ash. Lenna clutched at Ridha's arm as they pulled each other along. A cold wind blew, a brief respite from the dragon's onslaught, and Ridha drank it down gratefully, her lungs screaming for fresh air.

The dragon struck again, trying to bring the wall down on them. Ridha pulled Lenna with her, planks splintering over their heads and down the cliffside. The other Veder managed to dodge too, taking his first step onto the road down to the fjord, and safety.

Ridha's heart hammered in her chest, and Lenna's beat in time, singing out their fear. Another rhythm rumbled, beyond her own body, shaking up from the ground itself. It was almost familiar.

Hoofbeats? Ridha thought, a half second before the rider turned up the path, taking the sharp corners at a gallop not even an immortal rider would try.

The stallion snorted, blowing hard, almost roaring against its bridle, near to madness. He wore armor to match his rider, plates of onyx so dark they did not reflect the moon, or even dragonflame. The knight in the saddle urged him on, kicking with spurred boots, his face obscured by his simple helm. He wore no tunic and held no flag, his body covered from gauntleted fingers to booted toes. There was no insignia on him or his horse, no sign of any kingdom he might serve. Nothing but the black armor. It seemed made from precious, impossible stone instead of steel.

"Turn back!" the other Veder shouted, raising a hand to wave down the knight.

A sword passed through the air, cutting through his wrist in a clean, effortless line. The Veder fell to his knees, howling, as the stallion rode on, closing in on the broken gates—and Ridha.

"Do not stand in my way," the knight hissed, his voice low and serpentine. The chaos should have drowned him out, but Ridha heard him clear as a bell, even from a dozen yards, over the thunder of hooves and a dragon's rage.

She clutched at Lenna, gathering the chief to her body. There was no time to explain, no time to think. The dragon roared above, rearing up for another strike, as the knight ascended, his blade as black as his armor, dripping immortal blood. It seemed to swallow the world, and even the dragon receded from her mind.

Ridha ran, not for the gate, not for the winding path down the cliffside—but for the waterfall next to them.

The water was icy cold, a thousand knives stabbing at every inch of her skin. It was not the water Ridha feared, nor even the waterfall.

They went over the edge together, falling through open air. A single thought echoed in Ridha's mind.

The dragon did not come through the Spindle alone.

10
TO EARN THE WORLD
Erida

By nightfall, the smell of smoke was everywhere, clinging to her clothes, her hair, and perhaps her bones too. Campfires, cook fires, and flame within Rouleine, from the same and worse. The catapults had begun their onslaught, slinging rocks and rubble from the outskirts. Every few minutes, Erida heard the distant thunder of them. She wondered which blow would be the one to open the city gates and bring the flag of surrender.

The Queen's sleeping tent was as grand as it could be in a siege camp, with carpets on the bare ground, a small salon consisting of a low table with mismatched seats, and her bed hidden behind a screen. Her handmaidens and ladies had their own tent to the right, connected by a covered passage, as the council tent was to the left. The latter was large enough to hold seemingly every person of marginal importance in the army, lest someone feel slighted and decide Lord Konegin had the right idea.

As always, Erida's skull throbbed with the difficulty of keeping such a balance. Scales weighed in her hands, bobbing up and down.

Lucky there was only one scale to balance at the moment. Ronin sat before her in the salon, his dinner set on his knees, while Taristan kept up his steady prowl along the edge of her tent. His imperial cloak and armor were gone, but his shadow loomed large against the canvas. His constant, silent motion put her on edge. *Perhaps that's the point*, she thought.

Even though her armor was light, made for show and not function, it was good to be rid of it. Her long green gown with trailing sleeves was more comfortable. Slowly, she worked the braids from her hair, easing away a little bit of the tension in her head and neck.

Taristan's black eyes caught the candlelight. They followed the motions of Erida's hands as they combed through her hair.

His gaze sent a chill down her spine.

"I need to name more members to the Crown Council," she said, leaning back against her cushioned seat.

Ronin paused over his tray of greasy chicken bones and raised his red eyes. "I would be honored."

Erida laughed in his face. "I did not realize you had such a wonderful sense of humor, Ronin."

The quivering priest scoffed and went back to sucking on bones like a child scolded. *But he is no boy*, Erida knew. *Even if he is not so old, barely older than me, Ronin is a man, and a dangerous one.* She watched Ronin's eyes again, both scarlet and bloodshot. She had never seen such eyes. Part of her knew Ronin's eyes were unnatural, some gift or curse of What Waits. *No person alive could be born with such eyes.*

"Your focus should be on the Spindles," Taristan said to her, halting at his wizard's shoulder. "He would not like for your gaze to stray."

The Spindles. The march pushed most thought of them from her mind, out of both exhaustion and fear. She remembered Castle Vergon, ruins made by the echo of a Spindle. And now split by another, the one Taristan tore open only weeks ago. It was almost too sharp in her mind. The smell of his blood on the Spindleblade. The sun on broken glass, the image of the goddess Adalen shattered by his fist. The air itself seemed to crackle with energy, like the sky before a lightning storm. And she could never forget the Spindle itself, a single thread of gold that formed a doorway to another realm.

To think, there were more to open. More realms to draw forth.

And What Waits beyond them all, biding his time.

She wondered how they communicated, her husband and the Torn King. *Through the wizard priest,* she assumed. *They certainly aren't exchanging letters.*

Though a thousand questions ran through her mind, as they did whenever the Spindles came up, the Queen held her tongue. She was no fool. There were things she did not wish to prod, not yet.

"We should not tarry long here," Ronin said, cracking a bone with his teeth. He slurped out the marrow with a disgusting noise.

Erida pulled a face. *Clearly What Waits has not given him table manners.*

"The siege will not last," she said aloud, swallowing her revulsion. "They may have water and stores, but not stone. Their walls are already beginning to crumble, and when the siege towers are built—"

The red wizard shook his head. "That is still too long."

"And why is that?" Erida shot back, eyeing him across the low table.

"I exhausted your archives in Ascal, and found little in the way of Spindles. The Gallish records of anything *not* Gallish are sorely lacking." He set down his plate and cast another loaded glance at Taristan. "The Library Isle will be of far more use."

Erida sighed, frustrated.

"The Library Isle is in Partepalas," she said slowly, as if speaking to a child. "The Madrentine capital is the object of our entire campaign. And after we break Rouleine, it will be an easy march, right down Robart's throat."

Ronin snapped another bone between his white hands. The crack sounded through the tent. "You have twenty thousand men with you. Leave a thousand, five thousand—ten, even—to besiege Rouleine. But we must continue south, and we must continue our hunt for Spindles."

"Corayne is far more dangerous than we understood," Taristan rumbled.

The Queen sighed at him. "She is a child, and she is nothing without her allies. But fear not: I've set things in motion. I have not forgotten the danger of Corayne an-Amarat." She took another breath, steadying herself as she would during any council meeting.

"But it will be just as dangerous to leave Rouleine and split our forces. You may know Spindle lore, but you know nothing of warfare, Priest."

Ronin jumped to his feet, his robes falling around him in a crimson curtain. "Your war is in service to What Waits, Your Majesty," he said hotly. "Not the other way around."

"But she isn't wrong."

Taristan's voice was low but unyielding, his face stern.

The wizard cast up his hands in frustration. But to the Queen's great relief, Ronin did not argue. He stalked from the tent, muttering to himself in a strange language Erida could not place. In that moment, she hardly cared. Sieges were a tiresome business, and she had little energy left to fight with the wizard tonight.

Part of her wanted to crawl into bed and sleep. A stronger part kept her rooted in her seat, unmoving and silent. A mirror to Taristan's own brooding form, his shadow stretching behind him like a cloak. She expected him to follow the wizard and return to their own tent nearby. Instead he crossed the carpets and lowered himself into Ronin's chair.

Erida watched him as she would a great tiger. Her consort was a handsome man. She knew that since the first moment she saw him, half covered in mud, carrying only a jeweled sword and his own ambition. Even the lines down his cheek, the scratches wretched Corayne left, looked distinguished on his face. He had not softened after months as her husband, all but a king. If anything, he seemed harder and sharper than that day. More drawn, somehow. Even the shadows seemed darker on his face.

He let her watch him, silent in his own inscrutable thoughts.

"What you did to Orleon . . . ," Erida began, hesitant. For some reason she could not understand, her voice trembled.

She saw the fallen prince in her mind, his corpse disemboweled, his throat slit, his limbs severed at hip and shoulder. Killed a dozen different ways. There was still some blood on Taristan, despite his best efforts to wash it all away. On his neck, behind his ear. Even a drag of it along his hairline.

Without thinking, Erida stood and ducked behind the screen hiding her bedchamber. She filled a basin with water and grabbed a cloth before returning to the salon.

Taristan eyed the bowl, confused.

Before he could speak and steal her nerve, Erida pulled a chair to his side. She dipped the cloth and began to clean his face, wiping away the speckles of Orleon's blood still clinging to his skin.

"I am capable of cleaning myself," he forced out, sounding rather strangled.

"If you were, I wouldn't be doing this," she answered with a tight smile. The cloth stained quickly; the water in the basin turning pink.

Taristan offered no more complaint and sat stock-still, as if moving would break the world. She felt the heat of his skin even through the cloth, and she wondered if it was the realm of Asunder burning in his heart.

"What you did to Orleon . . . ," she began again, this time with as much resolve as she could muster.

His eyes met her own. "Did I frighten you?"

Erida paused in her work, pulling away to face him fully. "No," she said, shaking her head. "I felt nothing."

It was a strange thing to admit, having no sympathy for a man being butchered alive. *But I am a ruling queen. The life of one man is but a feather on the scales I must balance.*

"I only mean to say—I understood it. What you did to him, and why."

"Enlighten me." His teeth clicked together with every consonant, his eyes growing dark.

She drew back in her chair. "I know what you saw in him," she said, dropping the cloth. "Fine armor. A good sword in a trained hand. A prince born and bred for greatness, for power. A man with the world at his feet, who did nothing to earn it."

Taristan tightened under her scrutiny, until she feared he might snap. At least the red sheen did not return to his eyes.

"I saw the same," she murmured, choosing her words with utmost care. His eyes widened a little, blazing over her face. "But for you—he was everything your own brother was given. And you were denied."

Her consort drew a breath through his bared teeth. "I have not thought of my brother since the day I put a sword through him."

"I don't believe you," she answered, blunt.

His reply was just as quick, like a volley of arrows across the battlefield. "I don't care what you believe."

"Yes, you do." Erida folded her hands in her lap and set her feet on the ground, her back straight as a spear. She faced him as she would a councillor or a general. Though no councillor or general had ever made her heart beat so quickly. "Tell me about it. Where you came from."

Taristan eyed her, silent for a long moment. "I came from nowhere."

The Queen scoffed. "Don't be dramatic."

His lips pursed, but he bobbed his chin in something akin to a nod. He ran a hand over his cheeks, scratching the dark red stubble growing in.

"I've been told my parents died, or that they abandoned me to live out their years in comfort in some Elder castle. Perhaps I was the price they paid. Either way, they're gone now," he said. "I don't remember them. But I remember an orphanage in Corranport."

Erida winced. Corranport was a port city, a smudge on the map. Ascal if Ascal had no palace or gardens or well-to-do citizens. If most of the criminals in the world lived in Adira, the rest lived in Corranport. She knew the difficulty of growing up in such a place, and she saw what it had made him. The hard edge of a hard life, and a seed of mistrust planted so deep no man could uproot it.

"Everything stank of piss and fish," Taristan muttered, his face souring with memory.

"Ascal is not much better," Erida offered, trying to be helpful.

Instead he scowled. "Funny, I don't remember your palace smelling as foul as a dock orphanage."

She could only lower her eyes. "True."

Thankfully, the misstep didn't seem to push him away. If anything, he sank deeper, eyes sliding out of focus. The candlelight played in his hair; a gleam of gold against scarlet. A few strands fell across his eyes, and to Erida's pleasure, he did not brush them away. The light softened his features, even as the shadows pooled in the harsh planes of his cheekbones.

"I didn't want to fish, didn't want to sail, didn't want to trade. Barely learned to read," he said. "Most of us ended up begging or thieving. I was better at the latter."

Erida kept her jaw tight, her mouth shut, watching as he spoke. She found she could not imagine Taristan of Old Cor begging anyone for anything.

"But I couldn't stay. My feet were always moving, as if something were pulling me along." Taristan swallowed, pushing down something Erida could not see. "I know now, it's in the blood."

"Corblood," she said, almost reaching for his hand, his fingers braced against the table. They were bare but for the red still crusted under his nails.

He looked at her sidelong, those black eyes of his cutting as any knife. "A blessing or a curse, depending on who you might ask."

"Well there's only two of you left," Erida muttered, shrugging. "Corayne might call it a curse."

A corner of his mouth lifted. "She might be right."

His fingers drummed against the wood, the crescents of his nails like red moons.

"I was twelve when I ended up in a Treckish war camp. They put a sword in my hand and food in my belly and told me to fight." His eyes flashed, still black as jet. "I was best at that."

Judging by the release in his shoulders, his memories of Trec were far better than most he had. Erida balked at the thought. The Treckish war camps were home to soldiers no better than wolves, loping the countryside to defend borders and hunt bandits. Most of the men there were mercenaries, Erida knew, though once they had been slaves no better than human shields. *At least that foul practice is long ended*, she thought with a scowl.

"I saw a war camp once," she said, remembering the grim sight. Nothing but mud and stupid, leering men who had not bathed in a decade. All of them corded with muscle and bad tempers, as unyielding as the steel Trec built their kingdom upon. "At my northern border."

Taristan raised an eyebrow. "And?"

"Prince Oscovko was with them." She wrinkled her nose in distaste. "He enjoys it, apparently."

He half smiled. "Another disappointed suitor?"

Erida nodded, laughing. "He said they were defending the Gates of Trec from Jydi raiders. But I think the only thing he fought was gravity." She shook her head at the memory of the boorish prince, bloody and drink-stained. "Oscovko was wine-blind. I don't think he even knew who I was for the hour we spoke."

"I'm surprised you didn't marry him and kill him the moment your child came of age. Take his crown and his country," Taristan said, his voice low, without a hint of humor.

Erida tipped her head. "I'd rather give my children the realm entire."

The words echoed in her head, and in the tent, reverberating between the two of them. Like always, the mention of children, of a royal line sprung from their divided trees, unsettled them both. Erida leaned into the discomfort. She'd long since learned it was the only way to hurdle her fears. And while children were absolutely necessary to their reign, she still feared the concept, as any sensible person would.

Taristan reacted as he always did, retreating into himself. In fact, it was the only time Erida ever saw him do such a thing. *Is he afraid too?* she wondered. *Or simply disinterested?*

A man like him survived life seeing each step as it came, not the long path of the journey. *I cannot afford to think like that.*

"I can't believe you survived a war camp," she said, steering the conversation back to something safe. If a child growing up in a war camp could be considered safe at all. "You fought Jydi raiders?"

Taristan shrugged. "And the Countless too, during the wars of the Temur emperor."

She tried to picture the sight in her mind. A twelve-year-old boy against the ruthless raider folk and then the Temurijon, facing down the most fearsome cavalry in the known realm. It was a foolish endeavor, impossible even in her imagination.

"And then Ronin found you?" she breathed, trying to trace the line of his life.

"I suppose we found each other." Taristan looked to the tent flap, as if the red wizard might return. Erida half expected him to. *The little menace has a talent for interruption.* "I was in my wanderings again. Jydi don't raid in winter, and I went south with what coin I had. To what, I didn't know. But something called me to Ronin. And called Ronin to me."

Erida felt her eyes go wide. Her breath came hard, as if pressed from her lungs. "What Waits."

His gaze snapped back to hers, black and ruinous. Slowly, he leaned forward in his chair, until his face was only inches away. "What else?"

The closeness of him sent prickles down her spine, playing along each bone. Erida did not move, her back still straight, her feet still planted on the carpet. She would not give him the satisfaction and surrender her space to him, even if it meant feeling his every breath on her cheeks. Up close, his eyes were not the empty, flat black she knew. They seemed more like the surface of a pool beneath a starless sky, too deep to fathom, hiding more than she could ever know.

He expected her to pull away. She could see it in the set of his teeth, the tightness of his brow. Her stillness rankled him, but Taristan was not one to back down either. They remained, nose to nose, unyielding on either side.

It delighted Erida.

"I wouldn't have believed him," she said, sporting a winning smile. It felt like victory. "Some strange wizard wanders up and tells you you're Spindleborn, a Corblood mortal with a stolen destiny?"

Taristan did not laugh. "You believed your father."

The Queen blinked, the mention of her father like a slap across the face. She steadied herself quickly. "What?"

"When he told you what you were, what you were born to. When he told you what your crown and your throne meant," Taristan explained. She tried not to look at his mouth as he spoke. "Why did you believe him?"

A sorrow Erida kept at bay swept through her faster than she thought was possible, like the first flag of sickness. Tears pricked at her eyes, rising too quickly for her to hide. She gasped a breath, struggling for an answer. *Because he was my father, because I trusted him, because I loved him. Because I wanted to be what he needed and wanted of a son. And . . .*

The tears disappeared as swiftly as they came. Her sadness fell away, wrestled back into the box where she kept her useless things.

Taristan waited, patient as ever.

"Because I felt it to be true," Erida said. "In my bones."

His touch was nearly blistering, his fingers closing around her wrist with ease.

"So do I," he answered, studying her hands as an artist would a painting, or a soldier a battlefield.

She dared not move, either forward or back. They remained, Taristan and Erida, connected by a strange, tightening circle. Erida felt it loop around her throat, like a necklace she never wanted to remove.

The candles flickered, sputtering for a moment in a phantom wind, though the air did not stir. They danced in his eyes, and red glared through the black, a burst of blood from a wound too deep for Erida to see.

Taristan dropped her wrist without ceremony and stood from his chair. He took the bloody cloth in hand, focusing on the stained fabric instead of her. Suddenly, the tent felt too hot, as if it were high summer instead of autumn.

"You should sleep," Taristan ground out, striding for the flap.

Erida clenched her fists, every muscle in her body going tight with frustration. "Sleep will be easy. We are in for a long siege."

He reached the entrance to the tent, pulling the canvas aside. He did not look back.

"Not so long as you might think."

A fresh breeze washed in as he left, and Erida burned within, new sweat already cooling on her skin.

Too much of her wanted to go after him. Far too much.

"Fine," she said to no one.

11

HOW FARE THE WINDS
Corayne

The coast was only a night's ride from the Heir's encampment. The journey reminded Corayne of a royal procession, with lin-Lira and the Falcons riding in broader formation, allowing the Companions more room to move. Isadere and Sibrez rode with them, their own guardians tailing along, the flags of Ibal held high. The royal blue silks were dark beneath the night sky, but the dragons flashed in the moonlight, gold turned to silver.

Corayne kept her eyes on the horizon, squinting into the night, waiting for the first glimpse of sunrise—and the Long Sea.

Hour by hour, the world faded from inky black to shades of blue. A sapphire line gleamed in the distance, reflecting the moon. Corayne knew it was the coast, and the waters beyond. She sucked in a fortifying breath, the air tinged with the smell of saltwater. It hit her like a blow, and she thought of home. The Empress Coast, the docks in Lemarta, the Cor road along the cliffs, where the waves kicked up sea spray every morning. The old white cottage on the cliffside had never seemed as far away as it did to her now.

By the time sunrise came, the sky streaking pink and gold, they were close enough to the water for Corayne to feel the cool breeze on her face. When the horses met the beach, the sand fine as powder beneath their hooves, Corayne nudged hers into the shallow, lapping waves. The others gathered behind her, out of the water.

Corayne dismounted with a splash and nearly wept. She wanted to go farther, until the waves were at her throat, the salt in her teeth. She wanted to feel the sting of the Long Sea, the smallest piece of home. *Would it bring me there, if given the chance?* she wondered, as the waters kissed her boots. But Corayne knew better. The current ahead of them did not flow the way she wished, just like the path she walked now. Neither would take her anywhere she wanted to go.

Isadere's galley anchored offshore, a shadow against the sky. It looked nothing like the *Tempestborn*, her mother's ship, but if Corayne squinted, she could pretend.

There's no time for this, she told herself, wiping away a single tear with the heel of her hand. Her cheeks flushed with embarrassment. It felt silly to cry over something so familiar as the waves.

Corayne looked back over the sand dunes glowing golden. From the beach they were beautiful, shimmering in the sunrise, almost inviting. Corayne knew better. The Great Sands were as good a defense as anything in the realm, protecting the kingdom of Ibal as the fleets and armies did. The desert was no small thing to cross, and she felt as if some marvelous, dangerous creature had allowed her to pass unscathed.

After a moment she dipped her head, acknowledging the long road behind them. The oasis, the Spindle closed, the soldiers dead, and their footsteps all the way back to Almasad.

Sorasa came up alongside her, leading her oil-black mare. She glanced between Corayne and the desert, her brow furrowed in confusion.

"How did you know to do that?" she said. It sounded like a demand.

Corayne mirrored the assassin, looking back to the landscape and then to her. "Do what?"

"Show gratitude to the Sands." Sorasa gestured, bowing her head as Corayne had. "Did your mother teach you?"

Corayne shook her head, confused.

"My mother has never been this far into Ibal," she said. Meliz an-Amarat was never out of sight of saltwater, if she could help it. And though Meliz's father gave her some Ibalet heritage and her Ibalet name, she had never lived in this golden kingdom.

"It just felt right, I guess," Corayne added, shrugging. "Good manners."

"Well, it is," Sorasa replied, her sharp manner softening a little. She offered her curling smirk, then faced the Great Sands, her body squared to the dunes. With her free hand on her chest, she bent forward, lowering her eyes in deference to the desert.

All along the beach, the Falcons, the Dragons, and the king's children did the same. Isadere swept lowest of all, despite their royal birth.

"The King of Ibal only bows to the desert and the sea, the two things he can never command," Sorasa offered, following Corayne's line of sight. "It's the same with Isadere."

Andry bowed with the others, matching their customs as any polite, well-trained courtier would do. But the other Companions were not so observant. Sigil and Charlie were eager to be gone, putting their backs to the dunes and never looking back. Valtik was too busy combing the edge of the waves, looking for seashells and fish bones, to honor anything beyond her own two feet. And Dom simply glowered in his usual way, staring out to sea. The northern continent was too far, even for Elder eyes.

He watched the galley and Corayne followed his gaze.

She splashed out of the shallows, falling in at his side.

"It's a good ship," she muttered, assessing the hull and sails. Both were immaculate, fitting of royalty. The galley wasn't as large as the *Tempestborn*, but looked just as swift, built for speed. Where the *Tempestborn* was meant to eat ships, Isadere's galley was meant to outrun them.

Corayne glanced around at her Companions. They formed a circle, their faces turned to her. Their attention still felt strange, unwarranted.

She eyed the galley again, if only to put their focus somewhere else. "She'll make good time across the Long Sea."

"I'm surprised you didn't send us back to Adira," Andry said, a playful grin rising to his lips.

Corayne matched his smile. The criminal outpost was a haven in her memory, their last bit of quiet before recruiting Sigil and crossing the Long Sea.

"Don't tempt me."

Isadere stopped beyond their knotted circle, waiting to be acknowledged. Their brother was not so tactful. Sibrez shifted from foot to foot, impossible to overlook.

"Your generosity might save the realm. Allward is forever in your debt, Your Highness," Corayne said quickly, before Dom, Sorasa, Charlie, Valtik, or Sigil could ruin the entire endeavor. *Andry and I should be the only ones allowed to speak in mixed company.*

Again Isadere looked pleased, but also grave. They stepped forward, arms outstretched. Their traveling robes were the same deep blue of their silks, woven with threads of gold.

Corayne took their hands. Thankfully, Dom did not interfere, content to watch from a very close distance.

"I see so much in you, Corayne an-Amarat," Isadere said, looking her over. Their face grew more grim, and Corayne felt her heart twist.

"I know what you see, Your Highness," she murmured back, trying to ignore the Spindleblade across her own shoulders. "A girl, barely more than a child. Too small for the sword, too small for the task put in front of me." Her breath caught. "And you may be right."

Isadere's dark eyes narrowed.

"But I'm all we have." Corayne tried to sound strong, but her voice quavered anyway.

"And for that, I am grateful," Isadere said, taking Corayne by surprise. "I see the gods in your eyes, and bravery in your heart. I see the Spindle in your blood, burning hotter than any flame. I only wish I could give you more."

A flush warmed Corayne's face. "Passage and horses is enough."

Isadere's grip tightened, fingers strong and fierce. "I give you promises too. The mirror showed me the white wolf. Oscovko *will* help, and I will make my father listen, both to your tale and to Lasreen. The goddess wills us to fight." They looked back to the desert again, eyes filled with resolve. "I will not stand by and let Erida of Galland devour the realm. You must trust in this."

Corayne bit her lip. "I will certainly try," she muttered.

The lies had fallen so easily from Erida. In that small room, where she pretended to care about Allward, pretended to be their savior. Corayne had wanted to believe the Queen so badly. *I was an easy target, eager to give my task to someone else,* she thought. *And I still am, though no one will ever be able to take it.*

She tried to see past her own weariness and fear, to look into Isadere and find the same lie Erida told.

Isadere stared back, their eyes like iron.

"Thank you," Corayne forced out, giving Isadere's arms a squeeze before pulling back.

"And I do have something else for you. *We* do, I mean," Isadere said, gesturing to their brother.

Sibrez bowed his head and unclasped his vambraces, the black leather guards around his forearms. They wrapped from the wrist to below the elbow, the leather patterned in gold with the same scaled design as his armor.

"You will be the first person beyond the *Ela-Diryn* to wear them," he said, holding out the pair to Corayne. She looked them over, wide-eyed, before taking the vambraces with trembling hands. "*Dirynsima.* Dragonclaws."

They were heavier than she expected, a good weight, with worn leather buckles on the underside to keep them in place around her arms. She turned them over, examining the finely made armor. With a gasp, she realized the extra weight came from a steel splint reinforcing the vambraces. Tiny but lethal triangular spikes stood out along the long outer edge, marching from wrist to elbow. Corayne tested one, and nearly drew blood.

Sibrez looked on proudly. If he missed his Dragonclaws, he did not show it.

"These vambraces can absorb the strike of a blade, if used properly," he said, tapping a finger against the steel-enforced edge.

Sorasa appeared then, peering at the vambraces with discerning eyes. Whatever she saw in the leather guards, the Amhara certainly liked.

"She'll learn," she said, eyeing Sibrez.

Begrudgingly, he nodded in return.

"Thank you both," Corayne said, her fingers tight on the gift. She wouldn't wear them yet. Sailing with a set of spikes strapped to her body didn't seem prudent. "I hope we meet again."

Isadere nodded, sweeping back their arms, their trailing sleeves like the wings of a beautiful bird. "The mirror has not shown me the end of this road yet, but I hope so too."

With another low bow, Corayne stepped back. A rowboat waited to take them to the galley, the Ibalet captain already at its prow. The others followed, breaking off to unload the saddlebags. It would take some time to ferry the horses to the galley, and Corayne knew it might be hours until they truly set sail. Still, it felt good to get on another ship, to set off in the right direction again.

The Companions made to go, but Isadere reached out, stopping Charlie with a hand, bidding him wait a moment.

Charlie met Isadere's eye in silence. He could not have been further in appearance from the Heir: a short, heavyset young man with inky fingers and pale skin streaked by sunburns. But something seemed to unite them too. A reverence Corayne could not understand.

"We may not see eye to eye, but the goddess sees us both," Isadere said, taking on the grave air of a prophet again. "She is with you, whether you feel it or not."

Corayne braced for Charlie's reply. To her surprise, he touched his brow and kissed his ink-stained fingers. A salute to the gods. Isadere matched it.

"On that we can agree," Charlie said before tromping off to the boat. His saddlebags dangled from one shoulder, his many parchments, wax seals, and bottles of ink poking out.

What they would need on the road ahead, Corayne did not know yet. But she was eager to find out.

Once the horses were on board and settled below, thanks in large part to Sigil's gentle coaxing, the galley left the coast behind, heading north. The oar deck held twenty-five rows split down the middle, with two rowers on each side, and they made good time into the Long Sea. Corayne stood at the rail, breathing deep of the sea air again. It fortified her somehow.

Sailor-soldiers crewed the Heir's galley. Many were trained archers, taking turns defending the raised forecastle at the rear of the deck. They waited for the monsters of Meer, for krakens and sea serpents, but the Long Sea stretched blue and empty in every direction. No enemies, at least not any Corayne could see.

But she certainly still felt them. Erida and her army marching through Madrence, gaining mile after mile. Her uncle Taristan growing stronger by the second, hunting for Spindles to tear apart. *How long until he tears too many?*

Every passing moment could be the last, Corayne knew, though she tried not to dwell on it. Such a burden was too much for her to bear on top of everything else. She flagged against the ship railing, content to stay still, glad for the moment of quiet. Behind her, stacked crates hid her from most of the deck, and most of its occupants.

But for one.

"How long until we make port again?"

Corayne smiled as Andry rounded the crates. He leaned up alongside her, his elbows on the rail, his long brown fingers knitted together. The sea breeze played in his hair, rustling the heavy coils.

"Your hair's getting longer," Corayne said, remembering what he looked like when she first saw him. A young man at the door to his mother's apartments, his eyes kind and welcoming, ready to help the unknown girl before him. But there had been a darkness to him even then, the memory of a massacre tearing at his insides. It clung to him now. She hoped it would not last.

The squire ran a hand over his scalp with a sheepish smile. A few tight curls spiraled against his fingers, growing more defined by the day. "I've been a bit busy for haircuts."

"Shocking," she answered with a dry laugh.

His eyes flickered over the waves, searching the depths. She saw unease in him.

"I'm beginning to suspect you don't like sailing," Corayne said, shifting to face him. Her hip bumped the rail.

"Not when there could be krakens and serpents under every wave."

"Well, there's one less than when we crossed. That's something."

"That's something," he echoed, his eyes distant. "I'm beginning to suspect you're hiding."

Corayne glanced at the stacked crates around them and shrugged.

"If Sigil and Sorasa see me idle, they'll make me train," she muttered. A wave of exhaustion broke over her at even the thought of more fighting lessons. "I just wanted a moment to myself. Give the bruises a little more time to heal."

Andry nodded, his grin still fixed, but it no longer reached his eyes. "Of course, I'll take my leave."

"No, don't you run off." She caught his arm before he was out of reach, pulling him back to the rail. His smile widened, and so did Corayne's. "You're too polite for your own good, Andry Trelland," she said, nudging him with her shoulder. "Remember, you're running with criminals and castoffs now."

"I've been aware of that for some time."

His eyes hardened and found the sea, looking not to the waves, but to the horizon beyond it. *East*, Corayne knew, tracking his gaze. *To his mother? To Kasa, her homeland, where she waits for a son she might never see again?* She remembered Valeri Trelland, ill but resolute, a pillar of strength in her wheeled chair. *Or does he look to Ascal, where he left his honor in the shattered hall of Erida's palace?*

"You should let your bruises heal too," Corayne said in a low voice, hesitant.

He sucked in a harsh gasp. "There's a difference between healing and forgetting, Corayne. I will never forget what I've done."

The words stung. "And you think I will?"

"I think you're trying to move forward in any way you can, but—"

"But?"

"Don't lose your heart along the way."

Corayne felt her heart now, still stubbornly beating inside her chest. She put a hand to it, feeling the pulse beneath her skin. "It's not going anywhere. I promise."

It wasn't a lie. But it certainly felt like one.

"Less than a week to land," Corayne said, looking back to the sea for an easy change of subject. "If the weather remains favorable."

"Will it?"

She twisted her lips, thinking. "The worst of the autumn storms are to the east, where the Long Sea meets the ocean." The sky above them was perfect, a sailor's dream. "I think the winds will hold for us. It'll be the first bit of luck we've had."

Andry squared his shoulders to Corayne and looked her over. His expression pulled in confusion. "I think we've had a great deal of luck."

She tossed back her windblown hair. "We must define the word differently."

"No, I mean it." Andry drew closer, his voice firmer than before. "We came to Ibal to close a Spindle. We did it. And we're all still breathing. I certainly call that luck."

"And what about me?" Corayne's mouth filled with a sour taste. She knew it as regret. "Would you consider me lucky?"

His eyes flashed. "You're alive. That's enough."

"Alive," Corayne scoffed. "Born to a mother who leaves with every good tide. A father I never met, who still *somehow* holds sway over me, his influence in my very blood. His *failure*, this *curse* of what I am—and I don't just mean the Spindles." Her hands shook at her sides, and she shoved them behind her back, trying to hide her emotions as best she could. But she couldn't hide the way her voice quivered. "Corblood makes us restless, rootless, always yearning for the horizon we can never reach. It's why Old Cor conquered, spreading in every direction, searching for some place to call home. But they never, ever found it. And neither will I."

Andry looked stricken, his face twisting with pity. "I certainly hope that isn't true."

She could only flush, embarrassed by her outburst. She put her back to Andry and the sea, one hand white-knuckled on the rail. The deck of the ship creaked beneath his boots as he took a step, closing the distance between them. She heard him draw a breath, felt the lightest brush of a hand on her shoulder.

And then Sorasa rounded the stack of crates like a leopard prowling her den. She crossed her arms, looking them over. Corayne pursed her lips, trying to will all trace of her feelings away.

Thankfully, Sorasa Sarn felt pity for no one, Corayne included.

"Hiding?" the assassin said, ignoring Corayne's blotchy face.

"Never," she answered, pushing off the rail.

"Good." Sorasa spun on her heel, gesturing for her to follow.

Corayne did so eagerly, happy to leave Andry and all thoughts of her wretched blood behind. "Let's teach you how to use those Dragonclaws."

But Corayne did glance back, finding Andry still at the rail, his warm, soft eyes following her every step.

"I'll put on some tea," he said, going for his pack.

And so the days went, slipping by like the waves against the ship. Corayne's eye was true. The weather remained clear, though the air grew thick with moisture the closer they came to the shores of Ahmsare, the nearest kingdom. Clouds formed on the western horizon, toward the warmer waters of the Tiger Gulf, but no storms came close to the galley. Neither did any serpents or krakens, though the sailors and the Companions kept watch every night, lanterns blazing the length of the galley. It was the only time Corayne ever saw Dom, who spent most of his time with his head in a bucket, retching up whatever he'd managed to eat that day.

Sigil and Sorasa worked Corayne through her lessons in the morning, allowing her the afternoons to recover. Valtik would join them to watch, her rhymes dancing between Paramount, a language they all knew, and Jydi, which Corayne could barely comprehend. She even prayed over Corayne's new vambraces, rubbing the Dragonclaws down with her old bones. As usual, the witch made little sense, but her presence was a comfort all the same. Especially after what she'd done to the kraken at the oasis, shoving it back into a Spindle with some spell. The sailors avoided the old witch as best they could, giving her a wide berth on the deck. A few made signs of the gods in her direction, sneering at her collection of bones.

Charlie passed the time in far more interesting fashion.

Still fighting the aches and pains of the morning, Corayne found him one afternoon, tucked away at the bow of the ship. He was standing, bent over a small workspace, little more than a plank set across two barrels.

Corayne chose her steps carefully, letting the crew and the slap of waves mask the sound of her boots on the deck. It was almost too easy to sneak up on Charlie and peer over his shoulder.

His fingers moved painstakingly slow as he inked a piece of parchment. Corayne eyed the page and recognized the emblem of Rhashir—a four-tusked white elephant on bright orange. It was excruciatingly precise work, and he timed his marks between dips of the sea.

"I do not enjoy being spied on, Corayne," he drawled, making her jump.

She flushed, but he turned around with a half smile. The fugitive priest had ink on his brow and a spark in his eyes.

Corayne grinned, nodding to the parchment behind him. "Practicing?"

"Something like that," he answered, careful to keep himself between Corayne and the tabletop.

"Can't say I've ever seen a Rhashiran sigil before." She tried to step around him, but Charlie moved with her, using his broad frame to keep her back. "Teach me?"

He chortled, shaking his head. "I'm not going to tell you my secrets. You think I want to give your pirate mother free rein throughout the Long Sea?"

Corayne all but rolled her eyes. She pursed her lips, huffing. "You assume I'll see her again, and if I do, I'll tell her what you teach me." *Certainly not after she left me to rot in Lemarta.*

"Bitterness is unbecoming, Corayne," Charlie replied. "I should know," he added with a wink.

"Well, Sorasa did turn you into live bait. It's warranted."

"On the long list of things I have to fret over, Sorasa Sarn dangling me in front of my own personal bounty hunter is not one of them," he sighed, turning back around.

It was a tactic Corayne knew too well. Charlie was trying to hide the sadness welling in his eyes. Her natural curiosity flared, but her sense of propriety won out, and she let it be. She was no fool either. Charlie wore the look of heartbreak. Though Corayne had never felt it herself, she saw it in the sailors of Lemarta, and in their families left onshore. Charlie was the same, going distant in the quiet moments, his mind and his heart elsewhere.

Slowly, he slid the parchment away, leaving the work unfinished.

"Teach me how to cut a seal, then," Corayne begged, weaving her fingers together in a mocking prayer. She didn't bother batting her eyelashes, knowing full well Charlie had no interest in her—or any other woman, for that matter. "Just one."

A corner of his mouth lifted. He was a man defeated, a castle overthrown. "Just one."

She jumped with glee. "My choice?"

"You are a Spindlerotten little *imp*," he snapped, poking her with the quill. Then he reached for his pack. "Yes, your choice."

Delighted, her mind whirred with possibility. *A Tyri seal would be most useful, but Ibalet is more valuable—*

"Sail!" a voice shouted from above.

Charlie shaded his eyes, turning his face up to the mainmast, where the lookout kept watch. Corayne didn't bother, more focused on the forger's wares. It was not uncommon to spot other ships in the Long Sea. The Strait of the Ward was positively crawling with them. Her mother liked to joke they couldn't raise an oar without striking another ship. And they were in Sarian's Bay now, only a few days from the coast. Other ships would be common, heading for the port as they were.

The Ibalet sailors scuffled up and down the deck in a flurry of activity. There wasn't much cargo to secure—Isadere's galley was no trade ship—but they checked it over anyway, tightening ropes and rigging. They muttered to each other in hurried Ibalet, too fast for Corayne to catch.

But not for Sorasa Sarn.

"They don't like the look of it," she said, sidling up to Charlie's workbench. She listened to the sailors and watched the horizon with a cruel, keen eye.

Corayne barely glanced at her. She weighed a set of seal dies in her hands, both wooden cylinders with silver ends. They were heavy, so well made she suspected they'd been stolen from a treasury. One held the emblem of Tyriot, the mermaid brandishing a sword, and the other was the Ibalet dragon. Her mouth watered at the prospect of either.

But Charlie plucked the seals from her grasp, stuffing them back into his pack. "Let's put those away until we know we aren't being boarded by pirates," he said, offering a tight smile.

"Sarian's Bay isn't a hunting ground," Corayne scoffed back. She knew better than anyone aboard where the pirates of the Long Sea stalked their prey. "No pirate with sense hunts in these waters. It's just a passing trader."

At the rail, Andry pointed to the horizon. A dark smudge bobbed in the wind, almost too small to make out.

"Purple sails. Siscaria," he said, squinting into the distance. "They're a long way from home."

The waves rolled beneath the deck and Corayne's stomach rolled with them. She raised her eyes to the horizon. Her heart leapt and sank in equal measure, as if torn in two.

"Where's Dom?" she hissed, crossing to the rail.

"Sharing his lunch with the sharks," Sorasa sneered, jabbing a thumb in his direction. The Elder hulked at the bow, head over the side. "I'll get him."

He'll know. He'll see what the ship is—and isn't, Corayne thought, her lip caught in her teeth. She braced her ribs against the rail, leaning forward as if a few more inches might reveal the shape on the waves. Andry stood at her side, torn between watching the ship and watching her.

"Do you think—" he muttered, but Dom shouldered between them, his pale face whiter than usual. He swayed a little, unsteady, and Sorasa rolled her eyes behind his back.

The Elder gripped the rail, using it to straighten himself. "What are we looking at?"

Corayne only pointed, her finger finding the distant ship. "Describe it to me."

He blew out a shaky breath and fixed his stare far out to sea, his emerald gaze sharper than anyone else's.

"I see a galley," he said, and Corayne clenched a fist. "Purple sails. Two masts, a lower deck. Many more oars than we have."

Even though the ship was still too far off to see properly, the ship took form in Corayne's mind, drawn together from too many memories to count.

"How many oars?" she ground out. Her throat tightened, threatening to close.

"Forty rows," Dom answered.

"What flag are they flying?" Her eyes fluttered shut. She tried to picture the Siscarian flag, a flaming golden torch on purple. But it would not hold in her mind's eye.

The Elder shifted next to her. "I see no flag."

Her eyes snapped open and Corayne pushed off the rail.

Noise roared in her ears, a buzzing to drown out her Companions even as they shouted after her. She felt Andry match her steps, with Dom behind him, both trailing her. But she didn't turn, her boots hammering against the deck as she wove through the errant sailors, fighting her way to the forecastle at the rear of the galley. Oars slapped on either side of the ship, every splash a taunt.

The Ibalet captain saw her coming and abandoned his post, leaving his second on the raised forecastle. He met her at the bottom of the steps, dark brows furrowed.

"Put every man you have to the oars," she barked. "Let's see how fast this ship is."

He blinked back at her, perplexed. *Two days ago this man sailed for the Heir of Ibal, and now he sails for our ragged band of nobodies.* Thankfully, he bowed his head.

"We can handle pirates," he said, nodding back to his second. Orders carried down the deck, commanding every sailor to prepare for battle. Below deck, a drumbeat went up, setting a faster, more brutal pace for the oarsmen.

Corayne nearly bit her tongue. *Not this pirate*, she wanted to say.

A warm hand took her arm. Andry Trelland glanced down at her, his soft brown eyes looking over her face, noting every twitch and tightness. Corayne tried to mask her fear and frustration, and even her excitement. But there was nowhere to hide, on deck or in the waves.

"Corayne?" he said, his voice still distant, almost inaudible.

She clenched her teeth, bone grating bone.

"It's my mother."

Immediately, she wished she could call the words back and somehow make them untrue.

Instead Corayne looked back to the horizon, and the ship growing closer.

The *Tempestborn*.

"I've never seen her this way," she murmured, half to herself. But Andry listened. "On the open sea, in the wind. A wolf on the hunt instead of returning to her den."

The galley was a marvel, cutting through the water with ease. She seemed to be gaining speed, despite the many oars working beneath their own deck. The *Tempestborn* would be on them soon, and no power upon the Ward could stop her.

"She's beautiful," Corayne whispered, meaning both the ship and the woman she couldn't see, the captain upon her ferocious, hungry throne.

Sigil swaggered past, joining the flow of sailors down to the oar deck. She rolled up her sleeves, probably eager to show them all up.

"I don't know what the problem is," she called out. "Certainly your own mother can't be worse than krakens and sea serpents."

The sails above filled with wind, as if the Ward itself were pushing them onward. Corayne willed it to push harder, but deep down she knew better. She looked to the *Tempestborn* once more, now even closer. *This race was lost before it even began.*

She scowled.

"Clearly, you've never met her."

The minutes stretched, each one more painful than the last. Corayne almost wondered if the *Tempestborn* was holding back, inching along at the perfect pace, closing the distance so slowly it might drive them all mad. She stood at the bow of the Ibalet galley, beneath the Heir's blue-and-gold flag. It flapped over her, its shadow wagging back and forth, dragging Corayne between sunlight and shade. The Spindleblade dug into her back, bared to the world.

Her gaze never wavered, fixed on the galley a hundred yards off. Glorious as the ship was, she saw signs of its battle with a kraken. One of the masts was new, and there were long sections of replaced railing. The prow ram was gone entirely, probably snapped off by a curling tentacle. But Corayne still knew the hull, the ropes, the wine-dark sails. She knew exactly how many rowers sweated below deck, how large the boarding party was, and how fearsome the crew.

She could almost see them, the familiar faces crowding the *Tempestborn*, the most familiar of all at the helm.

"Hell Mel," she heard one of the Ibalet sailors cry, his voice stricken. The rest of the crew mirrored his dismay, the message carrying down the ship.

Her mother's reputation was known throughout the Long Sea to sailors of many kingdoms. The Ibalets were no exception.

When the captain joined her in the forecastle, a sword belted to his hip, she knew the time had come. There would be no outrunning the *Tempestborn*.

Corayne wanted to scream. Even after the Spindle in Nezri, the blood she'd spilled, Taristan's torn face, Erida's betrayal—no matter how far she'd come, she was no match for her own mother. *You don't have the spine for it*, Meliz had told her once. It felt like another life, and yet here it was again, catching up with every passing second. Corayne heard her voice now, the words surrounding her like the bars of a cage.

"You won't need that," Corayne said to the captain.

The captain blanched, putting a hand to his blade. "I don't intend to surrender my ship."

"She doesn't want your ship; she wants me."

Corayne pushed past him, numbness stealing over her. She took measured steps back down to the deck, her fingers shaking on the rail.

"Take up no arms and no harm will come to your crew," she

called over her shoulder, loud enough for the captain and his sailors to hear.

"Do as she says," Sorasa snarled, the Amhara assassin shouting down any opposition before the sailors could think to voice it. "Even Hell Mel would not attack her own child."

Dom fell in next to Sorasa and Corayne. He had his sword too. Despite his nausea, he was still an imposing sight. "But she will try to take her."

"Not if we have anything to say about it," Sorasa spat back, her copper eyes flashing. She tightened the belts around her body, checking her daggers. There wouldn't be any need for blades, but Corayne suspected they were a comfort all the same.

Even Valtik seemed on edge, slumped against the mast, her bare feet splayed out in front of her.

"You should get below deck," Corayne muttered, looking down at the witch. She tried not to flinch as Dom and Sorasa took up her flanks, and Sigil the rear.

Valtik leered up, smiling her manic grin. "The bones will not speak," she chuckled. One gnarled finger pointed, not to the *Tempestborn*, but across the deck at the empty north sky. "The way beyond is bleak."

"Enough, Witch," Sorasa grumbled.

"Enough, Forsaken," Valtik shot back, her lurid blue eyes like two blades. Sorasa flinched, feeling their bite, and dropped her gaze, a child scolded. Satisfied, the witch looked back to Corayne. "You are not mistaken."

"About what, *Gaeda?*" she said. Her eyes darted between

Valtik and the *Tempestborn* gliding closer and closer. The oars pulled in. Neither galley needed them anymore. Slowly, the *Tempestborn*'s shadow fell across the Ibalet ship, its sail blocking out the sun.

"You walk a different line." Still grinning, Valtik slashed her bony finger through the air. "You hold a different spine."

No spine. A cold jolt shot through Corayne. She started forward, meaning to kneel. *How could she know?*

"Valtik—"

"Prepare to be boarded!" someone shouted, his voice carrying the short distance between the two ships.

It was Kireem, the navigator of the *Tempestborn*. He stood at the galley's rail, one boot planted, a rope in hand. He looked better than he had in Adira, when Corayne saw him last, battered and bewildered by the kraken that had nearly destroyed the ship. His single good eye found Corayne among the crew, and his black brow furrowed.

The Ibalet captain stepped forward. Though clearly outnumbered, he showed no fear. "This is the royal galley of Their Serene Highness, the Heir of Ibal. You have no right nor cause to waylay us in our voyage."

"I have both right and cause, Captain."

Meliz an-Amarat's voice carried all the storms her ship was named for. She climbed up the rail alongside Kireem, using the ropes for balance. Her salt-worn coat was gone, leaving only breeches, boots, and a light shirt. Nothing marked her as the captain of the *Tempestborn*, but no man alive could have mistaken her for anything less. The sun blazed at her back and she cut a terrible silhouette, her black hair wild around her face, the edges going red. She leaned into the space between the two galleys, her teeth bared. She seemed more tiger than woman.

Corayne couldn't help but tremble under her gaze.

"Give me my daughter, and you'll never see the *Tempestborn* again," she said. It was not a question, but a command. Meliz didn't draw her sword, but her crew behind her was armed to the teeth, axes and swords and daggers loose.

No one moved.

Meliz's fingers curled around the ropes, her grip tightening in frustration. They were red with welts, her knuckles bruised and cut. There was a healing bruise on her exposed collarbone too, purple and yellow. Corayne knew the marks of a kraken's tentacles all too well.

Pursing her lips, Meliz stared at Corayne. She radiated rage.

"Corayne an-Amarat, do as I say."

Corayne's fear dissipated in the steady breeze. *You might be a pirate captain in all your glory, but you are my mother first.*

"I will not," Corayne shot back, raising her chin. She inhaled a steadying breath, gathering herself. *I have faced worse than you,* she told herself.

Meliz drew her sword with ease, never losing her balance on the rail. The blade danced a looping arc. "Get off this ship, or every person upon it dies."

For once, Corayne conquered the urge to roll her eyes.

"Not even you would stoop so low, Mother."

The ropes snapped and a dozen pirates of the *Tempestborn*

swung between the ships, landing hard on the deck. Corayne knew them all, her mother's most fearsome sailors. And Meliz was worst of all, burning brighter than any flame. She stalked across the deck, her sword raised in warning. The Ibalet sailors gave her and the others a wide berth.

Meliz sneered at them, snapping her teeth. Hell Mel reared her terrible head, threatening them all.

"For your life, I certainly would," the pirate captain snarled, rounding on her daughter.

Corayne held firm, bracing herself. Meliz stopped only at the last moment, her face but inches away. She glared, the anger rolling off her.

It took everything to keep still. But Corayne held her ground, even if she felt like a little girl again, one who made a stupid mistake and needed to face the consequences.

The Companions did not move, unyielding. They had seen far worse too.

Meliz eyed them all, her gaze flickering from one Companion to the next. She barely looked at Andry or Charlie, and Valtik was gone again. But Sorasa and Dom, they gave her pause. Corayne tried not to gloat. She knew her mother well enough to see the hesitation cross her face.

"An Elder and an Amhara?" Meliz muttered, looking between them. "You've made strange friends in my absence." Then the Spindleblade caught her eye, as Corayne had meant it to. She stared, wide-eyed, her fascination eclipsing her anger for a moment. "And this?"

"The sword of my father," Corayne said. "Cortael of Old Cor."

Meliz raised her eyebrows. She *hmm*ed low in her throat. "I suppose he's dead, then."

Dom glowered at Corayne's shoulder. "Speak of him with respect or not at all."

"I think he spoke of *you* once," Meliz said neatly with a cold smile. She looked Dom over again, reading his figure as she would a tide. "I'm afraid I can't remember the name—it was something long and ridiculous. But he said you were somewhere between brother and nursemaid." A sneer Corayne knew all too well crossed her face. "Were you his undertaker too?"

Wincing, Corayne whirled to Dom, but Sorasa Sarn was already there. She stepped between them, planting her body in Dom's path. He growled over her head, near to an animal, his eyes alight with vengeful green fire. Sorasa was hardly enough to stop him, should he wish to defend Cortael's honor, but she was enough to give him pause. He growled again and fell silent.

"I didn't realize Elders were so feral," Meliz scoffed. "Come, Corayne. It's a miracle you've survived so long with these people."

"Indeed," Corayne answered, steely. She crossed her arms and set her feet. *You will have to drag me off this ship, Mother.* "I survived skeleton shades, the Queen of Galland, sea serpents, a kraken, a Gallish legion, and a Spindle torn. Because of them. Not you."

Her mother's eyes went round with shock, then fear. She wasn't the only one. It rippled through the crew like a wave. They knew the monsters of Meer too. And some, Corayne realized, would never know anything else. She looked through them again. Familiar faces were missing. *Dead,* she realized. It felt like a kick in the gut. *Lost to the Spindle and the Long Sea.*

Meliz stumbled for the first time Corayne could remember, her mouth working to form the right words.

"You met the kraken too?" she said, the air of command dropping away. There was only fear in her now. "My dearest love—" she whispered, her voice breaking.

Corayne's muscles were stronger, her body leaner, her fingers and feet surer after weeks of training. Even so, she felt like a child when she took her mother's arm, pulling her close.

Meliz let her without question and Corayne maneuvered them both into the forecastle. The door shut behind them, closing them off in the tiny, low-ceilinged room. It felt so much like their cottage, Corayne nearly wept.

But Meliz beat her to it. Tears sprang to her eyes, and her battered hands shook as she wrapped Corayne in her arms. With a gasp, Corayne realized that her mother's knees had given out. Her own eyes stung and she did her best to hold them both up. Corayne an-Amarat refused to fall, even here, with no one but her own mother to see. She looked at the ceiling, little more than stained canvas bowing in the wind. The tears almost won, but she blinked them away, heaving a deep, bracing breath.

She counted out ten long seconds. Ten only. Within them, she was Meliz's daughter, a young girl safe in her mother's arms. Nothing could harm her here, and Corayne let herself forget. No monsters. No Spindle. No Erida and Taristan. There was nothing but her mother's warm, familiar embrace. She held on too tightly, but Meliz did the same, clutching her only child like a rock in a stormy sea. Corayne wished she could stay in those seconds forever, frozen in that single moment. *I was drowning*, she realized, sighing out another precious second. *I was drowning and she is the surface. She is air.*

But I must go down again. And I don't know if I'll ever come back up.

"Ten," she murmured, helping her mother into a chair at the captain's table.

Meliz wiped a hand over her tearstained face, her bronze cheeks ruddy with emotion.

"Well, that was shameful," she said, smoothing her hair. "I'm sorry for such a display."

"I'm not."

Corayne watched as Meliz changed before her very eyes, shifting from mother back to captain. She leaned forward in her chair, legs bent, her black hair falling over one shoulder. Her gaze took on that hard glint again. A challenge rose in her throat.

"There's more than one monster upon the Ward now, Mother," Corayne said, cutting her off. "And I'm the only one who can stop them."

The pirate scoffed, planting her elbows on her knees. "You're a brilliant girl, Corayne, but—"

"I am the blood of Old Cor whether I like it or not, and I carry a Spindleblade with me."

The buckles of the sword were second nature now, and she laid it across the table with a thunk. Meliz studied it with a skillful eye, accustomed to all kinds of treasure. The Spindleblade seemed to stare back, its purple and red jewels thrumming with Spindle magic. Corayne wondered if Meliz could feel it too.

"I am marked, Mother. I'm sure you know that by now."

"Why do you think I came after you?" Meliz snapped. "I abandoned all the riches of Rhashir to get you out of whatever mess you've made."

She reached into the sleeve of her shirt, pulling out a ratty piece of rolled parchment. She threw it to the floor. It was water-damaged and salt-stained, the ink running. But nothing could disguise Corayne's own face looking up from the wanted poster. Her bounty and her many so-called crimes were scrawled at the bottom. It looked similar to the posters in Almasad, though this one was scribbled in Larsian alongside Paramount.

"Queen Erida casts a wide net," Corayne said, tearing the poster in half. She wished she could do it to every scrawled drawing of her face all over the realm. "The mess isn't mine. But I have to clean it up."

Meliz narrowed her eyes. She had a new dusting of freckles over her bronze cheeks, born of long days at sea. "Why?"

Corayne's nails dug into her palms, nearly drawing blood. "I wish I knew," she sighed, focusing on the sharp bite in her flesh.

The pain anchored her and made it easier to recount the long days since Lemarta, since she stood on a dock and watched the *Tempestborn* sail into the horizon. She spoke of Dom and Sorasa, an Elder and an Amhara assassin united in their quest to find her. She told Meliz of the massacre in the foothills, when Taristan loosed an army and Cortael fell. Corayne was not there, but she heard the story so many times it felt like half a memory. Then there was Ascal, Andry Trelland, her father's sword. Erida's betrayal and her new husband, Corayne's uncle, who meant to rip the world apart. For himself. For the Queen. And for a hungry, hateful god—What

Waits. When Corayne spoke of Adira, and her near brush with the *Tempestborn*, Meliz dropped her gaze, staring at the floor with lifeless eyes.

Corayne could not remember the last time her mother kept silent and subdued. It was not in Meliz an-Amarat to listen, but somehow she did.

"The Heir gave us their ship, and we land on the Ahmsarian coast the day after tomorrow. From there we travel north, up the mountains to Trec, and then . . . the temple," Corayne finished, swallowing hard. She wished for something to drink but dared not move. The entire realm relied upon this moment, a pirate captain and her child in a stuffy little cabin.

Finally, Meliz stood. Her hand hovered over the Spindleblade, hesitant. She looked at the sword like it was a snake coiled to strike.

Then she raised her eyes, meeting Corayne's black stare.

"The *Tempestborn* is prepared for a long voyage," Meliz said.

Corayne's stomach dropped. This was Hell Mel speaking, not Meliz. Her tone was firm, unyielding.

The captain tightened her jaw. "There are pieces of the Ward even the Queen of Galland cannot reach."

Corayne wanted another ten seconds of her mother's love and protection. She wanted to say yes and fall back into a child's life, safe at her mother's side, sailing to the ends of the realm. Beyond the darkness spreading over the Ward, to new kingdoms and new horizons. Such a life was Corayne's to take. She needed only relent.

Instead she stepped back. Every inch was a knife. Every lost second a drop of blood.

"With all my heart, I wish that were true," Corayne whispered.

A single tear won its war and rolled down her cheek. "But nothing is beyond the reach of What Waits."

Meliz mirrored her, lunging for the cabin door. She fell flush against it, barring the way out.

"Don't make me run from you, Mama," Corayne begged, going to the canvas wall. She grabbed the Spindleblade, drawing the first inch from its sheath. "If I don't do this, all of us will die. Every single one. You. And me."

Meliz's chest rose and fell with desperate, shallow breaths. Her eyes danced over Corayne, as if she could find some loophole, some shortcut. Something snapped in Corayne's chest. *Is this what a broken heart feels like?* she wondered.

"Then I'll come with you," Meliz offered, taking Corayne in her arms again. "I can help."

Corayne stepped out of her grasp, keeping her mother at arm's length. She couldn't afford any more time lost, or any more temptation.

"The best help you can give is on the Long Sea. Not on the road ahead of us."

The coast, the mountains, the road to Trec and a prince's army— and the temple waiting. A terrifying path, Corayne knew. *No place for a pirate.*

Meliz tried to take her hands again, and again Corayne stepped away, continuing their twisted dance.

"Give me something I can do, Corayne." Her fingers curled over themselves, her cut and bruised knuckles impossible to ignore.

Corayne knew her mother was not a person to sit idly by and

watch the world crumble. *She needs something she can hold on to. Something that isn't me. She needs to feel useful.*

It was an easy answer to reach for. The truth always was.

"Erida tried to fill the Long Sea with monsters." Her chest tightened at the memory, and she remembered the scars on the *Tempestborn*. "Let's give her a taste of what that really looks like."

"What do you mean?" Meliz said, wary.

"I saw a dozen pirate ships in the Adira port," she said, trying to sound as commanding as her mother. "There are hundreds more across the realm. Smugglers and pirates and anyone else who dares to run the Straits outside crown laws. You can rally them, Mother. They'll listen to Hell Mel."

Corayne told herself not to hope, but hope burned within her anyway.

Meliz set her jaw. "And if they don't?"

"It's *something*, Mother," Corayne forced out, frustrated. Hundreds of pirates were nothing to sneer at, even for the Queen of Galland.

This time it was Meliz who took the long, endless seconds. She drew in a breath and stared over Corayne, her eyes moving so slowly they were almost still.

She's memorizing me.

Corayne stared back and did the same.

"It's something," Meliz whispered, stepping aside. Her hand went to the cabin door and wrenched it open, spilling bright sunlight across the floor.

Corayne winced, shading her eyes. And hiding the last rush of stinging tears. Meliz did too, sniffing loudly.

What a sight we are.

Corayne's feet moved too quickly, carrying her to the door too soon. She paused, half in the doorway, close enough to reach out to Meliz.

"Try the Tyri princes too," she said quickly, another idea taking shape. "They'll have run afoul of sea monsters by now. Between the Spindle creatures and the Gallish invasion of Madrence, they won't look kindly on Erida or Taristan."

Smirking, Meliz tossed her hair back. "The Tyri princes will put my head on the prow of a ship before they let me even open my mouth," she said with obvious pride.

Corayne laughed darkly. "The end of the world makes allies of us all," she sighed, stepping out onto the deck.

Meliz followed her out into the sun. The *Tempestborn* crew lazed about the deck like sleepy cats. Sleepy cats with a ludicrous amount of weaponry. The Ibalet crew and the Companions remained on guard, all but for Charlie, who had returned to his papers. Corayne supposed he had less cause to fear pirates than anyone else aboard. After all, they were criminals too.

Then he bustled into the fray, a stack of parchment in hand, and seals too. They rattled against each other, the cylinders rolling.

"Here," he said, holding out both hands.

Meliz only blinked, startled. "Corayne . . . ?"

"Charlie, this is—" Corayne's voice failed her as she eyed the papers in his hands, and the precious seals on top. *Ibal. Tyriot.* One of the seals winked golden, showing the engraved image of a lion. *Even Galland. Marks of passage.* "This is brilliant."

But Charlie ignored her, staring at Meliz instead. "These should get you through any blockades or toll fleets. Erida's navy will be on the prowl soon, if it isn't already." He held out the papers again, his round, kind face looking stern for once. "Take them."

Both captain and crew knew the weight of such things. The seals alone were greater treasure than most of their bounties. Meliz took them with a deep bow.

"Thank you," she said. "Truly."

"Might as well help where I have the opportunity. Rare as it may be," Charlie sighed, waving her off. But his cheeks turned pink with pride.

Corayne caught his gaze, her own eyes stinging again. *Thank you*, she echoed, mouthing the words over her mother's shoulder.

He could only nod.

"The Ibalet fleets will join you, once things are in motion," Corayne said, urging her mother across the deck again.

The sun glinted red in her hair, warming Meliz's bronze skin. Her eyes were the same as always, sharp as a falcon's, a rich chestnut that went gold in the right light, ringed by thick, dark lashes. Corayne had always envied her mother's eyes. *At least one thing hasn't changed*, she thought.

Meliz watched her, perplexed. "The King of Ibal has declared war on Galland?"

"Not yet, but he will," Corayne said, still walking. She stopped only when she reached Dom and Sorasa, slipping between her two stalwart guardians. Andry was there too, a comfort and a crutch. "Lasreen willing."

"When did you find religion? Oh, never mind," Meliz replied.

She could not hide her tears anymore, not in broad daylight. They gleamed for both crews to see.

Her voice softened. "Let me come with you, my love."

I asked you that once. Corayne saw the same memory in her mother's face. It poisoned them both, an echo that would never fade.

It would be easy to respond in kind. *You stay*, Meliz had said once, leaving Corayne on the dock, alone and forgotten.

But Corayne would not forget.

"How fare the winds?" she said, trembling. It was the only farewell she had the strength to give.

Meliz's smile split her face, brilliant as the sun.

"Fine," she answered, "for they bring me home."

12

THE JADE SNAKE
Sorasa

Corayne barricaded herself in the captain's little cabin after the *Tempestborn* faded into the horizon. Though hours passed, Andry stood watch outside the forecastle, a mug of cold tea in his hand, as if that were of any use to anyone.

Dom kept a watch of his own, his back braced against the mast of the galley. It was the steadiest place on the ship and therefore the best spot for his weak stomach. He hulked in his cloak and stared at his boots, leveling his gaze on something still. But for the occasional blink, he could've been a pale statue fixed to the deck.

There was little to do on board, and nowhere to go. The below decks were taken up by oarsmen and horses. Sorasa debated the merit of a nap but decided against it. Naps only left her groggy and off balance, not to mention vulnerable. The Ibalet sailors were no different from the other guards. They hated her, her Amhara tattoos as good as a brand to them. She'd already run through her daily exercises twice, her muscles loose and strong. And if she cleaned her blades again, they might wear to nothing. Charlie would only shoo her off his papers, and she could not blame him. It was Sorasa's fault he was even here, tied up in the ending of the world. And Valtik was worse than a storm or a sea serpent. Sorasa avoided her more than anyone else, lest the old witch call her Forsaken again. Sorasa didn't even have Sigil to strategize with. The bounty hunter was below in the hold, tending the horses with her own Temur rituals.

Sighing, Sorasa reluctantly took a place next to Dom. *I have been long from the citadel,* she thought. *Boredom has never seemed so difficult before.*

Dom glanced down at her, too nauseous to scowl.

She pointed her chin at Andry. "He looks like a puppy waiting at the door."

"I don't expect an assassin to know what friendship looks like," Dom muttered, tipping his head back against the mast. He drew in a long breath through his nose before blowing out through his mouth, in a steady rhythm to soothe his body.

"If you think that's friendship, Elder . . . ," Sorasa chuckled, trailing off with meaning.

"Friendship is all it must be," he said, halfway between a whisper and a growl.

Sorasa raised an eyebrow in turn.

"Are you her father now?" she said.

A flush spread quickly over his cheeks. Not from shame, Sorasa knew, but anger.

"Igniting your temper is an easy game to play, and even easier to win," she muttered, smirking.

His lip curled. "I am an immortal of Glorian Lost. I have no temper to speak of."

"Whatever you say, Elder." Sorasa shook her head at him. "We're all going to die trying to save this wretched realm. Let Corayne enjoy her time left, at least."

He bent, lowering himself to her eye level. His emerald eyes went dark and cold, his lips pressing into a thin line. His blond beard was getting longer, but not long enough to overtake the scars. They were healing, but slowly. Sorasa doubted even centuries would erase the army of Asunder from his flesh.

"Your cynicism is not helpful, Sarn," he said, every word slow and deliberate, carved in the air.

Sorasa tossed her head, her black braid falling over her shoulder. She offered a wide, false smile, a weapon as much as any of her blades. "I'm the most helpful person on this entire ship, and you know it."

"Yes, until it no longer suits you," he replied, his eyes narrowing with a hateful twitch.

In spite of herself, Sorasa dropped her smile, stung. "It hasn't suited me since Ascal."

"I don't believe that."

Dom took a step forward, closing the distance between them. Even after the desert and many days at sea, he still smelled like mountains and forest, or a cold spring rain. He looked through her, as if he could see past every wall in Sorasa Sarn, right to her heart.

She knew he could not. Those walls were built long ago. Nothing and no one could tear them down.

"You're protecting an investment," he hissed.

Her eyes flashed to his throat. *Your head*, she remembered, knowing the price he'd agreed to pay. *His death at my hands, his blood a river back to the citadel, to Lord Mercury and the Amhara Guild.*

Domacridhan of Iona was an Elder, centuries old. It was written in his body, the way he held a sword, the swiftness of his limbs, the lethal strength of his hands. Now she saw it in his eyes too. Five hundred years upon the Ward, a longer life than she could ever fathom. He was stupid in most things Sorasa considered important. Dom could not blend into a market or use poison. He knew little of kingdoms or language or currency, and nothing of human nature. But he was an immortal prince, a warrior made by centuries, and he meant so much more than she did, an orphan child of the Amhara Guild. Even though her days upon the Ward were hard-won, they mattered little to a son of Glorian. She used people as weapons and tools, and he was using her too.

"You Elders see yourselves beyond the rest of us," she said, leaning forward to put him off balance. "The bridge between mortals and gods."

He said nothing, raising his chin to look more stoic than ever. He seemed a statue again, too noble and proud to be real.

She showed her teeth, sneering. "But that isn't true. You are the bridge between mortal and beast."

"Who are you to judge, Sorasa Sarn?" he answered. Instead of growing louder, his voice only deepened, until she could almost feel its timbre in her chest. "As soon as the wind changes direction, as soon as another path appears, you'll take it."

The Amhara learned how to guard their emotions as well as they could guard their own flesh. Sorasa did not flinch, her face unmoving and empty, clear as the sky above them. But a storm broke in her chest, behind her high walls. She warred with an anger she couldn't understand, and her confusion only fed the storm.

"You are ruthless and selfish, Sorasa Sarn." He drew back, straightening up again. As usual, he towered over her, casting a long shadow. She was used to it by now. "I know little of mortals, but of you, I know enough."

"I can't believe it," she said, never dropping his gaze. Her voice was flat, hollow, another wall to hide behind. "You've finally said something intelligent."

She expected him to snarl after her, but she heard nothing but the return of his rhythmic breathing, and the lapping waves of the sea.

The northern coast was a welcome sight. Sorasa stared over the kingdom of Ahmsare, its beaches and hills half shrouded in mist. The clouds burned off with the rising sun, and light glinted off the port city of Trisad. Compared to Almasad and Ascal, it seemed a backwater, barely an afterthought for ships making the long voyage to far wealthier kingdoms. A walled fortress looked down on Trisad, perched on a hill above. It had a single bell tower, brightly painted in pale orange and vibrant blue. Sorasa knew it to be the home of Ahmsare's queen, Myrna, who had held her throne for six decades, longer than any ruler living upon the Ward. As they sailed past the port, the Ibalet galley cutting through calm waves, the sun flashed off the fortress gates. They were hammered copper.

The city soon faded behind them as they sailed on. Erida's bounty was too high. They could not risk making port in any city, Gallish or otherwise. They would not chance the Ward on a greedy city garrison, or Queen Myrna's mercy.

They anchored some miles on, and ferried everything they needed to shore, including the horses. The Heir had provided them with everything anyone could need to cross the Dahlian Gates and head north. Sorasa suspected they would not have to replenish until Izera, or Askendur if the hunting was good in the foothills.

Her horse pranced beneath her, happy to be back on solid ground. Sorasa felt the same, strangely excited at the prospect of their journey. By her reckoning, it was nearly a straight line from their landing to the Gates, the gap in the mountains. A week of riding through farm and hill country. The road ahead of them was safer than they'd seen so far. *Unless some other hellish creature decides to pop out at us*, she thought as she jumped up into the saddle.

"Is that a smile I see, Sorasa Sarn?" Sigil teased, sitting astride her own horse. She looked more herself in the saddle, her shoulders loose, her manner easy.

Sorasa raised the hood of her sand-colored cloak, her lips pursed in a mock scowl.

"Don't be foolish, Sigil. You know the Guild cut the smile right out of me." Then she nodded back. "And speak for yourself. This is the closest you've been to home in how many years?"

"Nearly a decade," Sigil answered, grinning. She fussed with her leather armor, brushing away invisible specks of dirt. "The Temurijon calls us all home eventually."

Though they had only just left the kingdom of Ibal, Sorasa felt a low current of jealousy. Sigil's country was ahead; the steppes of the Temurijon were vast, its people far flung beneath the endless sky. And while the Companions' road would not take them into the lands of the Temur emperor, they would certainly come close.

"Hopefully it doesn't call you too soon," Sorasa said, lowering her voice. "I can't do this alone."

The bounty hunter hooted out a laugh and clapped her on the back. It felt like being hit with a shovel.

"Fear not, Sarn. The iron bones of the Countless will never be broken." She put her fist to her breast in salute. "And I'm having far too much fun to leave now."

Chuckling, Sigil snapped her reins, urging her mare up the gentle rise of the beach.

Thank you, Sorasa wanted to say, but her jaw tightened, her teeth clenching tight.

The rest of the Companions followed, letting Sigil lead their strange band into the woodlands. The rainy season in Ahmsare had ended, and the woodlands were drying out, their leaves going golden. But it was warm, far more comfortable than Ibal's heat.

And far less dangerous.

As they left the beach and the Long Sea, Sorasa looked back, her tiger's eyes scanning the horizon. The Heir's galley was already sailing away, dragon flag waving in farewell. Long miles stretched between Sorasa and Ibal, its dunes and coast many days off. She saw it in her mind's eye, a flawless band of gold against sapphire. Her heart clenched and she sighed, turning away from shore. Some tension lifted from her shoulders, a heavy weight melting away. The ache for home returned, but it was easier to bear than before.

Return and I'll pick your bones clean.

Lord Mercury's threat echoed, a promise as much as a warning. Those were the last words he ever spoke to her, before she was cast out of the citadel and the Amhara Guild.

I am Forsaken, Sorasa knew, hating the word. *Ibal is not safe for me, and never will be again.* She blew out a breath and urged her mare onward, taking up the rear of their number. Every second in Ibal was a second deep in fear. But no longer.

Deep in her hood, Sorasa could not help but grin. She had defied the old snake again, and it felt like victory.

Inch by inch, mile by mile, day by day, the landscape changed. The woods grew thicker as the hills rose, and they left the farmlands of the coast behind. There were no more cities, and towns were few, little more than clusters along the Cor road. The Companions took no chances in their journey north. Sigil ranged ahead, directing them around villages and half-forgotten castles. They avoided every danger they could, from farmers and traders to old watchmen along the way.

The Mountains of the Ward loomed, their great peaks lost in the clouds. A warm wind blew from the southwest, bringing up moisture from the lush lands of Ghera and Rhashir. It was a balm after long weeks in the desert, especially to Charlie. His sunburn finally began to fade, and he dared to travel without the shadow of his hood again.

Dom took care to ride between Corayne and Andry, as if that were of any use to anyone. Sorasa doubted the clueless Elder even knew what attraction felt like, let alone how to thwart it. At least his bumbling antics were amusing enough to watch and a good way to pass the time.

Valtik always swayed in her saddle, singing her Jydi chants. Most days Sorasa wanted to knock her right off her horse, but refrained.

When they reached the Dahlian Gates, the great gap in the mountains, Sorasa urged them off the road and into the foothills. It was easier than chancing bandits or patrols along the various borders. The small kingdoms in this part of the world held a shaky truce, allied together lest the Temurijon and its emperor decide to break the peace of the last few decades.

As they crossed the Gates, the Companions stayed within a mile of the ancient Cor road, with Dom keeping watch for any traffic. There was little—traders mostly, a few pilgrim priests, and a sheep farmer driving his flock. The air thinned and the temperature dropped as they rode forward, gaining elevation through the great mountain range that cut Allward in two.

"This land is quiet," Corayne remarked, her breath clouding in the early morning chill.

"It wasn't always like this," Andry said from the horse next to her. "Old Cor ruled here in ancient times, when Ahmsare and the surrounding kingdoms were provinces beneath their empire.

It was the last land to fall before the Corblood conquerors, and the Dahlian Gates controlled the way into their northern provinces. But that was long ago."

Sorasa's lips quirked into a half smile. "You have a talent for history, Squire."

He only shrugged. "We all learned it, growing up," he said. "The old empire. What used to be. And what Galland might become again."

Despite the sunlight dappling his brown skin, Andry's eyes seemed to darken.

He set his jaw, a muscle feathering in his cheek. "Erida learned that lesson a bit too well."

To that there was no reply. Sorasa settled back in the saddle, a chill running over her. She glanced at the landscape again. Only ruins of the old empire existed here, the decrepit towers sticking out of the woods.

Sorasa wondered if Corayne felt a pull to them, the remains of her father's people. She did not want to ask, and risk another avalanche of questions from the intrepid, insufferable pirate's daughter.

In the week of traveling since they left the coast, the Companions fell into a rhythm. Camp, ride, camp, ride. Training Corayne when they stopped to rest the horses or sent Sigil ahead to scout. It rankled Sorasa. Rhythm meant comfort, and comfort bred carelessness, something none of them could afford. She did her best to remain vigilant, but even she felt her instincts dull.

The Dahlian Gates were behind them before she even knew it,

and they began their slow march down into Ledor, a land of sheep and green-gold plains. The forests clung to the foothills, and the flat land below opened up like a book, stretching in all directions. The city of Izera was a dark spot to the west, smaller than Trisad, little more than an overgrown paddock for the many thousands of sheep and cattle grazing over the landscape. Luckily, their provisions were more than enough, and the Companions had no reason to approach the city.

Sorasa whispered a grateful prayer to Lasreen, thanking her for keeping them out of the cow-shit streets of Izera.

Their road continued northeast, through the foothill wilderness. There were no Cor roads this side of the mountains, only the Wolf's Way. Halfway between path and road, it ran northeast from Izera, winding all the way into the steel jaws of Trec. Sorasa knew less of these lands. Her work with the Amhara had rarely brought her north of the mountains. Sigil took the lead, a wide smile never leaving her face.

We follow the Wolf's Way for a month at least, Sorasa knew, grinding her teeth. *Even longer if Charlie and Corayne have anything to say about it.*

But even she had to admit that both the fugitive priest and the pirate's daughter were improving. Not just in the saddle either. Corayne could finally hold a blade properly. The Spindleblade would always be too big for her, but the long dagger bought in Adira all those weeks ago suited her. Charlie did his best too, occasionally joining Corayne as a sparring partner. He was also a tremendous cook, foraging along the journey, collecting herbs and plants whenever he could.

To her own chagrin, Sorasa found herself ready for dinner now. She laid a hand on her stomach, trying to quell her hunger with will alone. It did not work.

"We'll need to hunt tonight," she said aloud, calling over the trailing line of Companions. They bent their heads against the slanting sun, now beginning its descent into the west. "There's deer and rabbit in these hills. Perhaps a boar if we're lucky."

"I've still got some rosemary," Charlie answered, patting his saddlebags. "Boar would do nicely."

In the Amhara Guild, acolytes were fed bland food, and only enough to stay strong. Exactly what their bodies needed and no more. The practice served Sorasa well for many years. *Until Charlon Armont*, she thought, her mouth watering.

She reined her horse, turning the mare out of formation.

"Sigil, make camp on that rise," she said, pointing to a flat bluff ahead. It stuck out a little higher than the foothills around it, with a copse of trees providing shelter from the wind and prying eyes. "The Elder and I will return in an hour or so."

It was earlier than usual for them to make camp, but no one protested. After many long days riding, they were grateful for rest.

With a thump, Sorasa slid to the ground. She took her bow but left her whip and sword, its sheath tied in with her saddlebags. Andry took her reins, tying her sand mare to his with quick fingers.

Dom did the same, giving his horse over to Sigil. The Elder wore his cloak, his sword, and his scowl.

As much as Sorasa hated to admit it, hunting was much quicker and more successful with the Elder at her side. He could hear and see for miles and smell nearly as far. They almost never returned empty-handed from a hunt.

She followed him dutifully through the woods, keeping pace a few yards behind, moving as quietly as she could. The Elder moved more silently than any Amhara, even Lord Mercury himself, and Sorasa cursed her own mortal feet every time they rustled a blade of grass.

They walked for some minutes over hilly terrain. A cool air crept down from the mountain heights, bringing mist with it. The sun broke gold, its rays like arrows through the tree branches. They had another hour or so of daylight, Sorasa knew, though she did not fear darkness in these hills. The Mountains of the Ward were at their back, stretching for hundreds of miles in an impenetrable wall. The Gallish armies could not follow them here. Even Queen Erida would not dare send her hunters so close to the Temurijon, and risk the emperor's peace.

She kept a tight grip on her bow, a quiver at her hip, ready to take aim whenever Dom pointed. Sometimes he did it too quickly, indicating a deer already sprinting away or a bird far out of range. Sorasa suspected it was his way of insulting her without speaking.

When he suddenly dropped to a knee, she did the same, crouching to the ground. Without a word, he raised a hand and pointed a long finger through the trees, toward a clearing.

Sorasa needed little more than that. She saw the doe, fat with the bounty of autumn, her belly round as she dipped her head to graze. She was alone, thankfully, without a fawn. Sorasa had never relished the idea of killing a mother in front of her child.

Her arrow met the bowstring quietly and she drew, taking aim. She timed her heartbeat, feeling the pulse of blood through her body, letting the rhythm steady. She blew out a long, slow breath and the arrow flew through the trees, finding home below the doe's shoulder, directly through her heart. The deer let out a wet grunt of pain and slumped over, her legs flailing once against the grass. Then she lay still, eyes glassy in the dying light.

"Venison tonight," Sorasa muttered, standing back up.

Dom said nothing and strode toward the clearing.

Silence fell over the foothills again. The hem of his cloak dragged over the undergrowth, the only noise besides the sigh of wind in the branches. His hair blended with the autumn trees, the leaves yellow and fading green. For a moment he seemed a creature of the forest, as wild as anything in the foothills. Dom held the shape of any man, broad-shouldered and tall. But he was set apart somehow, in a way Sorasa could not explain.

She slung the bow back into place. He wouldn't need help carrying the deer, and she hung back to wait at the clearing's edge.

Wind and birdsong filled the air. Sorasa leaned against the trunk of a pine and tilted her head, looking up through the needles. She filled her lungs with the clean, fresh scent. In spite of all her training, her mind wandered to dinner.

"It feels different, this side of the mountains," she said, if only to herself. "Wilder somehow."

Dom bent to the doe's body, working an arm under her neck to lift her onto his shoulders. He spared Sorasa a withering glance.

Then he froze, half kneeling, his face turned to the woods. Slowly, his eyes scanned the tree line.

Sorasa straightened. She saw nothing, heard nothing. The forest seemed peaceful.

But the birds stopped singing, the woods falling silent.

"What is it—"

A twig snapped across the way, from the undergrowth. It echoed sharply, deliberate. Dom whirled to the noise.

Another crack of wood answered, this one on the other side of the clearing. Sorasa's stomach twisted, a hand straying to her bronze dagger. She prayed to Lasreen, to every god.

For the first time in her life, Sorasa Sarn wanted to be wrong.

"You are a long way from home, Osara."

The voice turned her blood to ice.

Fallen. Forsaken. Broken. Everything that cursed word meant boiled up inside Sorasa, too many emotions rising with it. The strongest of all—fear.

In the center of the clearing, Dom made to get to his feet. Sorasa lunged, a hand outstretched, a shout in her teeth, her eyes wide with terror as she leapt into the clearing.

"Don't," she snarled, a tiger.

A tiger surrounded by hunters.

A dozen arrows waited. Their points gleamed around the tree line, glittering like the eyes of a hungry wolf pack. All aimed at Sorasa and Dom. She braced for the cold bite of familiar steel in her flesh.

Shadows took form around the clearing, bodies melting out of the woods. Sorasa named each one. She did not need to see faces to know exactly which Amhara surrounded them. Their figures were enough.

Agile, tiny Agathe, with her dancer's grace. Hulking, mountainous Kojji, bigger even than Dom. One-eyed Selka, with her twin brother, Jem, never far away. There was Ambrose. There was Margida. On and on, all children of the Guild, acolytes who had survived as she had, to become ruthless and lethal killers, the loyal hunters of Lord Mercury. Only Garion was missing. *Perhaps he is still wandering Byllskos, waiting for another contract to land in his lap.*

Sorasa raised her chin and her empty hands. The arrows moved with her. On the ground, Dom tried to stand again, and an arrow twanged, digging into the earth half an inch from his boot. The Elder froze in step, one knee still in the dirt.

A warning. The only one we'll ever get.

"I have no home," Sorasa said to the clearing.

"Is that so?" the voice answered, and her eyes found Luc.

The assassin leered out of the trees, stepping into the light. He was as she remembered, always moving, shifting to some song no one else could hear. He wore leathers like the rest, black and brown, patterned to blend into the terrain. In the citadel, Luc excelled at all his lessons, especially persuasion. He grew up beautiful, with milky skin, raven hair, and pale green eyes ringed with thick black lashes. The Guild found many uses for him once he came of age. *And now they think they can use him on me.*

"Lord Mercury is a forgiving man," he said, splaying his hands wide. Both were tattooed as hers were, the sun and moon on either palm.

"Not in my experience," she answered, counting weapons.

Sword and two daggers on Luc. Six daggers on Agathe. Margida's whip. An ax on Kojji...

Luc donned an easy, winning smile. He tossed a lock of dark hair out of his sea-foam eyes. "You'll find he can be persuaded," he said, taking a loping step toward her.

She felt the air shift, and Dom's gaze moved, spotting something over her shoulder. He caught her eyes and blinked forcefully. Once. Twice.

Two more behind me.

Her body moved as it had been taught, her muscles sliding into place. She shifted her weight to the balls of her feet, bending her knees and squaring her shoulders. All her lessons in the Guild boiled under the surface of her skin. She dared not reach for her daggers lest the clearing erupt in a tornado of blood and steel.

She kept her composure, still facing Luc. He was a dangerous man, equally skilled with blade and poison. They had blooded together, their first kills only a week apart.

"I remember when you used to cry yourself to sleep," Sorasa said, reaching for the only weapon Luc duCain wasn't trained to fend off.

Memory.

His razor smile faltered.

"The Amhara took you from a village in Madrence, somewhere on the coast." She ran her tongue over her teeth, as if savoring a delicious taste. "You used to whimper its name."

"We may have different pasts, but our future is the same," Luc answered stiffly, reciting the old Amhara teaching like a prayer. "We serve the Guild, and its lord."

The others echoed his sentiment. "We serve" sounded among them. Sorasa even felt the words on her own lips, begging to be spoken. She snatched them back.

In the center of the clearing, Dom shifted toward his sword, his movements so slow and silent, near imperceptible.

"I used to envy you, Luc," Sorasa breathed, taking a step toward him.

Luc did not move, unbothered by her closeness. He knew her measure, and she knew his.

"You envy me still," he said, shaking his head.

"You were so lucky. You remembered your family, your home. Something outside the citadel walls." Sorasa feigned a smile of her own, riling him. "I never could."

"We have only one family, you and I," Luc growled, his black eyebrows drawn together. Then, to her surprise, he put out a hand, the sun on his palm facing her. "Let us bring you home."

He's mocking me, she thought, her cheeks going red as anger flared in her chest. Her ribs itched and she snarled.

"Oh, Luc, I carry your home with me wherever I go."

She violently pulled her tunic aside, showing the long design inked into her skin. It ran the side of her body from ribs to hip, oil black tattooed on bronze skin. Most of it was beautiful, her name and her deeds, her great glories and achievements laid out in a trophy no one could ever take away. The script was Ibalet, the tongue she'd chosen, and something more ancient, the tongue of the Amhara long dead. She felt a dozen eyes run along the tattoo, tracing each letter. The assassins all had ones just like it, their own ribs marked and inked.

On the ground, Dom stared too, his emerald gaze roving over her exposed ribs and stomach. It wasn't difficult to guess at the Elder's thoughts. *Here is a lifetime of death written in my skin, impossible to ignore or forget. Here is everything he hates in me made flesh.*

The wind picked up, chilling her skin, but Sorasa refused to shiver. She wanted them to see it all. She wanted them to remember the last time they'd seen her, pinned to the floor of the citadel atrium.

Luc's eye snagged on the place where her abdomen met her hip, muscles flowing taut and coiled. The last piece of her tattoo was not beautiful, nor intricate. The final lines were half carved, made of ink and scar.

Osara. The word was a brand in her flesh and her mind. *Osara. Osara.* It burned still, naked to the world and a dozen eyes, her shame and failure laid bare. Sorasa wanted to scream.

It was Kojji who held me down, his knee between my shoulder blades. Pain flared in Sorasa's memory. *And Agathe kept her dagger to my throat, a breath away from slicing me open.*

"You all watched while this was made," she breathed, her voice going ragged.

Luc nodded, slowly pulling his eyes up her ribs, over the ink, through her history, until he reached her face. "I remember," he said. "We remember."

Sorasa Sarn did not expect an apology from any Amhara. She knew them, and herself, too well for that. They would never show regret and never speak against the Guild. Neither would she. She ached for it still, even now, when every Amhara blade in the world was set against her.

The wind stirred the trees again, shaking the branches. The Amhara stood out more sharply, unmoving against the wind, their dark forms anchored in place. Sorasa's grip loosened on her tunic, and the soft, worn fabric fell back into place. She took a steadying breath, tasting death in the air. She glanced at Dom again. His chest rose and fell as he heaved a breath of his own. His sword remained at his side, the massive blade all but begging to be drawn.

"And you remember too," Luc said, closer. "Lord Mercury can be bought."

Sorasa barked a true laugh, in spite of everything. "Name his price, then."

"Walk away now, Sarn," Luc said sharply, every word a knife. "Leave the Elder, leave the Cor girl. And be welcomed back."

She laughed again.

"I'm supposed to trust your word, Luc?" she spat. "I'd sooner kiss a jackal."

"That can be arranged," one-eyed Selka rasped from the edge of the clearing. A few yards away, Jem laughed.

Luc silenced them both with a twitch of his fingers.

"It is written in citadel stone. Your pardon," he said. "And Lord Mercury sent a token of goodwill. It will grant you safe passage."

Then he slipped a hand into his leathers, grasping for something. Sorasa braced for his dagger, the same one they all carried, black leather and bronze. *A token of goodwill*, she thought, scoffing to herself. *Lord Mercury sent you to slit my throat. No more, no less.*

Instead Luc pulled out a polished jade the same shade as his piercing eyes.

Sorasa did not move or blink, even as her body nearly collapsed, every muscle going weak. Her lips parted, her breath coming in tiny gasps. She stared at the solid jade cylinder, one end set with an unmistakable silver seal. *Mercury's own—a winged snake, its jaws wide and fangs bared.* The solid stone was the length of Luc's fist, a precious object even without the markings on its face.

But the markings made it priceless. She remembered the jade stone on Lord Mercury's desk, quietly waiting to stamp another contract and steal another life. He would never part with it, not for anyone. *Or so I thought.*

To Sorasa Sarn, the jade seal was the most valuable thing in all the realm.

Her voice shook.

"Safe passage," she murmured, her heartbeat racing. The world blurred before her eyes. "All the way home?"

In the center of the clearing, Dom's pale face went even paler, all color draining away. His lips parted, forming silent words Sorasa refused to recognize. He was miles away now, across the Ward in another life. A rushing noise filled her ears.

Luc extended his hand and the jade, pressing the cold stone into her palm. "Come back to us, Sorasa. Let the rest of the world bother with their great doings."

The seal was heavy enough to break a skull. Sorasa closed her fist around it until her knuckles went white. Its cool surface was a balm against her suddenly hot skin.

"This contract is not for you," Luc murmured, his impossible eyes boring into her own. "Do we have a deal?"

She almost couldn't hear him over the roaring in her ears.

The citadel. Home.

With a will, she tucked the seal into the pouch at her belt, among her powders and poisons. She carried so many weapons, but the seal was the greatest of all. She eyed Luc, then Dom, her gaze burning. The Elder drew himself up, puffing out his broad chest in one last show of bravado.

Her lip curled into a half smile.

"Kill the Elder slowly."

13

COME AND SEE
Erida

The council tent stank of alcohol and fish. The servants were slow in clearing their dinners, trying not to get in the way of nobles and generals arguing back and forth. Erida sat at the head of the long table, the spine and tail of a trout on her own plate. The bones swam in butter and salt. Neither had improved the taste much. After long days at siege, all the food began to taste the same, no matter what the cooks did. She did not partake in the ale like the others, nor wine, like Lady Harrsing two chairs away. Instead Erida sipped on a bracing cup of mint tea, a rich golden color to match her gown.

She wore no armor, ceremonial or otherwise. They had been two weeks at siege. But many of the nobles still wore mail and steel plate, despite never going near the city walls. They sweated now in the close air of the tent, their pale, pink faces piggish in the candlelight.

At her side, Taristan drank nothing, and his plate was long empty. Even the bones were gone, swept onto the floor for the wolfhounds to chew on. While he openly despised most of the people in the room, the dogs escaped his ire. Taristan let one hand dangle so that the dogs might nuzzle up against his fingers if they pleased. The animals did not fear him as Erida's councillors did.

Most avoided his gaze, the memory of the bridge and Prince Orleon's dismembered body fresh in their minds. They clucked about like overdressed chickens, with Taristan a fox in their midst.

"Rouleine was built to weather sieges," said Lord Thornwall, surveying the long table. Erida knew her commander did his own fair share of balancing, weighing the brainless opinions of self-important nobles against the wisdom of common soldiers. "We're intercepting everything we can on the river, but the Madrentines are good at slipping supplies into the city. And they'll never want for fresh water. But rest assured, the city will be worn down. It's only a matter of time."

Lord Radolph made a guttural noise barely cousin to a laugh. He was a small man, in stature and character, and he was no soldier. Erida doubted Radolph even knew how to hold a sword. But his lands were vast, encompassing most of the countryside outside Gidastern. His holdings afforded him a title and enough confidence to speak at Erida's high table.

"Time enough for Robart to gather all his strength," Radolph scoffed, picking a fish bone from his teeth.

"And do what? Meet us in open battle?" Thornwall answered, smirking beneath his red beard. "He could call every man and boy in his kingdom to war, and it would not be enough. Galland can outlast him, and near every kingdom upon the Ward."

All but the Temurijon, Erida knew, and so did anyone else with sense. Emperor Bhur and his Countess were the only army capable of matching the Gallish legions. *For now.*

Radolph shook his head. To Erida's dismay, more than a few other nobles mirrored his sentiments. "And what of Siscaria? Their alliance?"

The Queen raised her hand only an inch, letting her emerald ring catch the candlelight. The gemstone winked, more than enough to draw every eye in the tent, including Radolph's. He clamped his mouth shut.

"Thank you, my lord," Erida said, her manners perfect. She would not give anyone cause for offense, even if it meant bloating the egos of small, stupid men. "The alliance with Siscaria was built on a marriage that no longer exists. Orleon can hardly wed a princess when he is dead."

Around the table, a few of her more hawkish councillors smirked. A few glanced at Taristan, uneasy at the memory of Orleon's death.

Radolph grimaced and motioned for more wine. A servant jumped to attention, a flagon in hand.

"Murdered beneath a truce flag," the lord muttered as the servant poured.

Many pairs of eyes widened and Erida fought hard to keep her mask of poise. She forced a smile instead and leaned back in her seat, curling her fingers over the arms as if it were her throne. In her mind, Lord Radolph's name joined a certain list.

At her side, Taristan barely stirred, his callused fingers drumming a slow rhythm on his leg. She heard the notes in her head, a death march.

"Do you accuse my husband of something?" Erida said, her voice low and icy cold.

Radolph was quick to retreat, scurrying like a rat.

"I only mean to say that the death of Prince Orleon will create complications," he said, glancing at his fellow nobles for support. Thankfully, he found none. "King Robart, other nations—they will not look upon us kindly."

Erida raised a slim brow. "Have they ever?" she asked.

A murmur went around the table, and a few heads nodded to her point.

Lady Harrsing even rapped her new cane on the carpeted floor. "Indeed," she said.

Though her body had grown frail, her voice remained firm as ever. Erida wanted to smile at the older woman, to thank her for such stalwart support, but kept her composure.

"The realm has always been jealous of Galland. Our wealth, our strength," Erida continued. She closed a fist on the table, her knuckles going white. "We are the successors to Old Cor. We are an empire reborn. They will never love us, but they will certainly fear us."

Radolph bowed his head, surrendering. "Of course, Your Majesty."

Under the table, Taristan's fingers ceased their drumming.

"We must be mindful of the winter," another lord said, raising a finger.

Erida's smile tightened. She held back a frustrated scream. *As soon as one hole is plugged, the bucket springs another leak*, she thought, cursing in her head.

Thankfully, Harrsing leaned into the fray with her usual dismissive manner. She chortled and sipped at her wine. "Lord Marger, we're marching south. You'll be eating oranges in Partepalas by the time snow falls in Ascal."

"It was a good harvest, and the supply trains will hold for now," Thornwall added, shrugging. "The navy will take up the load when the deeper snows set in, and supply us on the coast."

That at least seemed to satisfy Marger, and Thornwall's own lieutenants, who nodded in approval. Erida cared little for the economics of war. What it took to feed and water an army, to keep it moving, of this she had little interest. But she knew better than to ignore Thornwall.

And she knew the council meeting was already running long. The food was mostly gone, but the wine and ale still flowed. They wouldn't make any more progress tonight, at least not in a direction Erida wanted to go.

She stood, extending her hands out to both sides of the long table. Her golden sleeves trailed, edged with a finely embroidered pattern of green vines and ruby-studded roses. Many chairs scraped across packed earth and carpet as everyone else jumped to stand, rising to their feet in deference to their queen. Taristan rose quietly, unfolding his long limbs.

"I plan to celebrate the new year on Robart's throne with a case of his own wine for each of you," Erida said, raising her cup in a toast. They mirrored her, holding up tankards of ale and sloshing goblets. "Let the Palace of Pearls ring out with Gallish song."

They boomed a resounding cheer, even Marger and Radolph, though Erida noted they wouldn't meet her eye. At least the rest seemed placated, eager to continue their drinking away from the Queen and her wolfish consort. *If they want to treat a siege camp like a feasting hall, let them*, Erida thought, meeting their raised glasses with her own. *They want glory, they want power—and I will give it to them.*

So long as they don't get in my way.

The promise of Madrence was enough to send the nobles chattering out into the night, clutching at each other as they schemed. Some jabbered over castles or treasure, striking bargains for a victory not yet won. Erida tried not to do the same. She had never seen the Palace of Pearls, the seat of the Madrentine kings, but she'd heard enough of its alabaster walls and high towers, every window polished like a jewel, its gates set with real pearl and moonstone. The magnificent castle watched over Vara's Bay, a gleaming beacon to sailors and the city alike. And within was an even greater prize—the throne of Madrence. Another crown for Erida of Galland. The beginning of her great empire, and her greater destiny.

Harrsing idled by the tent flap, but the Queen shook her head, gesturing for her oldest advisor to go as well. She did as commanded, moving stiffly with her cane. Erida watched her slip into the night, a member of the Lionguard going with her. *Bella is growing old before my eyes*, she thought with a sharp pang of sadness.

She fell back in her seat, leaning hard against the chair back.

The warm air made her tired, and she braced her chin against her hand, too exhausted to hold her own head up.

By now the Lionguard knew to leave their queen when only Taristan and Ronin remained. They swept out, taking up their posts at the entrance to the council tent and the adjoining passage to Erida's bedchamber. The tent suddenly seemed much larger without them, the long table all but empty, with only Ronin at the far end, and Taristan still standing. It was a rhythm they kept, the strange trio of the queen, her consort, and his pet priest.

Finally Taristan crossed to the sideboard, helping himself to a glass of wine. He drank deeply, licking his lips. Only a little remained, like blood in his cup, thick and dark.

"I'm beginning to despise these council meetings more than I ever did my petitions," Erida sighed, squeezing her eyes shut. They felt itchy and bloodshot, irritated by candle smoke and camp dust. Despite her ladies' best efforts, there seemed to be dirt and grime everywhere. "At least the petitioners could be dismissed. But these idiots and hangers-on must be coddled like children."

"Or whipped," Taristan answered, his tone flat. It wasn't a joke.

"If only things were that simple." Erida motioned for wine and Taristan obliged, filling her goblet. She nudged the tea away. "I wish I could send the lot of them back to Ascal and leave only the generals. At least they know what they're talking about."

She took the glass, their fingers brushing. His skin sent a bolt of lightning down her spine.

"And why can't you do just that?" he said, looking down at her. The black void of his eyes seemed to swallow the candlelight.

Erida blanched, forgetting his fingers.

"Send the court back to Ascal? Without me or any of my closest advisors? I might as well give Konegin my throne this very night." She swallowed a bracing gulp of red wine. It steadied her. "No, they have to stay here, and stay satisfied. I won't drive more allies into my cousin's arms. Wherever he might be."

"Lord Thornwall's scouts still haven't found anything?"

Ronin's preening hiss sounded from the end of the table. He stared out from his red robes, his white face a moon against scarlet. Not for the first time, Erida debated commanding him into a new set of clothes. The red was so garish. He looked foolish at the council table, and made her husband look foolish with him.

"No," she said hotly.

Ronin arched an eyebrow. "Or perhaps they aren't trying at all?"

Erida grew stern. After four years as queen of a vicious court, she knew manipulation well.

"I trust Lord Thornwall more than most people upon the Ward."

"Can't imagine why," Ronin grumbled, shrugging it off. "Two weeks we've been stuck here. Two weeks wasted in this mud. Get off, you," he added, waving off the last of the dogs. They yelped and bolted out of the tent.

"You are welcome to go wherever you will, Ronin." Erida wished she could banish him outright but knew better than to try. She had not forgotten Castle Lotha and the Spindle there, or the snarl within it. If anything had come forth, she did not know, but Ronin still seemed satisfied, and that unsettled her enough. "Sieges take time, as you must know."

"Yes, indeed. Sieges take time," Taristan ground out. He put his empty glass on the table, still standing. Like Erida, he wore no armor. He had no use for it, not while archers and catapults did the fighting. There was only the Spindleblade belted at his hip, settled over his red tunic and leather breeches. "For men, at least."

Erida opened her mouth to question him, but Ronin shoved back from the table, his chair falling to the ground with a thud.

"What have you seen?" he demanded, his red-rimmed eyes all but glowing across the tent.

The wizard stalked forward, his bone-white fingers trembling on the tabletop. The crimson folds of his robes fell back from his wrists, exposing too-thin arms. He looked like a spider crawling through its own web. Behind him, the candles guttered, their flames jumping yellow and red.

At the head of the table, Erida drew back against her chair, only an inch. She hated Ronin at all times, but this she feared. And for that she despised him even more.

Taristan showed a trickle of emotion.

Triumph.

"I dreamed of them," he answered.

"Who?" Erida hissed, but her consort didn't look away from the red wizard.

Instead Taristan took up his prowl, circling the other side of the table, until he stood opposite Ronin. His grin was a terrible thing. There was something predatory about it—unnatural, even. Erida hated the way it made her heart skip.

His eyes roved over the tabletop, a graveyard of half-empty plates and cups. Bones, skin, the dregs of ale and wine. The mess made Erida itch, but Taristan looked through it, as if nothing else existed in the world.

"They come tonight," he said, raising glassy eyes. Erida squinted, trying to catch the telltale red sheen, but there was nothing but the black abyss. "From the river."

Ronin could hardly disguise his glee. For a second, Erida thought he might jump up and down. Instead he rounded on her, closing the yards between them with short, scrambling steps. He grinned, showing small teeth.

"I would tell your ladies to start packing," he said, as if gloating.

The Queen of Galland did not like confusion. It made her feel weak. She tried to hide her bewilderment but couldn't help it. She glanced to Taristan, waiting for some kind of explanation.

He met her questioning stare.

"Rouleine will be broken by dawn," he said.

"Dawn?" Erida echoed. The warm air of the tent went thick on her skin, a blanket wrapped too tightly. Her throat worked, trying to swallow back the odd sensation. "What is happening tonight, Taristan? *Who* is coming?"

Taristan reached through open air, white palm up and out. His hands were long clean of Orleon, but Erida could still see the prince's blood all over them.

Again he smiled.

"Come and see."

At Castle Lotha, she had not known what she walked toward. It was foolish faith that had sent her into the ruined castle, tracking her new husband without even a single Lionguard to protect her. It was the first time they'd been alone since their wedding, an afternoon that had left Erida fuming and her sheets ruined in the least satisfactory way. She had been eager to see him again, horribly so, and eager to see exactly *what* great power he commanded, the kind that he'd promised would win her control of the entirety of Allward. She was not disappointed. The Spindleblade had cut through the air, slicing a portal between the realms, bringing Taristan one step closer to his god. And Erida one step closer to the ultimate throne.

She left the Lionguard behind again. She was growing accustomed to the absence of their sphere of protection. Taristan was her shield too, a better one. Knights could be bribed or blackmailed. But not Taristan. He would not betray her. *Could not*, she thought. *He is nothing without me, and he knows it.*

She followed Taristan and Ronin through the night, hoods drawn as they rode through the great siege camp. After two long weeks, the camp looked years old, the tents streaked in dirt and pit-fire smoke, the roads rutted or churned up by thundering horses. Mud splattered the hem of her gown and cloak, but Erida barely noticed. *What is a ruined dress against the surrender of a city?* She urged her palfrey on, the soft gray mare fighting to keep up with Taristan's charging destrier.

Taristan sat easy in the saddle, not like the lords and knights who bounced around on their poor horses. He rode with singular focus and perfect form, his long red cloak billowing out behind him like a flag. If the soldiers in their tents noticed the prince consort, they did not say so. Whispers of his exploits on the Rouleine bridge were well known by now, and none would dare stand in his way, even to gawk. As for Erida, she drew deeper into her hood, hidden in a plain wool cloak, with only the golden edges of her gown visible.

Thornwall will scold me for this, she thought. Even though these were her own soldiers, riding through them alone was a dangerous prospect. There could be any number of spies among the legions, or, worse, assassins. Like most monarchs of the Ward, Erida knew of the Amhara and their skill. But she did not fear them. They, at least, understood the language of coin.

The palisade wall at the edge of the camp rose, gray and jagged against the moonless sky. There was a gate, reinforced on one side by an old farmhouse. Erida made to slow her horse, but the wardens jumped to attention at the sight of Taristan and Ronin. *This is not the first time they've done this*, Erida mused, following them through the hastily constructed barricade.

After the council tent, Erida relished the cool night air as it whipped over her face. But as the gate closed behind them, a chill went down her spine. They were out of the siege camp now, past her walls, beyond her Lionguard. It startled Erida to see the open world yawn around her, its jaws wide. She faltered in the saddle, catching her breath.

Is this what everyone else feels like?

The river was a flowing band of iron, barely reflecting the starlight. The Rose was wider than the Alsor, the current slower. At the river's edge, Taristan reined his horse back toward the city. Torches flared along its walls, the yellow and orange lights growing with every step forward.

Erida gritted her teeth. They were beyond the camp, without a guard, and now riding *toward* a city under siege? A city that would do *anything* to fight her off?

"Taristan—" she ground out, trying to be heard over the horses. "Taristan!"

He ignored her, and she almost yanked on the reins, ready to turn back. But something pulled her along, a tug in her heart, the cord that ran between the Queen of Galland and her prince. She wanted to sever it. She wanted to pull it closer. Wanted less and more, all at the same time.

More lights flickered along the base of the walls and Erida let out a small sigh of relief. There were Gallish patrols moving along the marsh that protected half of the city. The rivers secured the rest, flowing together behind Rouleine, another obstacle for any approaching army. No matter how many men or how many catapults she brought, they could never cross the Rose or the Alsor to assault the walls from the south. Some mountains even the Queen of Galland could not climb.

Before she could ask exactly where they were going, Taristan reined his horse down the riverbank, into shallows choked with mud and reeds. Ronin followed and Erida did too, bracing herself against a splash of cold water. They waded until the flowing river kissed her boots and the horses could go no farther, lest they be swept away in the current.

"They come tonight," Taristan said again, without any further explanation.

She followed his gaze, searching the river, and then the base of the walls a few hundred yards away. From this angle, she could see where the Alsor met the Rose, foaming white before charging away south, deeper into the kingdom of Madrence. The joined rivers were a road to Partepalas, King Robart, and victory.

Erida ran up against the limits of patience, hard-won in the court of Galland.

"Exactly what are we looking for?" she whispered, though there was no one else to hear her. "Who are *they*?"

Ronin looked on, clearly enjoying her confusion.

"Is there another Spindle here?" She eyed the sword at Taristan's side, knowing its power and its danger. Her fingers worried the reins of her horse. The air felt still, silent but for the distant sound of the city and the camp. She felt no crackling charge of energy, no searing hiss of Spindle power. "Another crossing?"

Taristan did not answer. His red hair looked black in the starlight, curling slightly. He stared through the darkness, brow furrowed, jaw set, a shadow of stubble across his cheeks. His eyes ticked back and forth, searching the waterline where the river met stone, splashing up against the city walls.

It began as a wind swaying in the tall grass along the river, bowing the plants at the far bank. Erida barely noticed it, until she realized there was no wind at all. The air on her skin was still, the trees in the distance unmoving. Her lips parted as she watched, wide-eyed, trying to understand.

They looked like shadows at first, strangely sharp, their figures jagged against the dim light. Without the moon, they slipped through the grass undetected, silent, with barely a clink of armor or rasp of sword. But they carried both. And there were so many. Suddenly more than Erida could count, each figure stepping into the Rose River, wading into the water until it disappeared beneath its surface. One of them caught the starlight before it slipped below the current, a white gleam curving over its face.

No, that is not a face, Erida realized, a scream rising in her throat.

Taristan's hand closed over her mouth, rough skin hard on her parted lips. He pulled her back, nearly out of the saddle, pressing her body to his own to keep her from falling or making a sound.

Her teeth met hard flesh, and she expected the iron tang of blood. It never came; his skin was impervious to any wound she might give him. He held firm, enough to stifle her voice, but not enough to cause her any harm. She struggled anyway, an elbow digging into his chest, but it was no use. Taristan of Old Cor was as stone.

"That is the Army of Asunder," he hissed, his breath hot against her neck, his voice weaving through her mind. She felt his lips moving, the rough stubble of his cheek pressed against her own. "The first gift What Waits ever gave me."

Her heartbeat rammed in her chest, threatening to burst right out of her body, and lightning worked through her blood. She grabbed for the reins, trying to move her horse, but Taristan held firm, his grip unbreakable.

Ronin looked on, silent, his face blank.

She breathed hard against Taristan's hand, trying to calm herself, trying to think through this madness.

Trying to *see*.

Not faces, she knew, watching as more and more, dozens, hundreds of those *things* slipped into the water. Corpses, skeletons, all in varying states of decay, but somehow still *alive*. Her breathing steadied, her pulse still racing. She saw skin worn away to skull, empty eye sockets filled with shadow. Dangling flesh. Greasy, knotted hair. Missing limbs, mouths without tongues or teeth. Erida nearly retched against Taristan's palm. Their armor was battered, rusted over or bloody or both. It was the same with their weapons, a range of swords and axes and knives, all cruel, all terrible. *Creatures from the Ashlands. The Army of Asunder* echoed in her head, louder than her heartbeat. *The first gift of What Waits.*

I knew they existed, she thought, trying to make sense of the impossible scene. Dead men walking, dead men *swimming*. She followed their progress, rows of them slipping through the tall grass and into the river. Only ripples remained, small tugs through the current. The first wave reached the river walls, the ripples breaking against the stone. Slowly, they emerged—and began to *climb*.

These things killed Sir Grandel and the Norths. Her Lionguard had met these monsters first, when Taristan was just a mercenary with ancient blood and a more ancient sword. *This is what he brought from the first Spindle.*

She ceased her struggling, and Taristan lowered his hand to her neck, lest she try to scream again.

"I knew, but . . . ," she murmured. She swallowed, her throat bobbing against his palm. Her mind raced, words forming too slowly to speak.

Taristan remained, warm and solid against her back. "You did not know," he said, his voice as low as his morals. "Not truly. How could you? They cannot be known without being seen."

"Behold," Ronin whispered, pointing to the corpses. His white finger poked out from his robes. In the dim light, his hand looked skeletal, stripped of flesh, a knobbled bone.

The Ashlanders climbed like spiders, skittering over uneven stone, ascending what no mortal man could climb. Some fell back into the water with quiet splashes, their rotten hands breaking as they scrambled. But most made it up the walls, undaunted by the height. Erida wondered if they knew fear, or if they even felt anything at all. The first reached the top, and a scream followed. Some of the torches flared, kicking up, before falling over the parapet, plunging into the river with a hiss. And so it went down the ramparts. The Ashlanders crawled onward, leaving darkness and bloodcurdling screams in their wake.

Queen Erida of Galland watched, unable to move, unable to do anything but stare. She tried not to tremble, but she quivered in Taristan's grasp, shuddering with every clang of metal. *Hundreds*, she thought, trying to count the corpses again. *Thousands*.

She raised her chin, picturing herself in Rouleine, the city gates flung wide. Then Partepalas, on the throne of Madrence, two crowns encircling her brow. After a long moment, she stopped shaking, and Taristan pulled away, forcing Erida to hold herself up alone. She dared not move lest she fall from the saddle, or be sick into the shallows. Again she thought of the crown of Galland. The crown of Madrence. The glory of her forefathers, their dreams made flesh in a young, vibrant queen.

When the screams began in the city—man, woman, and child—she did not flinch. The flames came next, licking up within the walls. Smoke followed, clouding over the weak stars, until even they disappeared. The world took on a hot red light, pulsing like a beating heart, heavy as the smoke and ash falling across the rivers. In the siege camp, shouts went up, orders ringing through the legions.

"We must be ready for the surrender," Erida said in a hollow voice, feeling detached from her body. Her limbs moved without thought, and she reined her horse out of the river, urging her to a trot.

Minutes that felt like years passed, washing over her as a massacre broke through Rouleine. The sounds of slaughter echoed between her heartbeats, iron on flesh, shrieks and weeping.

She rode back to the gate, her hood thrown back to show her face. Taristan and Ronin rode at her side, keeping pace, grim as their master across the realms. The wardens balked, recognizing the Queen. The gate swung wide, allowing them to pass without stopping. Soldiers knelt but Erida ignored them, riding onward.

"I was fifteen when I took the throne. Far too young. Only a girl," Erida said.

Taristan turned in his saddle. His eyes were blood red. From the flames or his god, Erida didn't know. She didn't care either way.

"When the high priest put the crown on my head, I told myself to leave that girl behind." The siege camp woke around them, rising to find the city on fire. "There was no room for her on the throne."

The wind kicked up, blowing a curtain of snowy ash across the camp. Soldiers blundered from their tents and ran for water buckets, ready to stamp out any errant embers. Erida continued past them, the taste of smoke curling on her tongue.

"But now I know," she said. "That girl held on, clinging to my edges. Holding me back with the wishes and foolish thoughts of a child."

Taristan glowered, the darkness around them giving over to poisonous yellow and red. "Where is she now?"

Even over the sounds of the camp, the roar of flame, the cracking of wood and stone, she could hear the screams. Erida did not bother trying to ignore them. They were a cost she was willing to pay.

"Dead."

They did not enter Rouleine until first light, the rising sun filtering through clouds of ash. Smoke drifted, heavier than mist, throwing a hazy veil over the world. The fires had burned low, contained within the walls, leaving the river and autumn forest untouched. But for the smoke and the ashfall dusting the landscape, nothing looked amiss.

It wasn't true at all.

Erida stood at the edge of the bridge, resplendent in her armor and green cloak, the emerald of Galland winking on her finger. Her hair was braided around her head, set with jeweled pins to mimic a crown. Her toes curled in her boots, set beyond the range of bowmen. But no arrows fell. The Rouleine garrison were either dead or in hiding, long driven from the high walls. She looked at the ramparts, bleary-eyed from smoke and exhaustion. She had not slept all night and could almost feel the shadows ringing her eyes. Rouleine was quiet now, but the screams still rung in her head. They pealed like the bell of some distant church, inexorable and impossible to silence.

Despite her lack of sleep, her ladies did everything they could to make her look the part of a conquering queen. The others were just as regal, drawn up in their finest armor and clothing. Lady Harrsing leaned heavily on her cane, weary but eager. Lord Thornwall wore his full plate armor for the occasion, the steel of it glowing in the morning sun. He wore a green cloak over one shoulder and fidgeted in place, uneasy. Erida watched him from the corner of her eye. It was not like her commander to be so unsettled, not before the gates of victory.

Even Taristan had made an effort, his own armor freshly polished. It gleamed like new, matched only by the Spindleblade secure at his hip, and the imperial red cloak around his shoulders. He had even bathed, his dark red hair slicked back and his cheeks shaved clean. To the untrained eye, Taristan looked like the other nobles, a spectator instead of a soldier. But Erida knew better. She saw the wolf in him, the mercenary, the dark hand of a distant god. He returned her stare evenly, his expression grim, the long lines of his face set.

Ronin was the same as always, huddled in his red cloak, but today he smiled, his small white teeth reminding Erida of a rat in the cheese.

She kept her focus on the city, even as the whispers continued among the nobles. Some of them cowered behind her Lionguard, while others craned their necks for a better view.

What happened in the night? they murmured, trading theories back and forth. *Fires, assassins, traitors in the city?* Each explanation was more outlandish than the last, but never as impossible as the truth.

Erida steeled herself, raising her chin. She took a step forward, onto the bridge and into the range of archers long dead. The nobles gasped behind her, and Thornwall reached to pull her back.

"Your Majesty—" he said, reaching for her arm, but she shrugged him off gently.

"Rouleine, will you kneel?" Erida shouted up to the ramparts. The sun danced on her face, bouncing off her armor, warming her cheeks.

As expected, no one answered. Not even a rooster crowed.

"Where is the garrison?" someone muttered among the nobles, sounding afraid.

"Is it a trap?" another said, to a chorus of whispered agreement.

The marsh below the moat buzzed with flies, a sour smell rising with the sun's heat. Erida covered her nose against the odor and looked down to see a few broken bodies in the moat, half hidden by weeds. She avoided their faces, but their identities were easy to guess. Two soldiers, judging by their chain mail. A serving woman in a rough woolen dress. All three had jumped from the walls, escaping flame or blade. They'd met death anyway.

Erida set her jaw against the sickness twisting in her stomach. She extended a hand, waving her retainers forward. Taristan was first among them, striding without fear, while the rest edged out reluctantly.

Thornwall eyed the bodies beneath the bridge and pursed his lips.

"Not a trap," he said, pointing at the corpses. "Bring up the ram."

Wheels creaked and chains sang, the long battering ram

swinging on its frame as it rolled into position. The garrison had not even dropped the portcullis of the city gate, leaving the wooden doors exposed without so much as an iron grate to defend them.

The capped iron nose of the battering ram splintered the gate too easily, shattering charred wood. The doors burst inward after a single blow, the gates dangling from their hinges. Erida's heart rose in her throat as she caught her first glimpse of Rouleine.

Thornwall's ram team went first, career soldiers all, grizzled in their armor with proven swords and hard eyes. Whatever they found was to their liking, and they shouted for the Lionguard, who passed through the gate next.

Erida breathed hard through her nose and out through her mouth, counting the seconds. Waiting for her turn.

The knights took longer than Thornwall's men. A few minutes passed in odd, stilted silence, quiet but for the buzzing of corpse flies and errant whispers. Even Ronin kept his mutterings to himself, his lips pressed together into a thin white line.

When the all clear came, Erida's nerves fired under her skin, jolting in fear and anticipation. She almost motioned for Taristan to go first but forced her own steps forward. *This is my victory. I must be strong enough to see it.*

Her boots hit the bridge with a hollow thwack, one foot in front of the other, each step like the hammer of a nail. *But in what?* Erida wondered. *My coffin or my throne?*

The smell hit first. Smoke, mostly, with blood beneath, and something fouler. Erida took her first steps into Rouleine with as much resolve as she could, her head held high as she passed through the gatehouse. She was keenly aware of the murder holes above her head, bracing for a surprise attack or a splash of boiling-hot oil. But the grates in the passage were empty, the guardians long gone. The Ashlanders did their job well.

She emerged into the smoky light of the main avenue through Rouleine, where houses and shops crowded either side of the wide thoroughfare splitting the city. Doors dangled on their hinges, with shuttered windows beaten in or splintered. Bodies clung to the shadows. She spotted a woman collapsed across a doorway, her skull a ruin of bone and matted hair. Madrentine soldiers lined the road, fallen in their formations, overwhelmed by the Ashlanders as they rolled through the city in a hungry plague. Everywhere she turned, Erida saw evidence of the night's battle. It had ended as quickly as it began, the besieged city overcome by an attack no one could have ever predicted. Ash coated the ground in a thick carpet, broken by footprints and drag marks. The silence was most disturbing of all. Thousands of people had walked these streets only a few hours ago. Now they were quiet as a graveyard.

Her knights, stationed through the street, peered out from beneath their helms, both to guard the Queen and to take in the impossible sight. Erida saw the surprise in them and the wariness too.

"Where are they?" Erida muttered, feeling Taristan's warmth at her side.

He surveyed the main street, and the many roads branching off. "Waiting," he said quietly.

Erida pursed her lips, agitated by the lack of explanation.

"This way," Ronin said, and shuffled off down the street,

heading deeper into Rouleine. He showed no fear at all, even as he passed massacred bodies and smoldering ruins.

For once, Erida felt inclined to follow the red wizard. She did so with purpose, her Lionguard falling into step with her, their swords and shields at the ready. Her dread faded with every passing minute. She grew accustomed to the smell of blood. Every body they passed was the price of empire, the cost of her new throne. She let her eyes slide over each corpse, barely seeing, until the bodies were as broken doors and burned buildings. Collateral damage, and nothing more.

Behind her, the nobles were growing more upset by the second. One of them vomited, and more than a few turned back to the gate. The Queen did not care. She had no interest in their weakness.

The city garrison was small, as evidenced by the fewer and fewer soldiers she saw crumpled along the way. There were signs of the Ashlanders too. Severed limbs, rotting bone. Notched swords, half-decayed corpses in rusty armor. The Madrentines had fought back. *But not enough.*

When they reached the market square, Erida bit her lip to stifle a gasp. She kept her head up and her eyes forward, unwilling to break. Behind her, though, many nobles did. Their cries of surprise echoed through the smoky air.

The horde stood before them, terrible and staring, too many of them to count. They filled the wide market square, packed together like a school of cursed fish.

"The Army of Asunder," Ronin breathed, spreading his arms wide as he bowed, facing the many thousands of skeleton soldiers.

They were even more horrible in daylight. The corpse army

seemed plucked from a nightmare, unreal but standing right before her eyes. They spread from the square, waiting in every street and alley behind their unbroken front line. There was no commander Erida could see, no organization beyond their ranks. Nothing to control the swarm of Ashlanders beyond what she could only assume was What Waits and—

"Kneel to your queen."

Taristan's voice was low and gruff, barely a growl, but it echoed across the square and down Erida's spine.

The corpses did as commanded, lurching forward in a faltering mess of flesh and bone. Their armor and weapons clanked like a thousand chattering insects. More than a few skulls dislodged and rolled across the stone square. Erida didn't know whether to laugh or be sick.

"My queen."

Thornwall stuttered at her shoulder. He was bone white beneath his beard, his small eyes fixed on the corpses, his mouth opening and closing like a fish plucked out of the water.

"Your Majesty, what are they?" he forced out. "What is this?"

At his back, the nobles mirrored his terror. The Lionguard were not much better, trembling in their armor, their swords raised to fight. In their midst, even Lady Harrsing quivered. The usually unflappable Bella went pale as a ghost, her face drained of any color. She alone tore her eyes from the Ashlanders and found the queen, studying her face, searching for something.

Her lips moved without sound. *Erida?* she mouthed, stricken with horror.

Erida looked back at the Ashlanders, now kneeling, their heads or whatever remained of them facing the ground. But for their decaying bodies and exposed bone, they could be her legions, dutiful and loyal unto death.

And that is what they are.

Before anyone else could speak for her, Erida spun on her heel, putting her back to the Ashlanders even though every instinct in her body screamed otherwise. She needed to look unafraid and powerful, not a young girl but a woman crowned, a ruler in every quivering inch of her body.

"I am the Queen of Galland, and I will be Empress of Cor Reborn," she said, her voice steel. The words rang out through the square, echoing in the eerie silence. Even her nattering nobles fell quiet. "I live the dream of my forefathers, your kings, your own blood, who died for what we will build together. Alongside Prince Taristan, I will forge a new empire with Galland at its heart, the brightest jewel in a mightiest crown. I sit upon the throne of the world, with all of you beside me."

They stared back at her, thin-lipped, their eyes darting between Erida and the skeletons. She swallowed and wished for a sword. But she had a better weapon, something no one could even see.

"And the gods will it too," she said. Instead of raising her brow, she lowered it, and kissed her palms in holy reverence. A few of the nobles, the more religious ones, responded in kind. She noted each one. They would be the easiest to sway.

Thornwall narrowed his eyes and tipped his head. "The gods?" he asked, perplexed.

Erida raised her face and smiled. "Who else but the gods could raise an army such as this?" she said, spreading her arms wide, letting her green cloak fall back so the sun illuminated every curve of her ceremonial armor. "Look upon the blades of Syrek, the soldiers of Lasreen. This army is the work of our gods, their own will made real in this realm."

Behind her, the corpse army continued to kneel. Erida tried to see what her retainers saw, if only so she could manipulate their perspective further. Every performance she'd ever given, in the council chamber, in the throne room, in the feasting hall—every single one had been training for *this*.

She brought her hands to her heart, her royal emerald glowing. "We are the chosen ones, blessed to bring about a new age of glory." Then she extended one palm again, beckoning to them all. "Will you join me in it?"

Most hesitated to answer, but Lord Radolph frowned, his small body coiling up like a snake. "These creatures, they aren't natural, they aren't—*godly*," he spat, still eyeing the skeletons. His face took on a green, sickly pallor.

To Erida's surprise, Bella looked sick too.

The old woman puffed out a breath. "So much blood," she murmured, looking back along the streets.

But Erida was undeterred, even by Bella's misgivings.

"A small price to pay for the crowns of the Ward," she offered quickly, almost without thought. Erida was not a senseless person, nor an unintelligent queen. "Let them know what we can do, so they may kneel before we are forced to do it again."

That seemed to stir most, especially Thornwall. He dipped his chin in a shallow nod.

Even Ronin looked impressed, his pale yellow eyebrows all

but disappearing into his hairline. He inclined his head in her direction. His lips twitched, fighting his weasel grin, and Erida recognized an unfamiliar feeling: Ronin's approval.

And, beyond it, What Waits.

"The gods will make it so," Ronin said, and Erida knew exactly which god he meant.

Radolph made a noise of disgust. "Why must we still tolerate the red wizard? Be silent, you Spindlerotten imp."

"It is you who should be silent, Lord Radolph," Erida said hotly, cutting between them. Her eyes flashed, blue and dangerous. "Be silent or go. I have no use for cowards, or nonbelievers."

The older lord quailed, both shocked and afraid of her sudden temper. He even took a step back. "I am neither, Your Majesty."

"Good," she bit out.

Radolph is a dead man, she thought, and turned back to Bella and the rest.

"This is only the beginning, my friends," Erida said. "Rouleine is a message to all the Ward. The Lion of Galland bows to no one. And the gods are with us."

"The gods are with us," Taristan murmured, and Ronin quickly echoed the call. Then Thornwall, then Bella, her voice wavering. But the rest followed, joining the new cry. It filled Erida with delicious pride.

The cheering carried them all the way out of the city and back into the siege camp, where word spread among the common soldiers. *Rouleine has fallen. Madrence will follow.*

The gods are with us.

As she made her way back to her tent, Erida tried to imagine she felt them. *It*. Her own gods or What Waits. Whatever deity watched over her and had set her on this path. If it was the red presence in her husband's eyes, gleaming now, brighter in sunlight, so be it.

"The gods are with us?" Taristan whispered, his breath hot on her ear. He leaned in close, all but enveloping her with his presence.

"Am I wrong?" she whispered back. Her skin crawled, as if she could feel the skeletons scrambling all over her. She shuddered, fighting the sensation.

Taristan shrugged. "I suppose not."

Never far behind, Ronin pulled a face. "What of the next Spindle?"

"If Robart values his head, the gates of Partepalas will be open to us, and the throne too," Erida murmured, waving him off. Her tent loomed up ahead. After the morning, it looked like a sanctuary. "You'll have your archives as quickly as you can reach them."

"Very well," he said, satisfied for once.

"Your Majesty!"

Thornwall's booming call stopped Erida in her tracks. She whirled, wanting nothing more than to disappear into her bedchamber and tear off her armor. Instead she fixed her expression into something more respectful and befitting of her general. Taristan halted at her side, his usual glower still burning on his face.

Thornwall only gave him a passing glance as he approached. He moved slower in full armor, showing his age, and his bow was shallow at best.

"What of Rouleine?" he said, straightening up.

Erida wanted to shrug him off. *What do I care of Rouleine now?* Instead she lowered her eyes demurely. "What do you think, Lord Thornwall?"

The older commander settled back on his heels and turned to eye the city, its smoking shadow falling over the siege camp. He sighed, assessing the walls and gate. "We can leave a thousand men behind to clear the streets and make safe the city."

"Or?" Erida prodded.

Thornwall turned grim and hard, and she saw the soldier he had once been. Talented, intelligent. And brutal.

"We burn it to the ground, and let no other kingdom build a fortress upon our border again."

"Soon there will be no borders anymore," Erida answered, smiling. She turned back to her tent, and the ladies waiting within. "Let it burn."

14
PUT THE PAIN AWAY
Dom

"Kill the Elder slowly."

Her voice was a blade. It cut him in two.

Dom expected nothing less. He'd said as much a week ago. But he didn't expect Sarn's betrayal to come so soon. Or for it to be so final, so inescapable, even for an immortal prince of Iona.

"Sorasa," he snarled through clenched teeth, still kneeling. Her name was a prayer and a curse in his mouth.

You know what this will do! he wanted to shout. *You know what you're doing to us all.*

Everything flashed so quickly—Corayne, Andry, Iona in flames, Ridha gone, Cortael dead for nothing. The whole of Allward falling beneath Taristan and the shadow of What Waits. All for the selfish, vile desires of one wayward assassin, Sorasa Sarn. He wanted to break her with his own hands. *If she will be my ending, I will be her ending too.* He weighed the distance in his mind, measuring himself against the many assassins around the clearing. Dom was faster than any mortal, but was he faster than an Amhara's arrow? He didn't know—and he wasn't willing to risk the world to find out.

"Sorasa!" he shouted again.

She didn't answer and turned her back, stalking into the tree line. She left without even so much as a flicker of her blazing copper glare, either to Dom or anyone else. He gnashed his teeth, wishing she would look back and see his hatred, his rage, his utter revulsion. But she denied him even that small comfort. In her sandy cloak and brown leathers, with her black braid swinging below her shoulder blades, she blended into the woods with ease. Her shadow disappeared, even to his eye, leaving only the fading sound of footsteps through the undergrowth.

His focus snapped back to the Amhara assassins and the points of their arrows, still aimed and ready to run him through. Twelve steady heartbeats, eleven raised bows. His mind spun, grasping for a plan. Brute force could only take him so far here.

Eleven assassins watched in silence, unmoving. The twelfth, the one called Luc, looked satisfied with Sorasa's retreat. He took his time, a smile on his lips as he prowled around the clearing. Somewhere, a bird began to sing, mourning the sunset.

Dom still knelt, though every muscle tightened, ready to spring. He felt the grass beneath his hand, cool and lush. He inhaled deeply, filling his lungs with fresh air and the smell of earth. This was not Iona. But there were hints of it, a few wistful notes within the bird's song. He tried to think of home, to remember a place he loved and draw strength from it. It pulsed in his blood, alive in his body. He prayed to his silent gods of Glorian—Ecthaid for guidance, Baleir for courage, Melim for luck.

The lanky, green-eyed assassin stopped over him, relishing his treacherous victory.

Dom fought the urge to cut his legs off and damn the world with his rage.

"My death will doom the realm," he said, looking up at Luc.

The assassin shook his head, reaching for Dom's greatsword. "You have a very high opinion of yourself, Immortal."

Dom tried to pull away, but bowstrings creaked all over the clearing, their arrows a constant warning. Freezing, Dom realized he could do nothing while Luc drew his sword from its sheath, the steel of Iona gleaming red against the sunset. The assassin drew back to inspect the sword, turning it over in his hand. Again Dom measured himself against the arrows. In half a breath, he could put the sword through Luc's heart. But he remained still, as if chained to the ground. He nearly flinched when Luc tossed the sword away into the grass.

"I thought you Amhara were supposed to be brave," Dom bit out. "You will not even allow me my blade? I must die on my knees?"

Luc only shrugged. "We Amhara are smart. There's a difference."

Then he raised a hand, crooking long, pale fingers to signal the others. Dom read the scars on his hands. His fingertips were burned and mottled, singed by acid or poison. He remembered Sorasa's own scars, tiny cuts between her tattoos, all the marks of many years of training at her precious guild. The Amhara were not gentle with their own, and Dom knew exactly what kind of person that made. But for the circumstances, he might feel sorry for these venomous mortals, raised to know nothing but death and obedience.

Luc ordered something in Ibalet, the language too fast and flowing for Dom to follow.

The bows answered, as did the eleven surrounding heartbeats. He heard them all, the archers steady, their pulse slow and cold, unfeeling. Luc made twelve. His heart beat a bit faster.

Luc took a single step back, removing himself from the firing lines. He stared at Dom, his pale green eyes wide and unblinking.

He's never seen an immortal die before, Dom realized. He remembered Sorasa's bargain, her price for her service. His own death. *I suppose I'm paying it.* He drew another fortifying breath, and thought of home.

Their twelve hearts were the only sound.

No, not twelve.

He swallowed hard, every nerve standing on end.

Thirteen.

The bronze dagger caught the sunset, filled with flame as it spun through the air, its arc true and brutal. Without thought, Dom reached, and his fingers closed around the black leather grip of an Amhara blade. It was still warm from her body. His arm swept in a broad arc, fast enough to deflect two arrows as they sang from their bows. Four more passed through the air where his stomach had been half a second ago, the Amhara too slow to catch a Veder in motion. Another two arrows went wide, far off target. Their archers collapsed in the trees, clawing at their own opened throats. The smell of blood spilled through the forest, filling the air with its sharp iron tang.

Dom winced as the last three arrows found their target. One grazed his cheek, cutting a path along the bone. The other clipped his bicep, another stinging flesh wound. The third took his shoulder, the arrowhead embedded in the hard muscle. He wrenched it free without a thought, snapping the arrow like a twig. He growled low in his throat. The centuries welled up inside him, every year of his long and bitter life boiling over.

Luc's sword met the dagger, metal on metal, a shrieking sound as Dom rose to his feet. He towered over the smirking assassin, his cloak thrown back in a mighty flag of defiance. Dom was a thunderstorm, gathering dark and high, ready to break across the land without thought or mercy. He was a beast unchained.

Luc's smirk disappeared.

Out of the corner of his eye, Dom tracked the thirteenth heartbeat, a familiar sound after so many days at her side. He knew her gait, knew her breath, knew the small grunt of exertion as she hurtled through the trees, tackling one of the assassins to the ground. Two more lay dead behind her, their blood on Sorasa Sarn's dagger. She grappled with one of the Amhara women, a short-haired blonde armed to the teeth with knives of all sizes. They matched each other blow for blow, trained in the same movements and defenses. They moved together like dancers. It was a magnificent sight, but there was no time to watch. The other Amhara lunged out of the trees, their teeth and weapons bared. They fell upon them both, the immortal and the exile.

Dom bore down on Luc, using his considerable strength to

hold back his sword. He kicked hard and broke the assassin's ribs. Luc staggered back, clutching his torso, wheezing. Another arrow twanged, this time catching Dom in the meat of his thigh. The pain was fuel, feeding his anger and his resolve. He ripped the arrow out and stabbed it through Luc's eye. The Amhara's anguish echoed through the forest in a bloodcurdling scream.

Before Dom could put Luc out of his misery, he ducked, dodging the swing of a massive ax. The immortal whirled to find the biggest assassin in the circle towering over him.

The assassin swung again, this time with Dom's own sword clutched in his off hand. He was of the Temurijon, alike to Sigil in appearance, and somehow twice her size. Dom caught him around the middle and wrestled him to the ground. The greatsword fell from the assassin's hand, but the ax remained, pinned flat between them. The immortal wasn't used to being the smaller one in a fight and found himself thrown back, landing hard on his wounded shoulder. Dom hissed through another sting of agony and straightened just in time to catch the shaft of the assassin's ax, stopping it short before he could cut him in half. The assassin only grimaced and brought up one giant boot, stomping down on Dom's chest.

Dom gasped, arms locked to hold the ax at bay. He used his own legs, sweeping them around to knock the Amhara down again. This time Dom got to the greatsword first and swung, severing the Temur assassin's hands. They fell with the ax, fingers still curled around the grip.

Something cracked through the air. Dom sputtered as a whip curled around his throat, cutting off his breath. He turned, sword in one hand, but another whip lashed around his free hand. Dom snarled at the assaulting Amhara, a smaller woman with a tattooed face and close-cropped red hair. He worked his arm, spooling the whip, using it to drag her forward. She dug in her heels, her boots skidding in the dirt. She shouted something in Ibalet, an appeal for help or a battle cry.

The shape of a bow flashed at the edge of his vision, the familiar curved arc turning to take aim. Dom braced for another arrow, wincing. The bowstring twanged but he felt nothing. The arrow had a different target, skewering the Amhara with the whips, punching through her neck. She gurgled and slumped sideways, her piercing gray eyes fixed skyward. Dom shoved free as Sarn put another arrow to the string, taking aim across the clearing. She fired off the shot before ducking beneath the vicious arc of another sword.

Without thought or hesitation, Dom lunged to her, his blade in hand to defend her back. She did the same, moving in rhythm with him, leaning when he leaned, ducking when he sliced. They muttered back and forth, her voice steady and measured, even as they fought for their lives.

Arrow, sword, wait, go, watch his feet, hold your breath.

Poisons and powders clouded the air, stinging Dom's eyes, but he fought on.

Sorasa knew each and every trick in the Amhara arsenal. These were people she knew better than family, Dom realized, watching as she picked on their weaknesses. Old injuries, old rivalries. She used everything to her advantage, bringing down one Amhara after the other, until the clearing grew quiet again, silent but for the last rasps of metal and their own harried breath.

"Wait."

The final Amhara collapsed on shaking legs, one hand raised to protect her face. She lay in a pool of her own blood, a fan of knives around her like a halo. Her other shoulder hung from its socket, dislocated, but her injuries were not severe. She would not die here, not without help.

Dom settled back, his greatsword still in hand. But he could not cut her down, not like this. She was no more threat now than a rabbit in its hole.

Sarn shoved away a corpse, letting another assassin drop with her dagger still buried in his chest. Blood smeared over her face and hands, her cloak a ruin, torn away. With a start, Dom realized her braid was gone too, severed at the nape of her neck. He blinked, spotting the thick black braid lying in the dirt, coiled like forgotten rope.

"Who paid the contract?" Sarn snarled, closing the distance to the last living Amhara. "Who bought the death of Corayne an-Amarat?"

The assassin drew a shaking breath. "You already know," she forced out, gasping.

Dom glanced at Sarn. She looked back with barely a flicker of her eyes, but he saw the answer in her, as he knew it in himself.

Taristan and Erida sent the Amhara after us.

On the ground, the assassin clutched at her broken shoulder. "Sorasa—"

"Is that mercy you beg for, Agathe?" Sarn hissed. Her eyes were wild, almost manic. When she spoke, Dom saw blood in her teeth.

He hung back, panting. The last rays of the sun filtered through the trees as the clearing gave over to shadow.

"Wait," Agathe said again, weaker now. Her eyes wavered between them. He saw fear in her, fear and desperation.

"Immortal," she choked out, holding his gaze. "Surely this is not your way?"

Sarn answered for him, her face pulled in disgust. "No, Agathe," she said, putting a hand into her tunic. She pulled out the jade seal, heavy in her grasp. "It is ours."

"Sorasa—"

The heavy jade shattered bone and flesh, until the green stone turned scarlet, and Sorasa's own screams echoed through the silent woodlands. Dom had to pull her off the body, but she crawled away, leaving the bloody jade seal in the dirt.

She went to every corpse in the clearing, moving on hands and knees. Her violent screams faded into fervent prayers, indistinguishable to Dom's ears. It did not matter if Sorasa killed them or Dom. She treated them all with equal care, speaking over them with whispered blessings, closing their eyes or touching their brows. She took trinkets from all of them. A scrap of their cloak, a finger knife, a ring. She even pressed her forehead to Luc's own, resting their bones together for a long, quiet moment. What she said to him was for Sarn and Sarn alone.

Dom wanted to leave but found himself unable to abandon Sorasa in her grief. Even so, they could not stay. Night came on too quickly in the foothills, the shadows spreading to full darkness.

"Sorasa," Dom murmured. He almost stumbled over her name. He said it so rarely, and usually in anger. This time his voice was gentle, coaxing, worn with regret.

She ignored him.

Three times he tried to reason with her. Then gently, slowly, he took her by the shoulders and peeled her up off the ground. The last time he touched her in such a way, she threatened to cut his hands off.

She bucked in Dom's arms like a fish caught on the line, her entire body fighting against him. He held her firmly, knowing her strength, her back braced against his chest. He let her rage through the black night. Every emotion she kept buried rushed to the surface, pouring out of her. The dam inside her heart burst, spilling rage and misery. She cursed in Ibalet and a dozen other languages he couldn't place, but the meaning was clear. She mourned for the dead around them, for the only family she had ever known, for her single chance to return to their midst.

For the last pieces of herself, lost to the Ward and the good of the realm.

Her voice failed before her sorrow did and her lips moved in silence, running through prayer and curse alike.

Dom wanted to give her time to grieve, and privacy to do it. But they did not have the luxury of such things.

He braced her head in his hands, his thumbs brushing along her cheekbones. She felt so fragile between his fingers, her bones like eggshell. She tried not to look at him, her eyes darting in either direction.

"Sorasa," he breathed, his voice low and trembling. "Sorasa."

Her silent prayers continued, but she met his gaze slowly, reluctantly. Sorrow raged in her eyes, churning within those copper flames. It was like looking in a mirror, and for a moment Dom could not breathe. He saw himself, mourning for Cortael, the brother and son murdered at his feet. He saw his own anguish, too deep to dig out, impossible to overcome. Failure, loss, rage, and grief. He saw it in her, as he felt it in his own bones.

"Put the pain away," Dom said, and her breath caught, the harried rise and fall of her chest stopping. She said the same words to him in the desert, her oldest lesson in the Guild. "Put the memory away. You don't need it."

She shifted in his grasp and squeezed her eyes shut. Her prayers ceased, her lips pursing together. Her breath returned, ragged and rasping. She turned her head weakly, trying to free herself.

Dom held firm, pale fingers bright against her bronze skin. Blood dried on her cheeks, sticking to his hands.

"We need to run, Sorasa."

The others are in danger.

Sorasa's eyes flew open and her head moved against his hands, forcing a nod. Her fingers closed over his wrists, her grip strong as she pushed him away.

They left the deer behind. There would be no venison tonight.

They sprinted back as fast as they could. Dom would not let himself fear the worst. *More Amhara, more assassins.* He leapt through the undergrowth, hurdling tree roots and dodging branches as they worked their way back to the hill. *No, they came for us first, to pick off the rest after we were dead.* Sorasa kept pace behind him, her arms pumping in time with her legs. Branches and undergrowth lashed against her, but she didn't stop, even when they scraped at her face. The pain meant nothing now.

Her tears were spent by the time they reached the others.

The light of the campfire filtered through the trees, and the woods echoed with their voices. Laughter and gibes passed back and forth, as if the entire world did not hang in the balance and this were all some merry game. Dom slowed and let out a sigh of relief, the tension working out of his body. *Safe*, he knew, eyeing their shadows against the fire.

He only hoped Andry had the tea ready. Sorasa Sarn would sorely need it.

We look atrocious, Dom thought then. Bruises blooming all over his skin and his bloody knuckles, battered by the fight. His tunic and flesh were peppered with arrow holes. Blood smeared across Sorasa's face like war paint, making her eyes stand out more than usual. Tear tracks worked through the gore on her face, drawing ragged lines down her cheeks. And her hair hung in a jagged line, sliced just above her shoulder. It stuck to her face and neck, clinging to blood and sweat.

Dom slowed his pace, if only to buy Sorasa a few more moments before rejoining their circle. She only sped up, ignoring her appearance. Instead she squared her shoulders and straightened. The others would not see Sorasa as he had, broken in two, her insides hollowed out. She'd shuttered the pain away once more, locking it behind clenched teeth.

"Clean your face at least," he murmured. "The worse you look, the more they'll ask."

She answered with a glare over her shoulder, thrown like a dagger.

Wincing, he followed her into the camp, the gentle bluff looking northwest across the plains. Night rolled on across the landscape, the distant western horizon only a band of dark red light.

Andry and Charlie stood over the teakettle, adding leaves to the boiling water, while Corayne looked on, chattering about nothing. Sigil sat on a stone, sharpening her ax, her leather armor shucked off for the evening. Valtik was a silhouette at the edge of the bluff, her face to the wind. Her braids trailed like ribbons. After the clearing and the twelve Amhara corpses, the peaceful camp was almost jarring.

"Dom and Sorasa coming back empty-handed? I'm shocked—" Charlie began, but his playful smirk died on his lips. His warm brown eyes went wide, running over Dom and then Sorasa.

Even Corayne was silent, her jaw dropping open. She glanced between them, trying to piece together some idea of what had happened. Between the blood, the bruises, and their blades, all stained red, it was not a difficult puzzle to solve.

Sigil jumped up from her seat, the ax swinging in her hand. "What happened?" she demanded, her eyes on Sorasa. "Bandits? A Treckish war band? They shouldn't be this far south."

"Spindle monsters?" Corayne prodded, her voice catching with fear.

Andry moved to them and gestured for their weapons, which Sorasa gladly handed over without a word. "Let me clean these for you," he said softly. "Sit down, rest."

Even without a knight, Andry Trelland was still a squire, and still more observant than all the rest of them. He took her daggers and sword, gathering them with care to lay out for washing. Stone-faced, Dom drew his own greatsword and put it down with the rest. The steel mirrored the red horizon, bloody through and through.

Sorasa ignored Sigil and fished her waterskin out, strolling toward the bluff. She dumped it over her head as she walked, letting the water roll over her ragged hair and bloody face.

Sigil made to follow, her face drawn with concern. But Dom caught her by the bicep.

"Leave her," he said.

"What happened?" Sigil asked again, her teeth bared.

Dom saw the same question in all their eyes, even patient, quiet Andry's. He hesitated, wondering the best course of action. One thing was clear: it would be his responsibility to explain. Sorasa certainly could not and would not. *Bandits. War bands. Spindle monsters.* There were so many easy lies to reach for, but none to explain Sorasa's behavior, or her empty eyes. *The truth is best*, he decided. *Part of it, anyway.*

"Assassins," Dom said, wringing all emotion from his voice. He threw off his dirty cloak, wishing there were a stream nearby. "Taristan and Erida have paid the Amhara Guild to kill Corayne. They were unsuccessful."

Corayne's gold face paled, the firelight dancing on her cheeks.

"Well, of course they have," she muttered, shaking her head. "I suppose it's only fair half the realm wants to kill me."

Sigil was more subdued. Judging by her tight face, she knew better than to celebrate this victory. "How many did you kill?"

"Twelve," Dom answered. Their faces were already fading in his mind.

At the fire, Charlie stood stock-still, staring into the flames.

His round body cast a long shadow behind him, thick as a wall.

"Was Garion there?" he ground out, still looking into the fire.

Garion? Dom tried to place the name, racking his memory. He sifted through what he knew of the fallen priest, until he remembered Charlie's paramour—an Amhara like the ones dead behind them.

"I don't know," he replied. It sounded like an apology.

Charlie's lips moved without sound, forming a prayer.

When Sorasa finally returned to the circle, her face was clean and her short hair slicked back. She carried her tunic and cloak over her arm, grimy and bloodstained. Her undershirt wasn't as dirty, but still pitiful, torn at the neck to show more of her oily black tattoos. Dom glimpsed a new one; a winged snake to match the emblem on the jade seal. He grimaced, remembering the markings down her ribs. All her deeds and all her mistakes inked into her skin, forever.

Sigil didn't say anything, though he could tell she sorely wanted to. She took a seat as close to Sorasa as she dared, her fingers twitching. Even Corayne managed to wrestle her natural curiosity into submission.

Charlie could not.

He stood over Sorasa, his hands balled into fists. His body shook with fear.

But his voice was even and steady. "Was he there?"

When she didn't answer, he crouched, level with her eyes.

"Sorasa, was he there?"

Dom held his breath but could not hope. He did not know who remained back at the clearing, which bodies lay to feed the crows.

Sorasa's jaw tightened, her mouth resolutely shut. But she met Charlie's gaze, and found it in her heart to shake her head.

With a long sigh, Charlie fell back from her, his body trembling.

Sorasa shivered too and pulled her dirty cloak back around her shoulders. Slowly, she raised her hood, her face all but hidden. Only her tiger eyes remained, a little bit duller than the days before.

Dom kept watch that night, unable to sleep. She never shut her eyes either.

When the next morning dawned, she did not speak. Nor the morning after, despite all Sigil's and Corayne's coaxing. It set Dom on edge, the loss of her voice and cutting remarks.

A Veder could spend a decade in silence and lose little in the scheme of their time. But she was a mortal, and her days meant more than his own. They ticked by like sand through loose fingers, each one lost to the quiet. He found himself stricken, far more concerned for the mourning assassin then he would ever admit.

We need Sorasa Sarn whole, in mind and body, if we are to save the realm.

It was an easy thing to tell himself, to explain his growing concern for an immoral, selfish, and all-together infuriating assassin. She was a killer. A murderer.

And a hero too.

15

AN HONEST FACE
Andry

Every night Sorasa stared into the fire, rolling a jade seal between her hands. What it meant or who it stood for, Andry did not know, and even Corayne knew better than to ask. But she stared at the seal as if she could memorize it. Charlie actually did, practicing the shape on scraps of parchment when he was sure Sorasa wasn't looking.

They traveled north along the Wolf's Way, through Ledor and then Dahland and Uscora. Small kingdoms all, shadowed by the great mountains to the south, and the Temurijon to the north. The assassin continued their journey in pressing silence, the days sliding past. It came too easily to her, unsettling them all.

But worse than Sorasa's mood was the cloud overhead, the constant fear of Amhara. Andry watched every shadow, peered around every bend, his head snapping back and forth every time the wind rattled the branches. He wasn't the only one. Sorasa and

Dom kept sentinel watch, as did Sigil, all three of the great warriors worn raw by vigilance. While Sorasa stopped talking, Dom stopped sleeping. It turned both of them into ghosts.

Andry did his best to make things easy for them all. He was quick with his tea and his help, minding the horses with Sigil or foraging with Charlie. Corayne did what she could too, learning to clean horse tack and tending to their blades.

The realm was colder this far north, a vicious wind blowing all day and night. Cold from the mountains, cold from the steppes. The ground went hard with frost, the grass sharp and glinting in the morning light. The woodlands turned sparse, offering little cover, thin game, and poor, wet firewood that threw off more smoke than heat. Andry shivered against the chill. Winter loomed on the horizon, the mountain peaks growing whiter every day, the snows gaining more ground each night. Andry knew winter in Galland, but this land was harsher, more severe and barren. Golden hills went gray and empty, fallen leaves dying underfoot.

Sigil turned restless in the shadow of her homeland, her eyes drawn northwest, to the steppes. She didn't mind the cold, snug in her leathers, but Corayne, Charlie, and Andry were of warmer countries. They rode close, using each other for warmth.

It was Andry's only respite against the dropping temperatures.

Meanwhile Valtik delighted in the weather. The Jydi witch knew the frozen north better than any. It suited her, her pale cheeks going pink and her blue eyes gleaming in the cold sunlight. She sang every morning, when the frost glittered, a diamond coating beneath their horses' hooves. It was all in Jydi, unintelligible to any but Corayne, and even she could only translate small, bizarre pieces.

But one morning, near the Treckish border, Valtik's song rang out and Andry discovered he understood. He jolted in the saddle, wondering if the Jydi tongue had finally sunk in. But no, she was singing in Paramount that day, a language they all knew.

"The snow falls and the cold comes, with raider ships and battle drums."

Her voice was as thin and brittle as the frozen grass. As one, the Companions turned to the witch, watching as she rode along.

Even Sorasa looked out from beneath her hood. At least her scowl had returned, if not her voice.

"Brave and bold the raiders be, to sail across the Watchful Sea," Valtik sang on. Her sand mare plodded beneath her, unsure on the rocky ground. Or unsure of the rider on her back. "Broken swords and battered shields, from icy fjords to Gallish fields."

Corayne urged her mare up alongside Valtik, better to listen. She mouthed the words after the old woman spoke them, memorizing her song. Andry followed close behind, trying to puzzle out this latest impossible riddle.

Grinning, Valtik leaned between their horses, reaching out to tap Corayne on the nose. Her braids swung. The Ibalet jasmine was long gone from her hair, replaced by bright purple iris, the last flowers of the season.

"A fearsome thing, the world undone, but raider folk do not run," she finished. The shuddering wind continued to blow. It smelled of pine and snow and iron, of hard things.

"If only the witch took a vow of silence instead of you, Sorasa," Sigil muttered under her breath. By now they all knew to expect no reply, and the assassin carried on in silence.

"Raider folk do not run," Corayne echoed, worrying her lip.

"We're on the road to Trec, not raider country." Andry licked his dry lips and immediately regretted it when the cold hit them again. "Does she want us to abandon Prince Oscovko and look for allies elsewhere?"

Charlie scoffed. "Much as I dislike taking orders from dogmatic worshippers like Isadere, I wouldn't put much stock in the witch's song," he said. "It won't mean anything until she wants it to. Don't waste your energy on witch chants and Jydi foolishness."

Corayne eyed him sharply. "That Jydi foolishness pushed a kraken back into another realm," she said, and Charlie threw up a hand.

"We should keep on as planned," Sigil said, her strong voice booming from the head of the line. "The Treckish are good fighters, good enemies. They'll be even better allies if we can sway Prince Oscovko to our cause."

Andry nodded with her. "Even if he is a marauding drunk," he said through gritted teeth.

Corayne only shrugged. "He can drink whatever he likes, so long as he helps us fight."

Sigil's laugh shuddered in the cold air. "In that, we have a good chance. Oscovko's a warmonger. Spends more time with his mercenary war bands than on his throne."

"One of the many reasons Erida turned him down," Andry added. "He courted her for years, sending letters and all these awful gifts. He sent *wolves* once—real wolves. They terrorized the palace for weeks." He laughed at the memory, shaking his head. "It didn't go very well when they met, before—" He stumbled, the words going sour in his mouth. His manner dulled. "Before everything."

Corayne leaned toward him, looking up into his face. She raised her brows, as if to coax the smile back to his face. "I didn't know squires were so well trained in gossip," she teased, poking him in the chest.

His cheeks went hot. "It's impossible to escape, really." He cleared his throat. "Most people at court had little else to do besides bicker and scheme. The knights most of all. Sir Grandel used to . . ."

Andry's voice trailed away. His memories seemed to curl at the edges, rusting over, corrupted. Beneath them all lay Erida's betrayal, and his own pain.

Corayne's hand was warm on his forearm, fingers grasping over his sleeve.

"It's all right," she said, low and steady. "Tell me more."

Andry swallowed around the lump in his throat. "Sir Grandel used to complain about Erida's council meetings. Said they were just endless arguments about her betrothal." In his mind, he saw Sir Grandel in his golden armor, his face red from exertion, the gray in his hair turning silver in the candlelight. "He used to complain about almost everything."

And still he told me to run, told me to save myself. On the temple field, Sir Grandel had fallen fighting with his fellow knights. Dying for the Ward. Dying a hero. Andry could still hear his final words. *With me.*

"I wish I could have met him," Corayne murmured. The cold

wind stirred in her hair, and she drew her collar up, hugging herself for warmth.

Andry knew she mourned a ghost of her own, a face she tried to see in memories. *It isn't fair,* Andry thought. *I knew her father and she never did. None of this will ever be fair.*

Corayne offered up a weary smile.

Despite the cold, a burst of warmth flared in Andry's chest. Corayne was familiar as his own face now, after months on the road together. But her smile still ran him through, piercing as a blade. It was almost exhausting, to be so overcome by every flash of teeth.

"Oscovko will help us," Andry said, if only to convince himself. "He has to. His war bands don't turn from a fight."

"The war bands used to try the Temurijon too," Sigil called out, turning in the saddle. Her booming voice broke the quiet around them. "But even they will not dare break the Emperor's peace. The border has been quiet for twenty years."

Today she wore all her leather armor, and her ax on her back instead of tied with her saddlebags. She looked ready for a fight too.

"What about you, Trelland?" she asked, angling toward him. "Trec has had its fair share of troubles with Galland as well."

"I don't know if I'm Gallish anymore," Andry murmured, feeling the sting of it in his heart.

He wondered at their path since the capital—through criminal havens and perilous seas, across endless desert, and now hundreds of miles along the mountains. From his queen's most dutiful squire to one of her most fervent enemies.

"Erida betrayed the realm," Corayne said in a low voice. She nudged his shoulder, leaning into the space between their horses. "And she betrayed you. Not the other way around."

Andry tried to take her words to heart, to let them fill him with some resolve. He gritted his teeth and nodded back at her, forcing a smile he could not feel, even for Corayne's sake.

As a squire in the queen's palace, Andry had spent much of his time in the training yard, learning to swordfight, ride a horse, or brawl with his own two hands. But the squires were not ignorant of the world, or the court. Their lessons in the classroom were just as important as their training, with most knights relying on their wits as much as their swords. As such, Andry had learned his histories, the politics of the Ward, and good etiquette alongside how to clean armor and tend horses. Most of the squires cared little for their education, their eyes drawn to the windows, dreaming of the barracks or the alehouse. Not Andry Trelland. He bent to his work diligently, studying his books as much as his swordplay.

It was why he felt a shiver when they passed into the kingdom of Trec.

He looked down at his tunic, the blue star poking out between the folds of his cloak. With a twitch, he pulled on the fabric, hiding the emblem of his father and a Gallish knight.

Little served to mark the border with Uscora. There was only a stone at the side of the Wolf's Way, a pair of crossed swords carved into its face. They chanced the road now, with Dom guarding the rear and Sorasa riding on ahead, scouting the villages and farmland dotting the undulating landscape.

"I smell smoke," Corayne said, turning her face into the cold wind. She scanned the horizon, her black eyes eating up the hills.

The Gates of Trec loomed to the south, the wide gap in the mountains barely visible through the mist. Snowy peaks thrust into the sky like the spires of a cathedral. It reminded Andry of Ascal, the New Palace, and the home left far behind.

Andry took a breath. The air did smell of campfires and cooking meat, charred wood and ash. But there was nothing in either direction, only gray-golden fields and rocks, the outcroppings like giant fingers forced out of the dirt. Snow pooled in the shadows of the rocks, clinging to the shade.

"There must be a war camp somewhere nearby," he answered, looking sidelong at Corayne. She raised an eyebrow. "They rove the borders, fighting Jydi raiders, mostly."

"Mostly?"

"Sometimes the war bands get restless and a glory-mad captain or lord rides into Galland, spoiling for a fight." Andry sighed. Many knights went north to the Treckish border, dragging their squires with them. "War is sport to them."

Hoofbeats sounded around the bend and up the rise. Before Andry had time to worry, though, Sorasa's silhouette appeared, perched in the saddle of her sand mare. Her hair hung freely around her neck now, the ends still jagged from an Amhara blade.

"Trouble up ahead?" Sigil called, standing straight up in her stirrups. She made a towering sight. "My ax is ready."

From beneath her hood, Sorasa pressed her lips into a thin line. She shook her head back and forth, then held up one hand, displaying three fingers.

Sigil nodded. "Three miles to Vodin," she muttered to the rest of them.

Andry had never been so far north, but he had some idea of what to expect. Treckish ambassadors came to court often, dressed in knee-length coats trimmed in fur, with hats to match. They wore long curved sabers, belted at the waist, naked without sheaths, even to banquets and parties. Andry remembered them, sweating in their thick clothes, unaccustomed to the warmth and sheer size of the Gallish court. Erida liked to put them on display, her version of a joke. They stuck out like sore thumbs, and no one did anything to make them feel a little more welcome. Squires like Lemon would join in, picking on the Treckish page boys and servants who came south. Andry had never had a taste for it.

He was the sore thumb now, shivering beneath his cloak as they rode the Wolf's Way toward the Treckish capital. Again he adjusted his cloak, trying to hide any sign of Galland on his person. *The Treckish wolf holds no love for the Gallish lion*, Andry knew.

They passed two long lines of pike walls ringing the city, spaced out to stop a cavalry charge. The empty landscape was no more, the rolling fields and rocky hills now clustered with farms and villages, each one bigger than the last. Peasants, farmers, and merchants joined them on the road, forming a steady line of traffic toward the fortress city, which was only a mile away now. All of them were armed, Andry noticed, if only with a long knife. Most were on foot, with a few donkeys, horses, and carts rolling beside them. The travelers ambled in small groups, forcing the Companions to ride closer together, with Dom and Sorasa taking rear and lead.

Vodin sprouted over two high hills, each one ringed with a wooden wall fortified by stone gates and domed towers, the roofs painted pale orange. On one hill was the castle, where Prince Oscovko and the royals made their home. To Andry's eye, it looked more like a fortress than a king's palace, with thick stone walls, squat towers, and few windows he could see. On the other hill stood a magnificent church, twelve-sided, with an onion-domed tower at each point. Real gold gilded the church spires, each one the figure of a god or goddess. Syrek rose largest of all, his mighty sword thrust high into the gray sky.

Like Galland, Trec favored the god of war.

Most of the city lay in the saddle between the hills, and the road ran right to it, passing through the main gate. It yawned, a stone mouth of iron points, the portcullis raised to allow passage for the day. Orange flags flapped in the shivering wind, sewn with the black wolf of Trec. There was no moat, but a small ditch dug around the base of the wall. It, too, was lined with sharp pikes carved into murderous points.

"Trec remembers the might of the Temurijon," Sigil muttered, eyeing the moat with a flush of pride. Like the pike walls circling the city, it had clearly been constructed to fend off a mounted army. "They fear us still, even twenty years into the Emperor's peace."

They are right to, Andry almost said. Even in Galland, his lords and instructors spoke of the Temurijon with wariness, if not respect. Emperor Bhur and his Countless nearly broke the north in two, carving an empire of the steppes, forcing nations like Trec up against the mountains. Only a strange change of heart had spared the kingdoms from conquest, leaving them to their new borders and old rivalries.

Erida is not the same. Nothing can change her heart now. She'll conquer the realm with Taristan, or die trying.

Smoke trailed on the wind again, and not just from the city. Andry spotted a war camp to the east, barely more than a muddy smudge clustered around another city gate. Tents stood in haphazard lines, an eyesore compared to the camps of the Gallish legions.

Andry peered at the war camp as they approached the gate, his lip in his teeth as he counted the tents.

"What do you think?" Corayne muttered alongside him, also staring.

The squire tightened his grip on the reins. "Disjointed, unorganized. A mess," he answered. "But they're better than nothing."

A smile cracked across her face. Grinning, she raised her hood, ready to hide her face. "That's the spirit."

The gate traffic pressed in, but Andry didn't mind the jostle. He was used to Ascal, the largest city upon the Ward. The stream of travelers narrowed before the gray, old gate wardens, passing under the portcullis without difficulty. The two men waved everyone on with gloved hands and disinterest, the grip on their spears relaxed. Even though all of Trec looked ready to fight off a sudden invasion, it was just another day for the gate wardens.

The Companions approached the gate together, dismounting from their horses to pass through the city walls. They stood out sharply from the other travelers, who were mostly farmers, pale-skinned and fair-haired, with light eyes and heavy carts laden with the autumn harvest. The old ones eyed Sigil unkindly, their fear of the Temurijon giving over to blind disdain. They remembered the wars best. Andry glared back at them on Sigil's behalf.

"Gallish?" one of the wardens called out in Paramount, his long gray beard waggling.

Andry jumped, realizing the gate warden was looking at him.

The old man pointed to Andry's tunic beneath his cloak. The blue star on dirty white, his father's heraldry. Andry touched it softly, feeling the rough fabric. The star was earned in service to a crown that killed him and betrayed the Ward.

"I was," Andry answered instead, swallowing hard. His pulse thrummed in his ears.

The old warden grinned, showing missing teeth, and Andry sighed in relief. But it was short-lived.

The wardens waved the Companions forward, but not to pass through. They eyed their strange number with confusion, noting everything from Dom's size to the blade on Corayne's back to Sorasa's tattoos to Sigil with her smiling ax. Only Charlie and Valtik escaped scrutiny, both of them plain enough to the passing eye.

Andry bit his lip, his stomach twisting with unknown dread. He knew what a strange sight they made—and how distinct they all were.

"What is your purpose in Vodin, travelers? Yours is a strange number," the warden crowed, stroking his beard. With his free hand, he kept a tight grip on his spear.

Not that it would be of any use. Dom or Sigil could easily snap the warden in two.

The immortal opened his mouth to answer.

But before he could say a word, Charlie slipped neatly in front of him, a perfectly rolled scroll of parchment clutched in one outstretched hand. He fixed the two wardens with a winning smile, his cheeks red with cold, his brown eyes bright in the midday sun.

"We've been summoned here by Prince Oscovko himself," Charlie said, matter-of-fact, without so much as the hint of a lie.

Andry felt the falsehood on his cheeks and he lowered his brow, trying to hide the blush creeping over his skin. It hid his smile too.

The wardens balked, looking between each other and the scroll, then at the Companions assembled before them.

"If I may," Charlie said, clearing his throat. He casually unrolled the scroll and held it out for all to see.

"'I, Oscovko the Fine, Blood Prince of Trec, do summon the carriers of this scroll to Vodin, where they will treat with me at my seat in the Castle Volaska. Let no man or beast waylay my friends in their journey, for it is of dire importance to the safety of Trec and the survival of the realm. Signed, Oscovko the Fine, Blood Prince of Trec,' so on and so forth," Charlie added, his voice trailing off, one hand tracing circles in the air.

Andry could barely contain his glee as the fugitive priest waved the scroll again, displaying the signature and the seal on the bottom of the page. Orange wax, stamped with the outline of a howling wolf. Charlie even held out the scroll for the two wardens to examine, so confident was he in his work.

Both old men drew back, shaking their heads. Andry doubted they could even read, let alone identify a skilled forgery.

"What does our prince want with the likes of you?" one sneered, tugging on his beard again.

Andry moved without thinking and sidled up to Charlie, drawing himself up to his full height. He remembered the knights of Ascal and the courtiers too. Not just the gossip, but the pomp and pride they displayed without even trying. He made his best effort to feel the same in himself, digging it up from somewhere deep. Pursing his lips, he took the scroll from Charlie.

"That's the prince's business, unfortunately," Andry said, heaving a weary sigh. As if seeing the crown prince were a chore. "We must meet with him, and soon."

The crowd around the gate continued to grow, and a few travelers shouted at the delay, begging to enter the city. It felt like the first kindling to a roaring flame.

Andry made a show of surveying the unruly crowd, letting their frustration do the work for them. "Well, sirs, can we pass, or shall we summon the Prince of Trec to his own city gate?"

The wardens grimaced at each other. As much as they distrusted the Companions, they clearly feared their prince all the more. One of them cast a final glance at Sigil, sizing her up, before he relented and stood back from the gate. The other followed, inching backward to let them pass into Vodin.

"Well done, Squire Trelland," Charlie chuckled as the gate swallowed them up.

"Well done, Priest," Andry whispered back.

They followed the gate road straight between the twin hills of Vodin, with the castle to the left and the grand church to the right. Both watched over the city, the king and the gods standing in equal measure.

After weeks in the wilderness, the Treckish capital was jarring, but it reminded Andry of home. Vodin was a far cry from Ascal, but still busy, the city streets crowded with stalls, storefronts, and people wandering in every direction. The clatter of hooves, the shout of merchants, hammers ringing in a blacksmith's forge, a brawl spilling out of a gorzka bar—it was all achingly familiar. And yet so different at the same time.

Comforting as the streets were, they were a danger too. Still silent, Sorasa looked like a snake coiled in the saddle. She watched the streets and buildings, scanning every single face and cart. *Looking for assassins*, Andry knew.

Back on her horse, Corayne fished through her saddlebags. After a second, she pulled out a corner of dried meat and tore it in two, handing a piece to Andry without a word. She leaned against the flank of her horse, shuddering against its warmth. Andry's flush receded as he bit into the jerky, enjoying the savory burst of salt.

"Notice anything?" Corayne asked after a long second, casting a glance down their line.

Andry followed her gaze. Something like dread settled in his stomach. "Valtik's gone again?"

Indeed, the old Jydi was nowhere to be seen. When she'd disappeared or how, Andry had no idea.

Ahead of them, Dom shook his head. "The witch will wander," he said dryly.

"She's not the one I'm worried about," Sigil answered, looking straight at Charlie. "If another hunter steals my bounty—"

"Don't worry, Sigil, I won't try to run. Even I'm not that stupid," Charlie answered, rolling his eyes.

Corayne balked. "By the gods, Sigil, are you really still going to collect on him?"

The Temur woman shrugged her broad shoulders. She took the jerky from Corayne's hand. "I like to keep my options open."

Corayne snatched it back.

"She's getting faster, Sarn," Sigil said over the back of her horse. On the other side, Sorasa only blinked, less than impressed.

But Corayne grinned, ripping another bite. "Getting faster," she muttered so only Andry could hear.

"About time," he said, tipping his head to smile down at her.

She matched his grin, and the warmth of it spread through Andry's body, tingling in his cold limbs.

The top of the city hill leveled off at Oscovko's castle, with only a single gate. The other sides dropped off down the hill, too high for any army to climb. Wolves snarled from the ramparts, menacing and brutish, hewn of black granite, a stark contrast to the gray. Only one wolf was white, cut from pure limestone. It leered above the gate, wearing a crown.

This time there were no old wardens to hoodwink, but a garrison of bold young soldiers led by a sharp-eyed captain. Andry despaired of their plan even as he dismounted, joining Charlie with the parchment unrolled for all to see.

"The prince would not summon you to Volaska," the captain said with a scoff, indicating the imposing fortress behind the gates. He gave the scroll and the Companions a narrow look. "He lives in the camp outside the city, not the castle."

"Does he? How strange," Charlie said, pantomiming shock.

Andry was less skilled, feeling his face go hot again. His palms sweated in his gloves. He tried to think, wondering what a knight or even his noble mother would say.

But Corayne was faster, jumping off her horse to land on able feet. Dom followed close behind, her immortal shadow.

The captain gulped, craning his neck to look Dom in the eye, even as Corayne stood in front of him.

"My name is Corayne an-Amarat," she said sharply.

Andry sucked in a breath. *Assassins and bounty hunters and entire kingdoms hunt you!* he wanted to shout. He remembered every blade set against her. *But does she?* his mind roared.

"Corayne—" he hissed under his breath.

Luckily, the captain didn't know or care.

"Good for you," he answered, confused.

She held her ground. "Take that name to your prince and see what he has to say."

"The prince will throw you all in the stocks if he hears about this nonsense," the captain snapped, growing frustrated.

Corayne only grinned. "Let's prove you right."

An hour passed before Dom broke his vigil over Corayne, careful to keep the captain away from her. He craned his head, looking back down the road into the city. On the walls, the stone wolves cast long shadows cut by the dipping sun.

Andry followed his gaze, squinting down the hill, but saw nothing in the distance.

"A retinue is approaching the gate," Dom said, squaring his body so that Corayne was fully behind him. He twitched his cloak, freeing his sword should he need it.

Andry followed suit in a single fluid motion, throwing his cloak back over one side. Chill bit through his clothes, but he ignored it.

"Get back on your horse," he whispered to Corayne.

She didn't argue and climbed into the saddle with a step and a swing of her legs. Her fingers closed on the reins, and the mare beneath her pawed the stones, ready to bolt.

Andry's skin crawled as more of the garrison burst from the castle gate, orange cloaks over their chain mail and leathers. The black wolf ran through them, a warning as much as a symbol. Most were grizzled, veterans of many years, with gray beards and stern jaws. They did not move like the disciplined soldiers of the Gallish legions or the Lionguard knights, but they were fearsome all the same, bearing swords and spears.

A horn sounded, a low, throbbing noise to split the cold air. Not from the castle, but somewhere in the city, rising up to meet them. It sounded nothing like the bronze trumpets of Galland, the ones he heard in Ascal all the time. This was deeper, meant to carry for miles, rattling Andry's teeth. *A wolf's howl.*

The Prince of Trec was coming.

Andry knew Oscovko was older than Erida by nearly a decade, almost thirty years old, and heir apparent to the kingdom of Trec. He tried to remember all he knew of court and foreign royalty, expecting silk and fine brocade, a bejeweled crown, a permanently etched sneer. Something to earn the title *the Fine*.

Oscovko was nothing of the sort.

He approached with a half-dozen riders, all weaving their way up to the castle of Volaska. The prince sat astride a murderous red stallion, its head tossing against tight reins.

He drew up on the road and dismounted without so much as an introduction. There was no crown on Oscovko's head, and his hair was cut short, dark as pitch. He waved at the Companions with sharp, quick jerks of his white hands, urging them to come forward. But before they could even move, he strode into their midst, stopping only a yard from Dom.

He was nearly a foot and a half shorter than Dom was, but just as broad, all muscle beneath his black doublet and rust-colored cloak. The wolf's pelt across his shoulders made him even broader, its head dangling over his bicep, fastened with a dull iron chain. A pair of belts ran across his hips, holding a sword and a brace of daggers. The blades were the only clean thing on his body. The rest bore stains of gods-knew-what, but Andry wagered an even mix of wine and mud. Hardly a crown prince raised in a palace. He seemed as much a soldier as the rest of them, but for the single band of gold on his left thumb.

Prince Oscovko was perhaps the first person who looked on Dom not with fear, but fascination. His pale gray eyes barely flickered over the towering immortal, taking in everything from his sword to his half-ruined cloak.

With a snap, Oscovko pulled out a folded piece of parchment and held it out for all to see.

Fear leapt up in Andry's heart.

Corayne's face stared back at them, her name and likeness drawn on the parchment. Andry knew what the rest of the scroll said, remembering the posters plastered all over the Almasad docks. His own face among them, his own so-called crimes listed in black, burning ink.

Oscovko peered around Dom's great bulk, finding Corayne on her horse.

She did not flinch under his scrutiny, even raising her chin in challenge.

"This is awful," Oscovko barked, waving the paper back and forth. Then he grinned, showing several gold teeth. They winked in the gray light. "Looks nothing like you. No wonder you haven't been caught."

"Your Highness," Corayne said, trying to bow from the saddle of a horse. She did her best.

It pleased the prince.

"Wanted by the Queen of Galland herself, dead or alive," he said, letting out a low whistle. "What could you have possibly done to deserve such a sentence?"

Corayne dismounted in a single fluid motion. She landed gently, boots crunching in the frost. "I'd be happy to tell you."

Andry followed, falling in behind her like a knight behind his queen. It was almost second nature now, to guard her as he'd once hoped to guard Erida. *Corayne is far more important*, he knew. *To the Ward, and to me.*

"Hmm," the prince replied, tapping his lip. To Andry's surprise, Oscovko's attention shifted, snapping from Corayne to the squire. "You have an honest face," he said. "Tell me truly, is all this worth the time of a Blood Prince of Trec?"

Andry expected to feel nervous in the presence of a future king, but he'd stood before far worse in the past weeks. His answer was easy, a simple truth.

"It's worth all the time you have to give, Your Highness," he replied, careful to use his title before bowing.

As he straightened, he offered the prince a look of regret.

"My apologies, by the way," he added, offering an empathetic shrug. "Of all the men Erida could have chosen, I was rooting for you."

Andry had little skill in politics or intrigue, but he wasn't entirely ignorant of them.

Oscovko wrinkled his nose, going sullen. Andry knew it was a bold move, nearly overplaying their hand. But he knew pride. And while Oscovko seemed more soldier than prince, he certainly had the pride of a royal son. Erida's refusal had stung his ego if not his heart, and it was an easy wound to prod at.

"Very well," Oscovko said, sweeping his eyes over the Companions. His gaze landed on Sorasa, glowering next to her horse. "But I would be a fool to invite an assassin to my table."

Sorasa seethed, her ragged hair loose about her face. It was almost as good as her hood, hiding most of the tattoos on her neck. She heaved a breath, reluctant, and opened her mouth.

"I'm not Amhara anymore."

Her voice rasped with disuse. The shock of it ran through the Companions.

For a moment, Dom broke his focus, turning his head to face Sorasa. They locked eyes only briefly, but Andry saw something sharp and painful pass between them.

Next to her, Sigil whooped out a shout of glee, standing in the stirrups. She all but shook Sorasa out of the saddle, grasping her shoulder in one massive hand. The movement dislodged her hood and Sorasa let it drop, showing her entire face for the first time since the clearing, and the Amhara.

Andry's heart leapt in his chest, happy to hear Sorasa's voice, sharp as it might be. Next to him, Corayne beamed.

Oscovko didn't notice their collective joy, or simply didn't care.

"Sounds like something an Amhara would say," he muttered. "Well, Corayne an-Amarat, I promise not to sell you if your assassin promises not to kill me."

Sorasa growled, her voice unsticking. "I don't take contracts that small."

This the prince chose to ignore. He spun neatly on his heel, gesturing for everyone to follow. He continued shouting, though, his annoyed grumble carrying on the wind.

"If we're going to talk of the Lion Queen, I'll need a glass of wine. Or ten!"

16

THE WOLVES OF TREC
Corayne

This is much better than sneaking through wet tunnels and armed guards, Corayne thought, remembering how she'd once entered Erida's palace. The castle of the Treckish king was far less difficult, now that Prince Oscovko led the way.

He snapped his fingers and the castle gates swung wide, the portcullis rising with the clatter of iron chain. The prince stalked through without so much as a backward glance, his burly compatriots from the war camp in tow.

The city set Corayne's mind on edge, and she was glad to be leaving it behind, the castle walls swallowing her up. The smell of the streets alone had been almost unbearable. Sweet, savory, and foul all at once, clashing in her senses. Corayne's eyes still stung with smoke even as her mouth watered over the cooking meat and fresh-baked bread. There was no fruit in the markets. They were too far north and too far into autumn for it. In Lemarta, Corayne never found herself wanting for fresh food. She ached for it now, after so many days of meat and hard biscuits upon the Wolf's Way. She could barely even recall the taste of olives or oranges, or good Siscarian wine. With a twist of sadness, Corayne realized she missed home. The salty breeze, the cypress hills. Fishermen in the harbor, the cliff roads, and the little cottage. A blue sky over bluer sea. She thought of her mother, and the *Tempestborn*. Where they were now, she had no idea. *Still sailing on to Rhashir, seeking riches? Or will she do as I asked, and fight?*

Corayne knew her mother so well, and yet not at all. She couldn't predict what path the pirate would take. The uncertainty was a needle in her skin, never forgotten, but sometimes ignored.

With a will, Corayne shook her head and raised her eyes, casting aside her doubts as best she could. She noted the inner bailey of the castle, smaller than the square outside. A great keep frowned over everything, blackened by fire long ago. Corayne spotted a barracks, a stable, and a chapel built up within the curtain wall. Compared to the New Palace, it felt cramped and closed in, the high walls throwing the entire yard into shade. Briefly, Corayne understood why Oscovko preferred living in the war camp outside the city.

Dogs bayed near the barracks, a loping pack of hounds ranging in color from yellow to gray. Corayne eyed them, remembering what Andry said about wolves. But the only wolves she saw were made of stone or thread, in black or crowned white, sculpted on the walls or embroidered on the many flags and tunics.

Prince Oscovko ushered them through at a harried pace. Men stopped to salute but he didn't pause, climbing up the steps to enter the keep without so much as a wave. Corayne could almost see the nerves firing beneath his skin. He was clearly uncomfortable.

"Welcome to Volaska, the Wolf's Den," he said without fanfare, pushing the oaken doors open. They were thick as Corayne's arm was long, banded with Treckish steel, the strongest metal upon the Ward.

She shivered as she walked inside, blinking in the suddenly dim light of a long, torchlit hall. The windows at the far end were but slits, wide enough for archers, and the windows facing the yard were shuttered. Corayne willed her eyes to adjust and realized she stood in the center of the keep, in the court of the Treckish king. It was both feasting hall and throne room, with a raised dais in front of the dark windows. The throne of Trec sat empty, carved from a single block of the same white limestone on the ramparts. It was unadorned but for the wolf chiseled into the back, crowned with real gold.

Aside from Oscovko and his men, the hall was empty, even of servants. It smelled stale and unused, the air thick.

"Has King Lyev retired for the evening?" Sorasa asked, nearly blending into the shadows. Her voice sounded stronger already.

She ran a finger along the edge of a chair, disturbing the thick layer of dust. Corayne eyed the two soldiers behind Sorasa, following her every move from a safe distance. Corayne fought back a smile, if only for Sorasa's sake.

Oscovko scoffed and crossed the wide room, pulling the rest of them along with him. "King Lyev has not entered his own hall in many months," he said, sweeping through a doorway.

Three of his lieutenants followed, leaving the rest of his guard in the hall.

The adjoining chamber was long, thin, and brighter, its windows opening onto the steep side of the hill, looking out over the greater city. The Gates of Trec loomed in the distance, marked by the wide gap in the mountains. From here, the castle could see all the way to the Gallish border. Corayne squinted at it, as if she could see Taristan himself waiting on the other side. But there was only the gray haze of more forest and hill country, half dead with the season.

A feasting table ran down the middle of the room. It was too large for the space, clearly dragged in from the great hall. Oscovko gestured for them to sit and helped himself to a glass of wine from the sideboard. He downed a goblet in a single gulp before filling it again and taking a chair.

Corayne noticed he did not take the seat at the head of the table, but the one to its right. The other remained empty, left open for an absent king.

"Well," Oscovko said, crossing his boots on the tabletop. "Out with it, Corayne an-Amarat. I'm eager for a tale."

Corayne heaved a breath. First Erida, then Isadere, then her mother—and now Prince Oscovko. *Perhaps I should just write it all down, and save myself the trouble of explaining everything all over again.* She clenched her teeth and sat. The others mirrored her. Before Corayne could ask, Oscovko slid a glass of wine across the table, nudging it into her hand.

She took a fortifying swallow and spoke.

Her voice was low and hoarse as she recounted their tale. The gray light went gold in the windows, the clouded sky turning to brilliant shades of orange and yellow with the sunset. Dom did not sit, but stared out at the city, his figure casting a shadow across the narrow room, cutting it in two.

"Twelve Amhara assassins tracked us along the Wolf's Way," Corayne said finally. "They attacked a few days north of the Dahlian Gates."

She never saw the clearing where the assassins lay, their blood spent on the grass, but she remembered the aftermath. Sorasa's ruined hair, her hollow gaze, her silence. And Dom's great concern for her, more jarring than anything.

Corayne glanced at Sorasa, unmoving in her chair, staring at the pitted and stained tabletop, her face blank and eyes glassy. She hid behind a wall of her own making. Whatever weight she still carried from that day was not for any of them to see.

Oscovko watched her too, his eyes ticking over her tattooed hands, her neck, every mark of the Amhara on her skin. He pulled at his fourth glass of wine, somehow unaffected by the dark red vintage.

"They were clearly unsuccessful," he said, gesturing to the six of them. "I'm impressed. Twelve Amhara turned back by the likes of you." His gray eyes swept between Dom and Sorasa. "Though I suppose it's easy to kill what you know."

At the window, Dom turned to look over his shoulder. He sneered, his scars pulling at one side of his mouth. "Your Highness—"

"Don't." Sorasa's voice cracked like her whip, a single syllable filled with command.

The Elder knew better than to argue. He shut his mouth with an audible click of his teeth.

Corayne pushed on, eager to be finished. "After the Amhara, we continued north, meaning to enter Galland through the Gates of Trec."

The prince put down his glass and leaned forward, toward Corayne. His pale cheeks were stubbled, rough-shaven with haste. She guessed he had little need to keep up appearances in the war camp, with his father's court all but abandoned.

He looked her over. "But you are not through the Gates of Trec now. Instead you rode to my city, seeking Treckish blades and Treckish blood."

"Seeking an *ally*," she replied tightly.

"And what might I get out of this so-called alliance?" Oscovko pointed to his own chest, then to his quiet lieutenants. "Besides dead men."

Sigil drummed her fingers on the table, her face pulled in distaste. "You get to survive."

"Tempting," he shot back, his voice dry as old bone.

Corayne set her jaw. She felt the dagger in her hand, the correct answer so easy.

"Glory," she said, as if it were the most obvious thing in the world.

Oscovko's eyelids fluttered, his lips parting to show tongue and teeth. His eyes followed her as she stood, throwing back her cloak. Here was a prince who preferred battle to banquets, mercenaries to courtiers. If duty to his kingdom could not sway him, then surely his pride could.

"Glory for Oscovko the Fine, Blood Prince of Trec," she continued. "The histories will remember you, if they survive to remember anything at all."

The Spindleblade sang from its sheath as she drew, pulling the long blade over her shoulder in one smooth, clean motion. She set it gently on the table, letting the Prince of Trec examine the Spindleborn edge. He stood from his chair, hands outstretched, but he would not touch the blade.

"Finer even than Treckish steel," he murmured, touching the sword on his hip.

Indeed, Trec's mines and forges produced the finest swords and steel throughout Allward. But the Spindleblade was not of their realm. Even to his eyes, it stood apart, the metal rippling with the cold light of different stars. The gems of the hilt paled in comparison, beautiful as they were, winking red and purple with the sunset.

Oscovko licked his lips, as if he stood before an opulent feast. "I've never seen a Spindle before," he said, raising his eyes to Corayne.

"I can't say I recommend it, but . . . it's where we have to go." She crossed to the windows, joining Dom and his watch upon the Ward. "The Spindle in the foothills must be closed."

"Why? What happens if it remains open? What happens if I stay here behind my walls?" Oscovko jerked his chin at the windows. "What exactly is going on out there?"

For the first time in an hour, Corayne faltered, the words sticking in her throat. She had only seen shades of the Ashlands, images conjured by Valtik's own magic.

At the table, Andry cleared his throat. The memory pained him still, that was clear for anyone to see. "Taristan has an army like—like nothing the Ward has ever seen before. Corpses and skeletons. Alive but dead. And so many."

Oscovko cocked his head, bewildered.

"I didn't believe it either," Corayne said softly. "Once."

She remembered the girl she was, on the cliffs of Lemarta, who wanted only the horizon. Who was foolish enough to think the world would give it to her. Who saw an Elder and an assassin as merely stepping stones, a chance to escape the lovely cage of her mother's making. Corayne envied that girl, and hated her in the same breath.

Oscovko continued to stare, his pale eyes going hard, his jaw clenching tight. To Corayne's dismay, she realized it was not confusion on the prince's face.

"Bring me the letter," he said sharply, speaking over their heads to one of his lieutenants. The man jumped to attention and swept from the room, his boots hammering on the floor.

Fear gripped Corayne's heart, its icy fingers clawing her insides. "What letter?" Her voice trembled.

The prince did not answer, stone-faced. When the lieutenant returned, a parchment in hand, Corayne almost snatched it away to read for herself. Instead she tightened her grasp on the arms of her chair, trying to ignore the rising thud of her own heart.

With a snap, Oscovko unfolded the letter. Corayne leaned forward in her seat, as did Charlie, both trying to glimpse its contents from across the table.

"From the King of Madrence," Oscovko said, eyeing them both. He indicated the dark red seal, broken in half, the stamped image of a stallion cut in two. "The rider nearly died getting here, changing horses without rest."

Madrence, Corayne thought, swallowing hard. She exchanged

worried glances with Andry, who sat across from her, his brow deeply furrowed.

"Are you going to read the letter or dangle it in front of us?" Sorasa hissed.

Oscovko's throat bobbed. He looked to Corayne, and she saw fear in him, the destructive kind, the one that hollowed you out. The kind she knew too well.

"'Crown Prince Orleon has been killed,'" he said, reading from the smudged paper. "'The city of Rouleine has fallen to Erida. She has twenty thousand men marching to Partepalas, and another army of—'"

Something broke in his voice, and in his eyes.

Corayne felt it break in her too.

"'Corpses and skeletons,'" Oscovko whispered. He lowered the letter and slid it across the table. "Just as you said. An army like nothing the Ward has ever seen before."

Corayne's fingers trembled, shaking beneath the table. She stared at the letter and the inked message, the scrawl messy. Whoever had sent the message did so at great haste.

"Not a forgery," Charlie said, pulling the paper closer. He scrutinized the seal and signature with the eye of a master. "This is the king's own hand, his own writing. He is desperate indeed."

"For good reason," Andry muttered, his fist clenching on the tabletop.

Dom's massive form slumped against the thick window glass, his chest rising and falling. "The Spindle army marches."

Andry slowly collapsed back into his seat, taking his head in his hands. Corayne wanted to go to him but could not move. The shades of the Ashlanders ran through her mind, their decaying bodies coming through the trees of a quiet forest. A scream rose up in her throat, as the woods became buildings, the overgrown ground turned into city streets. She squeezed her eyes shut, trying to clear her thoughts. Trying not to see the skeletons as they fell upon man, woman, and child, laying waste to everything in Erida's path.

Rouleine is a border city, built to withstand war and siege. Her eyes opened, stinging with hot tears. *But not monsters. Not Taristan. Not What Waits.*

Her dreams flared up before her waking eyes, only for a moment. The red presence of What Waits leered at the corner of her vision, a hot and pulsing sheen. She turned her head, trying to catch it, only for Him to disappear.

The fear did not.

She could not imagine what Andry saw in his mind, or Dom. They knew far worse than she did. Both bowed under the weight of their memories, battling a storm Corayne would never weather. Instead she met Sorasa's copper eyes, sharing a sharp look. The assassin then turned to the squire and the immortal, her full lips pressed to nothing, her nostrils flared as she took in their pain, and despaired of it.

Oscovko watched them all, uneasy. He folded the letter with deliberate motion, creasing the paper.

He cleared his throat. "King Robart calls for an alliance of the Ward, all united against Erida and her consort. Against whatever evil they're using to roll through the realm."

"Will you agree to it?" Corayne blurted out. She expected that familiar burst of hope in her chest, but it never came. The situation was simply too dire.

The prince hesitated. "This letter was written last month, and I only received it two days ago," he finally bit out, and Corayne winced. "I must assume Robart is already dead. Or has surrendered his throne."

"The Spindle army is thousands strong." Andry raised his head, his brown eyes distant. Usually they looked so warm, but now Corayne saw only cold darkness in him. "Many thousands."

"And marching through Madrence," Dom mumbled, sounding lost.

Sigil's fist hit the tabletop with a boom, almost toppling the wineglasses. They all jumped at the noise, even Oscovko. She glared around at all of them, her black eyes narrowed, a flush in her bronze cheeks.

"If the army is moving, then it isn't guarding the Spindle," she hissed. "You can wallow when the realm is safe."

Oscovko's lips twitched into the smallest smile, amused.

But Andry looked grim. "More Ashlanders could be coming through all the time, and even if they aren't, certainly Taristan would leave a guard."

He ran a hand over his black hair, scratching his scalp. His close-cut squire's style was long gone, giving over to dense curls, falling like a soft, dark halo. Corayne certainly preferred it. He was unfettered by the rules of selfish court, becoming more of himself. Somewhere between squire and knight, boy and man.

Sorasa pulled her own short hair back from her shoulders, winding it into a small knot. The tattoos on her neck stood out more sharply, impossible to ignore. Oscovko eyed them again, a little too slowly.

"It's a chance," she said, and Corayne half expected her to set out at once.

Across the table, Sigil nodded and thumped her chest, her fist beating against her leathers. Charlie looked less than ecstatic but gave a tiny thump of his own.

"A chance," Corayne sighed, turning the words over. "Well, chance has gotten us this far."

She went to the table and raised the Spindleblade, sliding it back over her shoulder. The added weight had become a comfort in the long weeks, a reminder of what she could do—and how much they could still fight.

Dom remained at the window, his emerald eyes fixed without seeing. Corayne knew he was far away, standing at a forgotten temple, the spring grass rotting with blood and bone.

She put a hand to his cloaked shoulder. It was like touching a statue.

"We can't save the people already lost," she said slowly. The words were for herself as much as him. "But we can try to save the rest."

He was slow to react, a block of ice barely beginning to melt. His eyes thawed first, the hard chips of green wavering. "Yes, we can," he finally rumbled.

"If I could ride, I would go with you. Let these bones fight one more time."

Corayne whirled to find a feeble old man standing at the far end of the chamber, leaning heavily on a walking stick. He wore only a long shift of undyed wool, his feet bare, blue veins branching beneath frail, spotted white skin. His hair grew down his back, wispy and gray, his beard combed through.

Like Oscovko, he wore no crown or jewels, but Corayne knew him without them.

Lyev, the King of Trec.

A white film clouded the aging king's eyes, and he stared at the ceiling. The king was blind.

Oscovko hurried to the old man, taking his arm with an exasperated huff. He tried to turn him back toward the far door, into the private apartments of the castle. "Father, please. If you fall again, the healers—"

"We are all destined to fall, my son," King Lyev said weakly, his free hand running over his son's face. "What will you do before the end?"

The prince screwed up his face, stricken. His brow furrowed and his lips pursed; his forehead wrinkled with care.

"What will you do?" Lyev said again, and Corayne felt a sharp, cold chill creep over her skin.

"Nurse," Oscovko commanded, calling into the darkened doorway. He looked away before his father's carer appeared, shuffling forward to take the king by the arm.

Corayne's jaw dropped.

For once, Valtik wore shoes, a pair of mismatched boots. She winked one lightning-blue eye as she ushered the king away, pulling him from the chamber. Oscovko's eyes slid over her. He cared little for servants and old nurses. Around the table, the Companions went thin-lipped and teeth-tight, trying to speak without words.

But for the circumstances, Corayne would have laughed outright. Sorasa actually did, hiding a smirk in her hand, turning her face away.

Oscovko recovered slowly, running a hand over his own face, tracing the path of his father's fingers. "What will you do?" he murmured to himself, echoing his father's words.

Valtik's words, Corayne knew.

The prince's gray eyes ran along the table, then back to Corayne and the sword over her shoulder. A corner of his mouth twisted, curling into a black smile.

"My war camp has been quiet for too long. We will ride with you into Galland." He rapped his knuckles on the table, and his lieutenants responded in kind, cheering. "Few men can say they fought the apocalypse. I will be one of them."

Corayne nodded along with them, her own thin smile a front for the hurricane swirling in her belly. Terror, conviction, relief, and the seedling of hope battled within Corayne an-Amarat, each one wrestling for dominance. But all paled beneath Taristan—and What Waits. He was something worse than fear—he was doom.

"Call the camp up to Volaska," Oscovko said, shoving one of his lieutenants toward the great hall.

With a mad chuckle, he poured himself another glass of wine. The liquid pooled like blood, filling to the brim. It sloshed when he raised the glass, spilling crimson over his fingers. Oscovko didn't mind.

"Tomorrow we ride!" he shouted, his voice too loud for the room. No one matched his toast. "But tonight we feast."

* * *

They were given chambers throughout the castle, filling apartments long deserted by the shrinking Treckish court. With an ailing king and an absent prince, there was little cause for nobles and courtiers to remain. Most kept their own castles and halls, spread through the countryside. Luckily, Volaska still had many servants in employ, from the kitchens to the stables, and all were put to work cleaning out the dusty, unused apartments.

Corayne felt odd waiting for a maid to finish changing the linens on the bed, so she helped where she could, taking up the broom and refilling the water pitcher and washing bowl. She felt odder still with Sorasa standing in the corner, her arms crossed over her body tightly. She looked like a corpse in an upright coffin, set among the shadows. The maid eyed her warily and rushed through the room as quickly as possible.

Neither Corayne nor Sorasa spoke while the maid worked. While Corayne doubted Queen Erida had spies in the Treckish capital, it wasn't worth the risk.

A fire crackled merrily in the hearth and tapestries lined the stone walls. Both kept out the worst of the chill. There was even a tub before the hearth, half filled with steaming water.

Corayne didn't feel the cold anymore, but her skin prickled anyway, goose bumps rising under her clothes. Her eyelids drooped as she looked over a tapestry of the god Syrek, cloaked in red, the whites of his eyes all but glowing. A conquered army lay beneath his feet, the soldiers of many kingdoms, their faces every color.

His face was oddly familiar, woven with impossible precision. She stared, eyes running over white skin, long nose, thin lips, and dark red hair.

Taristan.

She clenched her teeth and blinked.

The threads changed, the face losing detail. Corayne hissed out a breath and wrenched herself away, crossing to the center of the chamber.

"This is fine," she said to the maid, first in Paramount, then in broken Treckish. There was still dust on half the furniture, but the bed linens were fresh, the chamber pot cleaned, and the bath full. That was enough. "It's only for the night."

The maid barely nodded and scurried out, eager to be gone from the room.

Sorasa wasted no time. She set to examining the bedchamber as well, but instead of investigating the tapestries, she pawed behind them, scouring every inch of the walls. Her fingers felt for cracks and gaps as she shoved aside a heavy wooden chest, sending up a cloud of dust.

"It's good to hear your voice again," Corayne said, sitting down on the bed. She watched, thoughtful, as Sorasa went through the room. "I've missed your training notes."

The assassin didn't turn around. "No you haven't," she shot back.

Corayne laughed outright. "No, I haven't."

With a sigh, she fell back on the bed, stretching out. After weeks in the wilderness, the stiff straw mattress felt like a cloud. It took all her will not to shut her eyes and fall asleep.

Sorasa kept up her searching, dropping to her knees to check the floor.

"Oscovko isn't going to hand me off to Erida."

"I'm not worried about Oscovko," Sorasa muttered, wriggling under the bed. "This castle has a rat problem."

She emerged on the other side, a tail and a wriggling, greasy body dangling from her grasp. Corayne pulled a face as the assassin tossed the rat into the hall.

"Oh, stop it, you've seen worse by now," Sorasa scolded, shutting the door behind her.

"That doesn't make rats better," Corayne snapped, drawing up her legs. She rustled the sheets, checking for any more rodents.

"We're about to feast with a Treckish war camp. Trust me, you'll wish for rats." Sorasa braced her hands on her hips and surveyed the room, finally satisfied. Then she poked at a folded pile on the table by the window, wrinkling her nose. "It seems Oscovko was kind enough to give us some clothes for the evening."

Corayne sniffed at her loose shirt, stained by weeks on the road. "Can't imagine why."

The clothes weren't much better, judging by Sorasa's expression. She grabbed a dress by the collar, shaking it out with distaste.

"You should make sure they aren't laced with poison," Corayne said, smirking.

But Sorasa was already going over the fabric, running it between her fingers, sniffing gingerly at the folds of linen and wool.

"I was kidding," Corayne said weakly. "Do people actually do that?"

"I have." Sorasa forced an overwide smile, tossing a dress and linen underclothes onto the bed. "You bathe first."

Corayne took the clothes gingerly, looking them over with some trepidation. The overgarment was plain wool, a pale blue color that must've been vibrant once. She ran a finger along the embroidery at the sleeves and neckline, feeling the craftsmanship. The dress was old but well made, perhaps for a lady or a princess in years gone by. White wolves ran through the embroidery, picked out in white and gold thread, weaving through a pattern of snowflakes.

The white wolf in a blizzard, Corayne thought, a chill running up her spine.

"Isadere saw this in their mirror," she muttered.

Sorasa made a dismissive noise. "Let me know when Isadere manages to turn the fleets of Ibal against Erida. Then I'll be impressed."

Slowly, Corayne pulled off her old shirt and pants, shucking them to the floor. It was like shedding her skin, peeling away layers of dirt and grime.

The warm water of the small wooden tub felt even better than the bed. She blew out a sigh as she sank, dunking her head. When she emerged, wiping her eyes, the water was already cloudy.

She winced. "Should we call for a fresh bath for you?"

Sorasa didn't bat an eye. "Just hurry up," she said, testing the latch on the window.

There was a small corner of soap and Corayne scrubbed her body all over, her toes curling with every scratch over her skin. Part of her wanted to just forget the feast altogether and sit in the bath until the water turned to ice. She finished instead, working the soap along her scalp before rinsing one more time. The fire roared at her naked back, and she barely shivered as she stepped out of the water, wrapping herself up in a thick blanket.

Sorasa was already out of her clothes, her tunic, pants, and boots neatly set in the corner with her many blades. Before Corayne could even blink, she dunked under the water.

Corayne couldn't help but notice Sorasa's tattoos. She had never seen so many before, not even on a member of her mother's crew. Sorasa had them almost everywhere. Up her legs, down her spine, across her ribs. A falcon, a spider, a constellation of stars.

"Which one is your favorite?" Corayne said when Sorasa's head emerged.

The assassin blinked, her usual swipes of black eye powder trailing down her cheeks. She narrowed her gaze. "Which what?"

Heat flared in Corayne's cheeks. "I'm sorry, that was rude." She ducked her head, pulling the blanket tighter around her body.

"The tattoos?"

"I don't mean to pry," Corayne answered, looking away.

Sorasa didn't blink. "But you always do."

Her face went hotter. "Yes, I guess so," she admitted. "I just— want to know. Everything. Always. If I know what's around me, every little detail . . ." Her voice trailed off, her mind a spinning mess. "I guess it helps me feel a little more in control. A little bit stronger. More valuable. It used to, at least."

Back home in Lemarta, knowledge had been her power. Knowing the tides, the trade routes, the passage of coin and gossip. All her information felt useless now, in the face of the ending of the world.

In the bath, Sorasa kept still, the water moving gently around her. *She* was the opposite of an open book. Corayne expected her to dunk her head and go silent again. Instead she swiped at her eyes, rubbing the black powder away, and grinned.

"These are my favorite," she said, raising both her palms.

The sun and moon faced out, inked into the flesh of her hands, distorted only a little by calluses and the lines in her skin.

Corayne glanced between them, fascinated.

"What do they mean?"

"These are Lasreen, the two sides of the goddess. Sun and moon, life and death. I carry them both in my hands." She turned her palms over, thoughtful. Her voice softened. "All the Amhara have them."

The assassin traced the sun on one palm, then the moon on the other.

Corayne watched her for a long, quiet moment. She felt herself edging out onto thin ice.

"Are you all right, Sorasa?"

Sorasa's hands dipped back into the water with a splash. "I'm perfectly fine," she snapped.

"You didn't speak for a month," Corayne said gently. She took a seat by the bath, perching on a small stool.

"I'm speaking now." The assassin sounded more like a petulant child than a killer. She turned her attention to the soap, running it over her arms. "And I say I'm fine." Her teeth gleamed in the firelight. "The Amhara made me what I am. I only did what they taught me."

It was a precarious balance, Corayne knew. Every question could push her—or Sorasa—over the edge. But she wasn't asking for her own curiosity, not anymore. She saw the pain behind Sorasa's eyes, burning even behind the wall in her mind.

"Did you know them?"

Sorasa sucked in a breath. Her eyelids fluttered. She balanced too. "Every single one."

Firewood splintered in the hearth and Corayne flinched, her gut twisting. *Every single one.* She knew little of Sorasa's life in the Amhara Guild, but enough to understand. The assassins had been her family once, whether she would admit it or not. And now twelve of them lay fallen in her wake, twelve brothers and sisters who had lived at her side and died by her hand.

"Why were you exiled?" Corayne's throat was dry.

Sorasa smoothed back her hair, pressing it away from her now-clean face. Without the dirt and black powder, the assassin looked younger. She fixed Corayne with a bold stare. "I thought you said that was my business."

Corayne shrugged out of the blanket and went to the clothes on the bed. "That doesn't mean I don't wonder," she said.

In the bath, Sorasa said nothing.

Corayne expected no reply and pulled the clothes on. She shivered at the feel of soft linen on her skin. Like everything else, it felt foreign after so many weeks in worn traveling gear. The dress fit snugly over the underclothes, skimming the curves of her body, with the neckline arcing below her collarbone. In Lemarta, Corayne hardly wore dresses at all. There was just no reason to, even for festivals. But she did not dislike them.

She watched her own reflection in the small looking glass. It was barely bigger than a piece of parchment, the glassy surface pitted and cloudy, but she swirled the skirt back and forth, admiring what she could see.

"A man hated his wife, and wanted to destroy her."

Turning, Corayne raised an eyebrow. Sorasa didn't react, staring into the fire, the soap forgotten, the waters of the bath swirling with road dust.

"He took out a contract," the assassin said, the flames jumping up. Heat pulsed through the room.

"But not for her," Corayne whispered.

"I've killed children before." Sorasa's eyes mirrored the hearth, dancing with hot red light. "But this—it felt wrong. And very little feels wrong to me." One of her hands dipped below the water, to her ribs, touching a tattoo Corayne couldn't see. "I went back to the citadel. But Lord Mercury had to make an example."

"Because you failed to kill the child?"

"Because I *refused*," Sorasa said. Her expression hardened, a flicker of anger crossing her face. "Failure is acceptable, but not disobedience. *We serve.* That is our deepest teaching. And I did not serve, could not serve. So Lord Mercury marked me as *osara*, and cast me into the sea." Memory welled in her eyes, and she tsked under her breath. "Men are so unsuited to power."

Corayne laughed darkly. "Women aren't terribly good at it either."

"Erida is a specimen all her own. And your uncle too."

It was Corayne's turn to harden, a terrible shiver going down her spine. She picked at her gown, trying not to think of Taristan and his army. His eyes an abyss, the memory of them frightening even now.

They would swallow her up if given the chance.

And swallow the world too.

The Spindleblade lay across the foot of the bed, nearly as long as the bed was wide. The sheath hid some of its magic, dulling the call of Spindleblade to Spindleblood, but Corayne could still feel its echo. She drew a finger over the leather. By now she knew each scratch and dent, the cracks and worn places, battered by her journey, by Andry's. And by Cortael's. Her thumb worked over the hilt of the sword, as if she could feel his fingers there.

"I don't want to die like my father," she murmured.

The water sloshed in the tub as Sorasa turned to face her, squaring her shoulders.

"No one wants to die, Corayne," she said sharply. "But we all do it, when the time comes." Some of the tension in her brow loosened, smoothing her forehead. "And then Lasreen will welcome us home."

Home.

Corayne's first thought was of the cottage, its small rooms and white walls, the flowers in the garden, her mother's citrus tea boiling in the pot. She breathed in, trying to remember the ocean and the cypress groves, but all she smelled was woodsmoke and soap. Her heart faltered. Lemarta was where she had grown up, but it was never home, not truly. It was a place to grow, but not a place to belong.

"Maybe we belong to each other, we who belong nowhere," Corayne murmured. They were Sorasa's own words, spoken so long ago.

The assassin remembered. Slowly, she nodded her head.

A booming knock at the door startled Corayne from her thoughts. In the bath, Sorasa lay back against the side of the tub, the water sloshing around her exposed collarbone.

She growled to herself, annoyed. "Yes, what is it?"

The door swung open and the Elder entered, stooping to get through the doorway, his towering blond head nearly scraping the ceiling. He had fresh clothes too, a black tunic and leather pants with his sword belted at his waist. His ratty old cloak was finally abandoned for the night.

"I—" he sputtered, his white face turning blood red. His eyes flew from Corayne fully dressed to Sorasa stretching in the bathwater.

His gaze lingered for a moment, then shot to the ceiling, the floor, the hearth—anywhere but Sorasa's bronze skin. "Excuse me—you said *yes*?"

"I don't see what the issue is." Sorasa shrugged in the water. A tattooed horse undulated on her shoulder, galloping over her moving flesh. "Domacridhan, you are five hundred years old. Certainly you've seen a naked woman before, mortal or immortal. Or do immortals look different?"

Dom forgot himself for a moment, fixing her with his scowl. "No, we don't look *different*—" he snarled before turning away. He raised a hand to shutter his eyes. "That is beside the point, Sorasa."

Corayne had to cover her mouth to keep from howling with laughter. Dom looked like he wanted to jump off the roof, while Sorasa grinned lazily, a coy cat stretching in a sunbeam of her own making. She relished every second of his discomfort.

"Well, be quick about what you wanted to tell us, then," the assassin said. "Or do you intend to stay?"

He hissed out a breath, calming himself. "The feast is being laid out below, and Oscovko is already drunk, if the shouting I heard is any indication."

"We could have figured that out for ourselves, Dom," Corayne teased.

Dom grimaced, looking to her with one hand still pressed to the side of his face, blocking Sorasa from view. "I only mean to say he and his men are poorly behaved. I will be outside the door until you're both ready to join them in the great hall."

Sorasa shifted, sitting up in the bath. "Exactly what gave you the indication I cannot protect myself or Corayne?" she asked, the water line falling a little lower.

Corayne feared for Dom's heart.

Still refusing to look in her direction, he could only stumble over an explanation. It came out in fits and starts, broken words making little sense.

"Very well, I will go," he finally managed, and left, spinning on his heel.

He wrenched the door open again, almost tearing it off his hinges. With one hand still raised to block his vision, he lunged out, his broad frame bumping against the doorway with a meaty thwack that shuddered the room. The sheer force of the slamming door stirred the air, and Corayne half expected the wood to splinter.

She gave Sorasa a mischievous grin. "I don't think he's ever seen a naked woman before."

Water spattered over the hearthstones as Sorasa rose from the bath, a twisting smirk on her lips.

"No, he certainly has."

Corayne's eyebrows shot up into her hairline. "How can you tell?"

"He knew exactly where to look," she answered calmly, drying herself off with a few quick swipes. Then she slipped into underclothes and wrung out her hair, glaring at her own dress laid out. Her smirk turned to scowl. "Treckish fashion is abysmal."

Her gown was the color of charcoal, edged in black and gold thread forming a pattern of tiny flowers. It had long sleeves and lacing at the neck, which Sorasa tightened, better fitting the overlarge gown to her form. Like Corayne's dress, the neckline dipped below her collarbone, showing more of her Amhara tattoos. If Sorasa minded showing black ink and bronze skin, she didn't show it. With quick hands, she braided her wet hair back against her scalp, weaving it into a knot at the base of her neck. She donned her eye powder again, swiping sharp, fresh lines of black over her eyelids. It made her copper eyes stand out, brighter than any fire.

She made a striking sight, a beautiful Ibalet woman with brown skin and black hair, done up in Treckish skirts. She seemed to glow, her high-boned face and full lips looking as fine as a lady in a painting.

Corayne felt the familiar sinking sensation in her stomach, the kind she felt standing next to her bold, magnificent mother.

"Abysmal or not, you look lovely," she said, waving a hand at Sorasa.

The assassin only shrugged. "I've looked better, I'll say that," she muttered, lacing her sleeves tight. "If only we could travel through the south properly. The court of Ibal is a glorious sight indeed."

Corayne tried to imagine it. In Almasad, they were more focused on passing through, but she remembered glimpses of fine silks and precious jewelry. Gold, turquoise, amethyst, lapis, and finest silver. Cloth draped to protect the wearer from the desert sun, but also to show off a fine figure or muscular build. Until now, she had only seen Sorasa in her leathers and tunics, her cloak never far away. Corayne could hardly picture her in silk.

"I've never been to a feast before," she muttered, picking at her gown again.

"I have, but I've never been invited," Sorasa shot back, hiking up her skirt to show a lean length of leg. She belted a dagger to her thigh before sliding another into her boot. "Firsts for both of us."

Corayne looked to the Spindleblade. "I suppose I can't leave that here," she said, imagining how foolish she would seem with a sword down her back.

"Have Dom carry it for the night, or Andry. I'm sure the squire would do anything you ask," Sorasa said, a sly look on her face.

Corayne's face burned and she grabbed the sheath. "Andry is just kind," she muttered, fighting the sudden swell of emotion in her chest.

Out in the passage, jeers echoed, sounding even through the door. She was suddenly grateful for the distraction. *The prince's men are drunk indeed.*

"How many ride with Oscovko?" she asked.

Sorasa shrugged. "Five hundred at most. I've never known a war camp to number more."

Corayne frowned. "He treats saving the Ward like a game, with glory as his prize."

"He can treat it however he likes, so long as he holds to his word," Sorasa said, crossing to the chamber door. She put a hand to the latch, her inked fingers curling. "Ready?"

"Starving. I mean yes."

To the surprise of no one, Dom was still waiting outside the door. He said nothing when they entered the passageway, and stalked off ahead, like a giant, lumbering shadow. But he kept pace with their steps, never more than a few yards ahead. Corayne noticed that his beard was trimmed and he had new braids in his hair, two hanging in front of each ear, with the rest of his blond locks falling loose. He looked a prince again, an immortal son of Glorian Lost, imposing and powerful.

Corayne smiled to herself.

And completely undone by Sorasa Sarn.

17
QUEEN OF SKULLS
Erida

The towers and cathedral spires of Partepalas rose against a cloudless blue sky. White stone and flashing silver paint gleamed in the afternoon sun, a stronger beacon than even the city's famed lighthouse rising over the port. The autumn chill of the woodlands was gone, replaced by the calm, temperate air of the southern coast. Everything was still in bloom, the air perfumed with flowers and a fresh salt breeze. Erida drank it down, greedy for more.

The Madrentine capital sprawled alongside the bank where river met sea, the strong current carrying out to Vara's Bay. Part of it was dug out to form a moat around the city, a green canal forming a second barrier alongside the city walls. There were several gates, all formidable, far more imposing than the gates of Rouleine. And far richer. Partepalas was a city built not for conquest or trade, but for the eye. The Madrentine kings were wealthy, and their city showed it, down to the cobblestones. There were shields of hammered silver decorating the walls and watchtowers, each one etched with the stallion of Madrence.

King Robart's residence, the Palace of Pearls, more than lived up to its name. It jutted out into the river, walled with polished gray and pink stone, its many windows like jewels. *Smaller than my own palace*, Erida knew, *but far more beautiful. Built for pleasure and comfort, for a monarch without fear of war. Until now.*

Only one thing was missing from the city, conspicuously absent. There were no flags: no burgundy silk, no silver horse of King Robart. They were all gone, replaced by a single white banner hanging listless in the still air. The flag meant only one thing.

Surrender.

The entire capital was a perfect, delectable cake, ready to be devoured. And the feast had begun.

Half of her legions were already camped outside the capital, ten thousand of them ready for the occupation. Gallish ships floated in the bay. Only three war galleys, double-decked and green-sailed, but they were more than enough warning. Erida's fleet was coming. It was only a matter of time before the entire port was blockaded. Most of Robart's ships were already gone anyway, leaving the bay half empty.

Erida felt as if she could fly, all but vibrating in her skin. It took every bit of her court training to restrain herself and keep her horse at a trot, holding pace at the head of the column of courtiers. The wary murmurs of her nobles and generals were long gone, replaced with buzzing excitement. For once, Erida shared the sentiment of her court. They wore their finest—steel and silk and brocade reserved for a coronation or funeral. A rope of emeralds winked on Harrsing's neck, with Thornwall's gold chain strung between his shoulders, dangling the image of a roaring lion. Marger, Radolph, and all the rest shone like coins. They knew this was a day to remember, a day to be seen.

For Erida most of all.

Her ladies had outdone themselves in styling her, even so far from Ascal. Her braids were heavy, hanging to the small of her back, woven with gold pins and red silk ribbons. Erida's cheeks blushed the softest pink, the rest of her skin pale white, flawless as the finest Ishei porcelain. She knew she contrasted beautifully with her golden armor and red skirts, the edges embroidered with rose vines in green, gold, and scarlet. The Gallish lion snarled over her crimson cloak, the folds thrown back over her horse's flanks. Even Erida's mare looked the part, her red leather tack oiled to a high sheen, with gold buckles and a rose-patterned blanket beneath her saddle.

While most of Erida's jewels were still locked away in the treasury, she'd known to bring the crown of her father for this very purpose. It was hardly her most beautiful treasure, but certainly it was the oldest. A masterwork of black gold and rough-cut gemstones in every color, worn by the first Gallish king. It had been altered to fit her head, and sat snugly. The ruby at the center of her brow warmed against her skin, big as a thumb. The gem was older still, dating back to the Cor emperors, and the empire she sought to rebuild.

Her appearance was better than the green flags flapping over her army. None would mistake her for anyone other than the victorious Queen of Galland.

She swayed in the saddle as they approached the bridge and main gates of Partepalas. A thousand of her legionnaires were already stationed inside the city, welcomed in ahead of the queen's retinue.

The Ashlanders hung back, the corpse army unneeded. They loomed on the horizon, a dark ribbon over the hillside on the opposite side of the river. Their numbers fell long and black, heavy across the land. Far enough away for her lords and their discomfort, but close enough for Erida to summon; close enough for the corpses to intimidate any who might cross her. Even so, Erida was glad for their distance. The decaying bodies poisoned the air, the corpses stinking and sickly as they marched through the countryside.

Taristan watched them too, with cool satisfaction rather than disgust. He cut a sharp silhouette in his armor and red cloak, his face raised to the sun, though the light somehow never seemed to reach his eyes. They remained black and consuming, immune even to daylight.

Ronin, on the other hand, only looked increasingly agitated with every day of the march, the dust clinging to his robes and face. He sneered at the city ahead.

"What if the King of Madrence has a change of heart?" he hissed, his white fingers clawed on his horse's reins. The mare shuddered beneath him, wary of the wizard.

Erida twitched a smile. "I wish he would." She extended a hand to point, her long sleeve trailing. "There's your archives, Wizard. As promised."

The Library Isle was not an island, not truly, but a tower at the far end of a bridge, the river current breaking around its base. It rose like a sword set on end, taller than a cathedral, with silver-tipped ramparts and a domed observatory at its crown. The Library Isle was known the Ward over as an unparalleled seat of knowledge. If there was any clue as to whereabouts of the next Spindle, Ronin would certainly find it there, among the spiraling shelves and dusty scrolls.

The red wizard eyed the great archives of Partepalas with relish. Erida half expected him to lick his pale lips.

"What realm will it be next?" she said, dropping her voice. Thornwall and the others rode only a few yards away, her Lionguard around them all.

Taristan tore his eyes from the Spindle army to meet her gaze. As always, his stare felt like a sword through her chest. "I do not know."

What more could come? Erida wondered, gritting her teeth. Even with the crown of another country in her grasp, she still felt herself at a disadvantage. *What more could there be?*

"How many does What Waits need?"

Taristan only looked to the Spindleblade, then to Ronin. "I don't know that either."

"We have two still open, and one lost. More must come. Soon," Ronin urged, his expression going sour. "And Corayne must die. We can't afford to lose another Spindle to her."

"She will be dealt with," Taristan ground out.

"My bounty has brought no leads, for Corayne or Konegin." Erida sighed in frustration. *We can overthrow a kingdom but not find a single Corblood girl or my scheming cousin.* "And the Amhara are so far unsuccessful."

"She will be dealt with," Taristan said again, every letter cut sharp, his teeth on edge.

Strangely, his feral focus was almost reassuring. Erida wondered if he had some sort of plan already in place, but the gates of Partepalas rose up before she could ask.

The drawbridge of the city passed beneath her mare's hooves, iron shoes ringing on wood and nails. It felt like entering Rouleine, multiplied a thousand times. She feared her heart might burst, every emotion in her mind rising to the surface. Joy, pride, worry, relief, and regret too, everything steeped in an odd bitter sense. She wanted to laugh and weep in equal measure. But she was a queen—she kept her head high and her expression placid as she emerged from the gate onto the streets of the foreign capital.

Her legion lined the way. They shouted in unison, a mighty cheer to greet their queen and her prince. The people of Partepalas who hadn't been able to flee the city watched Erida's procession too. They stared out from every door, window, and street corner, tracking her movement. Most were silent and blank, their true feelings hidden, their children squirreled away. A few, the bravest, looked down on the conquering queen and her army with disgust. But none raised a hand against their conquerors. No one shouted or threw stones. No one moved at all, frozen to the spot as Erida rode deeper into the city.

"They hate us," Thornwall said, a raw edge to his voice.

Erida looked back to her commander. "They fear us more. And that is victory too."

* * *

The Palace of Pearls echoed, its great polished courtyard of white stone and pearl inlay quiet as a mausoleum. Lionguard armor clanked and cloaks swished, boots rapping across the square. The river lapped at one side, the walls open to the water. It threw off wavering sunlight, dappling the procession in gold and blue as they walked.

"No guards," Erida murmured, noting the emptiness of the palace. She glanced between Thornwall and Taristan. "No soldiers in the city either."

"Whatever army King Robart assembled is long gone from here," Taristan replied, his eyes narrowed.

Thornwall dipped his head. "The legions have their orders. The watchtowers are manned and ready; our scouts are ranging the countryside. If Robart means to catch us unawares, he will have to try very hard indeed."

For not the first time, Erida was glad to have the old commander at her side. "Good."

Her knights threw the doors of the palace wide, ushering them all into the great chambers within. The receiving hall came first, patterned in pink-and-white tile, each stone set with real mother-of-pearl. Erida wanted to tear down the palace brick by brick, so she could ship back every precious gem or stone to her treasury. The marble statues of the Madrentine kings glared down at her as she passed. Erida daydreamed about smashing every face to pieces, until nothing remained at all.

"Where are the courtiers?" she asked. Her voice echoed off marble and limestone, carrying up to the painted ceiling.

"In the throne room, waiting with Robart." Thornwall gestured onward, through another arch. "Not to worry, the Lionguard will be with you every inch of the way."

"I do not fear Robart or his sniveling nobles," Erida said hotly. "These Madrentines are weak." She eyed the chamber again. Every fleck of paint and pearl. Her lip curled with disgust. "They have grown lazy after years of peace, better suited to the coin or quill than the sword or crown."

When she stepped through, she found that the throne was empty, raised on a dais, standing in silhouette against a bank of diamond-paned windows. The blue waters of Vara's Bay flashed in the afternoon sun, a shield of sapphire and gold, the reflections dappling the pale walls of the chamber.

The King of Madrence waited some feet below his former throne, standing on the steps of the dais, his hands clasped behind his back.

Erida didn't break stride as she walked toward him.

"At least Robart is smart enough not to posture," Erida whispered to Thornwall, her eyes falling on the throne.

Even without his throne, Robart still looked a king, done up in burgundy velvet, a jeweled belt around his thick waist. He wore his silver crown, the rubies standing out against blond hair given over to gray. Erida saw his son in his blue eyes and strong jaw, as well as his natural disdain. They scowled the same way.

His courtiers, few as they were, stood in silence like the rest of the city. They looked sullen, eyes downcast, in rumpled clothing with mussed hair. Either these lords and ladies had chosen to stay or were forced to. Erida cared little for either explanation.

The Lionguard fanned out in formation, letting Erida approach the throne. Even Taristan slowed, standing only a few feet ahead of her retinue, with Ronin at his shoulder.

"All hail Erida, Twice Queen of Galland and Madrence," Thornwall shouted, his voice reverberating around the marble hall. "The glory of Old Cor reborn."

Her eyelids fluttered, a shiver of delight running down her spine. She felt as if wings had grown from her shoulder blades, spreading wide, filling the chamber with her majesty and power. Every eye followed her steps across the floor, and she reveled in it. *Twice queen.*

"Your Majesty." The title felt like an insult from Robart's mouth, but he bowed low, bending forward with all the skill of a court-born royal. Erida did not miss the disgust on his face.

It would serve little purpose to nitpick. The throne was already hers. Robart was a broken man, a king no longer. *I've taken everything else from him. I will leave him his ugly looks.*

"Robart," she said firmly, unbowed. Her cloak trailed behind her, the lion roaring across the floor of the throne room. "You are wise to kneel."

The deposed king flinched, his entire body jumping. His mouth worked, jaw clenching and unclenching. But he knew better than to fight back. Slowly, he sank to the floor, his old bones cracking as he fell to a knee.

"My queen," he said hoarsely, gesturing to the throne. His disgust melted to shame as she ascended, leaving Robart broken upon the steps.

The throne of Madrence was pearl and silver, cushioned with dark red velvet. It was magnificent but not imposing, nothing to fear. Erida sank into it with a languid sigh, exhaling all the failures of the men who came before her.

It is I who sits on another throne, who wears a second crown. A woman, and no one else.

Around the hall, the others dropped to their knees, Taristan and her own courtiers as well as the lords and ladies of Madrence. They were less reluctant than their king, more eager to get the whole conquest business finished. Erida could not blame them. Already she tired at the prospect of judging their loyalty.

But it needed to be done and done quickly.

Erida twitched her fingers, motioning for everyone to stand.

"I will hear your oaths and allegiances," she said firmly, folding her hands in her lap. Hawkish, she surveyed the room with a keen eye. She knew a few names already, the more powerful nobles of Madrence. "And I require a chair for my consort, the Prince of Old Cor."

Taristan's face didn't move, but Erida saw the satisfaction in the set of his shoulders, the steady motion of his hands, and his easy, deliberate steps forward, his loping wolf stride more fearsome than any knight in the hall.

Robart's restraint broke.

"That monster killed my son in cold blood," he snarled, coming to the foot of the dais with fists curled. He was of a height with Taristan, but still seemed so much smaller, a weak excuse for a king. Taristan halted a yard from Robart, unbothered. His manner incensed the king further, Robart's face going red.

"How dare you stand here among us," he hissed. "Have you no shame? No soul?"

On the throne, Erida did not move. She weighed the room quickly, eyeing the Madrentine nobles standing to one side. They shared their king's disgust, and for some, even his grief. Briefly, Erida wondered how many courtiers the charming Prince Orleon had bedded before meeting his end.

Not that it mattered. Orleon was a fool, far more useful as a corpse than a living prince.

"The death of your son, and the deaths of the people in Rouleine, have saved all your lives," she said coldly.

It was the truth, and they knew it, even Robart. The fall of Rouleine was a storm cloud over the continent, the news of its overthrow spreading far and wide, shouted in the streets and country lanes.

"Saved us—from something so low as hunger," Robart forced out, each word quavering. "They speak of it all over the Ward. The Lion of Galland is awake, and hungry. Erida's army has no equal upon the Ward, and she will make herself empress of all the realm, with a Corblood prince at her side. No matter the cost, no matter how much blood she and her armies spill."

There was something else he did not say, laced between his words. She could taste his terror, and felt it in the whispers that followed them all the way from Rouleine. Erida heard it on the road, and in the streets. She saw it in Robart now, and his silent courtiers.

Queen Erida controls an army of the dead.

"Are you finished?" she said, flicking her eyes over the fallen king.

Robart hung his head, dropping his eyes from Taristan. Slowly, he shuffled out of the way. Whatever fire the old king had left, it guttered and died, leaving only ashes.

A pair of servants materialized from the corner of the chamber, carrying an ornate seat between them. They put it down and Taristan ascended, taking his place at Erida's side.

Robart watched with watery eyes, his gaze wavering between them, but he said nothing.

"You are wise to surrender, Robart." Erida ran a hand down the arm of her new throne; the cool stone and pearl was carved into the likeness of a stallion, she noticed. "Will your daughter do the same?"

The king went white. "My—"

A delightful vindication curled around Erida's heart. "The Princess of Madrence. Your only living heir now that Orleon is dead," she said, steely. She did not miss the fear rippling through the courtiers in the hall. Nor the pride on Thornwall and Harrsing. "I do not see her here. Her name is Marguerite, yes? She would be fifteen by now."

"Yes, Your Majesty," Robart whimpered, falling to his knees.

Erida had learned many lessons, politics and history best of all. She knew the risk of a lost heir, and the danger of a young woman underestimated.

"The same age I was when I first sat on the throne," she pushed on. "*Where* is she?"

Robart raised shaking hands, as if to defend himself from a blow. "An Adalenian convent, near Pennaline. After her mother died, I thought it best for her education. She is a quiet child, with no aspirations to a crown; you need not worry—"

Erida cut him off with a dismissive wave, her emerald flashing. "I'm sure you are eager to see her again. May you both live out the rest of your days in quiet peace."

"And where might that be?" Robart said hoarsely. He didn't even have the strength to look afraid.

Thornwall crooked a finger, a silent command to his knights. A pair jumped to attention, swords drawn as they flanked the old king. Robart barely flinched, heaving a weary sigh.

"I can think of no quieter place than a jail cell." Erida watched, stone-faced, as Robart was led away. He did not fight, and she looked to his courtiers instead, weighing their reaction. Only a few looked stricken, fewer than she'd expected. "I will not win an empire just to lose it to pretender kings and errant princesses. I will not build a glorious land only to destroy it with civil war."

In his chair, Taristan made a small noise in his throat. Erida only shot him a warning glance.

"We have a long day ahead of us," she whispered through clenched teeth. "Don't make it more difficult."

His lips twitched and he raised a hand, hiding his mouth from the chamber. "Wouldn't it be easier to execute them all?"

Erida's first instinct was to roll her eyes. But she caught herself, slowly turning the option over in her mind. Rouleine was a massacre, difficult to forget. The memory of it still turned her stomach. *But it bought us the surrender of the entire kingdom. Would the slaughter of the Madrentine court bring us the realm?* She hesitated, holding Taristan's stare.

Then soft fingers on her arm startled her out of her thoughts. Erida turned to see Lady Harrsing standing over her, her other hand clawed on her cane. Her face was lined with age and worry, her pale eyes locked on Erida's. The chain of emeralds bobbed at her neck, moving with the motion of her throat. She offered a small, tight-lipped smile, before bowing her head to both Erida and Taristan.

"Your Majesty, you have won their fear," she murmured, still holding on to the Queen's sleeve.

Erida barely felt it, the touch light and gentle. She would have commanded away anyone else, but not Bella Harrsing. Even the Lionguard knew to leave her be.

"Go on, Bella," Erida said, putting her own hand over Harrsing's. Her skin was cold and white, bloodless.

Harrsing pressed in close. She smelled of rosewater. "You have their fear," she repeated.

"I do not want their love," Erida replied hotly.

"No, not love. They will never love us." She shook her head at the court, despairing of the Madrentines as any good daughter of Galland would. Her voice dropped, her eyes flicking over Taristan again. "But they must respect you. Let them live. Let them see what a *queen* you are. How much better you are than the soft kings who came before, who sat this throne and did nothing but drink wine and write poetry." Harrsing's fingers tightened on Erida's arm, her grip surprisingly strong. "Show them what *real* power is."

Real power. Erida felt it flowing through her veins now, as if drawn from the throne beneath her and the crown on her brow. It was more seductive than anything and anyone the Queen had ever known. She wanted more of it, but beyond that, she wanted to keep it.

She gave Harrsing a reassuring squeeze. "You are wiser than your years, Bella."

"A high bar to clear," her lady answered, offering her usual smile.

But Harrsing's pale eyes remained stern, without a spark. Shuttered like a pair of windows closed.

"You have steel in your spine, Your Majesty," she said, straightening up. Again she glanced to Taristan, and Erida saw him tighten out of the corner of her eye. "Hold on to it. But bend when you must, lest you—and your crown—break."

With that Lady Harrsing shuffled away, returning to her place alongside Lord Thornwall. Her smile vanished, replaced by a cool, blank expression, her mask forged by many decades at court, and she dropped her gaze to the pearl-and-marble floor.

Taristan continued to glare after Harrsing, his black eyes gleaming with that red sheen. Doubt twisted in Erida, uncomfortable as a hot hand on a fevered brow. But she dismissed the sensation quickly. Bella Harrsing was loyal to the throne, more than anyone else, her allegiance proven a dozen times over. They sat in a room filled with enemies, but she wasn't one of them.

And they had far greater matters to attend to than the likes of an old woman.

Erida of Galland and Madrence drew herself up on her throne, gesturing to the steps beneath her.

"Who kneels first?"

18

THE FIRST REMEMBERED
Sorasa

The assassin felt torn in two. Sorasa knew better than to sample the prince's ale, his wine, or his blistering gorzka. She could already see the white liquor burning its way down a dozen throats. But she ached for the numbing embrace of a goblet, if only to take the edge off the memories churning in her mind. She still saw her fellow Amhara in every person and every shadow. They dogged the corners of her eyes, her stomach lurching with each new illusion. Even Oscovko wore the face of a dead man, Luc's features obscuring his own.

She blinked the vision away, trying to focus. A feast was a good opportunity for an assassin, and Sorasa knew that better than anyone. She'd used her fair share of banquets and galas to disguise a kill, employing the cover of chaos to fulfill her contracts.

Chaos spiraled around them now.

The great hall, so empty only a few hours ago, had been swept clean, with more long tables dragged in and the shuttered windows thrown wide. Somehow, the hall seemed bigger crowded with hundreds of people. There were Treckish nobles, lords and ladies in fine clothes, with braided hair and beards. Most of the men wore naked sabers at their belts, the steel flashing with every step. Oscovko's war camp comprised both Treckish soldiers and mercenaries, all men, hailing from nearly every corner of Allward. Their faces were a rainbow, ranging from a milk-skinned Jydi axman to a Nironese archer with a jet-black face and telltale ebony bow. Clearly Trec had no issue with weapons at the dinner table.

Most soldiers sat on the long benches or roved around like errant jackals. A few brawled, exchanging blows as easily as handshakes. Sorasa paid them no mind. The Treckish were quick to fight, and even quicker to feast.

Plates of food ran the length of every surface, platters piled high with roast chicken, salted pork, and more potatoes than Sorasa knew existed. Barrels of wine and ale lined the far wall, overseen by a particularly loud Treckish soldier. Night pressed in at the windows, but many candles and torches flamed, smoking in the close, warm air. Everything smelled of alcohol and meat and sour breath, and Sorasa wrinkled her nose as they walked through the hall. Corayne didn't seem to mind, her eyes alight, while Dom soldiered on, cutting a path through the crowd of Oscovko's lieutenants.

The King of Trec was nowhere to be seen. Sorasa wondered if Valtik was still with him in his apartments, tending to the blind ruler, singing her rhymes and Jydi lullabies. She could think of nothing more bothersome.

To Sorasa's relief, there were other women in attendance. Wives, noble ladies, a few camp women in their finest dresses. But no warriors. *Corayne, Sigil, and I won't draw more attention than usual*, she thought. *Well, Corayne and I won't, at least.*

Sigil was already among the men, a foot taller than most of them, and easy to spot. Her black hair was getting long, hanging shaggily around her ears. She wore no dress but a tunic and leather vest instead, laced up to her neck, with tapered trousers and her old brown boots. Oscovko drank at her side, a horn of ale in one hand, a sipping glass of gorzka in the other. The history between Trec and the Temurijon was long, written in blood, but the prince's approval kept off the stares of older soldiers. At least for now.

Corayne eyed the crowd with focus, and Sorasa perceived. She looked for the squire, her head craning back and forth to search through the sea of faces.

"He's by the windows," Sorasa whispered in Corayne's ear.

She gave a grateful smile in reply and set off, crossing the hall to join Andry at the dais. He beamed when she reached him, gesturing to something beyond the open window, down in the city. The empty throne loomed over them, the white limestone like old bone in the candlelight.

Like Corayne, the squire was newly clean, the muck of the road scrubbed away. He alone seemed at home at the feast, used to life in a busy court. *Vodin is probably tame in comparison*, Sorasa thought, remembering the New Palace in Ascal, and its monstrous halls.

"Leave it to the squire to find the quietest place at a party," Sorasa muttered, her voice lost in the din of the crowd.

Lost to all but an immortal's ears.

Dom looked at her over his shoulder, his gaze green and withering. "It isn't wise to push them together, Sorasa. And don't feel like you must hover over me all night."

She shrugged, coming up alongside him. He frowned at her closeness but said nothing, turning his focus back to Corayne.

"Annoying as you are, Elder, you're also quite useful," Sorasa said.

She enjoyed the shock as it crossed his face. Dom blinked down at her.

"Have you gotten into the wine already, Sarn?"

"These Treckish would not dare approach an immortal prince," Sorasa explained, ignoring his jab. "I'm simply reaping the benefits of your long shadow."

She nodded to the men and women around them. They gave the pair a wide berth. Dom hardly seemed to care. Sorasa wondered if he noticed the mortals at all.

"Little do they know, you're the danger here," Dom grumbled. "Not me."

"That's the kindest thing you've ever said to me, Elder."

"Well, now that I have your attention, I say again . . ." He bent to her level, looking her square in the eye. Torchlight flickered in his emerald stare. "Stop meddling with Corayne and Andry."

"They're a pair of teenagers bound to save the realm or die trying, stuck together on this impossible journey. Believe me, there's no meddling needed," she said curtly.

Dom sighed, wrenching his eyes away from the windows. "I

suppose not. I only wish Corayne were better at hiding herself, her emotions."

"I don't," she said, taking even herself by surprise.

The immortal whirled, his brow set in a single tight line. "*You* don't?"

"Corayne can be herself without a second thought," Sorasa answered, finding the words only as she spoke them. "She can wear her own face instead of a mask."

Her cheeks went hot, and she wished for a hood or cowl. A Tyri veil woven with gold coins. Ibalet makeup and powder. Anything to hide the crack in her own mask. She felt it grow wider and wider, struggling to hold back all she kept at bay. Dom looked down at her, his eyes ticking over her expression. The Elder was hardly a perceptive man, but he wasn't blind. She saw the compassion well up in his eyes, the same terrible remorse she remembered from the hills, in the clearing, when her hands ran scarlet with Amhara blood. She hated every second of it, and nearly bolted from the hall. Her fingers jumped, eager to grab a glass of gorzka from the nearest table. If only to force it down Domacridhan's throat, and save herself from an entire night of his brooding judgment.

His lips parted, and she braced for an interrogation or, worse, *pity*.

"You are only encouraging heartbreak, Sorasa," he said, turning away. It sounded like a reprimand. And a mercy.

She let out a relieved sigh, the tension unclenching in her chest.

"Perhaps you should stop worrying about their hearts, and tend to your own instead," she muttered, sizing him up with a sly look.

Like Sigil, he was bigger than most of the soldiers in the room, cutting a fine figure. The Spindleblade on his back made him look more rugged than she knew him to be, like a warrior instead of a prince.

Dom prickled under her scrutiny. "I do not follow your line of thought."

She smirked and gestured to the room, waving her hand at the roving current of courtiers and soldiers. Men in finely embroidered tunics. Ladies in their dresses, their hair done up in traditional Treckish braids, their sleeves trailing long laces of precious gold and silver thread. More than a few eyed Dom as they passed, just as they eyed Sorasa, wondering who they were. And more.

"I count at least six people in this room, man and woman both," Sorasa said, "who would happily keep you company for the night."

A fluster came over Dom for the second time that night. Flushing, he reached for a small glass of gorzka and gulped it down. He gasped at the taste.

"Six," he finally muttered, sounding shocked.

Sorasa almost rolled her eyes. For all his Elder senses, he was still entirely clueless about many things, most of all mortal emotion. She jerked her chin, nodding in several directions, to lords and ladies around the room. One was far bolder than the others, a young woman with red hair, milk skin, and eyes as green as Dom's. She idled close by, unmoving, watching him like a crocodile. Patient and waiting.

"It may be the last chance you ever have," Sorasa said, shrugging.

He narrowed his eyes, going sullen, and grabbed for another

searing glass. "I have little desire to bed a mortal, let alone one I will never see again."

To Sorasa's surprise, he pressed the gorzka into her hand. Her fingers closed around it eagerly, but she couldn't make herself raise it to her lips.

"I should've known you were picky with your partners," she said, scoffing.

Dom sneered back at her, his annoyance palpable, all but rolling off his shoulders. He seemed more animal than immortal again, his teeth too sharp in the candlelight.

"I won't even try to count how many would eagerly join you this evening," he bit out, his eyes on the crowd.

"That isn't a compliment," she answered. "Half these men would fuck a tree stump without a second thought."

Sorasa watched him wince, his lip curling with distaste. It rankled something in her, and her grip tightened on her drink, the glass threatening to shatter.

"I've seen you cut people in half, Domacridhan," she snapped. "Don't tell me a few curse words and a few inches of skin have you so rattled."

"I am hardly rattled," he said neatly, his face going blank as if to prove a point. But like Corayne, he had little practice with masks. His cheeks were still flushed, pale pink blooming around his scars.

"Be careful with the gorzka." Sorasa took a step back, curtsying better than any courtier. Then she swallowed down the liquor in a single motion. "It sneaks up on you."

He growled in her wake, but did not follow her, content to let the crowd close between them as she stalked away. The gorzka blazed down her throat, stinging and soothing in equal measure. Sorasa yearned for another but ignored the many glasses around the hall, grabbing a corner of bread instead. She choked it down as she navigated the crowd. Like Dom, a mouth full of food was just as useful in keeping away conversation.

Brawling soldiers barreled past, forcing her to weave between the tables. Two Treckish nobles clasped hands, their elbows braced, each trying to force the other's hand over. Another Treckish tradition.

She almost jumped when Charlie crossed her path, a glass of wine in hand. Her stomach twisted. Looking at him was like looking backward in time.

Charlie was done up in the finest clothes the castle of Volaska had to offer—a gold brocade vest over pale orange silk, fur-lined boots, and a fine pendant dangling from his neck. His brown hair was loose and freshly washed, curling past his shoulder blades, his face clean-shaven again after weeks of travel.

This was the Charlon Armont she remembered meeting two years ago. A fugitive already, a legend in the making. Barely twenty years old, and somehow the best forger in half the Ward, both respected for and dangerous with his gift.

Part of her expected Garion to slink out of the crowd, his thin dueling sword at his belt, his half grin reserved for Charlie and Charlie alone. The Amhara assassin and the fallen priest made a formidable pair, deadly with blade and ink. But Garion was not here. *At least he isn't dead with the others, his corpse left to feed the crows.*

For that Sorasa was grateful. And she knew Charlie was too.

Charlie furrowed his brow, meeting her gaze. "Something wrong?" he asked, his voice bringing her back to the world around them. The easy smile on his lips fell a little.

She shook her head, chasing off the memories. "Nothing."

But Charlie leaned closer. He nudged her shoulder with his glass. "No drink?"

"Not yet. I must stay sharp." Sorasa's eyes roved the chamber again, each shadow a potential danger. Nothing escaped her attention. "If another Amhara comes, I want to be ready."

Charlie's smile dropped entirely. His round brown eyes went impossibly dark, even in the torchlight. Slowly, he sipped his wine. Not to savor the taste, but to collect himself.

"And if Garion steps out of the shadows?" he said, his voice too low, strangled with emotion. "What then?"

Sorasa wanted to take the glass from his hand and drain it down. She kept still instead, holding his black stare.

"I don't think that's my choice to make," she murmured. In her heart, she prayed such a thing would not come to pass. "It's yours."

The fallen priest finished his wine. He studied the empty glass, letting the facets catch the flickering light. A rainbow played between his fingers, and his eyes went far away. To where, Sorasa knew.

A different place, in a different life.

He gritted his teeth. "I suppose that's the best I can hope for."

"Hope," Sorasa scoffed. She forced a grin and knocked him with her shoulder. "You're starting to sound like Corayne and Andry."

Charlie's smile returned, sharper and smaller. But still there.

He clutched at his heart, rolling his eyes. "How you wound me, Sarn."

It took some shouldering and well-placed elbows, but Sorasa finally slipped through the throng around the prince's table. Tonight Oscovko wore his crown, a braided band of old iron and copper across his brow. His wolf fur was gone, replaced by a black overcoat and leather breeches. White wolves ran the length of his sleeves, his collar unlaced to show the top of his chest, his collarbone, and a thick gold chain. He sat on the tabletop, his heavy boots on the bench, the fawning soldiers of his war camp ringed around him. Sigil was still at his table, a massive tankard of ale in her hand, but she sipped it slowly and quietly. Far from her usual behavior.

"Everything all right?" Sorasa said, drawing up beside her. She eyed the ale with worry.

Sigil heaved a breath, leaning on her elbows. She ran a hand through her black hair, the ends falling straight and thick over one brown eye.

"The young men don't trust a woman to fight. And a few of the old men remember the wars with my country a bit too well." She shrugged. "Not to mention they're all drunk already. We'll be lucky if the night ends without a brawl."

Sorasa dropped her voice. "I'd bet on you."

"Even I know better than to punch one of these soldiers and risk losing our only ally," she replied, forcing down a gulp. Her eyes darted around the table. The prince's soldiers eyed her in return, their harried glances ranging from fascination to disgust. "But we're meant to ride with these men, fight alongside them.

How can I do that if they don't believe in my ax or your dagger? In *Corayne*?"

At that, Oscovko told the punch line of some crude joke, and his men roared out their laughter. They clanked their ales together to cheer, toasting their prince. He raised his tankard with them and clinked it against Sigil's with a meaningful nod. She smiled tightly in reply.

"At least the prince is doing what he can to smooth things over," Sorasa said as he returned to his tales, each one more boastful than the last.

Sigil pulled at her ale. Her eyes narrowed. "He's trying."

The men around them were Oscovko's favorites. Only a few nobles, to Sorasa's eye, but soldiers all, their worth proven on the battlefield and in the war camps. They were hard men, grizzled and red-faced with drink, with scarred hands and darting eyes. She was reminded of the wolves on Oscovko's clothes and his castle. Hardy, wild, but united in their cause. And loyal to their leader.

"The Treckish respect strength. Victory," the assassin said, leaning closer to Sigil. "Let the young ones see your strength. Let the old ones see you as an ally."

She quirked an eyebrow. "How?"

"Maybe you *should* fight half the room," Sorasa said. She felt a true grin rise to her face, delighted at the thought. "After a fashion."

Sigil's face tightened in confusion and she tipped her head to one side, waiting for an explanation.

Instead Sorasa leaned forward and braced her elbow on the table, her hand raised and palm open. Grinning, she wiggled her fingers in invitation.

The bounty hunter blinked, then smiled, her thin lips pulled wide across her face, until her white teeth gleamed in the candlelight. She mirrored Sorasa, extending her own hand with something near to a giggle.

She took Sorasa's hand in her own, her elbow solid against the wooden tabletop. Sorasa could already feel Sigil's bone-breaking grip, tight on her fingers, threatening to snap them in two.

"The iron bones of the Countless . . . ," Sigil began, all but licking her lips.

"Will never be broken," Sorasa finished, her knuckles crashing against the table as Sigil pinned her hand.

A roar went up from the Treckish men, with Oscovko loudest of all. There was nothing the Treckish loved more than an opportunity to show their mettle.

Charlie and Corayne took the bets, roving around the great hall, Charlie with a scrap of parchment in hand and a quill between his teeth. They calculated the odds quickly, the pair of them collecting coin and wagers from the soldiers and the Treckish court. Oscovko was most favored, naturally, and he took his place at the table with an easy, relaxed grin. He didn't even bother to put down his drink, having switched to gorzka for the strength matches. The prince put away his first opponent with ease, wrestling a soldier's arm flat to a chorus of applause.

So it went down the long table, to Sorasa's delight. Soldiers crowded the benches, sitting opposite their fellow countrymen, eager to show off their strength or too drunk to know they shouldn't. Even Andry found himself shoved into the competition, though he protested heartily. Corayne only laughed and put him on her list.

Sigil fell in with them, her sleeve rolled up over her forearm, showing bronze skin corded with sculpted muscle. Sorasa smothered a grin. This was Sigil's arena, and an easy chance to win over the men around them.

"Join us, Amhara!" Prince Oscovko hooted, trying to make room on the bench for her.

Her grin disappeared and she backed away, arms folded over her dress. "I know my own measure," she said. "My value is not at the match table."

The prince pulled an exaggerated frown but didn't argue, turning back to his next victim. When he won again, he gestured for another glass, barking to a nearby servant.

"He'll be blind by the end of the night," Dom said, standing back from the fray. "This is no way for a prince to behave."

Rolling her eyes, Sorasa looked him over. The immortal seemed out of place now, one of the only warriors in the hall hanging back. He stood away from the crowd, and a few eager-eyed ladies still floated nearby. The redheaded woman was there too, sipping slowly at a small glass.

"Scared to compete?" Sorasa sneered, if only to rile him up. She knew better than any that Dom could best any mortal upon the Ward.

Except maybe Taristan, she thought darkly.

"I will not rise to your bait, Sorasa," he answered in an even voice, his eyes on the long table. He followed Corayne as she flitted through the crowd with Charlie, adjusting the bets as the matches went on.

She shrugged. "Just as well. You'd ruin my plan, as you do most things."

"*This* is planned?" he blanched, gesturing to the haphazard collection of strength matches, spilled ale, and jeering courtiers. Oscovko bellowed through it all, stomping his boots and smashing glasses with each victory.

Sorasa kept her own watch on Sigil. The Temur woman drank more deeply of her ale, her smile growing with every win, even as the Treckish soldiers lined up to challenge her.

"Trec and the Temurijon are old enemies, with a long history of rancor and bloodshed," Sorasa explained out of the corner of her mouth. "Emperor Bhur nearly wiped Trec off the map in the last conquest. The old veterans remember the wars, and the young soldiers are wary to fight alongside us weak, whimpering women."

At that Dom laughed outright.

"So here we are. The match table is Treckish tradition, a display of friendship as well as strength. Let them see that Sigil is just as good a soldier as anyone in the room, and just as willing to fight *with* them, not against them."

Dom furrowed his brow, unconvinced. "And this contest will do that?"

"That's the idea," Sorasa said.

"I see."

She could tell by his tone he did not see, and she huffed a despairing breath. For all his years and all his immortal gifts, Dom had less court sense than a peasant child. The machinations and manipulations of a royal court were beyond his grasp, or simply beneath his concern. *He wouldn't survive a week of Amhara training, Elder or not.*

"Andry's doing well," Dom muttered, nodding down the table.

Indeed the squire had a tally of wins, remaining on the bench even as others were eliminated. But the match clearly didn't suit him, and after taking down an older soldier, Andry stood back from the table with raised hands. Sorasa had expected nothing less.

"And what of you?" the Elder added, his eyes trailing over Sorasa's own hands. He lingered on her tattoos, the ones she shared with all her brethren, living or dead. "Did they not teach this in your guild?"

"I'd rather cut a man's throat than hold his hand," she bit back, folding her palms away. "Besides, we Amhara are not meant to be remembered. We kill and we disappear. We don't stand around and beg for praise."

"Well, you'll be the first, then," Dom said, matter-of-fact.

She pursed her lips, confused. "The first?"

He only blinked at her, as if the answer were obvious.

"The first Amhara remembered," he said roughly, his green eyes boring into her own. "If we can save the realm, that is."

The first remembered. Sorasa turned the words over in her mind, trying to comprehend them. They seemed to stick together, refusing to come undone, like a tangled knot. Amhara served the Guild, served the legacy of the greatest assassins, served Lord Mercury, served each other, even, but never themselves. Never the singular. Never one above the rest, and especially not above Mercury himself. The Amhara valued glory above almost all things, but for the Guild. It was not their way to rise alone, to carry their own names beyond the walls of the citadel. She felt her cheeks go hot. Even thinking about it felt wrong, running up against the teachings hammered into her bone and blood.

Dom continued to stare at her, going quiet amid the chaos of the feast. He waited, a mountain unmoved by a storm.

"It is not the Amhara way," she muttered, her voice weak.

He shifted, the firelight playing across his face. "You are not Amhara anymore."

The words felt like a knife in her heart, a killing blow. But also a lifting weight. Her breath caught in her throat, both sensations warring in her mind.

"I have no desire to be remembered," Sorasa finally said, the words stilted and forced. "Surviving all this will be good enough."

"Agreed," he rumbled, going stone-faced. "We'll make it through."

Liar, she knew, noting the hard set of his jaw. But Sorasa kept her mouth shut. *If the immortal dies, so be it. So long as Corayne lives, the Ward has a chance.*

Though that chance is small already.

In her mind, she walked the path ahead of them, through the Gates of Trec and into the Gallish foothills, to a lost temple overrun with Taristan's foul creatures. It would be a daunting task, with too many variables for even Sorasa to count. She gritted her teeth, fighting off despair before it could set in.

But then a Treckish lord stood from the table. He was easily the biggest person in the room, taller even than Dom, barrel-chested and formidable, his beard forked into two braids, with thick iron bracelets at each wrist to mark his high status. He was no simpering courtier like the lords in Ascal, strangers to war and hardship. Sorasa sized him up as he walked toward her, his intent clear in his gray eyes.

She sucked in a breath and braced herself. Normally, she wouldn't think twice about turning down a man's advances, but she didn't want to offend anyone either, no matter how annoying they were. They needed the Treckish support. It was a small needle to thread.

But the Treckish lord stopped abruptly, his gaze jumping from Sorasa to Dom beside her. He drew himself up, puffing out his chest, and raised a glass of purple wine in his meaty fist.

"Lord Elder," he ground out, his voice heavily accented with sharp Treckish. "I challenge you to the table."

Sorasa fought a barking laugh, biting her lip shut.

Beside her, Dom went pale. Instead of preening like the lord, he looked like he wanted to jump out the nearest window.

"Oh yes, Lord Elder," the redheaded lady said, jumping to his side. He flinched when she took his arm, her green eyes going starry. "We have all heard legends of your immortal strength. Show us."

Sorasa bit harder, nearly drawing blood.

"I beg your pardon," Dom said, stumbling over his words. He looked between the lord and the woman, both of them gesturing to the match table. More than a few heads rose, eager to see the immortal prince in action. Gingerly, he removed himself from the lady's grasp, peeling her fingers off his arm.

"It is not my way," he finally offered, bowing his head to the lord. "The Vedera do not take part in"—he eyed the table, pointing vaguely—"*this*."

"But it is *our* way, Elder," the lord said gruffly, pressing forward, his voice a little more firm. Far harder than Sorasa liked.

"It is the way of the Temur too," she said neatly, slipping between them. Her mask rose, easy to don, even after so many years. With a soft smile and a bat of her eyelashes, Sorasa took the lord's arm, her movements quick and deliberate. "Sigil of the Temurijon has bested all upon the table. Has she bested you, my lord?"

The Treckish man looked down at Sorasa, going doe-eyed. Then he grinned, forcing down his wine. "No, she has not," he ground out, stomping off with Sorasa still on his arm.

She caught a flash of gold out of the corner of her eye as Dom followed, close as the folds of a cloak.

"May I have this dance, Temur?" the lord said, pulling another man off the bench in front of Sigil. He sat without invitation, hugging Sorasa close with one arm while bracing the other for the match.

Sigil eyed Sorasa first, her expression unreadable. Sorasa could only smirk.

"Don't break his hand," she said in Ibalet, and Sigil grinned.

Thirty seconds later the lord limped away, cradling his wrist. Sigil could only shrug.

"We can't fight an army if you cripple our own soldiers," Sorasa hissed.

"You didn't say anything about the wrist," she protested, forcing out an apology.

It was Oscovko who answered, coming up behind the Amhara with his oddly quiet steps. He took the bench.

"Shall we settle this, Sigil of the Temurijon?" he said, planting his elbow. "It seems you and I are the last ones upon the table."

Indeed, the benches had emptied, leaving only the Temur bounty hunter and the Prince of Trec.

The rest of the great hall looked on, the crowd dizzy with competition and heat and wine. Most cheered for their prince, slapping their hands on the table or their thighs, beating out the rhythm of a war drum. It spread through the feast, thumping like a rush of blood, until even Sorasa wanted to join in. But she refrained, stepping back from the table to watch with the rest of them.

Corayne shouted above the noise, collecting a few last bets for Charlie, with Andry acting as go-between. Valtik had reappeared at some point during the evening. She crouched in the corner, barely a blue-eyed shadow, cracking bones between her teeth. And Dom deflated, glad to be ignored.

A muscle worked in Sigil's jaw, her face thrown into sharp relief by the many torches. Her bronze skin seemed to glow, her eyes dancing with the light. She pushed back the usual lock of hair from her eye and set her elbow, her palm offered to the prince. If she felt the pressure of the moment, she didn't show it. Her grin returned, half-wild.

The prince matched her smile and took her hand, his fingers closing over her own, their palms pressed together. The rough edge of his stubbled cheek lifted, one corner of his mouth curling into a half smirk.

"For Trec!" he bellowed, to the delight of the hall.

"For the Ward!" she answered, to another resounding cheer.

Both grunted, and the match began, their faces going red in unison, their brows set into deep, unyielding lines. Oscovko puffed out a breath, his knuckles white beneath his skin, as the muscles stood out in Sigil's forearm, her own breath coming hard. She gritted her teeth, their hands trembling together, neither side budging an inch.

"Oscovko! Oscovko!" the Treckish shouted around the room, clanging cups and slamming tables. Sorasa was reminded of the tavern brawl in Adira. "The White Wolf of Trec!"

"Sigil!" Sorasa felt herself cheer in reply, raising her voice so it carried. "Sigaalbeta Bhur Bhar!"

At the sound of her full Temur name, Sigil's eyes flashed, her teeth wearing at the edge of her lip. She blew out another steadying breath and kept fighting, throwing her full weight into her fist. Oscovko let out a groan of pain, a bead of sweat rolling down his forehead. His face was beet red now, brighter than a swath of fresh blood. His muscles worked at his collar, tight beneath his skin.

The shouting and cheering continued, with more than a few of the Treckish clapping for Sigil as well as their prince. Sorasa kept up her shout, applauding, and gestured for the others to follow suit. Dom roared louder than them all, raising his fists in the air.

"The iron bones of the Countless will never be broken!" he boomed out.

It was the last nail in Oscovko's coffin.

Sigil let out a guttural cry, the war scream of the Temurijon, and slammed the prince's fist back against the tabletop. His body nearly went with it, twisting to keep his arm from snapping in two. As Sigil leapt to her feet, hands raised in triumph, so did he. The hall thundered with cheering as he took her wrist in his spare hand, the other cradled into his chest. With a shout, Oscovko raised their joined hands together, celebrating her victory for all the feast to see. And the soldiers celebrated with him, spilling wine and ale and good wishes.

"We ride tomorrow, for war and the Ward!" he called.

"For the Ward!" his men answered.

"For the Ward!" Sigil bellowed.

For the Ward, Sorasa thought.

Hope fluttered in her chest, flickering, the light of a single candle. But too small, too weak. The hall echoed with triumph, but all Sorasa heard was the tolling of a death knell. Even as she smiled, dread curled in her belly. It was never far away, but now it reached for her with icy claws, its sting sinking too deep.

19

THE RUTHLESS CHOSEN
Erida

Even covered in burgundy velvet, the throne of Madrence was uncomfortable, the stone cold through the fabric, the high back maddeningly straight. After a long morning of sitting in council, Erida was eager to walk off the ache.

With a forced smile, she left Thornwall and Harrsing in the throne room and swept out to join her retinue of waiting ladies. She wished she could dismiss the various girls and women outright. They served little purpose on the campaign, besides making her presentable for the day. And spying for their families or husbands. But appearances were important, maddeningly so, and therefore the ladies remained. They followed at a respectable distance, murmuring among themselves, their voices a low hum.

The Lionguard trailed her, silent but for their clanking armor, ever present as she stalked the unfamiliar halls of the palace. As they walked, Erida took stock of the oaths again, going over the many Madrentine nobles who pledged fealty to her yesterday. She spent hours listening to simpering praise and veiled insults. *Young*, most of the nobles called her, bowing their heads to their bold conqueror. Erida knew better than to think it a compliment. They saw her as a child, a girl, barely old enough to rule herself, let alone two kingdoms with the making of empire.

They are wrong, and soon they will know it, she thought.

In the windows, clouds rolled in across the bay, darkening the afternoon, with only a beam of gold on the western horizon. The once-brilliant halls went dull, the pearl tiles losing their luster. Robart's palace felt suddenly small and unimpressive, a pittance compared to Erida's home many hundreds of miles away.

She had not expected to miss the New Palace, but a small ache crept up inside her. She missed the gardens, the cathedral, the stained-glass windows filled with mighty Syrek and the many gods. Her peerless city, overwhelming in its size, filled with her many thousands of loyal people. They cheered even for a glimpse of their queen. Not like the people of Rouleine and Partepalas, who spat at her feet and spilled blood for spite.

Erida wandered with no real direction, but her feet led her out into the magnificent palace gardens. Trees and flowers bloomed, the air perfumed with all scents, and a fountain rippled somewhere, undercut with birdsong. Small ponies picked their way among the grasses, their round bellies like shiny golden coins. Part of Erida wanted to expel them from the palace. They were, after all, Prince Orleon's pets, and she didn't need any more reminders of the dead.

She glanced at the darkening sky, weighing the threat of rain. Against everything else, a storm felt like nothing at all.

The city is yours. The kingdom is yours, she thought. The many nerves in her body began to uncoil, releasing slowly. *The next will fall, and the next. Until all the map is your own.*

She smiled to herself, trying to picture Allward in her mind. From the Nironese rain forest to the Jydi snows. The sweltering Tiger Gulf to the glens of Calidon. Ascal, the jewel in her crown, to the steppes of the Temurijon and Emperor Bhur. So many thrones, so many kingdoms. Some would kneel, stricken by her rampage through Madrence. Many would not.

Erida's jaw clenched, her teeth grinding together. Whatever relief she felt moments ago disappeared, fading as she listed the great obstacles in her way. The many dangers on the road to her destiny.

"Twice Queen," a deep voice said, and Erida's toes curled.

The Lionguard knew to let Taristan approach.

He appeared from somewhere down the path, stepping out from a line of poplar trees. Erida felt her ladies react behind her, some of them whispering. A few knew better, going silent. With a single wave of her hand, she dismissed them all, sending them scurrying back into the palace.

The Lionguard remained, a loose ring around their queen.

"I thought you were still helping Ronin in the archives," Erida called down the path to him. He walked toward her at an easy pace. "Reaching high shelves and the like."

The corner of his mouth twitched, betraying the urge to smile. "I'm wasted in the pages."

Taristan fidgeted in the garden, out of place, as always. He wore no cloak or armor, leaving only his fine red tunic, a rose embroidered over his heart.

"It suits you," she said, indicating the heraldry on his clothing. "You look a true prince of Old Cor."

"It does not matter what I look like, only what I can do."

"Both matter. And you should look like what you are. A prince of the old bloodlines, a rare descendant of ancient emperors."

"The proof of that is in my blood and my steel, not my clothing."

Erida knew that more than anyone else. No other man could tear a Spindle or wield a Spindleblade. No other man could be what he had become.

The collar of his tunic was unlaced, showing the white veins rippling over his skin. Erida was seized by the odd urge to touch the branch-like lines and trace their paths across his skin. She chalked it up to fascination. *My husband carries a god in his flesh. Who wouldn't want to see it?*

Taristan closed the distance between them. The temperature seemed to rise with every inch, her skin prickling with warmth beneath her ornate gown. The fabric felt heavy and too close. Erida wanted to tear it off. Instead she watched Taristan without blinking, never breaking his gaze.

"Twice a queen," she echoed. "And thrice a prince." His titles flashed in her mind. *Old Cor, Galland, and now Madrence.* "Quite the journey for a Treckish mercenary."

He didn't blink either, and her eyes began to burn.

"I think on it every day," he said, stopping in front of her, still holding her gaze as a snare holds a rabbit. Erida finally broke, allowing herself to blink. He responded with a satisfied smirk. "A port orphan, to this."

"A prince of silk and steel," she said, looking him over.

The right hand of a queen and a demon god.

"What do you see?" he asked, still unblinking. His stare was nearly unbearable, boring through her, inhuman in its focus. She felt speared by it.

"I see you, Taristan." She swallowed around the lump in her throat. He was close enough to touch, but she laced her fingers together instead. "I wonder which parts of your face belong to your mother. Your father. Which parts are Corblood, which parts Wardborn."

She tried to remember Corayne, the mouse of a girl at the root of all their troubles. Black hair, olive skin. Different coloring, but the same eyes and face. The same distant manner, as if they were somehow set apart from other mortals. *Could Corayne feel that difference within her? Can Taristan?*

"No one alive can answer that question," he murmured, finally looking away. The edge of the gardens ran up against the bay, the gentle waves lapping at stone. The blue waters were dark, reflecting the lights of the city in pinpricks of wavering gold. "For you or me."

Erida felt her breath catch, the city lights like brilliant stars in his black eyes. For once she felt as if she could fathom their depths.

"What else do you think on?"

He shrugged, rubbing his hands together. His long, pale fingers were clean, but Erida remembered how much blood they shed. "My destiny, mostly."

"No small thing," she replied.

"It was once. To die in a ditch somewhere. No longer. Not after Ronin found me, and What Waits raised me to what I am."

Erida clucked her tongue. She felt bold. "Give yourself some credit at least. Neither wizard nor god taught you how to survive."

His stare returned, locking back into place. It felt like the blow from a hammer. "The same can be said of you."

She shook her head slowly. "I learned because I had to. Especially after my parents died. No one would protect a girl who could not protect herself."

He nodded stoically. To her surprise, she saw understanding in his eyes. "In a palace or the gutter, the rats are still the same."

Rats.

Her teeth set on edge. "I've had enough of vermin to last a lifetime," Erida sneered. "First Corayne an-Amarat and her meddlesome pack. I hope she's dead in a sand dune somewhere, her bones bleached by the desert sun."

She swallowed back a wave of revulsion. "And then Konegin, still evading capture. Gods know where my treasonous cousin is, or who aids him. No matter how many cities we topple, somehow these two remain beyond our grasp."

Heat curled in her belly, not from the heavy dress or Taristan's presence. But from rage.

"Anger suits you," Taristan muttered, eyeing her face. "It feeds that fire you keep burning."

Erida flushed and she looked away, working her jaw. She felt her own thrumming pulse, born of frustration as much as Taristan's attention.

"I want Konegin's head," she hissed.

"He'll make another mistake soon enough," Taristan said, oddly calming. "Or another noble will make it for him."

"I'm already working on that. The Madrentine treasury is vast, and Robart's wealth is already being divided up among my supporters."

Taristan huffed out a scoff, his face falling. He eyed the Lionguard around them, silent and unyielding. "Pay the soldiers, not the preening nobles."

"Many of my soldiers follow those preening nobles," Erida answered coolly. "And coin makes for the strongest allegiances. Konegin cannot buy what is already mine."

"Konegin is *nothing* in this world." His low hiss filled the gardens. "One day you'll see that."

She could only sigh, rolling her shoulders. Her ceremonial armor was so heavy, and beginning to dig into her ribs. "One day you'll be right. But for now he's still a threat. Just like your niece."

"Indeed she is." His lip curled.

Exasperated as she was, Erida couldn't help but find quiet amusement in her own circumstance—and Corayne's. *So much of the world rests on the shoulders of two young women, with men squawking at our edges.* She tried to take heart in it and sink back into the woman she was an hour ago, a queen of all she surveyed.

Instead she felt small, dull as the shrinking palace, a pearl without light to make it shine. *I am a conqueror today. Why don't I feel it?*

Taristan's voice deepened, so low it reverberated through the air, finding home in her chest. "Is it everything you dreamed of?"

She clenched her teeth, fighting the sudden rush of sadness.

Her eyes fell shut for a long second. The birdsong and the fountain washed over her, enveloping her in soft noise.

"I wish my father were here to see this," she finally said, forcing her eyes open again. The fire Taristan spoke of licked up inside her, consuming her pain, turning it into something she could use instead. Anger. Fear. Anything but sorrow. "I wish Konegin were here to see it. Chained to the floor, gagged, forced to watch as I become everything he ever tried to take from me."

Taristan laughed openly, his teeth flashing.

"You are ruthless, Erida," he said, moving so his shadow fell over her. "It's why you were chosen."

Erida's stomach twisted. Her breath caught in her throat. "Chosen by who?" she gasped out, knowing the answer already.

"What Waits, of course."

The name of his demon god sent a jolt through Erida's body. Both a bucket of cold water and a bolt of lightning. She tried not to think of Him, and most days it was easy. The campaign had many distractions.

"He saw a weapon in you as he saw it in me. Something to treasure, and reward." Taristan took her in, his eyes still dark, still empty of all but the fathomless black. "Does that discomfort you?"

She chewed her answer. "I don't know," she finally said. It was the truth.

Taristan remained, unwilling to step back—or move closer. He looked down at her, and Erida felt like a corpse on the battlefield, dead eyes open, staring up at her ending. She could not begin to know how many had seen her husband this way, in their last moments, bleeding and broken. Again she knew how foolish it felt to trust him, to follow him willingly down such a dark path. And yet it felt like the right choice still. The only one she could ever truly make.

"You chose me too," he breathed. "You saw what I was, what I offered, and you said yes. Why?"

Erida took a steadying breath.

"Another man would have been my jailer, his leash woven through my crown," she said, matter-of-fact. "I've known it all my life. But you are my equal, and you see me as your equal too. No other suitor upon the Ward can say the same."

Her words stilled him somehow, his eyelids growing heavy. He seemed like a dragon entranced by a lullaby.

Then Erida shrugged. "No other suitor served an apocalyptic god of another realm either," she said, half smirking. "But if this is the price for my own freedom, my own victory, I will continue to pay."

His eyes remained black and staring.

Somewhere out at sea, thunder rolled in the clouds, and a single raindrop fell, shockingly cold on her face. But the air was hot between them. Suddenly she felt the heat of his cheek beneath her raised hand, smooth and warm, near to feverish, but without any sweat. Like a hot stone in the sun.

He didn't flinch beneath her fingers. Again he would not blink, his wild eyes seeming to swallow the world around them.

"Is he always there, inside?" Erida murmured, brushing her fingertips over his sharp cheekbone. He inhaled sharply.

She studied his eyes, waiting for the telltale flash of red. It never came.

Another raindrop fell. Erida expected it to steam on his skin.

"No," Taristan ground out, nostrils flaring.

Erida circled an ear, tucking back a lock of his dark red hair. A muscle in his cheek jumped, his pulse thrumming in his neck. "Can he control you?"

"No," he said again, near to growling. Her hand trailed, finding the veins at the base of his neck. They were hotter even than his skin, jumping with the rhythm of his heart. "My will is my own."

She pulled her hand away, dropping it to her side. Her own heartbeat roared in her ears, like the thunder rolling over and over again. All her nerves stood on end, until the air itself felt electrifying. Her toes curled in her boots, pulling away from the cliff she felt herself standing upon. One move in any direction and she would fall.

To her surprise, Taristan looked just as off-kilter. Twin spots of color bloomed on his cheeks, and his lips parted, inhaling again. The air hissed past his teeth.

"Prove it," Erida breathed, her voice so soft she barely heard herself.

But Taristan certainly did.

His touch burned, his hands circling her neck, thumbs hard beneath her chin to tip her face. She gasped in surprise, but his lips swallowed the sound, closing over her mouth. It took only a moment and Erida went loose, all but collapsing in his grip. He held her up, bracing her tight against his own body, the silk of his tunic against the steel of her armor. Her palm went flat against his bare collarbone, pressing up against flaming skin, while her other hand gripped his wrist, fingers circling muscle and bone. His breath was her own, his heat was her own, the fire in Erida meeting the fire in Taristan, burning together. Erida was both the hurricane and the shore. She broke in his hands as he broke in hers. She nearly stumbled but kept her balance. Her nails dug into his skin, coaxing him on.

Then he pulled back, his breathing ragged, his eyes heavy-lidded.

Her eyes fluttered open to see Taristan still above her, only inches away, his hands clutching both her wrists. Rain glimmered between them, drenching them both to the skin. Erida felt nothing but the burning touch of his fingers, even as her gown soaked through. Her lips parted, sucking down a breath of air. The cold wet was bracing, bringing her back to herself.

She stepped back, using all her will.

He let her go without question.

Erida wanted more, wanted it so badly her body ached. Her heart ripped a ragged tattoo against her rib cage, so loud she feared Taristan might hear. She shivered at the shocking, sudden absence of his flesh. She drew another breath, rooting herself to the spot. Her mind warred, torn between royal duty and her own control. Certainly Harrsing would celebrate to know Erida had finally taken her husband to bed. Erida delighted in the thought as well.

But perhaps too much.

"I have business to attend to," she forced out, her voice breaking.

"Certainly," Taristan answered, his face blank again. But the flush remained, spotting his cheeks.

Her skirts wheeled as she turned, flashing green and golden, a mirror to the lush gardens in a rainstorm. Erida cursed herself as she walked away, the Lionguard in tow. But she commended herself too.

I am a ruling queen of two kingdoms. I cannot afford weakness, not now.

And as much as Taristan made her strong, he certainly made her weak too.

20

HOPE IS ALL WE HAVE
Andry

Dawn broke cold over the castle of Volaska.

Andry waited in the gateyard, his saddlebags packed, his teakettle clanking softly. Along with clothes for the feast, Oscovko had given them each a fur-lined cloak, gloves, and wool underthings. Andry was glad for them now. The layers of wool, chain mail, his blue-starred tunic, and the new cloak kept out the worst of the cold. His breath rose in clouds, spiraling with the lightest sprinkle of snow. The Treckish horse snorted, blowing clouds of its own. It was stockier and hardier than his sand mare, now sleeping contently in the stables. Andry would miss her smooth gait and bright eyes, but the new bay horse would do far better in the cold. It was only a week's ride to the temple, but winter loomed, a shadow on the horizon.

Stable hands and servants scuttled back and forth in the gateyard, shuttling between the keep and the castle stables. They carried stores and tack, preparing supplies and horses for the journey south. But there were no soldiers, no advisors, not Prince Oscovko or anyone else Andry recognized. Not even his own Companions.

He stamped his feet, shifting back and forth to stay warm. Volaska rose over the gateyard, its towers stark against an iron-gray sky. Andry stared at the keep, searching the windows for some sign of life. Nothing moved. Not a person, or even a flickering candle.

Andry bit his lip and, after a long moment of awkward hesitation, waved over a groom at the stables.

"My apologies," Andry began, dipping his brow.

The Treckish groom did the same, bobbing his sandy head. He smiled toothily. "Yes?"

"Where is everyone? The soldiers? Prince Oscovko?"

The groom blinked. "Oh!" he answered with a heavy accent, laughing in a kind way. "They're asleep, sir! After all the drinking, they won't be awake for hours."

"Of course," Andry muttered, forcing a tight smile in thanks.

With a long, embittered sigh, Andry grabbed the reins of his horse and stalked away, leading the stocky beast back to the stable. He kicked stones across the yard, sending them skittering like the servants.

He returned to the great hall of the keep to find most of the tables empty, but for Corayne and Charlie in the far corner. Both wore new fur cloaks as well, their bags piled on the floor beside them. They bent over paperwork and plain breakfasts, picking at hard bread and stew. Corayne ate without complaint, but Charlie pulled a face as he spooned through the gray liquid in his bowl.

"Pay up," Corayne said as Andry took a seat, sliding onto the bench next to her.

Charlie's scowl deepened and he flipped a coin through the air. The copper metal flashed, landing in Corayne's outstretched palm. She pocketed it with a satisfied smirk.

Andry glanced between them. "What's the bet?" he said, wrinkling his nose as a servant put a bowl of the stew in front of him. It looked less than appetizing.

"I bet you'd be ready first," Corayne answered, tearing her bread in half. She dropped the larger piece into Andry's bowl. "First one ready to save the realm."

Charlie snorted into his breakfast. He eyed Andry over the rim of his stew. "First one ready to die for it."

The squire clenched his jaw. He knew the joke was meant to be harmless, but it stung anyway.

"I'm hardly the first," Andry said darkly, tucking into the meal. It wasn't terrible, more tasteless than anything. The vegetables were cooked beyond recognition, bled of all color and flavor. He wished for his collection of herbs tucked away in his saddlebags, left with his horse in its stall.

Pity twitched across Corayne's face.

Andry dropped his gaze. He told himself not to feel ashamed, not to regret his own survival. Part of him knew the guilt was foolish. But he felt it anyway.

"We should already be on the road," he grumbled. "Time is of the essence, and every minute is a waste of opportunity." His voice caught. "Of the lives already gone."

And those still hanging in the balance. My mother. And us too.

He swallowed hard, forcing down a gulp of food. It did little to hide his frustration.

"You're right, Andry," Corayne said, folding her arms. "I suppose that's the trade-off. We have an army now, but we aren't in charge."

"That's a generous use of the word *army*," Charlie said with a smirk. "More like a pack of scavengers."

Andry did not disagree. Next to the knights and legions of Galland, the Treckish war band seemed no better than the wolves on their flag. He sighed, shaking his head at the empty castle hall.

"I'd trade all of them for Isadere's soldiers," he said, remembering the Falcons and the Dragons. Both guardian forces were elite, deadly, and most of all dedicated. "I wonder if the King of Ibal has decided to fight."

At that, Corayne and Charlie traded knowing glances, their lips pulling into equal smirks.

The squire eyed them both. "What?"

Charlie leaned back against his chair, looking smug. "Even if Ibal does not fight, perhaps others will."

"Madrence is fallen," Andry sputtered. He remembered the letter as well as any of them, and Oscovko's face while he read it. The fear plainly displayed for all to see. "King Robart is probably dead. But even if he's alive, he can't hope to form an alliance of anyone now. . . ."

Charlie shrugged his shoulders. His eyes flicked down to the stack of parchment. "King Robart isn't the one asking."

"What are these?" Andry said, grabbing for the papers laid out on the tabletop. The ink was dry, the seals cooled to perfection. He studied the pages, eyes whirring. "More writs of passage . . . ?"

He felt his jaw drop as understanding dawned.

"These are letters," he breathed, sifting through the parchment.

Across the table, Corayne grinned. "It was Charlie's idea. He's been working on them since we left Ibal."

Charlie beamed with her, his pale face filling with a little more color. "And Corayne helped immensely," he said, a proud teacher. "She's an excellent translator, and she's better with seals than she lets on. Imp."

Corayne gingerly took back the stack of letters, careful not to crumple them. "If the King of Madrence can call on the Ward to fight, we can too."

Andry almost laughed, eyeing the many seals from across Allward. Each of them false, the signatures forged. "These are not letters from you."

"Every kingdom in the realm needs to get ready for war. The earlier the better." She inspected the pages again, testing the ink.

Many languages passed beneath her careful fingers, as did the colored seals and imprints. The golden dragon of Ibal. Rhashir's elephant. The white eagle of Kasa. Calidon's shaggy unicorn. Ahmsare's sun. The wolf of Trec. Even the stag of Iona. Summonses from all over the Ward, calling to the other kingdoms for aid, false letters holding terrible truths. Erida's conquest, Taristan's dark endeavor. The Spindles torn, What Waits looming behind the veils of the realm. It was Charlie's skill and Corayne's savvy on full display.

Andry puffed out an impressed breath. "You think this will work?"

"It can't hurt to try." Corayne shrugged, trying to look indifferent. But a small, satisfied smile played on her lips. "If even one letter succeeds, it'll be more than worth it."

"Truth dressed as a lie," Charlie said, proud.

"We'll send them out with couriers before the march," Corayne added. "There's no sign of Oscovko yet, but we can have Dom break his door down if the sun gets any higher in the sky." She gestured with her spoon, pointing out a familiar, blocky silhouette in the nearest passage.

The immortal prince stood sentinel, watching the way to Oscovko's apartments with the focus of a hawk.

"Doesn't matter when we leave—with our luck we'll end up marching through a blizzard," Charlie said cheerfully. "Can't wait to freeze to death in a border ditch."

Sorasa appeared from another passage, clad in her old brown leathers again. Her fur collar was pulled tightly up her neck, hiding her tattooed throat. She glared as she took up her own post at the window, leaning against the glass to face their table.

"Pessimism becomes you, Charlie."

The fugitive gave the assassin a winning smile.

"You know, I hear that quite a bit," he said dryly.

"Who'd you have after me?" Andry muttered, nudging Corayne's shoulder. Even though talking to her was easy now, as natural as breathing, he still felt a jolt in his stomach. "For the bet."

"Sorasa," Corayne answered around another mouthful. "She's on the prowl. I don't think she likes being shut up in a castle."

The assassin frowned, eyeing the hall. "You're absolutely right.

Too much opportunity. And if Dom doesn't drag Oscovko out of bed, I will."

Corayne smirked, all mischief. "I doubt the prince would mind."

In the passage, Dom glowered, but Sorasa only shook her head, exasperated.

"Whatever gets things moving," she grumbled, helping herself to a hunk of bread. "Has anyone seen Sigil?"

"Not since she took some lord and lady to her chambers last night," Charlie said. He finally gave up on his stew, shoving the bowl away.

Sorasa took it without blinking. "Only two? She's getting slow in her old age."

Warmth spread across Andry's cheeks and he lowered his head, trying to hide his discomfort. He spooned at his stew, eyes downcast, but Charlie snickered at him anyway.

"Save your embarrassment, Squire," he chuckled. "Certainly the knights of Ascal were no better."

"Not by much," Andry mumbled. He'd served Sir Grandel long enough to know which courtiers shared his bed and when to make himself scarce.

"Is that right?" Corayne prodded, her dark brows rising. "First gossip, now beddings? I thought you knights and squires were meant to be so well-behaved."

"I—no—well—" Andry stumbled, flustered. Indeed, many of the squires did have their dalliances, both well hidden and not. None were allowed, but there were always ways around such things.

Not that Andry ever tried.

He swallowed down a spoonful of lumpy stew, attempting to collect himself. "We should be thinking of the march," he finally said, overly stern. "And planning for whatever Taristan left behind to guard the temple."

It worked too well, throwing a somber blanket over the table. Even Charlie dropped his grin.

Corayne pushed her bowl away too, going quiet. "Not to mention whatever Spindle he tears next," she muttered. "Or has already torn."

"Does he even need the Spindles anymore?" Charlie muttered.

Andry narrowed his eyes. "What do you mean?"

"You saw the letter from Madrence." The fallen priest eyed his papers. "King Robart called for an alliance. We are calling for one too. But it may not happen in time. Taristan won't need a demon god to take over the Ward if his wife has already done it, picking kingdoms off one by one."

At the windows, Sorasa pulled a face and shrugged. "I suppose Erida's empire would be better than the apocalypse."

"Well, when you put it that way," Corayne said darkly. "It's my head no matter what."

"Taristan of Old Cor isn't just fighting to win a crown or even the Ward." Dom stepped out of the passage to loom over the table, his face twisted with anger. "He owes a debt to What Waits, and so does his wizard. No mortal throne will satisfy his hunger, or his rage."

Charlie blinked up at him. "How do you know?"

"His eyes. His face," Andry heard himself answer. Suddenly

he stood on that hill again, looking down on the temple and his long-dead Companions, watching as Taristan stalked across the clearing. His eyes burning even behind his helmet, the Spindleblade like flame in his hand. "What Waits is in him, and the wizard too. This is still only the beginning of what they want to do. It's bigger than a simple conquest."

Andry remembered every second of that morning. It was burned into him like a brand. The smell of the blood, the hot ash blowing from the temple doors. The smallest glimpse of the Ashlands beyond, a burning realm of pain and torment. And the corpses spewing forth, driven by a master Andry could not see.

His hands trembled on the tabletop and he tucked them away, trying to hide the fear as it broke over him.

Corayne's fingers were suddenly cool in his sweating palm. She gripped hard. He squeezed back. She was an anchor and he clung to her eagerly.

But she clung to him too.

"We need to go," Andry said, his voice low. But it echoed through the hall, a command as much as anything else.

Snow fell over the city, blown in on a bitter wind.

By noon, the war band made it through the gates of Vodin, with half the city turning out to see Oscovko and his soldiers off. Andry heard little of their cheering, his focus narrowing to the rhythm of his horse's gait. He remembered leaving Ascal with Sir Grandel and the Norths, the Lionguard knights in their distinct golden armor. Back then, the sun was warm on their faces, the spring air fresh and crisp. It felt like a lifetime ago, or even a dream, so distant from the reality Andry lived now. Once more, the squire wished he could step back in time. Return with what he knew now. Save the Companions, and stop all this from unfolding.

He glanced sidelong at the many hundreds of soldiers stretching out behind him. *How many will meet their ending at the temple?* Andry wondered, his mouth filling with a bitter taste. *How many more will have to die there?* Try as he might, Andry couldn't get the image out of his head. He saw Corayne, Dom, Sorasa, and the rest all dead before the temple Spindle, cut apart like the old Companions were. Returning to the killing ground felt like madness, like suicide.

But we must, he knew, repeating it over and over again. *We must go back.*

Oscovko led the long column of riders, all astride strong, stocky horses bred for winter. The snow continued in a steady curtain, coating the landscape in a thickening blanket of white. The army traveled the Cor road for some miles toward the border, but turned off at the banks of the White Lion, riding south along the river. The road carried on west without them, to the Gallish city of Gidastern on the coast, some days away.

Nightfall came on quickly, the sky fading from gray to black as they followed the winding river through the mountain valley. The White Lion formed a clear border, with Trec on the hilly western bank and Galland to the east. Woods clung to both sides of the water, forcing the column to spread out as the paths narrowed. Andry glimpsed only branches and thick undergrowth on the Gallish bank. There were no watchtowers, either Treckish or

Gallish, not this far from the main roads linking Vodin and the rest of the realm.

Corayne sat the horse next to him, her body turned toward the river. She barely blinked, eyeing the far bank.

"I can't believe that's Galland right there," she said fiercely. The snow looked like stars in her black braid. "I feel like even the trees might reach out and grab us."

Andry looked over her, to the border. "I don't think Erida's lands can do that. Yet," he added, sighing. "If we hold this course, we'll be over the border by morning."

"And caught by nightfall," she said, her tone too cheerful.

He settled back in the saddle, one hand braced on his thigh, the other holding the reins. "Oh, that's right, you're a wanted fugitive."

"So are you, Andry Trelland," Corayne shot back.

Andry rolled his eyes. "Don't remind me."

"I'm sure everyone back at court is scandalized," she teased, leaning into the space between them.

"Absolutely," he said, playing along. "It'll be the gossip of the season. Other than, you know, the Queen trying to conquer the entire world." Then he looked ahead, through the bowing trees to the head of the column. His voice dropped. "At least Oscovko knows what he's doing."

As always, Corayne's interest was piqued. She turned away from the river. "How so?"

"Look at them: they certainly don't look like any army I've ever seen." He nodded forward along the column, to Oscovko at its head. "No flags. No matching tunics or uniforms. Nothing to mark their kingdom or their loyalties. And Oscovko looks like any other soldier. No crown, no fine armor."

The crown prince wore only black fur and brown leathers, blending into his men around him. Far from the knights and lords Andry remembered.

"He isn't proud or foolish enough to put a target on his own back," he said, half impressed. "Or make it easy for a scout to identify his army."

Corayne heaved a sigh. "Not that flags or crowns matter to the Ashlands," she muttered.

A chill ran over Andry. He knew better than most that the corpse soldiers would devour anything in their path if Taristan commanded it. They were empty husks in his memory, undead, a nightmare made flesh and bone.

He shook his head, refusing to let such thoughts swallow him up.

"Oscovko's smart to skirt the border like this," Andry continued, gesturing to the river. "There isn't a castle for miles, down out of the foothills. The closest real garrison will be in Gidastern, away on the coast. And no village watch is going to be able to stop an entire war band."

Corayne eyed him keenly, looking him up and down. She lifted the corner of her mouth in the shadow of a smile. "Is that hope I hear in you, Andry?"

"I think hope is all we have, Corayne," he bit out. "Painful as it might be."

Her smile remained but her eyes darkened. She looked back to her reins, dropping her gaze. "I tell myself not to do it. Hope," she said. "But I can't stop myself."

Andry leaned, bumping her shoulder softly. "Good. I'd hate to see you lose it. You and your hope have gotten us this far."

"Me?" She balked. "I'm nothing without the rest. Dom, Sorasa—and *you* too."

Despite the bitter cold, Andry went warm beneath his cloak. He furrowed his brow. "I'm just a squire."

"You can keep saying that, but it doesn't mean I'll believe it," she snapped back. "Let me give you a compliment for once."

Andry met her eye, noting the twin spots of pink on her cheeks. Her annoyance only made her more endearing, just like her curiosity and her dogged resolve. He wondered how much of that was her Corblood, the restless nature of her ancestors. And how much was simply Corayne, a girl from the end of the world, who only wanted to see the rest.

"Very well," he finally said, grinning. He felt his own cheeks go hot. "Just this once. But that means I can give you one too."

She rolled her eyes. "Fine."

His reply was quick, already formed. "I'm glad to know you, Corayne an-Amarat. You're the bravest person I've ever met. And no matter what you may think, you've done great things already. You will do greater still."

At the top of her fur collar, her throat bobbed. Something softened in her black, inscrutable eyes. Then she narrowed her gaze and turned back in the saddle, facing forward. She put her nose in the air and sniffed. "That's three compliments."

* * *

The snow had finally moved on, the sky clearing above the trees. Bare branches veined overhead, and the river was behind them now, the sound of it lost to the forest.

"Galland," Andry said, his breath clouding in the frosty air of dawn.

Beneath her hood, Corayne made a groggy, half-formed noise. She jolted and almost fell from the saddle. Only Andry's quick reflexes kept her upright. As always, he was astounded by her ability to sleep sitting up.

"Sorry," she slurred out, getting her bearings as they rode. "What?"

"We're in Galland," Andry said again. The name of his own country felt like a stone around his neck, weighing him down. He swallowed against the sensation.

Corayne pushed back her hood, freeing a head of wavy black hair. She blinked sleepily in the daylight, looking around at the half-dead forest, over the heads of men and horses. The Companions rode along around them, half asleep but for Dom and Sorasa, both straight-backed in the saddle.

"How can you tell?" she forced out, searching the woods.

Andry did not feel pride, but shame instead. "I've studied war maps all my life," he murmured. "It was supposed to be my duty to defend this border one day. And defend the rulers who kept it."

"You are defending it still," Corayne said, her voice sharpening.

He didn't reply, and she grabbed his reins, forcing her horse even closer to his. Their knees bumped together, and it took all Andry's willpower to keep still.

She didn't let go. "Andry."

But Oscovko's high whistle cut her off, the piercing sound echoing over the column. He called out to his horde and reined his horse right, turning the entire column westward, away from the White Lion.

Andry's heart squeezed in his chest.

"I know the way from here," he whispered.

He saw the path in his mind. *Through woodlands and frozen meadows, below the more rugged foothills of the mountains. Toward the Green Lion, another river. And the pilgrim road to an ancient temple, once forgotten, but no longer.*

He looked back, past Corayne, past the haunches of his own horse, to Dom swaying in the saddle, mountainous compared to the soldiers around him. The immortal met Andry's eye from beneath his hood.

They shared a heavy, grim stare. Andry knew that Dom bled as he did, if not worse. Slowly, the squire forced a nod. His lips moved, soundless, forming words for Dom and Dom alone. *With me.*

To his surprise, the Elder mouthed them back.

With me.

It was a small comfort, but Andry would take anything he could find. Anything to combat the terror rising in his chest, threatening to push out all else. He tightened his grip, feeling the leather reins through his gloves. Again he tried to anchor himself in something real, in the world in front of him instead of the memories behind.

But still the smell of ash and burned wood filled his nostrils. Andry winced, gritting his teeth against the sensation. It was sharp, stronger even than in his dreams. He squeezed his eyes shut, trying to will the memory away, even as it seemed to surround him.

"What is that?" Corayne's voice washed over him.

Andry's eyes snapped open to find that the smell was not part of some waking nightmare, a memory of the temple ruin.

It was real, and right in front of him.

Oscovko whistled again, directing the column to widen as they rode out into a clearing among the trees, where the ground was flat and empty. But it wasn't a clearing at all, not a natural one anyway. The trees were splintered and burned away to stumps, their branches turned to cold ashes. The fire was long gone, leaving a blackened crater and the lingering smell.

"I don't know," Andry murmured, dazed.

He looked back and forth at the jagged gash through the foothills, like a giant black scar dragged through the woods. It wasn't from a forest fire, or even a passing army. Something had burned these lands to embers, with great force and even greater precision.

Andry turned to Corayne; she was already staring at the scarred landscape.

"Another Spindle?" she breathed. He could see her mind spinning behind her gaze.

"I don't know," Andry said again. His stomach twisted. The scorched land felt wrong, the very air like poison on his skin.

Dom urged his horse up alongside them, surveying the obliterated landscape. He frowned, deepening the scars on his face. Under his breath, he cursed in his own immortal language, the words indecipherable.

Sorasa followed, a shadow upon her black horse, barely more than a pair of copper eyes beneath her hood. "What do you see, Domacridhan?"

"It's not what I see," he breathed, his shoulders tightening. "It's what I know."

Oscovko forced his way into their midst, circling his horse back. "And that is?" he demanded.

Dom raised his chin.

"A dragon is loose upon the Ward."

21

SLEEP AND DREAM OF DEATH
Domacridhan

The threat of a dragon loomed like a dragon itself, a black cloud over all their heads.

The column put the burned-out crater behind them, murmurs running through Oscovko's war band. His warriors both feared and delighted in the prospect of a dragon. The Companions less so, with only Sigil looking eager to test her ax against a dragon's fire.

"What do you know of them?" Sorasa murmured as they rode on, her voice low enough to be lost among the hooves and idle chatter. Her eyes shone with rare concern, her dark brows drawn close together.

Dom hesitated, casting a glance behind her to Corayne. She already had so much on her shoulders. He didn't want to put the full weight of a dragon on them too. Thankfully, she was deep in conversation with Charlie, the pair of them bent over some scribble of parchment.

The Amhara followed his gaze. "If you'd rather not say, fine. But if you die without telling me how to bring a dragon down, I wager I'll die soon after. And I'd simply rather not."

His breath hissed through his teeth, his face torn between scowl and smile. "For once you've overestimated me, Amhara," he muttered. "I was not there to watch the last dragon die."

"Useless immortal," she cursed, but the insult held no sting, her eyes no harshness.

His throat tightened. "I remember it, though."

Her copper gaze flared.

"The beast fell some three hundred years ago, and took many immortals with it. Burned, broken, crushed." Every word felt like a tiny cut, deeper than the scars on his face. "I do not know which ending my parents met, but I know they did not survive. Lord Triam and Princess Catriona, lost to the rocks and sea."

Sorasa only stared, still but for the rhythm of her horse, her tiger eyes unblinking.

"I can barely remember their faces now," he murmured, his voice fading. *Silver hair, green eyes. Milk-white skin. His sword. Her bow. Only their cloaks came back, burned nearly to ashes.*

But it was an old wound, long healed. Far easier to bear than the others.

"I remember when the warriors returned, the Monarch leading them. I was a child, and Isibel took me in, to raise her sister's son as her own." His sorrow turned to anger. His aunt had wielded the sword of war once, but no longer. And her cowardice might doom the Ward.

"She told me stories of that day. The way the dragon moved. The heat of its flame. They slashed its wings, using arrows and bolt throwers, siege engines. Anything they could to bring it down, close enough to drive spears through its jeweled hide, into its ember heart."

Sorasa ducked her chin. "Wings first, got it," she said stiffly. With a click of her tongue, her horse quickened its pace, carrying her forward through the column.

Dom was happy to be left behind. He wagered she did not know what to do with fear, nor sympathy. It was a confusion he understood, at least.

The immortal kept his eyes and ears trained on the sky, his focus outward instead of inward, so that he barely noticed every step farther into the foothills. The miles passed gently, with only his nerves a ruin, and not his weak, wretched heart. The weather helped too. It had been spring the last time he came this way, through lush green woods filled with birdsong. Now the forested hills were gray and skeletal, the tree branches like gnarled fingers, with only the pines still tall and evergreen. Dead leaves crunched beneath their horses and the wind blew bitter, smelling of snow and rot. Nothing was as it used to be, and for that Dom was grateful.

It was only when he dropped his guard that the memories crept back, slow but unstoppable. The figures around him changed, their silhouettes shifting. Sorasa became Marigon or Rowanna, black hair going red, bronze skin going white, brown leathers replaced by scaled purple mail. The rider behind him was no longer Sigil, but Lord Okran of Kasa, towering in his white steel armor, the eagle across his chest, a white smile like a crescent moon in his dark brown face. Oscovko, Charlie, the other Treckish soldiers and mercenaries, all faded. Even Corayne, who already looked so much like her father. She stared at him with Cortael's face and Cortael's stern manner, thin lips pressed into his usual grim smile. His face was as Dom remembered, not at the temple, but back home in Iona. Before the blood, before the slaughter. Before his body lay cold and still, torn apart. Dom wanted to reach out and touch the figure's arm, to see if the memory felt as real as it looked.

He refrained, hands too tight on the reins, cracking and creasing the leather in his grip. With a will, he looked skyward again, searching the gray clouds for the shadow of a dragon.

"It isn't far," a voice mumbled at his side.

Dom turned and startled at Andry, sitting tall in the saddle. For a moment he thought the squire was a memory too. But his brown eyes were too dark, stricken, as haunted by the landscape as Dom was. Andry glared at the trees, a rare hatred on his kind face.

Reluctantly, Dom surveyed the landscape around them. The gentle slope of their path up the hill, the nearness of the mountains. The distant sound of the flowing Green Lion, the river low and weak this time of year. It felt familiar but wrong, like an old coat grown too tight.

The immortal steeled himself, reining his horse out of the column. He'd known this moment would come, and hated it.

"I will scout ahead and assess the temple ground," he said. "To see what we might be up against."

Among the war band, the Companions turned to watch him go, their faces like glowing lanterns.

Andry followed, grasping for Dom's arm. The squire shook his head, dropping his voice.

"Take Sorasa with you."

"Sorasa doesn't know what to expect," Dom replied, though part of him wanted to acquiesce. Sorasa was certainly capable enough to creep up on a few brainless skeletons and make it back alive.

The squire gnashed his teeth and urged his horse on, matching Dom's pace. "I do. Let me come."

But Dom put out a hand and clicked his tongue, stopping Andry's stocky horse in its tracks.

"It must be me," the immortal said, even as every nerve ending lit with terror. He swallowed back his fear, trying to press it down into nothing. "Stay with Corayne," Dom added, his green eyes flicking to her. She stared at them from her horse, face tight with worry. "Keep a watch on the sky, and the wind. It will change quickly if a dragon is close."

Another horse pulled out of the line, joining the pair. Sorasa glowered from the saddle and threw back her furred hood, her short hair hanging around her face.

She sneered at Dom. "And where do you think you're going?"

The immortal angled himself away, barely looking at her. It was easier to keep moving than stop and give Sorasa a chance to join him.

"It's half a day's ride to the temple from here," he said, the horse quickening her pace. "I'll report back as quickly as I can. Like I said, keep a watch on the sky."

Sorasa's voice dropped to a snarl. "Dom—"

But he was already gone, his horse galloping beneath him, the autumn leaves spiraling in his wake.

After a few miles, Dom stopped to vomit into a nearby stream. He wiped his mouth with the back of his hand and splashed his face, letting the cold water shock him back to life. A sudden weight pressed down on his chest, as if a stone lay there, and he struggled to breathe against it. He was no stranger to panic, but it threatened to overwhelm him now, blurring his vision and slowing his reactions. His heart thumped a ragged tempo. The water helped a little, and he found some rhythm again, heaving long gasps in and out. He swung back into the saddle, spitting out the last sour taste. Luckily, the stout Treckish horse had a good temper and kept on at a solid pace, covering the rocky ground with sure legs and steady hooves.

Come home, Domacridhan.

The voice sent a bolt of lightning down Dom's spine. He straightened, eyes wide, and searched the forest around him, hunting for any sign of his aunt's magic. He had not seen a sending in decades. He almost didn't recognize the magic at all, the voice seeming to come from within his own body rather than the world around him.

But the Monarch of Iona's voice was unmistakable.

Isibel? he thought, calling out to his aunt.

She said nothing, but he could feel her smile, cold and small. He smelled Iona through the gray branches. It was the scent of rain and yew trees, moss, mist, the city's old stone. Home in a single breath. He nearly wept for the memory of it.

My beloved nephew, come home.

Then her white figure wavered between the tree trunks, a pale shadow failing to fully take shape. Grimly, he urged his horse on. Out of the corner of his eye, he glimpsed the edge of her face, a long nose and stern brow, gray eyes, blond hair trailing into nothing. Her magic could not truly reach him here. He was too far away, or the nearby Spindle was too strong. She existed only in echoes. And those were almost enough to ruin him.

I cannot, he answered, his thighs tightening on his horse. The beast responded in kind, quickening her pace. It wasn't enough to outrun the sending, which carried along beside them, a wisp at the edge of his sight.

Her voice wavered like her image. *The bonds between the realms grow thinner. The land of Allward will fall.*

Not if I have anything to say about it. Dom furrowed his brow, squinting through the trees. He saw no sign of corpses or skeletons, no cursed army of the Ashlands. He couldn't even smell them. The hill beneath him rose steadily, with the infernal clearing on the other side.

This is our chance to go home. To find the Crossroads. To open all the doorways.

Dom loosed a low snarl of frustration. His aunt used the same argument in the throne room of Tíarma, many months ago. *You'll die trying,* he thought, *and doom the rest of us with your foolish hope.*

Something broke in Isibel and she gasped, halfway between a scoff and a sob. *Where is Ridha? Where is my daughter?*

In the saddle, Dom flinched, pulling on the reins. The horse slowed beneath him as his body ran cold, his fingers turning to ice. Fear flooded his veins, matched only by the terror in his aunt's voice.

I do not know.

Isibel's sending flickered, bright with desperation. *I cannot reach her. Is she with you?*

He felt her anguish even through the sending, distant as her magic was. It mirrored his own pain as he thought of his cousin for the first time in many weeks. He tried to remember her that day in Iona, proud in her green armor, an immortal princess with the world at her feet. He hoped she was not yet a corpse. The weight on his chest increased tenfold, his throat tightening.

Evil awakes in this realm. Her voice took on an echo, growing further away. *I can feel it coming.*

Dom grasped for Isibel with his mind, willing her to stay. The sending came no closer, lingering in the trees, beyond his reach.

The evil is already here, my lady, he pleaded, throwing all his rage and desperation toward her, hoping her magic could carry it back. He thought of the dragon, somewhere in the Ward. And Taristan was even worse. *You helped birth it years ago, when you made one brother a prince and left the other to become a monster. All for what? The hope of the old empire? Cor reborn? The way to Glorian Found?*

Somehow, he felt Isibel wince.

Is that shame, my lady? You deserve it.

Even as he thought the words, Dom wanted to call them back. Truth though they were.

Isibel's choice had sent Taristan down a terrible road. Without her, he might have never become a puppet of What Waits, a blunt instrument for a demon king. Her decision, small as it had seemed, could doom the world.

But you can help stop what you began, he thought. Again he reached for her magic, trying to hold on to her. *Put down the branch, take up the sword.*

The sending failed, her light disappearing from the trees.

I cannot. Her voice echoed in his skull, growing weaker by the second. *Your time is running out, Domacridhan. Come home.*

"No," he whispered aloud, hoping she would still hear him. It could be the last word he ever spoke.

The hill above loomed, the temple close. The smell of Iona faded, replaced by the winter forest and something worse beneath. Like sickness, like corruption.

Dom slid from the horse, his sword in hand, his old cloak still fastened about his shoulders. As the last touch of Isibel's magic left him, he felt her absence as a sudden void in his mind.

Ridha, he thought instead, his cousin's name repeating over and over in his head. He had no magic and neither did she, but he reached for her anyway, bending his thoughts to wherever she might be in the wilderness. *Isibel could not reach her,* he knew, and that was a terrifying prospect. Either she was too far away to find, shielded by some magic he did not understand, or beyond the realm entirely. *Dead.* The prospect threatened to swallow him whole. But he would not give up on his cousin. He simply could not bear it.

Dom lashed his horse's reins to a tree at the base of the hilltop, hiding her from whatever might be on the other side. Now he relied on his memories of the temple instead of running from them. He tried to see beyond the corpses of his fallen company and remember the landscape that waited.

He dug his boots into the yellowed grass, finding his footing on the muddy hill. It was the same one Andry stood upon all those months ago, guarding their horses. He knew that the hill loomed over the clearing, with the temple on the opposite side. The temple was white stone, old and cracked, built by Vederan hands centuries ago. It had a single bell tower, its deep toll like a hammer. The bell was silent now, but Dom knew better than to trust such things.

Despite the need for stealth, he moved quickly, making no noise at all. He was the blood of Glorian, after all, gifted with great agility and speed as well as his heightened senses. Even terrified, he was still formidable to any foe in his path.

And there would be many.

Dom pressed in among the gray-brown trunks and scratching twigs, his cloak of Iona blending in with the autumn. Even his golden hair camouflaged well, the same shade as the undergrowth of dying grass and fallen leaves. He crouched, lowering to his belly, to crawl forward and peer over the lip of the hill.

Quietly, he prayed there would be no corpses he recognized, decaying in their Lionguard armor or Vederan cloaks.

The smell of death was overwhelming, making his eyes water. He wanted to turn around and run. He wanted to never move again, paralyzed on the spot. Only resolve outweighed his fear. And the promise of vengeance. Cortael died for this Spindle. Only Domacridhan could make sure his ending was not in vain.

The temple was as he remembered, white-walled and white-columned, its bell tower empty and silent. But the steps were crusted over, painted the color of rust. Dom knew it was dried blood. The grass of the clearing was gone, churned up by thousands of marching feet. Any bodies that might have lain there were long gone, trampled into dust. Somehow that was worse than skeletons, knowing the Companions were completely destroyed, left without even their bones.

He tracked the army's path down the other side of the clearing, following the pilgrim road Taristan had walked so many months ago. Dom remembered the first glimpse of him coming through the trees, moving at an easy pace, the wretched red wizard at his side. They were both far away now, with the bulk of the Ashlander army.

But the Spindle remained, and it was not unguarded.

Dom felt the familiar buzz of the portal, its existence a hum of power beneath the air. It crackled on his skin, raising the hairs on the back of his neck. If the Ashlanders felt it too, he could not say.

The corpses milled about in a strange circle, marching in time with each other, going round and round the temple in an impenetrable wall of iron and bone. They walked ten abreast, slumping along at a slow but steady pace. Only a few fleshy corpses remained. Most were rotted to the bone, jangling in their rusted armor. As he watched, one dropped a limb, its arm separating at the shoulder with a tear of disintegrating tendon. Dom clenched his teeth, biting back another surge of panic. He set to counting as fast as he could.

* * *

"More than a thousand."

Dom could still smell the rot of them, though the temple was ten miles behind him.

He faced the campfire, staring into the flames, letting the dancing light soothe his panicked mind. It was easy to lose himself in the jumping red and yellow. Easier than facing his Companions and Oscovko, all circled around him, awaiting his news. The Prince of Trec knitted his fingers together, hulking in his black furs, one eyebrow arched in thought.

The rest of his war band fanned out among the trees, bedding down for the last night before the onslaught. They were used to sleeping hard and rough, and did so without complaint. Dom could not look at them either. He didn't need any more ghosts.

Corayne eyed the many soldiers and mercenaries, scanning the woods. She didn't know what it was to carry such weight.

"And we number?" she asked, looking to Oscovko.

The prince curled his lip. "Three hundred."

She set her jaw. "And seven."

"And six," Dom countered sharply. "*You* will not be fighting."

Charlie tipped an inky finger, brows raised high. "And four. I hardly think you need me in this mess. And I haven't seen Valtik since we left Vodin."

Dom hissed out a breath, feeling his eye twitch involuntarily. It was so like the witch to disappear that none of them noticed until now.

"She'll turn up," Sigil muttered, perched on a stone. She flexed one massive hand and Oscovko smirked. The memory of their match was obviously still fresh in his mind.

Corayne heard none of it and stood from the ground, planting herself in front of Dom. It felt like staring down a particularly annoyed rabbit.

"What's the point of all this training if I'm not allowed to fight with the rest of you?" she demanded.

All manners forgotten, Dom leaned down to her eye level and growled. "What's the point of the rest of us fighting if you *die*, Corayne?"

She recoiled, startled by his sharp tone. Immediately, he regretted it.

"My apologies, but I have little patience for bravery anymore," he sighed, touching her on the shoulder. "It always ends poorly."

Corayne frowned and sat again.

From the other side of the fire, Sorasa raised her cup.

"That's the smartest thing you've ever said, Elder," she chuckled. She drank deeply, savoring her wine. Oscovko was quick to pour her more from his own wineskin, clearly elated to be seated between assassin and bounty hunter.

It rankled Dom, though he couldn't say why.

"Were there any more coming through?" Andry said, leaning forward on his knees. He alone knew the true danger ahead, his stormy countenance mirroring Dom's own.

Dom shook his head. His braids from Volaska had come undone, leaving his golden hair to flow free over his shoulders.

"No. The doors to the temple were flung wide, and the Spindle is still open, but I didn't see anything." He did his best to report without remembering, to speak without seeing that wretched place rise up before his eyes. "I think the Ashlands are spent, the bulk of their forces with Taristan in the south."

Oscovko grinned, his teeth catching the firelight. "I'll take these odds."

"A thousand corpses is nothing to sneer at," Andry muttered, forgetting himself. Quickly, he dipped his head. "Your Highness."

The prince only waved him off. "I've sneered at worse," he crowed. "My men are blooded fighters, all of them. You'll find no better force upon the Ward."

Snoring, belches, and otherwise gaseous noises echoed from the woods, rising from several hundred Treckish soldiers.

Sorasa snorted into her cup. "That is hardly true," she said, and Dom found himself agreeing.

Oscovko shrugged off the jab, his grin growing wider. "No better force willing to fight with you, I mean."

"Point taken," Sorasa grumbled.

"We're on horseback—that's another advantage," Corayne chirped, jumping up from her seat again.

Dom almost wanted to push her back down. Her excited, dogged nature would only get her killed, especially here. Slowly, he bent and took a seat before the fire. Even immortals faced exhaustion, and Dom certainly felt it now.

Corayne remained standing, undeterred. The fire danced at her back, turning her edges to gold. "A corpse army can't stand against a cavalry charge."

"They have spears," Dom said wearily, scrubbing a hand over his face. His fingers played over his scars. They didn't sting anymore.

"But no master," Corayne retorted. She planted her hands on

her hips and faced him down. "The Ashlanders follow Taristan and Ronin, but they aren't here. They're brainless, aren't they? Certainly we can outfox a few hundred walking skeletons."

Andry frowned. "Others had the same idea, Corayne," he said gently.

Her eyes narrowed to slits, a muscle jumping in her jaw. "I know that," she snapped, her voice dropping. She rounded on Dom again, eyes flashing. "It's my father you mourn, Domacridhan. Don't act like I'm detached from this, like I don't know what's at stake."

Dom's face went hot, but not from the roaring campfire. He dropped his eyes, examining his boots instead of Corayne.

She didn't let him chase her off, and instead went to her knees, taking his hands in her own. Her eyes shone, black as Cortael's.

"I know you're frightened," Corayne said softly. "So are we."

He gritted his teeth. "It isn't the same."

"Grief isn't a competition," she countered, dropping his hands. With a withering glance, she stood. "We're going to fight tomorrow morning. And we're going to win." She stuck a hand out, palm open to him, and wriggled her fingers in invitation. "It's the only option we have."

From his seat, Oscovko laughed into his wine. "If I didn't know any better, I'd say you were raised by wolves," he said, nodding at Corayne. "In my country, that's a compliment."

"Worse than wolves," she answered, her smile edged with bitterness. "Well?" she added, tipping her hand again.

It was warm in Dom's own, and so small, so breakable. He took it anyway, hoisting himself up.

"Very well, Corayne an-Amarat," he said, and her smile flared like a sunbeam. Behind her, all but Sorasa smiled too. "I will sleep and dream of victory."

Domacridhan slept and dreamed of death.

22

KNEEL OR FALL
Erida

The halls of the Palace of Pearls became familiar, to Erida's annoyance. She wanted to be gone from Madrence as soon as possible, but the days wore on, and her army remained in Partepalas.

She awoke that morning in the usual way. Too many maids, too many ladies, all buzzing around her like a cloud of flies. They washed, groomed, clothed, and coiffed her, a practice Erida was long accustomed to. They worked in silence, never speaking until the Queen spoke to them, which Erida never did. She kept her lips pressed shut, her eyes on the floor, her mind elsewhere.

Her skin tingled, even days after the rainstorm in the gardens. She could feel his touch still blistering on her face, his burning fingers still tracing her cheekbones and mouth. The hands of her ladies paled in comparison as they combed through her long hair.

Not that either Erida or Taristan had addressed the moment,

either in court or in their few private moments beyond the watchful eyes of her council. Ronin had said nothing either, meaning he did not know. Otherwise, the little red weasel would have squirmed with jealousy. After all, she was the wizard's greatest rival for Taristan's attention, a point he made endlessly clear many times. *Attention or allegiance,* she wondered idly, trying to ponder where Ronin's true ire came from. The answer eluded her, as did most things about the red wizard. Spindlerotten, her courtiers called him. A Ward mortal born with magic, touched by a Spindle somehow. Once a conjurer, and now the mouth of What Waits, the Torn King of Asunder. A demon from children's stories, a nightmare Erida knew to be all too real.

And Taristan's master too.

Erida shuddered, thinking of the red sheen in her consort's eyes. She barely noticed the gown as the ladies slipped it over her head. The skirts fell in sheets of white silk, the hem embroidered with roses.

She left the warmth of her rooms behind, the wider halls cooling with the autumn season. Her Lionguard fell into formation, flanking her on her walk through the palace. Like her ladies, they were silent, and for good reason. They guarded the most powerful crown upon the Ward. Nothing would break their focus.

Lady Harrsing met her at the staircase, one hand on her cane. The other reached for Erida's arm, which she gladly provided.

"Did you sleep well, Bella?" Erida said, surveying her old friend. Her brow crinkled with worry. Harrsing's years seemed to be catching up with her on this campaign.

But she only chuckled. "As well as I can hope for these days. Every moment brings some new ache."

"Something to look forward to," Erida scoffed, shaking her head.

"Is there anything for me to look forward to, Your Majesty?" Harrsing's grip on her arm tightened, her long fingers surprisingly strong. "I'm told I'm very good with children."

Erida's face went suddenly hot against the cold air, so quickly she worried her skin might steam. Again she felt Taristan on her lips, and the feverish sensation of his skin.

She forced out a laugh, giving no ground. "You are relentless."

Harrsing shrugged. "I'm old. I'm allowed."

Warm light bathed the grand hall below, spilling out from the windows overlooking the Long Sea. The waves looked golden and pink beneath the rising sun. A bitter wind blew, leaving whitecaps across the water. Only a week had passed since they marched into Partepalas, victorious, but the weather had turned quickly, the warm air of the south giving over to winter's damp. She could only imagine how Lady Harrsing felt, so thin and weak beneath her fine clothing.

The clouds were still red, streaked by dawn long since broken.

"The sky looks strange today," Erida muttered, stopping to observe the clouds. Indeed, everything had taken on an odd, glinting light, almost too harsh. Like the glass itself were colored, and not the sky beyond. "As it did yesterday."

Harrsing barely looked. "The season is turning," she said, shrugging.

"I've never seen a sky like that, no matter the season." Erida racked her brain, trying to place it. The closest she could think was firelight, giving off an orange glow, as if something burned just below the horizon, somewhere out to sea.

But that was impossible. It was only a trick of the clouds and the autumn winds, growing unpredictable as winter set in.

More Gallish ships bobbed in the bay, their green sails furled and oars stored. Erida smiled tightly at them, glad for their presence. They brought reinforcements and weaponry, and would return to Ascal with holds spilling over with Madrentine gold. Wars were won with coin as well as swords.

Her smile dropped as she counted, ticking off the ships on her fingers, one by one.

As if summoned, Lord Thornwall rounded the far corner, all but stomping down the passage with his own retinue of knights. The older man looked relieved to see her, but also disheveled, his gray hair mussed and cloak askew over one shoulder.

He dropped to a knee, dipping his head as she approached. "Your Majesty—"

"Lord Thornwall, there are half as many ships as expected in Vara's Bay," she said, and bid for him to stand. "Is there something I should know?"

"Yes," he said tightly, straightening up. "The captains are reporting trouble in the Straits of the Ward."

Erida raised a slim eyebrow and frowned. "The Ibalet navy?"

"Pirates, mostly," Thornwall answered, shaking his head. He seemed oddly jumpy, out of character for the stalwart soldier. His eyes darted between Erida and her consort. "But that's not what I need to tell you."

Erida felt Harrsing shift next to her, going stiff. The old woman knew Thornwall as well as Erida did, and they both read the discomfort on his face.

"What is it?" Lady Harrsing said sternly, sounding like a schoolteacher.

Thornwall's throat bobbed.

"A scout just returned with news."

He gestured to a dirty, overgrown boy in the midst of his soldiers, his face windburned and his legs bowed from weeks riding. He stared resolutely at the floor, determined to not look anyone in the eye.

"And what does he say?" Erida asked slowly.

Thornwall swallowed again. "Corayne an-Amarat and her compatriots have been spotted, far to the north. On the other side of the Mountains of the Ward. Riding for Trec."

The floor seemed to tip beneath Erida's feet and she nearly lost her balance. But the queen held on to herself, keeping her feet even as her mind spun.

She already pictured Corayne in her head, a half-dead, desperate girl astride a weak horse. Stringy black hair, a long, plain face, skin bronzed by too much sun. She was unremarkable in Erida's memory, neither beautiful nor ugly. An easy face to forget, but for her void eyes and her bold tongue. Did Andry Trelland still walk beside her, a traitor to his kingdom and his queen? Or was the squire dead, lost to the desert Spindle and the sand dunes? He mattered little, in the scheme of things. There was only Corayne and the blade on her back, the wretched power in her blood. She could undo everything they worked for and kill Erida's newborn empire in the cradle.

"Trec?" Erida muttered, narrowing her eyes. *So far from Ibal, half a realm away.* "Why Trec?"

Thornwall shook his head, mouth gaping. He had no answer.

"I know why."

Taristan loomed out of an archway, a red shadow against the pink-and-white walls. Erida's heart leapt at the sight of him, her eyes going wide. She stepped away from Harrsing, gesturing for Taristan to approach.

"Join us, Your Highness," she said, her voice thick.

The others bowed, allowing her consort to pass.

He snarled low in his throat and took Erida by the arm, leaning in to her. His fingers burned on her arm, his grip bruising.

"The temple," he said in her ear. His voice trembled with sudden desperation. "It's close to the border, a few days' ride."

Her jaw tightened, holding back a sudden string of curses.

"Send word to the garrison at Gidastern, with all speed," Erida commanded. Her gaze pierced through Thornwall. "A rider, a boat, whatever you think is quickest." *Most likely both*, she knew, thinking of the northern road. "Dispatch men from Ascal as well. I want Corayne breathing before me or I want her head. Nothing less."

Thornwall bobbed his head in acquiescence, but lingered, still uneasy.

It was not like him to hesitate, especially when ordered by the Queen herself.

Erida eyed him, feeling his agitation creep into her own body. Dread rose in her throat.

"What else, my lord?" Her voice dropped. "Konegin?"

"You'll see," Thornwall answered, gesturing for Erida and Taristan to follow.

They swept toward the great hall in a wave of silk and armor, the commander and his men barely a step behind Erida. She passed through pink marble archways, beneath gilded ceilings painted with pastoral scenes of meadows and farmland, bucolic coasts and green vineyards. Burgundy banners and draping still hung from the gallery above, though the flags throughout the city had been replaced by the Gallish Lion. The cold air seemed to flee before them, burned away by Taristan's presence. Erida even dropped her furs a few inches.

When they entered the throne room, the raised seat cut an impressive silhouette against the wall of windows, backlit by the oddly colored sky. The chamber itself was all but empty. It seemed smaller without a crowd of courtiers. Erida shuddered as they walked beneath a tapestry of silver stallions, the last testament of the Madrentine kings.

No, not the last, she realized, her eyes falling on the dozen people gathered before the throne. Most were Gallish soldiers in green tunics, an armed escort fresh from the road. They still smelled of horse. A girl trembled in their midst, her blond braid reaching the small of her back.

Erida sat the throne, schooling her face into cool disinterest, even as a thousand things swirled through her mind. The conquest. Corayne. Konegin.

And now the young girl in front of her, fifteen years old, a princess in name only, the last living heir of Madrence.

Marguerite Levard visibly quivered but did not kneel, her

hands clasped behind her back. She was dressed as a commoner, in a plain cloak and rough-spun wool, but there was no hiding her royal bearing. She was her brother's miniature, golden-haired and square-jawed, with skin tanned by the southern coast. Her blue eyes fixed on the pearl and marble beneath her feet. Erida weighed the girl's manner. Was it born of fear or disrespect?

She thought of herself at the same age. Just as small, just as frightened. *But I stood tall*, she thought, her lips pursing together. *I looked my enemies in the eye.*

"Marguerite of Madrence," the Queen said, surveying the young girl. The deposed princess flinched at the sound of her own name. "Where was she found? The convent as her father said?"

At her side, Thornwall bent to answer. "No, Your Majesty," he said in a halting manner. "My men found her on the road, riding for the Siscarian border. She had a detachment of knights with her, as well as these traitors."

He gestured to the two Madrentine noblemen flanking Marguerite. Both were white as fallen snow. Like the princess, they wore simple traveling clothes, and they quivered with fear. Erida recognized them easily, even without their finery. They swore their allegiance to her only a week ago, offering oaths of loyalty and empty smiles.

Erida bit her tongue, holding back a curse. *I've been queen of this kingdom for seven days and already they try to overthrow me.*

She did not address the two lords, barely looking at them at all. They did not deserve her disgust or her anger, only swift punishment. Taristan glared from his seat, his eyes burning holes through both of them.

"I see," she forced out. "And what did you seek in Siscaria?"

Marguerite kept her eyes on her feet, a picture of innocence. "Sanctuary, Your Majesty."

She spoke softly, sounding younger than her years. Erida knew the trick well.

"You could not find that in a convent?" she scoffed.

One of the lords stepped forward, dropping to a knee. He bowed his head, as if that would save him from her justice. "We thought it safest for the princess."

"I see no princess here," Erida sneered, her voice acid.

A long bolt of silence shot through the marble hall.

"For Marguerite," the lord mumbled, but the mistake was already made. "She is like a daughter to us, and no father could bear to see their child locked away, even in comfort."

Erida's hand curled on the arm of her throne. "Her own father *is* locked away, and would be glad to have a companion." She let the full weight of her glare land. "I'll not hear lies."

On the floor, the lord continued to snivel. "You are distant cousins, Your Majesty," he whimpered, begging. "Your *Magnificence*. Her mother is of the Reccio family, like your own."

"And?" she said coolly, shrugging.

He sputtered on his knees. "She is an heir to you."

Erida was glad for her mask, for all her lessons hard-learned at the court of Ascal. Rage flared in her chest, burning hot at even the thought of Marguerite usurping her throne. Slowly, she stood, and descended the steps of the dais at a steady, maddening pace. She halted beyond reach of the lords, too smart to come within range of a hidden dagger or clenched fist.

She eyed Marguerite instead, waiting for the girl to meet her gaze. After a long time, the once princess raised her face, reluctant but resolute.

With a twist of her stomach, Erida realized their eyes were the same nearly shade of blue.

"Did you learn embroidery at your convent?" she asked, trying to coax an answer from the young girl. "Sewing? Needlepoint?"

Marguerite barely nodded. "Yes, Your Majesty."

"Well done. I was never skilled with the needle. My stitches were always crooked. I didn't have the mind for it. Thread could never hold my interest." It wasn't a lie. Erida had despised all manner of sewing and weaving, largely because she held no talent for it. But she despised traitors even more.

She shifted, facing the lord on the floor. "Sewing your mouth shut, however, that would be very interesting indeed. Do you follow my meaning?"

He could only nod, clamping his teeth together so as not to provoke her further.

"A wise decision," Erida mused. "Now, what do you know of their plan, Marguerite? I can see you're a smart girl, smarter than your brother was."

The deposed princess winced at the mention of Orleon. Her eyes flew past Erida, finding Taristan still seated next to the throne. In an instant, the pageantry fell away, and Erida glimpsed the fury in Marguerite's eyes. Pure, unchecked, a deep anger built on grief. Erida understood that too, well enough to fear it.

The Queen tsked slowly. "No idea? Do you have a guess, at least?"

"To keep me safe," she answered, tight-lipped.

Erida raised her brows. "Safe for what? Certainly there was some reason."

The princess dropped her eyes again, trying to retreat behind her wall of quiet innocence. She was young, not as skilled as Erida had become, and the Queen saw through her.

"I do not know, Your Majesty," Marguerite murmured.

Erida could only smirk.

"I was a young girl once too. I know your weapons, Marguerite, for they were my own. And I admire your bravery, foolish as it may be," she said.

As Thornwall had a week ago, she crooked a finger, signaling to the soldiers guarding Marguerite. A pair of them stepped forward, seizing the young girl by both shoulders.

At least she knows better than to fight, Erida thought, watching the young princess break. The same deadened look King Robart wore came over Marguerite, but hers ran deeper. A single tear trailed down her cheek.

"Remember this moment, Marguerite. Remember that tear." Erida watched the single drop fall. "It is the last one you will ever shed as a girl. You are a woman now, the last of your childish hopes and dreams bleeding to death before your own eyes."

Marguerite forced her gaze up, her blue eyes ferocious as she met Erida's own. She said nothing, her lip caught in her teeth.

On her right-hand side, Erida felt the telltale ripple of heat. Taristan appeared next to her, his face blank as her own.

"There are no fairy tales in this world," Erida said, her eyes going soft. "No charming prince will come to save you. No god hears *your* prayers. You will not avenge your brother. Rise against me and you will fail. And you will die."

Marguerite flagged in the grip of her captors, almost falling. She hissed out a pained breath.

"But behave yourself, and you'll be well provided for," Erida offered, matter-of-fact. She even smiled. "I have no desire to torture a conquered king and his living child, so long as you both cooperate. Your father has a lovely apartment and wants for nothing. Neither will you, I can promise that."

It was hardly a comfort to Marguerite.

Erida cared little, and turned to stone again, eyeing the Madrentine lords.

"As for treason, *that* I cannot abide," she growled out. Her gaze bounced between the pair of them, trying to guess their measure. "The lesson need only be taught once. Who shall learn it?"

The one standing furrowed his brow. Sweat glistened across his forehead, despite the chill of the room. "Your Majesty?"

Erida ignored him. "Disloyalty is rot in the foundations of peace and prosperity. I will not have it in my empire. The first man to tell me where you were going, and who was helping you, will live. I give you this chance only once."

Both lords went wide-eyed, their faces pulled in exasperation. They glanced to each other, unblinking, their mouths tightly shut.

Again silence fell heavy through the chamber, palpable as smoke in the air. She remained still, relentless, giving no quarter to the traitors in front of her, no matter how much she wanted to look back, to draw strength from Thornwall or Taristan. Instead she drew it from her father, her own memories of him stalwart upon the Gallish throne. He dealt with treason and betrayers all his life, always with wisdom and always harshly. Anything else left room for treachery.

She would not break before the lords did. Her crowns depended on it.

"Byllskos," the kneeling lord sputtered out, even as his compatriot lunged for him. Erida's soldiers caught him around the middle, hauling him back as he yelled in Madrentine, spouting curses and threats.

The kneeling lord began to weep, his hands raised in surrender. "The Tyri princes," he gasped. "The Tyri princes rise against you."

Between her captors, Marguerite flailed. "Don't—"

"And him too," the kneeler said, throwing a letter to the floor at Erida's feet.

Again the other betrayer shouted, his deep bellow lacing with Marguerite's high pleading. Erida heard neither of their cries and grasped the letter, unfolding the parchment with numb fingers. Her eyes went not to the writing, but to the seal broken at the bottom.

The green lion stared up at her, and her skin went to flame.

Konegin.

Erida had not seen him in more than two months, since Castle Lotha, since before she won a crown her predecessors had only dreamed of. Since Lord Konegin put poison in her husband's cup and fled a failed assassination, disappearing into the borderlands. Suddenly he stood among them, golden-haired and fox-eyed, done up in all his silks and furs. He leered from every face. The lords, Marguerite, her own soldiers, even Thornwall. No one but Taristan was safe from the shadow of Konegin. She found herself wishing the specter in her mind were real, so she could strangle her usurping cousin with her own two hands. He wavered before her very eyes, his grin sickening, a scroll in his hand. It dangled over her still, all the names, every suitor, every person he'd ever tried to foist upon her. They burned in her mind alongside Konegin's face, each one a still bleeding wound.

"Who, Your Majesty?" she heard Thornwall ask. His voice sounded far away, as if shouted down a long passage.

Her vision spiraled as she walked, the letter in her grasp. She felt nothing, only the pounding rage at the back of her skull. Her breath came in short bursts, all her focus turning outward, to her appearance, to her mask of calm. She felt it slipping and tried to hold on, willing herself to keep moving. To remain a queen, and not a beast.

"Here," she murmured, pressing the parchment into Thornwall's palm.

The edges of her sight went black, the shadows spotting and spreading. A wave of sickness churned, but her anger was stronger. It guided her body and kept her upright, even as Taristan stepped closer. His lips moved but she could not hear him, all sound dying away. All sensation gone.

But for the leather in her hand, steel beneath it.

Thornwall's dagger was old, unused for a decade.

And still sharp.

Marguerite's flesh gave like butter, the blade finding home in her stomach. Erida heard nothing, even as the princess's mouth went wide, her teeth biting at the air. She felt her hand twist, the girl's organs give way around the dagger. Warm blood ran over her hands, scarlet like the sky outside, like the velvet on Taristan's chest, like the devil sheen in his eyes. The white-and-pink marble splattered with red as the young princess collapsed. She floundered, a fish on a line, choking on the blood welling up in her mouth. She pawed weakly at her own entrails, every swipe of her hand growing slower and more sluggish. Finally she stilled, her eyes blank and staring. The palace of her father stared back, filled with foolish paintings of idiot fields and taunting trees. Statues of kings long dead loomed close, watching with stone eyes as their dynasty bled to death upon marble and pearl.

Air seared back into Erida's lungs. She gasped one breath after another, her teeth bared. She felt like a lioness, like a sword, powerful and ruinous. For once, she held fate in her own hands.

One of the lords was sick all over himself, the smell cutting through Erida's dulled senses. She rounded on him with a scowl of disgust.

"Grow a spine," she snarled, nearly stumbling.

Burning hands caught her before she hit the marble, holding her in place. She tried to shove Taristan away, to stand on her own two feet, but he held firm, a crutch as much as an anchor.

Around the chamber, her subjects gaped. Even Thornwall was white-faced, the paper still in hand. His pale eyes wavered between Erida and the body, his dagger still in Marguerite's abdomen.

Erida forced down another breath, trying not to gag. Everything stank of vomit and blood. Her fingers clawed to Taristan, her head pounding, her stomach twisting over and over. She wanted to faint or fly.

"Thornwall," she growled, panting. Sweat broke out over her skin, and she shivered at the sudden damp.

Next to the throne, her commander trembled, slack-jawed. He dared not speak.

Erida smoothed her hair away from her face, leaving a smear of blood across her cheek. She sucked down a cold gasp of air, letting it center her.

"Send word to Siscaria and Tyriot. They will kneel, or they will fall."

Erida dismissed her ladies upon their return to the royal apartments. They skittered off like insects, disappearing into the palace without question. The sight of their bloodstained queen was enough to send even the boldest running.

Only Taristan remained, guiding her into the sitting room, a round chamber with windows looking out over the bay. The light was still odd, slanting orange across the floor, as if a wildfire burned somewhere close. Erida stared at the carpets, inspecting the complex designs with sudden intensity. She traced each thread, blue and gold and pink, forming diamond patterns and scrollwork. It was easier than looking at her own hands, her fingernails crusted in blood, the sleeves of her dress stained red.

Water sloshed somewhere, and Taristan knelt before her seat, a washcloth and a basin of water at his side. He set to his work with steady, slow motion, careful not to startle the Queen. Her breath came in fits and starts, the iron tang still hanging in the air.

"The first kill is hardest," he murmured, lifting one of her hands. The cloth dragged along her skin, turning red as her flesh went white again. "It stays with you."

Erida turned her focus from the carpet to the water. It splashed, going the color of rust every time he dipped the cloth. The blood of a princess was like any other, indistinguishable from the lowest peasant or common rat. She saw Marguerite's face in the water, eyes blank, mouth wide, blond hair splayed out like a godly halo. *The girl was only fifteen.*

Erida was reminded of the tent on the battlefield, when she wiped the blood from Taristan's flesh. Then it was Prince Orleon she washed away. Now his sister swirled scarlet in the water.

She swallowed back a sour taste. "Who was yours?" she murmured.

Taristan continued cleaning her hand, tracing every line of her palm.

"Another port orphan. Bigger than me, too slow to steal like I could. Thought he could beat me into giving over my dinner." His face tightened, a line furrowed across his forehead. Erida saw the memory in him, still a wound. "He was wrong."

She curled a finger, brushing it along his hand. "How old were you?"

"Seven," he spat. "I used a stone."

A far cry from a dagger in the hall of a king. Her eyes stung and her vision swam, not from nausea, but from unshed tears. She blinked fiercely, trying to force them away. She worried her lip, nearly drawing blood. Sensation returned, the numbness fading from her limbs, the buzzing in her ears fading away. *What have I done?*

Without thought or concern for the blood, Taristan's hand

closed on hers, gripping tightly. She gripped back, their bones pressing together. She ached for the press of his lips, for the burn of his touch.

"Don't apologize for doing what you must," he breathed, ferocious. Her heart clenched, feeling the dagger in her hand again, Marguerite's life bleeding out between her fingers. "This world will eat you if given the chance."

His other hand went to her face, turning Erida to look at him. Not the carpet, not the basin. Not her own wretched fingers painted with slaughter. She leaned into his grasp, holding his gaze, searching his eyes.

There was only the endless black. Only Taristan kneeling before her, reverent as a priest.

"You're strong, Erida. But strong as you are, you are the most appetizing piece of meat in all the realm right now." The concern on his face was foreign, a puzzle. Erida had never seen it before. "The wolves will come."

"One wolf already has," she said, leaning to brace her forehead against his. His skin flamed and his eyes flickered, lids growing heavy. "Will you devour me too?"

The breath he drew in sounded like a snarl. It shuddered through her, from skull to toes.

"Like this?" she whispered, barely audible.

Her pulse thundered in her ears. All the world seemed to shrink.

"Like this," he answered.

His lips were feverish and she shivered against them, sweat beading along her spine again. The fur fell from her shoulders, the blood forgotten. Something roared in her belly, taking hold, guiding her fingers as they latched in his hair and beneath his tunic. His own were already on her bare collarbone, her gown tugged over one shoulder, his lips trailing a path from her mouth to neck.

Every touch blazed, until Erida felt burned from the inside out. She never wanted it to stop.

As they lay together, limbs entwined, watching the bloody sunset across the windows of the Queen's bedchamber, Erida waited for the infernal red wizard to burst through the door. But he was still shut up on the Library Isle, transfixed by the endless scrolls.

Good riddance, Erida thought, running a hand over now-familiar ground. Pale skin, white veins, a muscular chest sculpted by years of battle and toil. There were many scars, knobbled and raised, but none to match the veins. She traced the branches, torturous lightning in Taristan's skin, spiderwebbing over his flesh. She had never seen anything like it, not even in her mother, who'd died of a wasting disease, reduced to barely bones before the end. This was something else. And it was spreading. She saw it, slowly but surely, the bone white creeping under his skin.

"I don't know what it is," Taristan said in a hollow voice, his eyes on the gilded ceiling above them. "Why I look like this now."

Erida sat up sharply, propping herself against the bed with her elbows. "It—He never told you?" she said, perplexed.

Her consort stretched out next to her, his torso exposed by the burgundy silk blankets tangled around his waist. He lay flat on his back, one hand tucked behind his head. The veins stood out on his arm too, weaving around the lean muscles. Though the court of the Madrentine king did not suit Taristan, the king's bed certainly did.

"What Waits doesn't speak the way mortals do," he said. His face tightened. "There are no words, only visions. And feelings."

Erida tried to picture it but could not. She brushed her fingers over his neck, where the thickest vein stood out. "What does Ronin think?"

"Ronin calls it a gift. The strength of What Waits flowing through me."

"Does it feel like strength?" she murmured, flattening her palm to his throat.

His skin flamed beneath her own, burning as always. By now she knew this was not unusual. Taristan ran hotter than fever. The feel of him was enough to make her sweat, in more ways than one.

"What else can it be?" he answered, turning his head to face her.

The red sheen was there, barely a glimmer. But Erida perceived. And while she knew this, knew it was in him, she felt sick anyway. *What Waits does not control him, but He is in his eyes, and in his head. In a different way than I will ever be.* And then it was her turn to be jealous, not of a wizard, but of a demon king.

Slowly, she rose from the vast bed, putting her red-eyed husband to her back. Without her ladies, she dressed plainly, slipping into underclothes and a green gown without much difficulty. Her hair was more of a struggle, still tangled from sleep, and she fought it back into a single braid. All the while she stared, not at Taristan on the bed, but at the Spindleblade by the window. It gleamed with the red light of sunset, a mirror filled with fresh blood.

Taristan quickly followed suit, slipping into his own clothing. He despised the silks and velvets, pulling a face as he laced up his collar, hiding the last of his white veins from view.

"At least your Lady Harrsing will stop bothering us about an heir," he muttered, stepping into his boots.

Erida couldn't help but scoff. "On the contrary, her questions will increase threefold. She'll probably inspect my sheets for my monthly courses, and track my appetite too," she grumbled. Already, the Queen despaired of Bella's meddling. "The court has started taking bets."

He wrinkled his nose in disgust. "We war for the world, and your nobles have nothing better to do?"

"My nobles are not soldiers. They prefer banquets to the battlefield." She threw a long vest over her body, golden fur brushing against her chin. "If betting on your seed and my belly is the distraction they need, so be it. Let them gossip while we grow stronger."

Suddenly Taristan was at her back, wrapping one arm across her middle. He did so slowly, gingerly, careful as he was in all things. As if she might pull away at any moment.

"Soon you will not need them at all," he growled in her ear.

She leaned into him, bracing her back against his solid form. Even through the fur, she could feel his heat. "I doubt even What Waits can do that, my prince."

"My prince," he echoed, testing the words.

"That's what you are," she murmured, putting her fingers to his arm. She circled his wrist. "Mine."

His stubbled cheek brushed over her face, scratching her skin. "Does that make you mine?"

To that, Erida of Galland had no answer. *Yes* welled up in her throat but could not pass her lips. It felt like a betrayal of herself, of her crown, of her father and every dream of her ancestors. *I am the ruler of Galland, queen of two kingdoms, a conqueror. I belong to no one, only myself.* Even Taristan was no exception, intoxicating as he was, powerful as he made her feel. There was no man she would chain herself for, not even the Prince of Old Cor.

At least that was what she told herself, staying silent.

Ronin's cough made Erida jump in her skin.

She startled, twitching away from Taristan, her braid flying over one shoulder. Her heart rammed, and she glared at the wizard.

"You have incredible timing," Erida snarled, sitting down at the window seat.

Taristan turned with cool indifference, but his usually pale face flushed red. He scowled at his priest, lips twisting with rare disdain.

"Ronin," he ground out through clenched teeth.

The wizard barely glanced at him. He eyed the bloody basin, forgotten on the floor, and the Queen's hands instead. She curled her fingers, feeling shame again. But it was too late to hide the evidence.

Ronin clucked his tongue, his rat smile returning. "Ah, that explains the mess in the throne room."

"How long have you been standing there?" Erida seethed.

"Irrelevant," he answered with a shrug.

In a swirl of crimson robes, he swept over to the windows, standing in silhouette to study the city and the bay. The odd light lined his body in gold, like a holy figure in a painting or tapestry.

"I've found much and more," he said. "The Library Isle is far more extensive than the archives in your own palace."

It felt like a jab, and Erida bit the inside of her cheek to keep from reacting.

Taristan's patience ebbed. "Well, Wizard," he growled. "Out with it."

When Ronin turned, he wore a smile Erida never wished to see again. It spread too wide, the lines of his face running too deep, turning his red-rimmed eyes into a pair of eerie moons. She did her best not to recoil in horror as the veins in his neck pulsed, white as Taristan's but sharper somehow. They jumped slightly, thumping with the rhythm of Ronin's withered heart.

The priest folded his hands together in mock prayer.

"What do you know of the realm . . . Infyrna?"

23

STAIRWAY TO HELL
Corayne

The dream was worse than any before. Too real, too close. She felt Asunder all over, the hellish realm both hot and cold, blindingly bright and void black all at once. Everything and nothing. Corayne reached with empty hands, pawing through air and mud. She tried to breathe, tried to scream. Nothing came.

But she felt her legs moving. Felt her feet. Heard the echo of her own boots on stone.

There was a stairwell. Her fingers trailed against a wall, rough to the touch, and warm.

Down and down she spiraled, the blackness pressing against her open eyes.

She wanted to scream again, but no sound came.

This is a nightmare, she told herself. *You are asleep, and nothing here can hurt you. You're going to wake up. You're going to survive.*

It felt like a lie, even in her own head, even as she knew nothing around her was real.

And yet it certainly was.

The staircase ended.

This was Asunder. This was Hell.

The realm of the Torn King, the Devil of the Abyss, the God Between the Stars. The Red Darkness.

What Waits.

"Corayne an-Amarat," a voice hissed, everywhere and nowhere, in her bones and in her ears. "I've been waiting for you."

The night air was cold on her face, searing into her lungs as she gasped for breath. Corayne jolted upright, her forehead damp with sweat, her body tangled in her own cloak. Next to her, Andry slept soundly, and Charlie on his other side. She panted, looking at their sleeping forms to ground herself.

It was just a dream. Just a nightmare.

Her heart threatened to jump out of her chest, her pulse pounding in her ears. Every breath was a struggle, searing through her teeth, the wind freezing on her face.

Dom hulked next to the closest fire, his silhouette edged with flame. He watched her without moving, his eyes glassy but alert. Corayne saw him raise one eyebrow and she shook her head.

"Just a dream," she whispered.

He nodded an inch and let her be.

With a will, she lay back down, flat against her cloak, her chest rising and falling. The stars above winked through the clouds and trees. She tried to count them and steady her heart.

Despite all her speeches, her plans, Corayne an-Amarat had never felt so afraid. She did not fall asleep again, her eyes on the stars all night long, watching as her breath puffed in the frigid air. She looked for dragons, looked for skeletons, looked for anything out of the ordinary as the clouds parted. She was warm within her furs, the campfire still throwing off good heat even as dawn streaked through the sky. But no matter how comfortable or how weary she was, she never shut her eyes again.

Andry rose first, as usual. He put his tea on, hanging his kettle over the fire to boil water as he selected from his tin of herbs. Corayne watched him through slitted eyes, finding peace in the quiet squire, dutiful in all things. He sniffed at a sprig of rosemary before putting it in the kettle with some sage and lavender. As the water boiled, it filled the woods with a soothing smell. Corayne greedily sucked down a breath.

Before she knew it, Andry stood over her, a steaming mug in hand.

"It won't make up for all the sleep you missed, but it'll help," he said, crouching down to look her in the eye. He kept his voice to a whisper so as not to disturb the others.

With a grateful smile, Corayne sat up and took the tea. She sipped at it, letting the embracing warmth ripple through her. It felt different from the heat of her dreams, the boiling inferno of Asunder and What Waits. The tea was the hearth in their cottage. It was a cup of mulled wine back home in Lemarta, the winter sea gray in the harbor. The tea was Dom's shadow and Sorasa's sneer and Andry's eyes. Her mother's laugh. All things that held her up, even when the world tried its best to knock her down.

"You seem a little smaller than you did last night," he said softly.

She took another bracing sip. "Can you blame me?"

The brew of herbs helped unwind some tension from her body. At least her old aches were long gone, her muscles used to days in the saddle, her hands callused to her long knife. Sorasa's and Sigil's training made the road easier these last days.

"Thank you," she murmured, her breath clouding in the cold air. "Are you ready?"

"There's no such thing," Andry replied, thoughtful. "What about you?"

"What about me? You heard Dom. He's probably going to tie me to a tree at this point."

"I mean the dreams." He dropped his eyes, a flush darkening his cheeks. "I heard you last night. It sounded—"

"Worse." Her voice went hollow. She looked to the nearby fire, trying to find some comfort in the flames. "Worse with every step toward the Spindle, and I have no question as to why."

Andry fell back on his heels, his brown eyes wide. Something like pain crossed his face, and Corayne wished she could wipe it away.

"What Waits?" he offered, all worry.

The flames jumped and crackled, red and yellow. Embers spiraled into the trees. Corayne followed their path, trailing the flashes of light as they hissed out.

"The temple portal leads to the Ashlands, a burned realm, cracked with Asunder. It's under his control. He can't come through, but maybe pieces, whispers of him can." Overhead, the branches seemed to scratch the dawn. Corayne studied the trees, if only to anchor herself against the fear clutching at her insides. "He knows me. He's watching. He can't touch me yet, not while Allward remains unbroken, but—"

Her voice caught, the words sticking together. For a second Corayne felt herself back in the dream again, unable to make a sound.

But the air was fresh on her face, sunlight streaking through the forest. And Andry's hand was warm on her shoulder, a steadying weight.

You are awake, she told herself.

"He comes when I sleep." Corayne swallowed back the tightness in her throat. "Night after night, stronger with every inch closer to the Spindle and the Ashlands. He's strongest there, at a tear in the world."

She did not have to look at Andry to know he felt her fear, and shared it. He had seen the temple with his own eyes. He knew what lay beyond the doors, in the ashes of another realm.

"Usually it's the same thing, the dreams. White hands, red eyes, a black void with no ending. It all cuts deeper each time, crueler somehow." She felt it still. "Last night there was a stairwell, and he spoke to me. Once, I could forget a nightmare upon waking. Now they never seem to leave."

Andry's eyes narrowed, his brows drawn together in a furrowed line. Corayne almost expected him to laugh at her. Instead he gripped her shoulder tighter.

"What did he tell you?"

"That he's waiting for me," she answered, teeth on edge. Then shook her head. "It's almost funny. You expect a bit more from a demon god."

Andry didn't smile, his focus unbroken. "And what did you say?"

"I couldn't speak." Even now, the words felt difficult to form. "I know. Who knew that was possible for me? But I couldn't make a sound, not even to scream. I could only stand in that strange place, waiting for something to wake me up."

She fixed her stare on the ground beneath her, in the dirt and dead grass. Her fingers grazed the frozen earth. "Now, so close to the Spindle, I thought—I was afraid I wouldn't be able to come back. That no one and nothing could pull me out."

"Bullshit," he growled, and Corayne almost jumped.

"Andry Trelland," she gasped, startled by his harsh tone.

She looked up to find him glaring, all softness gone from his warm eyes. But his anger wasn't for her. He looked through the trees, in the direction of the Spindle, the temple, and the ruin of the world. A muscle feathered in his cheek and Corayne saw the shadow of a knight in him, a warrior of many years. Not just the squire, but the man Andry Trelland was always meant to be.

"I'll be here for you. Always," he bit out, looking back to her without thought. "We all will. I promise."

Andry Trelland was the most honest person Corayne knew. He had no talent for lying. It was easy to see the hesitation in him. The doubt. *He can't promise we won't be dead in a few hours. But still he tries.*

She covered his hand with her own.

"I'll hold you to that."

"I hope you do," he answered, unmoving.

They broke apart when Charlie snuffled awake, shuffling out of his bed to take a seat by the fire. With a glance at the rest of the sleeping circle, he set a piece of parchment across his knees and began to write.

Corayne glanced at the parchment sidelong, expecting another forgery.

But the letter was nothing official, without his usual artistry. There were no false seals, no forged signatures. His penmanship wasn't even any good. But he scrawled and scrawled, brow bent in concentration as the quill skittered over the page. When his eyes went glassy, shining with some emotion, Corayne looked away.

The others roused soon enough. Corayne and Andry set to preparing breakfast for everyone, hovering over their stores of food.

Dom had finally fallen asleep at some point, but now opened his eyes and sat up sharply, his sudden awareness startling the others. Sorasa had crept off without even Corayne noticing, but returned with braided hair and black-lined eyes, her face done up for war. Her fur cloak was gone, her leathers tightly buckled and laced, every dagger she owned easily accessible. Even her pouch of precious powders hung from her belt, tucked in alongside her coiled whip and sheathed sword.

Sigil rose last, yawning like a lion.

She seemed excited for the morning, thumping her chest to greet the mercenaries as they stirred. Whatever animosity they had shared in Volaska was long gone. Oscovko pulled her away to talk tactics, chattering about the horses and a potential charge.

Corayne shook out her cloak and shoved on her boots, lacing

them tight. Each motion seemed both too quick and too slow. She wanted the morning to be over. She wanted the sunset and the campfire, the Spindle behind them, with every face she knew still around her. They could snipe and argue all they wanted, as long as they lived to see the stars again.

Andry looked her over, his eyes heavy-lidded. His anger was gone but the fear remained. "Dom's right. Stay out of the battle."

She gritted her teeth, a sudden heat rising in her face. "I can't just stand on the side and watch."

Andry blinked, thoughtful. "I did."

"And it haunts you," she shot back, gripping the clay mug too tightly. "It haunts you to this day."

His voice remained even and low, audible only to the pair of them. "It kept me alive, Corayne," he said, the words laced with frustration.

When she didn't respond, he reached out and touched her hand, his brown fingers drifting over her knuckles. It sent shivers up her arm and into her spine. Corayne told herself it was the cold, the terror, the doom looming over all of them.

His brown eyes seemed to melt, warm all the way through, inviting as a crackling fire in the hearth. They pressed into her own, impossible to ignore. She wanted to look away but felt locked in place, rooted beneath his gaze. Andry Trelland reminded her of a spring morning at dawn, when the light slanted golden and the grass glimmered with dew. Filled with promise and possibility, but fleeting. She wanted to hold him in this moment, and herself too.

"Please," he murmured.

The moment broke.

"Fine," Corayne answered, dropping her head. She couldn't bear to see his relieved smile, not for her own cowardice.

Instead, she focused on her vambraces, pulling the Heir of Ibal's gift from her saddlebags. *Dirynsima*, she knew. *Dragonclaws*.

The leather arm wraps gleamed, the gold detailing polished, the leather well oiled. As she buckled them into place, she felt the steel reinforcements within, hard against the length of her forearms. The scale design and embedded spikes made her stomach flip. She wondered if the Dragonclaws indeed lived up to their name, and if the dragon loose upon the Ward had the same hide.

"Gods willing you won't need those," Sorasa growled, walking past with her own bags slung over her shoulder. Her horse trailed behind, nosing for grass along the sparse ground.

Corayne clenched a fist and twisted her wrist, engaging the spikes along the edge. The vambrace went tight against her arm, the small but lethal row of steel triangles standing up.

"At least I know how to use them now."

Sorasa snorted back. "Keep telling yourself that," she said, throwing her saddlebags into place. "Ready, Elder?" she added, eyeing Dom already on his horse.

He stared grimly into the woods, his eyes half-focused.

"I don't think it's possible to be ready for this," he said slowly.

Charlie stood from the fire, tucking his parchment into the vest beneath his furred cloak. His eyes flickered between Dom and Sorasa, weighing them both. "You've seen these things, haven't you? You've killed them before?"

"Only their shadows, Charlie," Sorasa answered. With a single, graceful motion, she swung into the saddle and adjusted her reins. "But yes, they can be killed. And they will be."

Corayne knew Charlie took little comfort in that. His face went slightly green, but he soldiered on anyway, trudging over to untie his horse. Corayne followed, again wishing time would both speed up and slow down. She wanted more of the morning. She wanted it to be nightfall. She wanted to close her eyes and skip a few hours into the future, when all was well and her friends safe, alive, and victorious.

But that was impossible. No magic in the world could manipulate time itself, not the Spindles. Not What Waits. The mountain before them had to be climbed. There was no way around it. They could only go forward.

Corayne climbed into the saddle without thought, the action long familiar to her now, almost second nature. The cold air bristled against her face but her blood flamed, hot with anticipation and dread. She swallowed, surveying the landscape of trees and rocky undergrowth. The war band moved among the branches and trunks, their faces gray as the dead trees, clad in battle-proven leathers and mud-stained cloaks. Some clutched shields and swords; others wore axes. Oscovko himself carried a longsword near to Dom's in size, a grin on his face. Together the three hundred warriors rose, the ground itself seeming to rise with them.

Their horses stamped and snorted, blowing clouds of steaming breath. Chants went through them, small at first, but gaining in strength like a wave crashing toward shore.

First in Treckish. Then in Paramount, bellowed for all to hear.

"The wolves of Trec, the wolves of Trec," they called, raising their steel and iron. A few men howled. "We feast on glory tonight!"

Among them, Sigil swung her ax, a manic smile on her face. "The iron bones of the Countless will never be broken!" she called, raising her battle cry with their own.

Corayne's blood surged within her, driven by her thundering heart, the raucous cheers, and the call of the Spindle, the realms beyond the Ward. She felt her Corblood singing, reaching out to wherever her ancestors came from. It pulled in every direction, a siren's song. The Spindleblade lashed to the saddle called too, the power within the steel rising like the hum of some unearthly chorus. Like her, it felt the Spindle, the fiery heart in which it had been forged. For a moment, Corayne forgot they rode toward doom, and let the magic flow through her, filling her up. The way it was meant to do, the way she was meant to feel. She tried to hold on to the sensation, to turn toward the Spindle's light and not away. She gritted her teeth, the reins tight in hand.

She would cut this portal in two, as she had the one in the desert. She would make Taristan feel it. And she would make What Waits regret every dream He ever gave her.

Her heartbeat thundered, and the ground shook beneath the force of three hundred horses, all careening toward death itself.

24
THE DEATH BELL
Domacridhan

Every pounding step of his horse was like a sword in his heart. Dom wondered if there would be any piece of him left by the time they reached the temple. Or would he be little more than a shadow then, an echo of an immortal lost? But as every inch cut him apart, it also made him numb, until the fear was only a buzz at the back of his mind. The memory of Cortael caused no pain. For Domacridhan felt nothing at all.

Only hunger. Anger. Vengeance.

Few are given the chance to right past wrongs. Perhaps this is mine, he thought as he urged his horse onward, the stocky stallion careening through the half-dead woods. Hundreds of horses surged into the trees, the army pounding over the earth.

And then the hill came.

His stomach dropped but he kept his seat, leaning forward over the horse's neck. He did not remember drawing his greatsword, but he felt it in his hand, the leather grip worn by the decades. He knew the feel of it better than anything else upon the realm, even his own face. The sword was older than his scars; older than the men around him. The steel of it caught the sun, flashing like a manic smile. So did the rest, too many blades to count rising into the air. Out of the corner of his eye, he saw Sorasa with her bow, Sigil with her ax. Andry raised his sword high, the blue star on his chest a blazing sight. He was a knight in every inch.

And beyond the squire, to Dom's great relief, was Corayne turning aside. Not by her own accord, but Charlie's. The priest had her reins, forcibly pulling the both of them out of the fray and into the safety of the deeper trees. Neither would fight.

It was the last thing Dom saw before they topped the hill, a foaming wave of warriors and horses. He found himself at the crest, Oscovko alongside him, Sorasa to his right, her bowstring already singing. Sigil roared out the cry of the Countless, first in her own language, then in Paramount.

"The iron bones of the Countless will never be broken!"

Dom prayed she would not be proven wrong.

He prayed for them all, even himself. Even in a realm where no gods could hear him.

Oscovko howled like a wolf, and his men answered, taking up the battle cry.

Once more, Dom tried for a sending. He had no magic of his own, but he bent his thoughts to his aunt anyway, calling out for her across the many thousands of miles. He called for Ridha too, wherever she was. No answer came. There was nothing but the temple.

It loomed before them, the clearing laid bare at the base of the hill. Dom looked to the temple doors first, to the Spindle within and the Ashlands beyond. Still nothing came through, only embers and ashes blown on a hot wind. The corpse army churned around the white stone and smooth columns, like a whirlpool out at sea. For a moment they kept their strange formation, lurching along one after the other. Dom briefly wondered if they could break ranks without the command of their master.

His question was quickly answered.

The corpses perceived the army riding down the hill and stopped in their tracks, shifting to face the hill with their eyeless skulls and broken blades. Swords and knives and spears rose to battle, a thousand pieces of rusted steel eager for flesh.

"Close ranks—ride as tightly as you can!" Oscovko shouted over his men.

They did as told, knotting together to form a wall of horseflesh and steel. The army bore down.

Dom leaned, and the horse reacted beneath him, gaining speed.

The world stank of blood and rot. The only sounds were the screams of men and Ashlanders. Overhead, the sky was clear blue, empty of clouds. Peaceful, even, but hell boiled beneath. Skeletons and corpses formed a macabre wall between the army and the temple. Dom kept his eyes on the ground in front of him. Corpses leered up, reaching with bony fingers and rotten hands.

His was the first sword to swing, but far from the last.

Domacridhan of Iona was an immortal, a son of Glorian Lost. He was not taught to fear death. He did not know what it was to be so fragile as a mortal. But even he knew to be terrified. The thought of it broke over his head like shattering glass.

Somehow, the mortals and their horses fought through without faltering. Oscovko's war band kept up their demonic howling, even as the corpses fell upon them, tearing many from the saddle. Their screams of pain melded with shouts of exhilaration, even joy. Oscovko himself called out between bouts, raining down blows with his sword. His face was soon streaked with mud and gore, but he didn't appear to mind. The Prince of Trec was a veteran of many battles, thrilled by each one.

Without Corayne to worry about, Dom tried to narrow his focus to only himself. It was the best way to survive. But try as he might, he could not let go of Sorasa, Andry, and Sigil. Even as the tide of battle tried to sweep them apart, he did all he could to stay with them, only a few yards away.

Sigil pulled them both along, better in the saddle than even Dom. She maneuvered with incredible skill, letting her horse fight with her, its hoofs crushing skulls and rib cages as her ax shattered a dozen spines. In her leathers, against the sky, she was a mountain, and the corpses a crashing sea.

Sorasa followed in her considerable wake, her bow twanging in every direction. Her reins slapped against the horse's neck, forgotten. She did not need them, directing the horse with the grip of her thighs instead. Her arrows found home in many corpses, slowing most and felling a few.

The blue star flared at the edge of Dom's vision, away to his left. Andry moved in graceful arcs, his sword sweeping from one side to the other as he rode through. The squire knew how to fight on horseback as well as any. His brown skin gleamed like a polished stone, the rising sun reflecting off him like a person blessed.

If the gods protected anyone upon the battlefield, Dom hoped they would protect Andry Trelland.

The tide raged back and forth, the cavalry charge cutting through the churn of corpses. But the war band was vastly outnumbered, and they rode into spears and swords at every turn. Dom left dozens shattered behind him, but there were always more. They surged and stumbled, bones and flesh and rotting limbs in every direction. Worst of all, the Ashlanders had no fear. They did not tremble. They did not falter. Their resolve was absolute and unbreakable, driven by a will more vicious than any other.

Then Sorasa's horse toppled, tossing its head as it fell, a terrible scream cutting through the air. Without thought, Dom whirled his own horse toward the sound, only to watch Sorasa Sarn disappear into a sea of bodies, her bow lost to the mud.

"Amhara," Dom heard himself snarl. The rest of his body lost feeling, his limbs reacting without thought or care.

Sigil saw it too and howled out a call, her horse thundering through the press of bodies.

Then the whip curled, lashing through the air with a crack like thunder. It snared a corpse and with a violent tug severed skull from spine. The Ashlander fell to reveal Sorasa Sarn ankle-deep in muck, her whip in one hand, her dagger in the other.

"*Stay alive!*" Dom yelled across the battlefield, the words too familiar on his lips. They were his own language, he realized, the tongue of Glorian. Known to none of them.

Sorasa heard him anyway, her copper eyes finding him through the fray. She gave nothing in reply, her attention on the enemies all around her. She knew better than to break her focus. But he saw a prayer of her own slip from her lips, in her own language, even as she continued to level the corpses around her.

As she fought tooth and nail, her short hair whirled with every motion, worked free from her braids. This was not like her battle with the Amhara, an equal display of skill and cunning. This was all edges, all violence. Like the corpses, she showed no emotion and no regard.

For once, Dom was glad for her Amhara training. It would keep her alive.

Then his own horse screamed beneath him, rearing up on her hind legs. Dom jolted and a sick feeling came over him. He saw the spear, half broken, its head buried in his horse's proud chest. Before the horse could fall, he leapt from the saddle, his greatsword in hand. His immortal senses flared and he swung his blade, cutting through the nearest corpses with the momentum of his fall. The horse thumped into the mud behind him, but Dom was already moving. He could not turn back, not even for a moment. Somewhere, he thought he heard Corayne cry out, but she was still on the hilltop, he knew, safe with Charlie in the trees.

Sigil rode the perimeter, her path like a noose around the corpses. She nodded to both Sorasa and Dom as she passed, the edge of her ax dripping blood. Overhead, clouds rolled through the blue heavens, filling the sky with iron gray.

As he had on the Wolf's Way, Dom found himself standing back-to-back with Sorasa Sarn. But instead of Amhara, corpses ringed around them, too many to count.

She raised her blade, parrying the blow of a corpse sword. "Nice of you to join me, old man."

"I've survived worse," Dom said, the words more resolute than he felt.

Sorasa spared him a single withering glance. "I don't think the kraken was quite so difficult."

Even as his greatsword cut a corpse in two, Dom fought a manic grin. "I'm talking about you, Sarn."

"I'm flattered," she snapped back, leaping over an Ashlander with no legs. It dragged itself along on rotting fingers.

Out of the corner of his eye, Dom saw Andry still on horseback, following Sigil as she circled. Other horsemen joined them, forming another cavalry charge to hurtle through the dwindling number of Ashlanders. Dom felt his breath catch in his throat, hope rising in him, even as his sword danced back and forth, his boots crushing skulls underfoot.

They are losing, he thought, eyeing the battlefield with a harried glance. He could see more of the ground than he could before, albeit covered in broken bodies. Bones piled everywhere, the mud turning red. But his eyes did not lie. The corpses lurched in fewer numbers, with the living army bearing down.

We could win.

For the Companions fallen. For Cortael, somewhere beneath his feet, lost to the mud like so many broken bones. Unbridled joy leapt up in Domacridhan like a flame.

Then he heard the worst sound in all the world. No, not heard—*felt*.

High in the temple tower, the bell tolled.

Its hollow song dragged him back through time, and Domacridhan of Iona fell to his knees, his sword to the ground. Sorasa's shadow wheeled over him, never breaking rhythm. He heard her voice calling to him, but the words were inscrutable, fading even as she yelled.

Then Sorasa was no more. The Amhara disappeared.

It was Cortael he saw, standing over him with his stern face, the Spindleblade in one hand. The jewels gleamed with unholy light, off-kilter, flashing like red and purple flame. He raised the blade and Dom drew back, fearing the steel edge. But his old friend did not move. He remained frozen, exposed to all the horrors of the world.

The Ashlanders boiled around him and Dom wanted to scream. But he was rooted to the spot, chained to the mud. Doomed to watch it happen all over again.

In a blink, Taristan was there, a vision Dom could not chase away. His blade moved with precision, stabbing through Cortael's heart. The son of Old Cor fell slowly, as if through water, his fingers reaching with nothing to grasp.

Dom's throat ripped raw, though he could not remember screaming.

The bell tolled again and Dom flinched, cowering. The vision of Taristan swung again, raising his sword to strike. Dom could almost feel the steel and wondered what body part he would lose first.

The ash wind blew from the temple doors, and shadows moved within.

There was nothing Dom could do but close his eyes.

25

A SHADOW WITHOUT A MAN TO CAST IT
Corayne

Corayne still tasted rosemary and lavender on her lips, even as the smell of the corpse army fell over the forested hills. She clung to the memory of Andry's tea, wishing for another cup, wishing for the campfire and the long night of refused sleep. Instead she bent forward over her horse's neck, urging it onward with the rest.

Until someone grabbed her reins and pulled her aside, out of the column and into the trees. The others thundered on and up, the first of Oscovko's band howling like the wolves of their flag. Dom was with them, his golden hair a beacon as it caught the sunlight. Sorasa and Sigil followed, the first with her bow raised, the other her ax circling overhead. Andry went with them, and Corayne felt the first of many tears spring to her eyes.

The hand on her reins kept pulling, maneuvering both her horse and his own away from the charge, to circle around to a thicker part of the trees, where they could wait and hide.

"Charlie," Corayne forced out through gasping breaths. Screams rose from the other side of the hill, a bloodcurdling sound from both man and monster. "Charlie, we can't leave them."

The fugitive priest refused to look at her, stone-faced. It was the most serious she had ever seen him, his brow and lips tightened to thin lines.

"You're no use dead, and I'm no use in a fight," he said, urging on the horses. "We're more a danger to them down there. Let them focus on saving their own skins."

Corayne could barely nod, choking back a cry of frustration. She swiped at her face with one hand, brushing away the wet tears on her cheek. It was no use. They kept coming, silent and unstoppable, trailing down her face until she tasted salt in the rotted air.

They remained astride their horses and halted at the edge of the hill, the tree branches gnarled around them like a wall of splinters and thorns. Beneath, the skeleton army filled the clearing, circled around the temple in a wall of their own. Charlie kissed both hands and touched his eyes, mouthing a silent prayer before dipping his head. His lips moved endlessly, speaking to every god in the Ward's pantheon.

At first, Corayne didn't want to look and squeezed her eyes shut. The sounds were just as terrible. The Treckish howls. The rattling screams of corpse monsters. Dying horses. Sigil's battle cry. A deep voice calling in a language Corayne couldn't understand but knew anyway. She opened her eyes to find Domacridhan of Iona cutting a bloody path through the Ashlanders, his horse charging over bones as he swung his mighty sword through tattered flesh and broken armor. The churned earth before the temple turned to mud, coating all of them in streaks of brown and red. With a shudder, Corayne realized all the blood was their own. The Ashlanders did not bleed. Their hearts did not beat.

Her heart leapt into her throat as her stomach plummeted to her toes. She almost forgot to breathe, her knuckles white on her reins, gripping so tightly her own nails drew blood. She didn't notice any of it. The scene before them was too terrible, eclipsing everything else in the world.

The battle swung back and forth like a pendulum, advantage tipping from one side to the other. Corayne couldn't bear to follow it, so she watched her Companions instead, seeking them out in the roiling chaos.

The temple loomed over everything, the white bell tower like a sentinel. Corayne hated it. Only a little ash drifted over the steps, blown by the winds of another realm. She tried not to see within, to the barest glimpse of golden light. But the Spindle buzzed on her exposed skin, like lightning in the air. And something hissed beneath, different from the Spindle at the oasis. It played along her fingers and face, as if tracing her features, memorizing her flesh. Corayne wanted to slap it away, but there was nothing to push off, only open air.

The pendulum continued to swing in their direction, the odds tipping. The skeletons seemed to dwindle while the Treckish war band held firm, brutal in their work. The hope Corayne hated so much grew like a weed, springing up in her heart. She tried to ignore it, tried not to curse the battle before her eyes.

Hundreds lay dead, skeleton and mortal both, but the bones far outnumbered the bleeding flesh.

"Make ready your sword, Corayne," Charlie whispered, dazed. His eyes shone with disbelief.

She grappled for the Spindleblade, reaching down to touch the worn leather hilt. Again she felt the echo of her father's hand. His failure, and her triumph.

And then the bell tolled.

Crows scattered from the bell tower, cawing as they flapped into the iron-gray sky. Corayne watched them, wishing too for wings.

I was not there before. I never saw my father die, she thought, a pain splitting her head. She clutched at her forehead, all but falling from the saddle. *But I know enough. The bell brought them.*

Through slitted, watery eyes, she watched the doors of the temple. The light within flickered, wavering between gold and hateful red. It pulsed with the sharp pain in her skull, matching time like a beating heart. Whatever wind there was in the Ashlands picked up, blowing smoke and dust through the Spindle and onto the battlefield. It seemed to embolden the Ashlanders, who roared as one, their voices hollow and whistling, their impossible breath hissing through bone.

Dom stumbled with the bell, falling to a knee. Sorasa kept up her rhythm, standing over him with sword in one hand and dagger in the other. But she wasn't enough, and the circle closed in, the Ashlanders hungry for a kill.

Sorasa's voice carried over the toll of the bell. "Sigil!"

The Temur bounty hunter was already there, maneuvering her horse through the scrum. She leapt from its back with ax in hand, rolling to her feet on Dom's opposite side. Still on his knees, he clutched at himself, but there was no blood Corayne could see. He flinched with every toll of the bell.

She could only guess what he saw, what he remembered.

Andry.

Despite the fiery hammer threatening to split her head in two, she raised her eyes to search for the blue star. There was Oscovko, wounded but still fighting, his mercenaries rallying around him. But no Andry. No blue star of a Gallish squire, barely more than a boy but better than every man around him.

On the temple steps, the doors still yawned, the red light growing. Shadows skittered within, and the first of the Ashlander reinforcements lurched through. They were worse than the ones on the battlefield, more decayed, turning to dust as they walked.

But they would be enough.

"Oh gods, save us," Charlie mumbled.

Corayne swiped the tears from her eyes again, her skin prickling as the air turned hot. She snapped her reins.

"We must do that ourselves."

Before he could stop her, she flew down the hill, her mind on two things.

The Spindle—and the blue star.

She heard nothing, smelled nothing. She felt the pain but blurred it out, letting it numb her. She saw only the line in front of her, between the ears of her horse. Her thighs tightened on the mare's sides, gripping hard as Sigil had taught her. She left one hand free to hold the hilt of the Spindleblade, the other outstretched with her long knife, held at an angle to slice through any Ashlanders who might attack her flank.

The Treckish horse crashed down the hill, hitting the mud without losing speed. It was a sure-footed beast, strong enough to charge through rows of battle. Corayne tightened her thighs and dug in her heels. The mare quickened at her command, surging on.

"Corayne!" a voice roared, sounding miles away. She couldn't distinguish who it belonged to, man or woman, immortal or mortal. She only knew it wasn't Andry.

Then there he was, crumpled in her path, the blue star like a lighthouse across the ocean.

The agony in her head tripled, but it paled in comparison to the searing gash across her heart.

A yell ripped from her throat. "Andry!"

At her voice, he lurched, struggling to push himself up even as the mud tried to pull him back down. He was wounded but alive, a long cut across his face, another bleeding above his knee. *But alive.*

"Andry!" she said again, letting the long knife drop from her hand.

Her fingers remained stretched out, her arm reaching its full length. She gritted her teeth, willing him to move a little faster, to rise a little higher. Willing her own body to hold.

From twenty yards, he met her eyes, his head shaking slowly back and forth. A few Treckish soldiers held back the closest Ashlanders, but they were closing in again. It was all Andry could do to wave her off, his palm raised weakly.

"Get to the Spindle!" he forced out, gasping for air. "Corayne!"

A needle of pain went through her head again, nearly blinding. But she held on, one hand on the Spindleblade, the other open to the ground. Screaming against the splitting sensation, she leaned, angling her body, her palm facing out.

She knew a moment later she would never be strong enough. Andry was too tall, too big, in leather and chain mail. She could never hope to pull him up.

He saw her closing in. By the flash in his eyes, Corayne saw he knew it too.

But she didn't stop.

An inhuman howl of pain escaped Andry's lips as he scrambled to his feet, balancing with his wounded leg. He fought his way toward her horse, picking up speed even as he gnashed his teeth, his face stricken with anguish.

He reached for her as she reached for him. Her fingers found his collar, his hands either side of her saddle. With another roar, he hurled himself into the saddle behind her, his breath coming in great, laborious pants.

Corayne nearly wept again as he slumped against her back, one hand around her middle, the other dangling free. Fighting the ache in her own body, she grabbed his other arm and tucked it close, making sure he wouldn't fall.

Then the steps of the temple were beneath them, her horse's hooves like hammers on stone. She glimpsed Sigil from the corner of her eye, her ax a red smile. Oscovko took Corayne's other flank, both of them fighting to keep up with her horse. The three of them barreled forward together, a battering ram.

The temple doors loomed, its monsters lunging forward from the inner chamber. Between the Ashlanders, she glimpsed the Spindle. It bloomed pure gold and scarlet, the pounding in her head beating in time with the changing colors. A presence watched Corayne from within, its eyes like burning knives stabbing her body. She tried to throw them off, but it was no use.

What Waits was waiting. Waiting for her.

She rode on, Andry at her back, the monsters all around. With a will, she pulled the Spindleblade from its sheath.

The jewels glowed with the Spindle's light, pulsing red and purple, dancing at the edge of her vision.

Corayne raised the steel high, two hands on the hilt, her elbows up as Sorasa had taught her. Weakly, she hoped the assassin was still alive. Then the Spindle drove out all other thought. Nothing remained but the portal between realms, the crack in the doorway.

I need only push it shut, she told herself, her cheeks wet and streaked with tears.

Somewhere inside her head, What Waits laughed, a guttural, grating sound, like the pieces of the world rubbing together.

Her sword caught the light and she laughed back.

The horse stumbled beneath her, its legs failing, neck arched in sudden, jerking pain. Corayne flew forward, thrown from the saddle like a doll. She braced herself for impact, the stone walls of the temple rising up to meet her.

And then she hit dirt, her mouth filling with the horrendous taste of hot ash and bone dust.

Heat fell over her in a heavy curtain. The winter was behind, a flaming realm of pain and torment ahead.

Corayne sat up, trembling, the pain in her head extinguished like a candle blown out. She still had the Spindleblade tight in her hand, but nothing else. Not the horse. Not Andry. She stared, unblinking, trying to make sense of the red light around her.

"What is this place?" she murmured, if only to herself. In her heart, she knew. Her own realm lay behind, back through the portal.

The Ashlands were a wasting desert. Not like the golden dunes of Ibal, blue-skied and brilliant. This was a red world, a broken realm, its dirt like rust. She spat on the ground and clambered to shaking feet, her sword raised to fight. All around her the desecrated Ashlanders hung back, staring at her with empty eye sockets and slack jaws.

With a jolt, she realized she stood between them and the Spindle.

As if a girl were enough to do that.

Behind the Ashlanders, the landscape stretched horribly in all directions. This was a realm of jagged cliffs and drifting sand, with smoke trailing around the crimson horizon. It was day with no sun, night with no stars, existing somewhere between. Worst of all was the silhouette of a distant castle, shattered and abandoned, its towers crumbled beyond repair. A city lay around it, gone to ruin. Corayne trembled and knew she looked upon a broken realm. What Allward would become, if What Waits succeeded.

"It is a pleasure to meet you, Corayne an-Amarat," a voice said, sliding like silk, but sharp as new-forged steel.

It came from everywhere and nowhere, from the Ashlands and within her own mind. Corayne heaved a breath, searching for the voice. There was nothing but a shadow on the ground, the silhouette of a cloaked man.

But no man stood to cast it.

What Waits.

The Spindleblade still gleamed, its own light stronger than the red sky of the Ashlands. Corayne glanced at it, then at the Ashlanders still staring. And at the shadow, growing darker on the ground. It spread toward her like oil through water.

She forced a smile in His direction, running her hand along the edge of the Spindleblade. Her palm stung, fresh blood welling between her fingers.

Her toes wriggled in her boots, testing the ground. Corayne wanted to run, but her limbs felt heavy, as if the air of the Ashlands itself pressed down upon her.

"You can't pass through," she hissed, brandishing the Spindleblade. The steel gleamed between Corayne and the shadow.

It halted on the ground, and What Waits laughed again.

"Not yet," He said.

Corayne willed herself to move, but her foot only slid back an inch. Even that felt exhausting, like lifting an impossible weight. She gritted her teeth, trying to look strong. Trying to seem like any of her warrior friends behind her, back through the Spindle in a realm unbroken.

"Your world is lost, Corayne." The shadow rippled with His voice. "You do not know it yet. How can you? That wretched hope won't let you accept defeat. Oh, how I despise that flame inside you, that restless heart of yours."

She took another step, this one a bit easier. The sword grew heavy in her hand. "Allward still stands. And she won't go without a fight."

"You cannot fathom the realms I've seen, the endless ages, the limitless bounds of greed and fear. You cannot know how wrong you are. I almost pity you." The voice rippled over her, making her skin crawl. "And while I hate your heart, I admire it too."

The Spindle burned at her back, singeing the air with its power.

"Put down the Spindleblade. Step forward, not back," He said. "And I will make you queen of any kingdom you wish."

"Is that what you promised Taristan?" Corayne scoffed, spitting on the ground. "He was so easily bought."

What Waits's laugh turned high and shrieking, like wind through a crack in glass. It nearly split Corayne's head open and she flinched.

"What a specimen your uncle is," he hissed. On the ground, the shadow inched closer. "No, Corayne, my darling, my dear. He does not need my voice to be commanded, but you—you must be persuaded. Yours is a sharper mind, a harder heart."

Her eyes widened. Shock ran through her. "And why is that?"

"It is easy for me to claim what is already broken, and Taristan was broken long ago. But not you. Somehow, even now, I see no cracks in you."

Raising her head, Corayne narrowed her eyes at the shadow.

"And you never will," she said, turning with all the speed she could muster.

Back to the Spindle, back to Allward. Back to everyone she held dear.

The Ashlanders moved with her, snarling and hissing, falling over themselves as they lunged. She felt bony fingers in her hair, grasping at her cloak, closing on her ankles.

But they were weak things, brittle and wasted like their realm.

I am stronger.

She leapt, the Spindleblade lightning in her hand, swinging with all the force in her body. Something screamed behind her, an inhuman groan that shook the Ashlands in an earthquake.

It echoed even through the portal, following Corayne as she landed hard on the marble of her own realm.

And then the scream was gone, disappearing with the red light, the ash wind, and the Spindle itself. The golden thread blinked out of existence as if it had never been there at all, leaving no sign but the Ashlanders still lurching around the chamber.

Corayne fought to her feet, stumbling on weak legs as one came toward her, dropping ribs with every step. It raised a notched knife, stained with the blood of too many men. She countered its blow, using the Spindleblade to cut through its spine, severing its body in two.

Then she slid to the temple floor again, losing her footing on the slick, bloody stone.

"Andry," she murmured, her vision sliding back and forth.

The floor slanted, rising up to meet her, but she fought the urge to faint. It might be the last time she shut her eyes. She was too close to the Spindle.

"Don't let me sleep, don't let me— He's too close," she murmured, stumbling.

Strong hands lifted her up instead, carrying her out of the temple and into the bracing cold air. It still stank, but she gasped it down, eager to press all remnants of the Ashlands from her lungs.

Corayne shuddered and looked up to find Dom staring down

at her, his eyes alive with green fire. She was too tired for relief, too broken for words. He only nodded grimly, pushing onward through the remnants of slaughter.

"Is it over?" she mumbled, slumping in his grasp.

He merely threw her over his shoulder in reply.

Behind them, the hall of the temple went dark, filled with shadows once more. The bell was silent. The Spindle was gone, severed, its golden light extinguished.

"Is Andry alive?"

Again Dom said nothing. Corayne didn't bother to stop the tears this time, letting them fall, hot and furious against Dom's shoulder. If he felt them, he gave no sign.

Seconds or days passed. Corayne couldn't tell.

Finally, Dom laid her down, letting her curl into a ball at his feet. She looked up, eyes bleary, expecting some explanation from her Elder guardian. Instead he slouched away. The edges of her vision blurred, narrowing her sight to the ground in front of her. This time she wanted to faint. To lie down and let darkness take her for a little while. The Spindle was closed, as good as a wall between her and What Waits. She was safe again, if only in this moment.

Instead her eyes sharpened, and the veil around her head lifted.

The gray clouds hung overhead, unchanged. Barely an hour had passed. And Corayne sat on the hill again, looking down at the temple and the battlefield as she had with Charlie.

She wasn't the only one.

The wounded lay among the trees, in various states of injury. A few moaned but most sat up, nursing cuts and gashes themselves.

The Treckish men were good with pain, grinning through it. A few compared wounds. Oscovko strolled through his men, shirtless, his ribs wrapped in a bloody bandage. Corayne gaped, trying to comprehend.

Behind her, she heard a hissing breath. "You did it," someone said, his voice pained but strong.

Corayne sat up on her knees and turned, slowly at first, then so fast her head spun. When her vision cleared again, she gasped and fell to her hands.

"Andry," she said, moving toward him on all fours. "Andry."

He lay still, his head cushioned by his own cloak. Someone had dressed his leg and the cut on his face, cleaning the muck away from his brown skin.

Shaking, Corayne put a tentative hand to his cheek, hoping not to hurt him. He felt hot beneath her fingers, not from fever but from exertion. The battle hung on him as it lingered in the air.

He took her hand before she could pull away, pressing her palm into his cheek.

"Corayne," he murmured, his eyes falling shut.

His chest rose and fell in steady motion, beneath the still-brilliant blue star. No bed had ever looked so inviting, no blanket so soft and warm.

Her exhaustion finally broke, pulling her under. It was all Corayne could do to lie down beside the wounded squire, her head finding home over his firmly beating heart.

Sleep came to her quickly, but the nightmares never did.

26
FAILING TO DIE
Sorasa

Between the dragon crater and the skeleton army, Sorasa Sarn did not know what to believe in anymore. No god she prayed to had ever been so real. Not even Lasreen herself.

Sorasa stared at her own palms, eyeing the sun and moon inked into her skin. The lines of her hands were not as dirty as they should be after a battle, but then, the Ashlanders did not bleed. When a knife passed through their tendons and splintering bones, it came out clean. She'd never seen anything like it, not in all her years of killing and guild training. The Amhara had never faced an enemy like this.

Which explains why Mercury is stupid enough to take a contract on Corayne. He doesn't know that her ending is his own, she thought. *But perhaps he can be made to.*

She raised her gaze from her own hands to the scene around her, the crest of the hill slouching over the battlefield below. Battered men spread out like fallen snow, propped up against trees or laid flat on the ground. Most of the wounded had been removed from the muck, with only a few too critically injured to move. The dead were dragged away from the fallen corpse army, somewhere down the pilgrim road toward the stream. Oscovko watched over his own dead, attending to the burials as a prince and commander should.

Sorasa was glad she didn't have to do the same.

Corayne was alive. Dom was alive. Andry and Charlie and Sigil. Valtik was still gods-knew-where, doing gods-knew-what. Sorasa cared little for the witch's absence. At least the rest had lived to see the Spindle torn, the temple closed. The battle won.

She watched them all through the trees. She felt like a shepherd counting off sheep. Corayne and Andry were fast asleep, curled up together in a way that Dom greatly disliked. He slouched nearby, storm-faced, trying not to glower and failing poorly. Charlie passed through the wounded with his prayers, kneeling to mutter a few words here and there. The people of Trec worshipped Syrek above all, and Charlie obliged, kissing his palms and touching their eyes.

Sigil stalked through the camp, grinning as she approached Sorasa. Her teeth were red, bloody as her ax. She was still flushed with exertion, a sheen of sweat gleaming over her bronze skin. Her nose was horribly broken, the bottom half set at an odd angle. If it bothered her, she didn't show it.

"Hell of a morning," she said with a whistle, extending a hand to Sorasa.

The assassin took it without a word, letting the bounty hunter pull her to her feet.

"You should set that," she muttered, eyeing Sigil's face.

Sigil blustered and touched her broken nose gingerly. "I think it makes me look interesting."

"It's going to make you snore," Sorasa shot back.

With lightning-quick movements, she put her fingers to either side of Sigil's nose and snapped, the bone cracking back into place. Sigil grunted once in pain.

"You're no fun," she grumbled, testing the skin with a light touch. "And you smell," she added, nodding at Sorasa's body.

Indeed, there was muck and bone dust and sweat all over her. Down her collar, in her hair, smeared across her face.

Sorasa shrugged and gestured back, looking Sigil up and down.

"You aren't so grand yourself," Sorasa said, and stalked off down the hill in the direction of the stream.

Sigil laughed and followed close behind, her heavy boots crashing through the dead leaves and undergrowth. For all her deadly skill, the bounty hunter had no talent for stealth.

They found a place upstream, out of sight of Oscovko's burials, where the water was deep enough over the rocky bed. They stripped down to their skin, both women eager to be clean of the battle. Sorasa braced herself for the bitter cold, but Sigil sank into the current up to her neck, letting herself float among the rocks and eddies. She splashed a little, enjoying herself as Sorasa got to work, scrubbing the battle away as quickly as she could.

Sorasa turned her eyes to the sky, hunting the low, gray clouds. "It would be just our luck for a dragon to appear right now," she grumbled, her teeth chattering against the cold.

"Hold off a little longer, Dragon!" Sigil called, hooting up to the sky. "Wait for me to get my pants back on."

In spite of herself, Sorasa let out a long, low chuckle. It grew and grew, until her chest heaved with full peals of laughter. Sigil watched, overly pleased, her cheeks going pink with cold.

Then she sat up in the shallows, splashing herself.

"I sent word to Bhur," she said. Icy water ran from her broad shoulders, working its way down her back carved with hard muscle.

Sorasa paused and blinked at her. "The Emperor?"

"He is my cousin, after all." Sigil shrugged and slapped at the stream running around her torso. "I dispatched a letter from Volaska, before we left. I figured I might as well, what with Charlie sending scribbles to every man, woman, and child across the Ward. But who knows how long it will take to reach Korbij," she grumbled.

The Temur capital was many weeks away, over steppes already blanketed in winter.

Her angular eyes tightened, a look of anguish pulling at her wide face. "I wish I could've told him about this too. And the dragon, by gods."

Sorasa shivered in the water. "What *did* you tell him?"

"Everything I could," she answered, ticking off on her fingers. "The oasis Spindle. Corayne's uncle, Tarry something or other."

"Taristan," Sorasa said through clenched teeth.

"Right, him." Sigil heaved a breath and set to washing, splashing her face again. She spoke through her fingers as she worked the blood away. "I told him the Ward will fall without the Countless, and the full strength of the Temurijon. I told him Erida will swallow the entire realm. Even him."

Sorasa's teeth began to chatter. The cold water, snowmelt from the mountains, felt like needles in her skin. "Will he believe you?"

"I hope so." Sigil climbed out of the stream and onto the bank, her bronze skin a pop of warmth in the gray forest. "But he might not want to risk his precious peace."

The air was almost as cold as the river, and Sorasa wrapped herself up in her cloak, trying not to tremble. "Unfortunately, war is the only option left to save it."

"I said that. Not as well, but." Sigil shrugged, taking her time drying off. How she wasn't frozen, Sorasa had no idea. "That's in there. What about you?"

Her eyes flashed, black as a polished stone. Sigil had no skill for manipulation either, and her meaning was plain to see. Sorasa shuddered beneath her cloak and dodged the question.

"I thought I might send a letter to Mercury," she said, trying to rub her limbs back to warmth. "But he would never listen. Not after whatever price Erida paid. And—" Her voice caught. "Not after what I did."

Sigil scowled openly and spat in the stream.

"He cannot blame you for failing to die," she crowed in indignation, smacking a fist against her naked chest. Again Sorasa wondered how the Temur woman hadn't turned to ice. "Feel no shame for it, Sorasa Sarn. Your lord should be proud, really. It's a testament to his teachings."

In spite of herself and her mask of calm, Sorasa flinched and sucked in a painful breath. *Sigil is right. It isn't my fault I managed to survive*, she thought. *But it isn't their fault either. They were sent to kill me, raised to obey as I was.*

"Sorry," Sigil said quickly, her scowl melting, replaced by a soft look of pity.

That stung worst of all.

"It's fine," Sorasa muttered, waving her off. She tried to think of the corpse army, and not the assassins who had fallen to her blade. "The Amhara are small in the scheme of things."

She threw the cloak from her shoulders and braved the cold air, pulling on her underclothes and then her leathers. They were still grimy, but there was little to be done about that so deep in the woods.

Sigil did the same, donning her clothes and boots. A rare grimness set in, her broad smile far away. She eyed the stream, then the woods beyond, where Oscovko buried his men.

The bounty hunter threw her cloak around her shoulders, sighing. "Many things are now."

They could not linger in the Gallish foothills. There were no garrisons nearby, but Ascal was only a few weeks' ride to the south, and being so deep in Erida's territory set them all on edge, especially Oscovko. He made his war band ready to head home before nightfall, lashing the worst of the wounded on stretchers between their horses. Andry was one of them, a fresh bandage on his leg. As she secured him to a stretcher, Sorasa examined his stitches herself, expecting a hack job from a Treckish mercenary. Instead she was pleasantly surprised by the neatly treated wound. The squire would make a quick recovery, and be walking again by the time they crossed the border.

Returning to Trec felt odd, but it was safe and relatively close. Sorasa knew it was their best option to regroup, and even Corayne agreed. She was given a new horse, and rode alongside Charlie, with Andry strung between them on his stretcher. Sigil led the column with Oscovko, her silhouette standing out sharply against the smaller men. Sorasa and Dom took the rear, not far from Corayne, with another dozen or so men behind them.

Two hundred riders set out through the Gallish woods, leaving behind one hundred fallen, lost to the Spindle.

A small price to pay, Sorasa knew.

The ride north seemed quicker than the way south. Such was the way of things. The Spindle no longer loomed over their journey, the ancient temple left to be forgotten once more. It faded away among the trees, white against the battlefield. Perhaps in a few years the clearing would be green again, the grass fed by blood and bone dust. The tragedy grown over, lost to the inexorable march of time.

As he led them home, Sorasa saw that Oscovko kept a quicker pace, too. He'd lost some of his prideful swagger, the color gone from his face. Sorasa supposed the corpse army had something to do with that. Now that he knew what they faced, and what Erida of Galland had loosed upon the Ward, he was eager for speed. The horses moved swiftly, making for the old Cor road.

For once, Sorasa didn't shudder at the thought of the open highway. They needed speed now more than secrecy.

Built during the time of Old Cor, the roads spread wide across the former boundaries of the empire, linking together their great cities and many crossings. This particular road, the Watchful Line, ran back to Gidastern on the sea before following the coast all the way to Calidon. It linked with many other paths and roadways, all of them crisscrossing Galland, with Ascal at their heart.

The Cor road was the quickest way back to the Treckish capital, but also the quickest way for an army or garrison to travel. Sorasa's horse followed the rest onto packed dirt and paving stone, wheel ruts dug deeply into the road. They were able to ride three horses abreast without the slung wounded and even the litters moved swiftly, making better time than they would in the forest. Still, Sorasa felt too exposed, and she huddled in her cloak, her furred hood raised.

She looked back over her shoulder, through the many lines of riders and trudging soldiers. The horizon stretched beyond the forest, the winding blue ribbon of the White Lion bisecting the flat valley. Black clouds gathered to the east, toward the sea. If she squinted, they looked like a gathered army rolling over the gray and golden lands.

Then she shook her head. Things were hard enough without inventing new enemies to fear.

At her side, Dom seemed just as off-kilter. His immortal eyes hunted the last stretches of forested foothills, roving through the branches before shooting skyward. He barely blinked, his stare like a piercing sword.

Sorasa clucked her tongue. "I don't think Taristan is going to jump out of the trees."

"A dragon might," he replied in a low voice, near to growling.

"Add one more thing to the list," she grumbled, shaking her head again. "No chance you're wrong about the dragon?

Dom shifted in the saddle, squaring his shoulders to face her. "Nothing else could've done that to a forest."

"Could've been a fire, a lightning strike. A particularly idiotic woodsman," she offered, too hopeful. Even so, she felt a now-familiar dread curl in her chest. "The last dragon in Allward died centuries ago."

"Three hundred and seven years ago, to be precise." Dom's focus dropped, his gaze turning inward.

Sorasa clapped her mouth shut. Needling the immortal was no fun when the needles drew blood.

He answered her unborn question anyway, teeth on edge.

"I was too young to be there. But I wish I had been."

Strangely, Sorasa couldn't imagine Dom at a different age. The life spans of immortals were impossible for her to fathom. *What constitutes a child among his people? He seems only thirty to my eyes, and acts like it. How long did it take for him to reach such an age? Is he still growing older? Will gray hair ever streak his blond head?* She tried to picture it but came up wanting. Dom existed to her only as he did now, somehow both five hundred and thirty years old at the same time. Ancient in the world, and still so new to it.

Dom didn't notice her scrutiny, too deep in his own memory. She saw it rise up in his face, a bitter pain that pulled at his green eyes. It was the only time she saw the years on him. Pain aged him like nothing else. But this wasn't a fresh wound, not like the temple or Corayne's father. This was a deeper ache, familiar, easier to bear.

"The enclaves aligned and won, at great cost," he said, low and steady.

Beneath her hood, Sorasa swallowed hard, her throat rigid against her collar. Dom was an immortal prince, a glowering old anchor, too bullheaded for his own good. An annoyance at best. And somehow she felt sympathy well up in her heart, working between the cracks in the wall she gave so much to build. Sorasa fought the feeling tooth and nail.

She hated pity. She would not give it to Dom either.

But then he raised his eyes to her own, green breaking against copper-gold. He set his brow, relentless. His fingers went to the hilt of his greatsword, gripping the leather. The steel was cleaned of mud and ash, but Sorasa remembered him at the temple. He fought like a tiger, like a bear, together in a single form. Nothing but the bells could bring him down.

"The last dragon made me an orphan," he seethed. "I will not underestimate this one."

At that Sorasa could only nod, her breath oddly caught in her throat.

"Then neither will I," she managed, facing forward again.

A moment passed, allowing both assassin and immortal to collect themselves. Their horses walked on in step, hooves clicking against the broken stone. Sorasa felt herself tighten. Every second of daylight was a chance for Erida's men to ride out of the trees and take Corayne. Every step beneath the iron-gray sky could be their last before a dragon struck.

She didn't know what would be worse.

"If you're right about the dragon, then another Spindle is open," she said, finally looking back to Dom. His usual scowl had returned. "The dragon came through somewhere. Or maybe it was of the Ashlands too—"

"Dragons are not born of that realm," he bit out, killing her hope at the root. A muscle flexed in his clenched jaw. "Another Spindle *is* torn."

Sorasa blew out a long breath. Suddenly hot, she threw back her hood. A manic laugh rose in her throat, and she couldn't help but let it go, all but cackling to the cold wind.

"Well, fuck," she snorted, dropping her face into her hands.

On his horse, Dom nodded. "Fuck indeed."

No stranger to exhaustion, Sorasa let the waves of weariness roll over her. She raised her head and rolled her shoulders, though she knew no amount of stretching could chase away the bone ache. *Every time we climb a mountain, another one rises right behind it.*

"I should've just let the Amhara kill me," she muttered, throwing up her hands. "It certainly would have been easier than all this."

The joke sailed over Dom's head. He turned to her sharply, movements too fast, his Elder speed almost beyond her comprehension.

His green eyes flashed. "Never say that again."

"Very well," she mumbled, taken aback, feeling her cheeks turn warm.

Dom went back to searching the trees, all but sniffing the air. He reminded Sorasa of a wolfhound, growling at every noise.

Then he whistled and reined his horse off the road, pointing as he rode.

"In the trees!" he shouted, calling to anyone who would listen.

At the head of the column, Sigil started and Sorasa nudged her horse to follow, riding after him.

A few Treckish soldiers drew their bows, but Dom waved them down. He leapt from his horse, arms raised. "Hold your arrows—they're children," he called, stepping into the trees.

Children? Sorasa was only a few steps behind, parting the low shrubs and pine branches to see Dom kneeling at the base of a fallen oak. He peered into its hollowed-out trunk. On the road, the column halted, with Oscovko himself jumping to the ground.

Sorasa watched as Dom coaxed a trio of young girls from the oak tree, each one dirtier than the last. Their pale faces were black with ash, the smell of smoke clinging to their hair and rumpled clothing. Only two had cloaks, the oldest of the three shivering in little more than a wool dress and shawl.

Oscovko joined Dom, extending a hand to the girls. "Shh, shh, it's all right. You're safe," he said, bending down to meet them eye to eye.

The girls looked him up and down before recoiling as one, clutching at each other.

"A war band," the tallest murmured, looking past Oscovko to his men on the road.

Sorasa slid down from her horse. The three girls were clearly petrified, traumatized by something.

"Perhaps someone less terrifying should speak to them," she said dryly, gesturing for Dom and Oscovko to hang back. "Corayne!"

But she was already there, coming through the trees with Andry limping along beside her, Charlie behind them. The squire winced with every step but kept pace, holding himself up without help. Sorasa wanted to shout him back to his stretcher but bit her tongue. He wouldn't listen anyway.

Sorasa stood back, knowing her own face was hardly comforting, and let Corayne approach the girls.

Corayne looked between the children, weighing her options. Slowly, she eased down to a knee, with Andry at her back.

"Hello, my name is Corayne," she said calmly, offering a falsely bright smile. "Who are you? Where do you come from?"

The tallest clutched her two sisters, holding them to herself. At first Sorasa thought she wouldn't speak; then she raised her chin, her blue eyes clear.

"I'm Bretha," she said. "We're from Gidastern."

Corayne nodded in greeting. "Hello, Bretha. You are a very brave girl. I can tell." She eyed their clothes and worn shoes. "Gidastern is a long way to walk in the cold."

"We ran," the smallest sister mumbled against Bretha's chest.

"Gods above," Corayne said, her eyes going wide. "What did you run from? Was there a fire?"

Bretha nodded gravely. "Yes. Too many."

"The city is burning!" the little one blurted out, bursting into tears.

The sound of a child weeping snapped something in Sorasa, and she had to look away. At the ground, at the horses, at Sigil still watching the road. Again she wanted to move on. Grab the children and keep riding.

Andry's voice was low and calm, warm as his tea. "How did you make it so far alone?"

"Papa," Bretha said, her breath hitching.

Sorasa winced, hoping the oldest wouldn't cry too.

"And where is your papa now?" Corayne asked, hesitant.

The girls did not answer, though the little one continued to weep.

"I see." Corayne's voice broke but she pushed on, collecting herself. "I'm sorry to hear about your city, but you can travel with us. We're going to Vodin, to stay in a castle and get warm before the hearth. This is the Prince of Trec, you know," she added, sweeping a hand toward Oscovko. He gave a small wave. "He's very pleased to meet you."

The middle child watched him, her eyes going round.

"A prince set our city on fire," she said in a strange, dull voice.

Corayne tipped her head and furrowed her brow. Behind her, Sorasa wondered what idiot had left the wrong candle burning.

Bretha hugged her sisters in again, blue eyes narrowing. "A prince and a priest all in red."

All her annoyance melted away, and a jolt went up Sorasa's spine, the edges of her vision going black. At her side, she heard Dom suck in a searing breath, while Corayne almost lost her balance, leaning back against Andry. He held her steady, despite his injuries, his eyes flaring open.

Corayne sputtered, her lips flapping. "A prince and a priest?"

"He wasn't a priest. He was a wizard," the middle child said primly, looking up at her older sister. "Spindlerotten, like Mama said."

"Oh, sorry." Bretha lowered her face. "A *wizard* all in red."

"In Gidastern," Sorasa hissed.

The girl's eyes found her own. She nodded, her haunted gaze

running the assassin through. "Yes. I saw them come through the gate two days ago. And then the burning started."

Sorasa's mind spun. She could almost feel the others' minds spinning with her.

Corayne crumpled into the dirt, falling back on her seat. She ran a hand through her loose hair, her eyes going distant. She turned from the three children, looking back to the Companions, staring but not seeing.

Frozen to the spot, Dom all but shook with fury. His hand gripped his sword again, threatening to snap the hilt clean off.

Corayne's fingers clawed in the dirt. "If Taristan is there . . ."

"Another Spindle," Andry choked out. "Another portal."

Sorasa felt her knees buckle, and she put a hand to Dom's shoulder, using his bulk to keep herself up. It was suddenly difficult to breathe. Her skin still crawled with the memory of the skeletons, their bony fingers, their rusty swords. She tried to remember her training, to push down her fear. Let it guide, but not control. It felt impossible.

Another Spindle. Not just wherever the dragon came from, but another one open. She fought to count. *Two closed, and two torn. Every time we take one step forward, that wretched prince shoves us back.*

The words had the opposite effect on the Elder. He did not tremble or quail.

For the first time since Byllskos, Sorasa Sarn feared Domacridhan of Iona. There was no Dom behind his eyes, only hatred and rage. His feral edge took over, pressing out all thought.

"He's close," he growled, and the girls shuddered. "Close enough to kill."

It was Charlie who struck the final blow, his terrified face like a knife in Sorasa's gut.

The fallen priest leaned back against a tree, forcing a heavy breath. Slowly, he kissed his palms and raised his hands in prayer.

"The Burning Realm comes. Infyrna."

27

EMPRESS RISEN
Erida

Conquest was cause for celebration.

And a luxurious coronation ball was a lovely distraction for Erida's nobles, both Gallish and Madrentine, who now occupied the same court. She saw the same misgivings in them all, no matter how hard they tried to hide them. What had happened to Marguerite of Madrence was common knowledge by now, leaking out all over the palace. Word had probably reached Ascal, slithering back along the Cor roads to reach even Lord Ardath's failing ears.

Erida knew better than to ignore viperous gossip. If left to fester, it would eat at their loyalties and alliances, destabilizing all she sought to build. And drive more nobles to Konegin's cause, sending them scurrying from one overlord to another. His efforts would not stop with Marguerite. She was sure others had received letters of friendship and schemes, within her own court and without.

She curled in a chair in the salon of her chambers, staring out at Vara's Bay and Partepalas upon the shore. Weeks had passed since Taristan left, pursuing the next Spindle, and the strange red tinge in the sky had not lifted. He sailed out under the cover of darkness with Ronin at his side. The wizard had insisted on his garish red robes, but Taristan left his imperial finery, returning to his worn leather jerkin and old, stained cloak. She worried for him on his journey, but not truly. None could threaten her husband, not with steel or flame. And he was suited to the road, born a wanderer. She only hoped he returned quickly, his Spindle torn and his task finished.

Her ladies murmured among themselves as they flitted about the salon, preparing her things for the coronation that afternoon, and the ball afterward. She wished Taristan were with her, but the Spindle called, and so did her own duties. She needed to crown herself Queen of Madrence, cement her title, and forge on toward her own great destiny.

And the Spindle would only strengthen their reign, paving the road to the empire.

The sooner it's done, the safer we both will be, she thought, tipping her head back.

One of her servants brushed out her long, ash-brown hair until it shone, still wavy from her sleeping braids. Another rubbed oil into her hands and feet, melting away the calluses and aches. Erida sighed, allowing herself to slow and lie still in the moment, everything quiet but for her mind. Her ladies kept to themselves, as Erida preferred. She knew better than to trust the young noblewomen around her.

The odd light in the sky bothered her endlessly, as it did the rest of the court, though no one had an explanation as to what it could be. Not even Ronin, who scoffed at their questions and shook his head so dismissively that Erida knew he had no idea either.

She turned to see Bella Harrsing perched near the window, looking like an aging bird. She kept her cane in hand, leaning back against the glass. The older woman craned her head as best she could, moving slowly in her advancing age. The campaign had aged her, wearing new wrinkles into her face, new spots on her hands. Her pale green eyes seemed to have lost their color, even as she gained a rattling cough.

"You should sit, Bella," Erida said, watching her warily. The Queen had no illusions as to mortality, but still, she hoped to hold on to Bella a little longer.

Lady Harrsing waved her off. "It hurts to sit," she grumbled. Though her body failed, her character remained, sharp as ever. "All that riding and sleeping in cots did my terrible old back in for good. Standing is better."

"I told you to stay in the wheelhouse with the others."

"Since when am I like the others, my lady?" Harrsing said, her face creasing with smile lines.

"True," Erida conceded. The maid finished with her brushing and set to arranging her hair, dividing it into four distinct braids. Her fingers were quick on her scalp, firm but not painful. "I'm glad you're here."

Harrsing tapped her cane on the floor and studied the bay, frowning as the red light danced on the current. "Because your husband cannot be?"

"Because I love you, Bella, and I value your wisdom," Erida said quickly, standing from her seat. Her shift fell around her in a white cloud.

Her maids jumped to attention, bringing over her gown for the evening's ceremony. Erida barely noticed as they laced her into a kirtle. The gown followed. It had once belonged to a Madrentine queen, as evidenced by the rich burgundy silk and tight bodice, cut low beneath her collarbone. The sleeves trailed to the floor, freshly embroidered with the roses of Old Cor, Galland's golden lion, and Madrence's silver stallion. They made for a glittering parade, matched only by a belt of braided gold at her waist. And the crown that waited in the throne room. Erida felt Harrsing's shrewd gaze as her ladies pulled her cloth-of-gold cape into place, fastening the jeweled clasps at either shoulder.

"Just because I am twice queen doesn't mean I don't need you anymore," Erida said, extending a hand. A maid slid a ring onto each finger, rubies and sapphires to gleam next to her Gallish emerald.

Harrsing met her eye. The lines between her brows deepened, her face going tight. "Is that true, Your Highness?"

"I do not lie, Bella," she answered, feeling the lie in her mouth. *Queens say what they must, and none can judge them but the gods.* "Not to you."

Erida waved the maids off with a flap of her hands and reached out, taking Harrsing's fragile fingers in her own. The skin was soft and plump, painfully swollen.

"You can tell me anything."

Harrsing's throat jumped. "I only mean—that business with

Marguerite," she muttered, drawing Erida closer to the window. The odd light turned Harrsing a sickly shade, but it made Erida's gems gleam like fire. "It's so difficult to believe. Knowing you as I do."

Erida narrowed her eyes. She felt Harrsing's judgment, even as she danced around it. "I am not softhearted, Bella."

"That I do know," the old woman said quickly, almost placating. "But I have never known you to be so impulsive. At least not until . . ."

"Until what?" Erida said through gritted teeth.

Lady Harrsing took a steadying breath. Not because of her age, but because she knew this was dangerous ground. "Until your marriage to Prince Taristan."

Erida pursed her lips. "I thought you approved of him."

"My approval means nothing," Harrsing sighed, shaking her head.

"Indeed it does not."

"You care for him; you want him by your side; you see his value as you see mine, or Thornwall's." Harrsing's grip tightened in Erida's hands, surprisingly strong for her age. "And I support you in that."

Raising an eyebrow, Erida tipped her head. She told herself to listen, even if her advisor spoke nonsense. *Bella is getting on in years, but she deserves to be heard out at the very least.*

"But?"

"But he does not understand the realities of court," she answered, her whispers turning desperate. "Politics. Common human behavior, it seems." Her eyes shone, wavering as she searched Erida's own. "And you do."

Erida couldn't help but smirk. Gently, she pulled her hands away. "I believe that's called balance, Bella."

"Yes, Your Majesty," Harrsing said, sounding reluctant. "I just don't want to see you do something rash, and risk everything you've built for yourself since the day the crown touched your head. Few others would flourish the way you have. You are Queen of Galland, the most powerful person in the entire realm. You have Madrence already, with Siscaria looking close to surrender. But don't grasp at what you cannot hold. Don't risk your castle for another cottage."

You don't know what I can do, Bella, or what my destiny demands, Erida thought wearily. She patted her lady on the arm, offering a small, pleasant smile.

"I'll take that into consideration," she said, turning back to her maids.

Behind her, Harrsing dipped into the best curtsy she could still give. Her cane shook beneath her. "Thank you, Your Majesty."

The maids resumed their work. One put the finishing touches on Erida's hair, setting the four braids into a single long plait, the length spangled with jeweled pins in gold and silver. Another dabbed rouge onto her cheeks and lips.

Harrsing watched her for a moment, as she used to do. Like a grandmother, filled with pride and contentment. But it was not the same as their days in Ascal, when Erida was a queen alone, a single throne beneath her. Now something darkened behind Harrsing's eyes. Erida wanted to blame pain or age. Lady Harrsing was an old woman before they even left the capital, before a hard march across the continent. The girl Erida used to be would have dismissed the strange look on her lady's face. The woman, the queen Erida had become, could not ignore it.

"By the way," she said, "have you had any news from your daughter, Bella?"

Harrsing sighed, looking grateful for the change in subject. She smiled truly. "Which one, Your Majesty?"

Erida's lips twitched. Lady Bella had three well-connected daughters across the continent, each with a fleet of children and a powerful husband.

"The one married to an Ibalet prince," Erida said sharply.

A shadow crossed Harrsing's face. She dropped her gaze, eyeing her cane as she weighed an answer.

"No, not recently. She sends letters, of course, but we've been long from Ascal, and anything would be slow in finding me," she said, her words coming too quick. "Why?"

Erida hid her own disappointment well. She knew what it looked like when Harrsing lied.

"The Gallish navy is having issues in the Long Sea. Pirates, Thornwall says," she said, forcing an exaggerated shrug. She wore a look of disinterest, keenly aware of her many maids and ladies following their conversation. "But I've never known pirates to cause such trouble. I suspect something else is at play."

Harrsing fluffed up like a startled bird, her skirts sweeping around her. "Certainly Ibal would not cross you, even with their fleets."

"Certainly," Erida echoed.

A maid offered a looking glass and she barely glanced at it, knowing exactly what she looked like, down to every fold of her gown. No longer a queen, but an empress risen. She needed only her crowns now, specially forged for the occasion.

Erida clapped her hands once, signaling her approval. The maids stepped back and dropped their eyes, glad to be finished.

The ladies fell in quickly, already dressed in their finest clothing. But none outshone the Queen. They knew better than to make such an easy, foolish mistake.

Erida eyed them once, just to make sure. Even Countess Herzer, doll-like, looked demure and drab, simple in a gray silk gown.

Satisfied, Erida looked back to Bella, fixing her with a stare, her eyes hard as sapphires.

"Ibal would challenge Erida of Galland, but I am twice queen now, with two kingdoms in my fist. It would be good to remind them of such things," she said, her voice filled with meaning. "Daughters do listen to their mothers, especially ones as wise as you."

Again Harrsing dropped into a shaking curtsy. Erida tried not to notice the discomfort on her lady's face.

With Taristan gone, Erida entered the throne room alone, the Palace of Pearls yawning around her with its pink-hued walls and precious paintings. It still felt like walking through clouds, iridescent after a rainstorm, cut with gilt molding and crystal-paned windows. The light in the sky deepened with the sunset, making for a splendid sight, as if all the realm hung beneath a shield of hammered gold.

The light flamed across the marble floor, throwing Erida's shadow jagged onto the walls. She kept her pace steady and even, neither too fast nor too slow as she strode the length of the hall, down the long aisle of assembled courtiers. Her Lionguard flanked her, their golden armor brilliant in the waning light of afternoon. Their armor and boots were the only sound in the room, Erida realized with a burst of satisfaction.

The nobles were not whispering around her anymore.

They dare not.

The throne of Madrence was familiar by now, after many weeks upon it. She was already their queen, but the pageantry served a purpose. And Robart was part of the display, forced to stand at the front of the crowd and watch. She caught his eye as she passed, noting the gold shackles at his wrists and ankles. He stared at her without seeing, lifeless as the corpse army camped in the hills outside the city. The loss of his daughter and son dragged him down like two anchors, making for a pitiful sight.

But an important one. Erida wouldn't give his nobles the hope of a restoration, not with a king so perfectly conquered.

In Madrence, they worshipped Pryan above the rest of the pantheon. The charming god of art, music, celebration, and storytelling occupied little of Erida's mind, but it was an easy tradition to honor. His hand upon the realm, a priestess known as Pryan's Joy, stood before the steps of the throne. She was a tall, beautiful woman with white hair and golden-brown skin. She wore the same lavender robes as her circle of priests, set apart only by the silver tiara across her forehead, thin as thread.

In her hands rested a velvet pillow, where the crowns lay.

Erida eyed them as she passed, ascending the steps of the Madrentine throne.

The Joy began to sing, her voice weaving through many

languages. Gallish, Madrentine, Siscarian, Tyri, Ibalet. All the tongues of the Long Sea braided together until they became Paramount, known to all. Erida heard none of it, beautiful as the Joy's voice was. She could only focus on the crowns, the throne, the sun setting red and burning.

There were too many faces, too many eyes. She fixed her gaze over the heads of the crowd, letting them blur before her. It was an old trick learned long ago in the court of Ascal. She looked stoic and resolute, even as she quivered within.

One of the dedicant priests put a scepter in her hand, a blooming flower made from silver and precious ruby. Another dotted her forehead with sacred oil that smelled of roses. They sang with the Joy, going through all the trappings of a Madrentine coronation. Somewhere, a harp trilled to life, filling the air with sweet music.

Inside, Erida tightened. She wanted the Gallish sword. She wanted the lion's wrath, Syrek's own strength and power beneath the patterned light of a mighty cathedral. Not this airy nonsense. But she kept still, back straight against her throne, the folds of her golden cape thrown aside to trail down the steps. *At least I look like a conqueror, and not some minstrel on a stage.*

The first crown settled over her brow, a braid of gold and emerald. It warmed against her skin and she relaxed. When the Joy raised the second crown, Erida sighed, letting all her nerves escape with her cool breath.

The silver circle, studded with rubies, slotted together with the gold braid, forming a double crown to encircle Erida's head. It felt lighter than it should have, the double crown of two kingdoms, but Erida liked it that way. It would be easier to wear, and more would soon join.

The Joy finished her song, a gentle smile on her face, but her eyes were empty of any emotion. She bowed low and Erida stood, the jeweled flower clasped in her arms like a child.

"Arise, Erida, Twice Queen of Galland and Madrence," the high priestess said, her face still tipped to the floor. Behind her, the courtiers echoed her words, dropping to their knees. "The glory of Old Cor reborn."

Erida told herself not to smile. It would be unbecoming. Instead she stared over her nobles, the light of sunset nearly blinding them. They could not hold her gaze, positioned as she was, silhouetted against the blaze across the sky. But she could see them all, each courtier bent and sworn. None wavered.

None but Robart, still standing, his shackled wrists dangling at his sides.

"You will kneel," Erida said, her voice high and clear. It was her first command as a twice-crowned queen.

He did not, his mouth hung wide, his eyelids drooping and empty. Robart was a shell, but even shells held power. Erida's fist closed on the golden flower. She winced as the sharp petals drew blood.

Lord Thornwall reacted first, crossing the aisle to reach for Robart. "Kneel for the Twice Queen, the rising Empress," he said sharply, and Erida felt a flush of delight.

But before Thornwall could reach him, Robart sprang, lunging forward. His chains clattered, ringing like bells. Behind him, the crowd of courtiers gasped and startled, wide-eyed.

The Lionguard jumped to attention, closing ranks in front of Erida even as she ducked, expecting the worst from a grieving father. Robart sprinted right past them, moving well despite his shackled feet and hands. He clanged with every lunging step. Thornwall gave chase but wasn't quick enough, stumbling on old legs.

Among the nobles, Lady Harrsing shut her eyes.

Erida did not, watching through the gaps in her guard. The world seemed to slow as Robart ran, charging for the windows behind the throne. The glass gave beneath the force of his body, shattering out into the bay.

The old king followed, plunging into the lapping waters of the sea.

For a moment, Erida forgot herself and her crown. Gasping, she ran to the windows and looked out, expecting to see a ship or a boat beneath the palace. Some traitor sent to recover the fallen king. Maybe even Konegin himself. But there was nothing in the water, only the ripple of white where Robart had plunged in.

His chains were gold, and gold was heavy.

Thornwall leaned out next to her, stricken. His face went as gray as his hair. "He will not resurface, my lady."

The ocean breeze kicked up, driving a wash of spray across Erida's face. She shivered, still searching the golden waves. "Surely Robart can swim."

"Swimming is not his aim," Thornwall said thickly.

Erida wanted to spit into the sea but refrained. "How fitting. A present for my coronation," she hissed, snatching herself back from the broken window. "Leave it to Robart to ruin my day, even in death."

Disgust flashed across Thornwall's face, but he knew better than to let it stick. He fell into step beside Erida, escorting her back to the throne in silence.

The Queen had far greater concerns than her old commander. She clenched her jaw, assessing the once-silent nobles now buzzing with interest. Most cared only for the gossip, craning their necks to try to see more than a broken window. But a few, both Madrentine and Gallish, looked worried—distressed, even. That rankled Erida more than the man drowning beneath her palace.

"All hail the Twice Queen," Thornwall cried, rallying the courtiers as he would his troops.

Lady Harrsing was the first as always to take up the call, gesturing for others to follow.

Once, their loyalty would have been a balm to Erida. Now unease wriggled at the edge of her thoughts. Thornwall and Harrsing could not be trusted, as she could not trust any other noble in her court. They were courtiers too, veterans of long years in the royal household. They knew how to navigate as well as any, and survive.

I have only myself, Erida knew, letting the cheers and oaths wash over her. None satiated as they had only a few weeks ago. *Myself and Taristan, the two of us allied against the rest of the world.*

But Taristan was far away, seeking the Spindle in Gidastern. They could not protect each other from so far apart.

And it was terrifying, striking a chord so deep Erida didn't know how to stop it. She could only weather the feeling, clinging to her mask of indifferent calm. It was her best weapon upon the throne, the only one she had today.

No, said a voice in her mind, a voice that was not her own.

It hissed and shouted, ringing like a tiny bell or the blow of a hammer on an anvil. A lion's roar, an eagle's shriek. A lover, a child. All things at once, and nothing at all.

You are not alone, darling. I am here with you, if you let me stay.

Erida's hands quivered, the jeweled flower trembling in her grip. Her heartbeat quickened, blood racing. The air went heavy on her skin until she felt both held and trapped, comforted and captured in equal measure.

Again she looked through her courtiers. Again she saw Konegin's face in them all, and Corayne's too. Then Marguerite. Then Robart. The many kings and queens who still lay in her path to victory.

She took a steadying breath, air hissing between her teeth.

Who are you? she whispered in her head.

His laughter was felt as much as heard.

You already know, darling. Let me stay, He answered.

Queen Erida clenched her hand on the jeweled flower, again drawing blood. The pain steadied her and cleared her mind. Her eyes watered, seeming to burn.

Twice Queen, Rising Empress.

She faced the room and smiled, feeling the world in her teeth.

28

BLESSED ARE THE BURNED
Andry

He stared into the crackling fire, waiting for dawn to break. The war band was still asleep, spread out in the open field, but waking early was second nature to Andry Trelland. It was drilled into him after so many years in the barracks, rising with the sun to train and to serve the knights.

Ambara-garay.
Have faith in the gods.

Andry heard his mother's Kasan prayers in his head, gentle but strong. She was across the Long Sea by now, safely returned to her family in Nkonabo. He tried to imagine her tucked into her chair, sitting in the courtyard of Kin Kiane's villa. The warm sun on her face, the purple fish swirling in the little pond, the air perfumed with orchids and paradise flowers. He only knew her home as she described it in her stories, but it felt real enough. In his mind, she breathed deeply, without effort, her green eyes bright and open.

Her sickness was gone, her frail limbs restored. She stood from her chair and walked toward him, brown hands outstretched, her smile wide and white. He wanted to go to her so badly. He wanted to believe she was alive and thriving, protected from the looming apocalypse. There was no other reality in Andry's mind. None that he could bear, anyway.

The squire had more than enough on his shoulders.

Embers crackled in the fire, glowing red, throwing off a low heat to keep away the frost. Without the protection of the foothills or the trees, the Gallish plains were cold and barren. A sharp, cruel wind blew in from the east, carrying the chill of the Watchful Sea and the acrid sting of distant smoke. Gidastern burned, and now they were close enough to smell it.

A silhouette stirred, sweeping through the camp with the wind in his cloak. It rose like gray-green wings. For a moment, Dom was a god instead of an immortal, his face raised to the early sky. His scars held on to shadow, a memory of what lay behind.

He moved toward the horses, all gathered together in a hasty rope paddock. With a jolt, Andry jumped to his feet, his leg stinging beneath him. He watched, wide-eyed, as Dom slung a saddle over a horse's back. Then the immortal loosed his sword belt and fixed it to the straps, buckling his blade into place.

Pained breath hissed through Andry's teeth as he limped, picking through the sleeping camp as quietly as he could. His stitches held, the gash on his thigh still aching but healing well enough.

"What are you doing?" Andry whispered, ducking under the rope fence. He puffed out a breath and leaned against the flank of the closest horse, taking weight off his injured leg.

Dom turned from the saddle and eyed him coolly. The dawn light turned his pale skin to alabaster stone, his gaze bright green. The first streaks of sun crowned him in gold. He seemed an immortal in every inch, too tall and beautiful to be born of the Ward.

"Do you think I would abandon you, Squire Trelland?" he said thickly.

Andry flinched, stung with accusation. "I think you're going after Taristan alone."

Curling his lip, Dom whirled around again. "I can move faster than the war band," he growled over his shoulder.

"Speed won't save you, Domacridhan," Andry whispered, limping to his side. Already he saw Dom fading into the horizon, a doomed immortal on a doomed horse, riding for a burning Spindle and the monsters within.

Dom fit the bridle over his horse's head and the bit into its mouth.

"It did once before," he ground out, giving the mare a pat on the nose. "I won't let him slip through my fingers again. I cannot abide the pain of it."

"We're two days from Gidastern. Two days only," Andry said, hearing his own desperation. "You heard what those girls said: the city is on fire. It's probably ashes by now, with a Spindle at its heart, spewing gods only know what. The terrors of Infyrna—"

His argument glanced off Dom like a sword off a shield.

Andry huffed in frustration. "We don't even know if he's still there."

He grabbed for his reins. But Dom snatched them away, Elder

quick, towering over Andry's lanky form. His nostrils flared, his green eyes going wide.

"I know enough of him," Dom snapped. His immortal beauty gave over to immortal rage, a fire burning for centuries. "Taristan is taunting us, trying to draw Corayne out. I won't give him the satisfaction of killing her too." His fists clenched, knuckles turning white. "He's waiting for her, and he'll have to cross me first."

Andry had seen far worse than a battered, heartsick immortal. He held his ground even as Dom loomed up to his full height, somewhere between mountain and storm.

"*Us*. He'll have to cross *us*," he said neatly. Again he reached for the reins.

Like a petulant child, Dom snatched them away.

"Don't go," the squire said, wincing as his leg stung beneath him. "Either way, you can't do this alone."

"You should listen to the squire."

As Sorasa Sarn stepped out from behind a horse, Andry let out a sigh of relief. She prowled toward them with her arms crossed, her copper eyes filled with a rage to match Dom's own. She sneered up at the immortal, her short hair loose about her face.

Dom sneered back. "I suppose you can handle things for two days, can't you?"

"Certainly," she answered. "Can you?"

His breath hissed through his teeth. "Sorasa, I am an immortal, the blood of Glorian Lost—"

Without hesitation, the assassin grabbed the hilt of Dom's greatsword and drew it, spinning quickly on her heel. To Andry's surprise, Dom didn't react with his Elder speed. Instead he slumped against the flank of his horse and put a hand to his forehead, the picture of exasperation. Sorasa didn't break stride, disappearing into the horses with a blade nearly the size of her own body.

"Can't go anywhere without a sword," Andry muttered, shrugging. He glanced at Dom sidelong, watching as his perfect nature seemed to fade, the fire in his chest burning down to embers.

He seemed, for a moment, not so immortal at all.

Dom sighed again, some tension easing from his brow. "Two days to Gidastern."

"Two days," Andry echoed, clapping him on the shoulder.

With a grunt, Dom straightened and began untacking his horse. "You'd think I'd be used to this by now."

"Sorasa?"

"Death," Dom clipped. "Though I suppose they are interchangeable."

Andry tried to smile, if only for Dom's sake.

"There's no getting used to it," he said quietly. His words hung in dawn light, silent but for the horses around them. "Not even for us mortals."

Dom tried to smile too. "That's oddly comforting."

"Glad to be of service, my lord."

Andry's muscles remembered how to bow. The skill had been drilled into him at a young age. When he bent at the waist, sweeping back his arms, time seemed to shift. Dom could be Sir Grandel, the grassy plain beneath them the marble of a palace.

But all those things were gone, eaten up by time and the turning of the realm. Even so, Andry closed his eyes, holding on to the sensation for just a little longer. It would have to be enough to carry him through.

When he returned to their smoldering fire, Corayne was awake, bundled up against the cold. Charlie snored heavily at her side, curled up beneath his cloak.

"The Burning Realm," Corayne muttered, staring at Andry from across the embers. Her black eyes danced with the firelight.

Andry eased himself to the ground beside her, stretching out his wounded leg with a low grunt. Again he looked into the flames. They sparked and spit, eating at the last of the firewood, turning all to ash. *The Burning Realm*, he thought. *Infyrna*.

"*Gambe-sem-sarama. Beren-baso*," he muttered, speaking in Kasan, the language of his mother. It was an old prayer, with an easy translation. "Let the fires wash us clean. Blessed are the burned."

Corayne's dark brows drew together. "Where did you learn that?"

"My mother." Again, the memory of her rose up in his mind. This time, Andry saw Valeri as she was in his childhood. Vibrant, full of life, praying before the hearth fire in their apartments. "She holds the faith of Fyriad the Redeemer. In Kasa, they pray to him before all others in the pantheon."

"I've heard his temple is magnificent," Corayne said. "The fires burn night and day."

Andry nodded. "For the faithful. They whisper their sins into the flames and are forgiven." He squinted into the embers, trying to remember the god his mother loved. "Blessed are the burned."

"I suppose we're about to be very blessed," Corayne mumbled, picking at her gloves. She didn't bother trying to hide her apprehension, or her fear. "Do you have any idea what Infyrna might hold?"

Andry shrugged. "I know what the tales say, what my mother's scriptures whisper. There are stories about burning birds, fiery hounds, flowers that bloom in embers. A river of flame."

He thought of Meer, the realm of the water goddess, its Spindle torn in the middle of the desert. Sea serpents, krakens, an ocean spewing forth over the sand dunes. Andry had seen Nezri with his own eyes and yet he still couldn't believe the sight. *Will Infyrna be even worse?*

"I can barely tell what's real anymore," he murmured, lowering his head. The motion created a gap at his collar, and the cold wormed in, drawing an icy finger down his spine.

Warmth at his wrist made him jump, his head snapping up.

But there was only Corayne, her fingers circling his arm as best they could.

"I'm real, Andry," she said, staring back at him. "You're real."

Then she leaned across him and Andry went numb, his breath caught in his throat. Only for Corayne to press down on his injured thigh, testing the stitched wound beneath his breeches. He gritted his teeth, hissing in pain.

"That's real," she said with a sly grin, pulling away.

"Yes," he bit out. "I see your point."

"At least you can ride again," she offered, looking over the camp to the horizon.

While the sky above them was clear, turning a steady, bright winter blue, clouds hung low in the east. Andry knew they were not clouds at all, but drifting columns of heavy smoke. The sun filtered through them strangely, throwing a red-and-orange light, streaking the sky with clawed fingers. The wind blew again, cold and smoky.

Corayne shivered against it, her jaw tight.

"Those poor girls," she said, her gaze wavering. "It was good of Oscovko to give them an escort. They'll be in Vodin by now. Part of me wishes we were too."

"Well, one can hardly expect to close a Spindle every single day," Andry said, a poor attempt at a joke. "It's exhausting work."

She didn't answer and picked at her gloves again, then at the vambraces on her arms. She'd worn them ever since the temple. Together with the Spindleblade, they made her look more like a soldier.

"You're sleeping better," Andry said.

Corayne blanched. "You noticed?"

"I mean you don't wake me up quite so much as you used to." He leaned back on his hands, tipping his head to the sky above. From his new vantage point, there was only the empty blue. "No more nightmares?"

"No more nightmares," Corayne answered, resting her chin on her knee. "No more dreams either. Just black. It feels like dying."

Andry looked at her sharply, abandoning the quiet peace of the sky. "Do you want to talk about what happened?"

She cut a glare at him. "You'll have to be more specific, Andry."

He bit his lip.

"You fell through the Spindle," he finally said, fixing his eyes on her face. *She is still here. She's right in front of me.* "At the temple. The horse bucked and you went flying. You disappeared through the portal and I thought—I thought you were never coming back out."

Corayne's olive skin went sickly pale, her lip trembling as he spoke. Immediately, Andry wished he could take it back and steal away the pain the memory caused her.

"He was there," she whispered. Her eyes glassed over. "What Waits."

Andry's heart dropped. He clawed his fingers in the dirt. Before the temple, What Waits was just a fairy-tale villain or demon in scripture, little more than a way to keep unruly children in line. Now Andry knew better. What Waits was as real as the ground beneath his hands.

Corayne's voice wavered. "He didn't have a face or a body, but I knew. I saw his shadow."

Andry saw that shadow now, deep in her eyes, taking hold of her heart.

"And I saw what he does to the realms he conquers," she hissed. "I used to dream about him, even before Dom and Sorasa found me. I didn't know then, what He was. Or what He wanted." For reasons Andry could not fathom, she blushed, as if ashamed. "I suppose Taristan had the dreams too, once, long ago. And he gave in to them."

He took her fingers gently, wishing he could tear away her gloves and feel her skin on his.

"Not like you, Corayne," Andry said, holding her hand as he held her gaze. "I know you fear your uncle. So do I. But you're stronger than he is."

She glanced away, exasperated. "Andry—"

"I don't mean with a sword or a fist or anything like that. I mean in here." He tapped his own chest. "You are stronger."

Her smile was weak, but brilliant still. She gave his hand a squeeze.

"I'm only as strong as the people beside me. In that, at least, I've been lucky," she said, withdrawing her hand. "Even if I'm fated for trouble at every turn."

Andry scoffed low in his throat. "You're not the only one."

"I grew up alone, you know." Her eyes burned into his, the red lines of dawn breaking over her face. "There was Kastio, of course. My guardian. Too old to sail but strong enough to watch over me when my mother was gone. But still, I was alone. I played with maps and coins instead of dolls. I had contacts, business partners, my mother's crew, but no friends."

Corayne put a hand to the Spindleblade at her side, running a finger over the jeweled hilt. It seemed to strengthen her, ground her somehow.

"Then the world decided to end, and I am the only person able to stop it." Her smile soured. "Can you think of anything more lonesome?"

Andry wanted to take her hand again, so badly his fingers stung.

"No, I can't," he said.

"But I don't feel that way at all. Somehow, all this, terrible as it's been—" Her breath hitched. "I'm trying to say thank you, Andry. For being my friend."

You are so much more than that, Corayne, he wanted to say. The words rose up in his throat, begging to be spoken, fighting for air. But he clamped his teeth and held his tongue. Spindle monsters and Erida's hunters were not as frightening as the truth in his chest, rattling his ribs like a cage. *You might not know what friendship feels like, but I do. This is deeper,* he knew.

Corayne held his gaze, going quiet. Waiting for a reply Andry could not force himself to make.

When she turned, he felt something inside himself deflate.

"Thank you to this lump too," she said, batting Charlie on the shoulder.

He snorted himself awake, bolting upright with a grimace. The young priest blinked at her and frowned.

"I am not lumpy; I am round," he said, yawning. "And I hardly consider you a friend. A nuisance, maybe, but nothing more."

Even Andry knew that was good as an embrace.

"Now, where are our stoic sentinel guardians?" Charlie said, looking around the camp with one eye. He rubbed his face, wiping away the last remnants of sleep.

"You know Dom, never far away," Corayne said, pointing off through the grass. "And you know Sorasa, only a few feet behind, making sure he doesn't step on someone."

They snickered together, the three of them. It reminded Andry of his life in the palace barracks, together with the other squires. Some were terrible, like Lemon, but they weren't all bad. Their training had united them, giving them a common obstacle. Taristan and the Spindles were the same.

Charlie sighed and climbed to his feet, his cloak still wrapped around him for warmth. "Let's see if I can't convince Sigil to let me go after all this is over," he muttered, straightening up.

Something small and tan slipped out of his clothes as he did, fluttering to the ground. Charlie stooped, but Corayne was quicker, snatching up the folded piece of paper. She turned it over in her hand but knew better than to open it.

"Give it back," Charlie said sternly, his jovial manner gone.

Corayne startled at his tone and held it out quickly. She flinched when he snatched it back.

"You should've sent this off with the girls and their escort," Corayne said, narrowing her eyes. "I doubt there are any couriers left in Gidastern."

He shoved the letter back into his jacket, going red-faced. "I can't exactly send a letter if I don't know the destination."

Andry quirked an eyebrow. "You don't know who it's to?"

"No, I know him well enough," Charlie answered, sounding bitter. "But not where he is."

"Ah," Corayne said, her brow smoothing over with realization. "Garion."

The name rang a distant bell in Andry's brain as he struggled to remember where he'd heard it before. It came to him slowly, as if through mud. The look on Charlie's face was more telling than anything.

Garion had been his paramour, some time ago. And one of Sorasa's Amhara brethren.

"That mind of yours is quite annoying," Charlie muttered.

"Don't I know it," Corayne answered, slinking down a little. "Sorry."

But Charlie waved her off, the folded letter still in hand. "It's fine. It's not a love letter or anything so foolish."

She quirked an eyebrow. "Oh?"

Charlie's face fell, the cloak slipping from his shoulders. He pursed his lips. "It's a farewell."

"Burn it," Corayne said, her voice suddenly sharp. "You didn't die in the oasis, you didn't die at the temple, and you won't die in Gidastern. None of us will. I won't allow it."

Her teeth bared, she glanced back to Andry. Again she looked more like a soldier than the young woman he'd first met. He thought of his commanders back at the palace. She was fearsome in comparison. After meeting her pirate mother, he found it easy to guess why.

Her blustering worked on Charlie, and he nodded grimly. But Andry knew better. Corayne needed to say the words, for herself as much as anyone else. It was the best thing she could do, and he held on to her conviction, false as it was.

Wincing, Andry stood. He wavered but held himself up, ignoring the pain.

"With me," he said, extending his arm.

The old battle cry of the Lionguard felt good on his lips.

"With me," Corayne answered, clasping his forearm.

They waited, expectant, as Charlie blinked between them. He eyed their joined hands with a withering look, his face pulled in disdain.

"This is silly," he said dryly, shuffling off.

Andry and Corayne chuckled in his wake, the laughter of one feeding off the other, until they both doubled over, gasping into their hands. It felt strange and ridiculous, but freeing too, to laugh so openly with fire on the horizon.

Something cold landed on Andry's cheek as he recovered, wiping his eyes. He looked up through slitted lashes, searching the cold blue above. There were no clouds over them, only the smoke blowing from the east.

But the snow began, one flake after another, spiraling on a wind no one could see.

29

WORN TO BONES, WORN TO BLOOD
Domacridhan

The snow fell over the war band, flakes drifting on the smoky air. It was never enough to white out the horizon, though Dom wished it would. He saw Gidastern first, a burning bruise to the east, throwing off clouds of black smoke underlit by flame. He half expected the dragon to be there too, already circling. But there was nothing but smoke above Gidastern.

Like any Gallish city, it had high walls and towers, the battlements of a keep rising at its center. Now the defenses were useless against an enemy already inside. Indeed, the walls served as another weapon, hemming in the city. Everything within was fuel for the raging fire, filling the air with the smell of charred wood and ash. The smoke drifted, trailing down the coast like black ink over the Watchful Sea.

Again Dom wanted to dig in his heels and gallop the last few miles. Hammer down the gates. Hunt Taristan through the city. *It is his life or mine. One will end today*, he promised himself. It was all he could do to keep on at their steady, maddening pace.

But what if Taristan is already gone?

Dom didn't know what he feared more. Taristan's absence, or his sword.

He eyed the city again, staring down the old Cor road across the coastal plain. It headed straight for the gates of Gidastern, bisecting the farmland ringing the walls. To Dom's dismay, the road was empty of travelers. After meeting the girls in the woods, he expected more refugees, but no one headed toward the city or away. There was only snow and smoke, spiraling in a hellish swirl of gray. Even the iron sea faded into nothing, obscured by smoky clouds only a few hundred feet off the shore. It felt like riding into the arms of a ghost.

Sorasa kept pace at his side, her furred hood lowered. She squinted into the distance, black brows drawn together, her full lips set in a grim line. Her mortal eyes couldn't see as far, but the clouds of smoke were enough to darken her countenance.

"How many live in Gidastern?" Dom asked out of the corner of his mouth. The smell of smoke was sharp in his nose, and his heart clenched.

She glanced at him, impassive. "Thousands."

An arrow of pain lanced through Dom's mind and he winced, loosing a low growl. "The Queen of Galland cares little for her own people."

"Have you never met a ruler before?" Sorasa scoffed. "No, she only cares for power. They always do."

Dom swallowed a retort, thinking of his own monarch back

home in Iona. Isibel's sending was still fresh in his mind, her white figure trailing him like a shadow. *Come home.* He'd called her a coward once, and he meant it still.

The walls grew larger ahead of them, made of mortar and stone, three times a man's height at least. They caged the fire and the city, their gates firmly shut. Dom tried not to imagine who or what barred the gates out of a city burning.

Oscovko's men numbered two hundred, many of them injured. Dom despaired of their ability to mount an assault on anything, let alone a city on fire.

He leaned toward Sorasa, lowering his voice. "Did they teach you siegecraft in your guild?"

"Somehow I missed that lesson. I can slip a gate or cross a wall, but not with an army holding my skirts," she grumbled, eyeing the soldiers around them. She faltered on Corayne and the Companions, battered but not broken. "Perhaps Oscovko has some ideas."

Dom frowned. "He'll probably just slow the march even more."

"His band is wounded, fresh from a battle not his own. And still they ride on," she shot back hotly. "He deserves some credit, at least."

The immortal felt a low current of angry heat ripple through him. "It isn't like you to give credit at all."

She waved him off, her inked fingers cracked raw by the cold. "I'm many things, but mostly a realist."

"Well, I think reality is catching up with the prince," Dom said. He tipped his chin and gestured to the front of the column where Oscovko rode, Sigil close to his flank.

Like Sorasa, the mortals couldn't see much of the city. Even so, the Prince of Trec lost a little more color with every step of the march. His face seemed drained of blood, his easy smile forgotten. He looked back and forth, turning in the saddle to survey his war band and the city. His lips pursed, turning white.

Sorasa looked just as stricken.

"How bad is it?" she whispered, still staring at the horizon. "Tell me truly, Domacridhan."

A muscle ticked in his cheek as he studied the city beyond. The fire reflected against the underbelly of the smoke, turning black to glowing red. Sparks danced along rooftops and within the clouds, flaring and jumping. The watchtowers and battlements of the keep were empty, unmanned by any garrison. Flames licked up against the stone, red flowers in bloom.

"At best, we face an inferno," he murmured. "The fire our only obstacle."

Sorasa nodded once, all steel. Her hands tightened on the reins of her horse.

"At worst, we face the flames, Taristan, and whatever else he drew from the Spindle portal." Dom set his teeth. "We face the unknown."

If the prospect frightened Sorasa Sarn, she gave no indication. Instead she unclasped her cloak and folded it away, showing her old leathers beneath. They were still battered from the temple.

"I can guide us through the city," she said.

Dom sighed, shaking his head. "I don't need to know how many people you've killed here."

"Fine, I won't say," she shot back. "So, we get through the gates. We close the Spindle. We get out alive."

In Dom's mind, the thread of a Spindle glowed, thin and golden, surrounded by roiling flame. A silhouette stood against the fires, his figure lean, his head bare. He wore Cortael's face, but Dom knew better. *Taristan.*

"Domacridhan."

Sorasa's voice snapped, her tone and his full name jolting him back.

"Our goal is the Spindle. Protecting Corayne," she said. Behind her, Corayne sat firmly in the saddle, her head bent with Charlie and Andry. "She is our first and only priority."

Dom wanted to agree, but his tongue stuck in his mouth. He glared at the mane of his horse. It was coal black, the same color as Taristan's eyes.

"If he dies, this ends," he ground out.

He felt Sorasa's furious, piercing stare but refused to meet it.

"What if she is the cost?" she asked coldly.

At that, his head snapped up. He looked her over with a flick of his eyes. She was the same as ever, a viper in a woman's body. Her daggers were her fangs, her whip a lashing tail. She had her poisons still.

Sorasa tightened under his scrutiny but held her ground, unblinking as the horse trotted beneath her. The snow landed on her upturned face, white flakes clinging to dark lashes and black hair.

"Have you grown a heart, Amhara?" Dom said, incredulous.

She smirked.

"Never, Elder."

Oscovko halted the march a mile from the Gidastern walls, on a rise above the windswept beach. From there, even the mortals could see the ruin of the city. The prince dismounted from his horse and stared, stone-faced. Flames consumed the streets and buildings, tracing an eerie red light. The roar filled the air, the smoke stinging Dom's throat. Ash fell with the snow, coating them all in gray and white, until one rider was hardly distinguishable from another.

Murmurs ran through the war band. The Treckish language far escaped Dom, but a few spoke Paramount too, and that he understood too well.

"Where is everyone?" one whispered.

"Have the people all gone?" another asked.

Oscovko eyed his men once more and Dom understood his aim. He was taking their measure, balancing their strength against the obstacles ahead.

"You say another Spindle is open within the city, and that she must close it," the prince barked, pointing to Corayne with his unsheathed sword.

"We've done it before," Corayne called back, but she sounded small, unconvincing. She shuddered beneath her ashy cloak, a gray ghost. Only the Spindleblade gleamed, its red and purple jewels catching the firelight.

One of the prince's lieutenants scoffed at her. "We should make camp. Wait for the fires to burn down, then mop up whatever's left inside."

"Or turn back," another chimed in. He sported a fresh cut across his face. "Let the Gallish burn for all we care."

Dom slid from the saddle, making for the prince. Both

lieutenants leapt aside to clear his path. They knew better than to get in the way of an immortal Veder.

"You will burn with them, if this Spindle is left to fester," Dom said, glaring between the two. His voice carried, spreading through the war band.

He wished he could show them what he saw in his head, what they'd fought on the Long Sea. The creatures of Meer were still loose in the waters, even with the Spindle closed. And there was another Spindle somewhere else, spitting out dragons, of all things. One of those monsters might even be close, burning its way through the hills and forests. They couldn't afford to leave another tear in the realm of Allward, another chance for What Waits to walk through.

"Our best hope is to close it now." Dom turned back to the prince, looking down on the stout warrior. "Before anything more terrible can enter this realm."

Oscovko stared back, holding his gaze. "And what has come through already? Could this be the dragon?"

To that, Dom could only shake his head.

But Sigil jumped down from her horse and clapped a hand on Oscovko's shoulder, giving him a hearty shake.

"Won't it be fun to find out?"

Dom winced. But Sigil's bravado was infectious, spreading through the war band. A few rattled their swords, and some color returned to Oscovko's cheeks. He put a hand over her own, giving her a wide grin spotted with gold teeth.

Overhead, the snow fell quicker, carried on a sharper wind.

The Prince of Trec regained his swagger, raising his sword high above his head. "I will not command you to fight if you cannot, or will not," he shouted, facing down his war band. "But this wolf feasts on glory tonight."

In this realm or the next, Dom thought darkly as the war band howled over the wind. The battle cry passed through them all, even the injured, who raised whatever they could in a flashing wave of iron and steel. To his surprise, he felt a cry of his own rise up in his throat, begging to be freed. He locked his teeth, waiting for the sensation to pass.

And then something answered the wolfish howl.

The horn sounded from the sea, a low, guttural noise that reverberated in Dom's chest. He turned toward the beach, eyes narrowed against the clouds offshore. But they were a gray wall, obscuring the horizon, even from Dom. Another horn picked up the tune, a bit higher and keener, and Oscovko flinched.

His eyes went wide.

"What is it?" Corayne asked from her horse, standing up in the stirrups.

Dom dismounted without thinking, moving to the edge of the rise to get a better look. Sand shifted beneath his boots. He squinted, seeing the vaguest of dark shapes cutting through the haze.

Behind him, Oscovko jumped back into the saddle.

"Raiders of the Jyd," he spat. "Vultures, scavengers, come to feast on the still-burning carcass. Will we give them the satisfaction?"

His war band brayed out their opposition, bashing shields and breastplates. Their horses pranced beneath them, catching the rising excitement of their riders. The kingdom of Trec was no stranger to the clans of the Jyd.

Dom hissed out an exasperated breath. He didn't have the stomach for these mortal squabbles.

Among the clouds, the shadows solidified into longships, their prows curling high above the water, sails flung wide to catch the frozen wind blowing from the north.

Then the first longship broke through the cloud bank and all his frustration lifted, his entire body going numb. Dom's legs gave beneath him and he fell to his knees, landing in the soft yellow sand of the beach.

Battle-ready men and women crowded the deck, working the oars. Their wooden shields hung over the sides of the ship, painted in every color. Their iron and steel flashed red, reflecting the burning city. Dom stared, not at them, but at the woman at the prow of the ship. He almost didn't believe his own eyes. *It can't be*, he thought, even as the ship came into sharper focus.

Still on the rise, Oscovko peered down, silhouetted against the smoke.

"What do you see, Immortal?" he called. The other Companions clustered next to him, concern on every face, even Sorasa's.

"Victory," Dom answered.

She wore pale green armor, her black hair wild and streaking over her shoulder. To Dom, it was as good as any flag.

More and more longships broke through the heavy clouds, bristling with shields and spears, but Dom saw only Ridha, the blood of Iona returned.

His cousin was not a vision, not a sending. Her form was real and solid, her own cloak of Iona catching the wind. She saw him as he saw her, and raised a hand. Dom did the same, his palm turned out to the waves.

Strange, unfamiliar joy surged through his body, growing with each new ship on the horizon. It felt like lightning in his veins. It felt like hope.

Ridha's ship reached the beach first, running up onto the sand. A dozen others followed close behind, cutting through the shallow waves. Dom cared only for his cousin and ran for her ship, arms wide. She leapt from the deck, landing gracefully despite her full plate armor. Others followed, most of them Vedera, but one was clearly mortal, with blond hair and whorled Jydi tattoos. Ridha matched his speed, closing the distance between them. He laughed as she caught him around the middle, nearly lifting him off the ground. For a split second he was a child again, dragged back through the centuries.

"You've lost weight," Ridha muttered, grinning.

Dom took her by the shoulders and looked her over, smiling so wide even his scars twinged. He steered them both up the hill, back toward the Companions and the war band.

"You look the same as you did months ago, when you rode off seeking a miracle," Dom laughed as they crested the rise. Then his eyes flicked past her, as the rest of her ship emptied onto the beach. "It seems you found one."

Hope rose up inside him as the Vedera of Kovalinn descended to the beach, outfitted in furs and mail, carrying greatswords like his own. A red-haired woman led them, taller even than Dom, with an iron circlet on her brow. She climbed the hill up to them with long strides and surveyed him with a cold eye, her white face raised.

Though they stood on some ash-blown plain and not in the halls of an immortal enclave, Dom bent at the waist, bowing low to the mother of Kovalinn's monarch.

"Lady Eyda," he said, putting a hand to his breast. "It is a pity we must meet in such circumstances. But we thank you for your aid."

She approached with fluid grace, a sword of her own in hand.

"My son's command is clear. Kovalinn will not doom the Ward to ruin," she said, her gaze going beyond Dom to the mortals behind him.

The Companions looked on with great interest, none more so than Corayne. Oscovko blinked between Eyda and Ridha, slack-jawed. Dom nearly reached over and tapped his mouth shut.

Eyda was unbothered. "My warriors are few, but they are yours for this war."

Dom nodded, bowing again. This time the others followed suit, blanching in the face of so many immortal warriors.

"May I present Lady Eyda and the army of Kovalinn, as well as my cousin Ridha, Princess of Iona and Heir to the Monarch," he said, overproud. *At least one member of my family is useful.*

"And the raiders?" Sigil said, eyeing the shallows below.

The longships ran aground one by one, hulls hissing up onto the sand. Four had already landed, with still more coming. The Jydi spilled out, less graceful than their immortal counterparts, but far more numerous. Dom spotted men and women, both fair and dark-skinned, all armed to the teeth. With only a glance, he understood why so many feared the people of the Jyd.

Ridha shifted, allowing the blond raider to step forward. She was short and wiry, with a wolf tattooed over half her head. She curled a wicked smile, her incisors sharp, made of gold.

"We are ready," she said, raising a fist to her raiders. They shouted back, answering her command. Then she clapped her fist to her chest, her eyes flashing. "But Yrla came first."

Dom had no idea what she meant, though Ridha clearly did. She all but rolled her eyes.

"Yes, Yrla came first, we know," she muttered, shaking her head with a small, soft smile. But it quickly dropped, her gaze landing on Corayne's face. Her breath caught in her teeth.

Before Dom could intervene, Ridha dipped her brow, touching it gently. "I apologize, but . . . ," she murmured, her pale cheeks turning red. "You look so much like him."

It was a knife in Dom's chest. Judging by the sudden look on Corayne's face, she felt it too.

"So I'm told," she bit out, her face going blank. "Seems everyone knew my father but me."

Ridha bowed lower, her armor clanking. "I apologize again."

"Well, I certainly see the resemblance between you two," Corayne mumbled, eyeing Dom. "How did you know to find us?"

The Jydi woman answered instead, jabbing a thumb over her shoulder, indicating a figure down on the beach.

"So the bone tells," the raider said.

Dom shivered, and a gasp ran through the Companions. They traded confused glances, all sharing the same thought.

He followed the raider's gesture to see the figure climbing to meet them. Her blue eyes were the brightest thing on the beach, her gray hair braided into many plaits all tied with bone. She wore black paint across her eyes and the bridge of her nose. It turned her fearsome, a warrior as much as the rest of them. Her old wool dress was gone, replaced by a long black robe. She cackled and sang a melody they all knew but could never re-create, waggling her bony fingers. At her waist, her pouch of bones rattled.

Annoying as she was, Dom breathed a low sigh of relief. He never worried for the witch, but he was glad to have her back all the same, even with her rhymes.

Valtik did not disappoint.

"Worn to bones, worn to blood," she chortled, walking up to them. "A Spindle torn for flame, a Spindle torn for flood."

He recognized the rhyme. She said it before, so many months ago, in a tavern at a crossroads. The Spindle for flood was gone. But the Spindle for flame remained, burning now, close enough to smell.

Ridha eyed them all, her brow furrowed in confusion. "We found the old witch floating out to sea, clinging to some driftwood. The Jydi said she is one of their own, and she led us through the clouds. Right to you," she said. "Do you know her?"

Valtik's laughter cracked like split bone.

"The Spindle looms," she sang, puttering along. "The dead tree blooms!"

Corayne took her arm, as if the Jydi woman needed any kind of help. "She's right—there's no time to explain."

Ridha threw her hands up in disbelief. "Baleir's wings!" she cursed. "You understand the old witch?"

"Don't fret over it," Dom muttered. "We have worse to face."

Beyond the beach, the city still burned, its gates still shut fast. Dom's fear rose to life again. He tried to breathe evenly and slow his quickening heart.

The others looked out, watching the flames.

"Into the jaws of death we go," Ridha murmured.

Sorasa was the first to climb back into the saddle, snapping her reins.

"You get used to it," she said over her shoulder.

They wasted little time forming up, the war band on their horses, the Jydi and the Vedera on foot. The raider chiefs stood out in their war paint, white and blue and green swiped across their eyes, the colors denoting their clans. Only Valtik wore black. She returned to the Companions astride a horse none of them had ever seen before. Dom thought little of her mysteries now, long used to her strangeness. And grateful for it too. His mind was ahead, on the gates of Gidastern. They were only oak banded in iron, but cracks ran through the wood. Flames licked up inside the walls, burning against the other side of the gates.

The gates will fall easily, Dom thought, though they had no siege engines and no battering rams. From a few hundred yards off, he could already see them crumbling. A few Vedera would not struggle to bring them down.

Oscovko raised his sword, roaring out a cry to rally his war band. They answered in Treckish, a rousing shout, their swords ringing against shields. The Jydi joined the fray, haunting in their chant. Their voices thumped like a drum, like a heartbeat, in a language beyond reckoning. Dom felt it pounding with his blood, and his horse pawed the frozen ground beneath them, eager to run. He was eager too, his sword in hand. The steel edge gleamed with the fiery light. Beneath the clouds and falling snow, he no longer knew what time it was, day or night. All the realm seemed to narrow, until there was only the burning city and their force. Even with Ridha's ships, they numbered less than a thousand.

Will it be enough?

This would not be like the temple. Corayne could not hang back and wait, not with Taristan nearby. And not with the Spindle burning in the city. She would have to ride with them, safe within their company, the Spindleblade at the ready.

She waited now between Andry and Dom, her face indifferent and still. But her horse betrayed her emotions. The mare whickered nervously, feeling Corayne's fear.

Dom wished he could take it from her, but there was nothing he could do but fight. It was his best use now: a weapon and a shield, not a friend.

Ridha stood with Lady Eyda and the Vedera of Kovalinn, the sight of them Dom's only comfort. A single Veder was worth many good soldiers, and at least a hundred stood at Eyda's back, armed and flint-eyed. But he feared for them too, Ridha above all. He could not even fathom the loss of her, not now when she was real and breathing before him.

Something clattered behind the gate, and every immortal turned, hearing what the others could not. Dom narrowed his eyes, trying to see through the wood itself, to whatever waited on the other side. Something was *scratching*, its claws breaking against the charred wooden gates.

Many somethings, Dom realized with a jolt.

Their roar was sharp and short, like a dog's bark but deeper. Bloodthirsty. It rose from the city, echoing out over the coast, louder even than the crashing waves. The cry settled deep in the pit of Dom's belly. His jaw tightened as the creatures roared again, his teeth gritted so hard they threatened to shatter. Many of the riders flinched, ducking down in the saddle or looking to the sky in fear. Others glared at the Companions or the immortals, searching for some explanation.

But there was none to be had.

The Jydi alone did not quail, raising their axes and swords and spears. Their chant deepened, louder now, rising to match the barking roar of the Spindle monsters beyond the gate. Oscovko followed suit, howling out his wolf call, and his war band reacted in kind, ringing their shields again.

Sigil added her voice to the cacophony, raising the cry of the Temur.

Then Charlie kissed his palms in prayer, looking to the sky. His lips moved without sound and Dom hoped some god heard him. After a long moment, Charlie looked down their line, his eyes finding each of them. He lingered on Corayne, offering her a grim smile.

"Don't die," Charlie said, dipping his head to her. "I won't allow it."

Her lips tightened, her smile tight but sure.

With a nod to the others, Charlie rode out of the column to

await the end of the battle, or the end of the world.

Sorasa's own language curled under her breath, so low only Dom could hear. He did not understand the Ibalet, but she kissed her palms as Charlie had, offering prayers to her goddess.

Next to him, Andry and Corayne clasped hands, bending their heads together.

"With me," Dom heard Andry mutter, and Corayne repeated the words, turning to draw the Spindleblade.

The ancient sword sang free of its sheath, joining the melody rising with the smoke.

Dom knew death now, better than many. He could not pray. His gods were not upon this realm to listen. He could not sing, with no cry of his own to add. The Vedera remained silent, still, coiled in wait for the fight ahead. Even now they seemed detached and cold, set apart from the lives around them.

But we all die the same.

As he had before the temple, Dom thought of Cortael and so many already dead. So many lost for Taristan's foolish greed. He drew on that rage, letting it fill him up. The anger was better than fear.

"The gods of Infyrna have spoken, the beasts of their fires awoken."

Dom shuddered and Valtik's voice rang out through the army, as if she spoke in every ear. Her horse bucked, rearing up on its hind legs. The old woman held her saddle without blinking, her focus trained on the gate and nothing else.

"Storm and snow, wind and woe," she chanted, reaching into the folds of her long coat. To Dom's disgust, she pulled out a leg bone far larger than any in her pouch. It was old and yellow, and human. Her skeletal fingers clawed to either end.

All down the line of the Jydi, other raiders did the same. Like Valtik they wore braids and long robes. *More witches*, he realized. Almost a dozen femurs rose in the air, brandished like spears.

They mirrored Valtik's movements, each witch holding a bone skyward, their eyes on the spiraling snow. Their lips moved as one, chanting the language of the Jyd.

The wind howled cruelly at their back, blowing over the army toward Gidastern.

Valtik's horse bucked again and she held firm, grasping the horse with only her knees. The old witch went grim, her maddening laughter long forgotten. Her grip on the bone tightened, her knuckles white beneath her pale skin. Her eyes stood out against the black paint, blue as ice, blue as the heart of a roiling hot flame.

The roaring and scratching kept on, nearly drowned out by the rallying army. Pieces of the gate fell away, the iron bands peeling back as the wood splintered. Fire licked between the planks, and then came a pair of long, clawed paws. They scratched and kicked, slamming into the gate over and over again, like a prisoner rattling the bars of his cell.

"Let the ground quake," Valtik hissed. "Let the storm *break*."

The leg bone snapped in her hands, split clean down the middle. The crack drove through the air, louder than any sound, even the wolves. Twelve more cracks answered, as the bone witches broke a dozen femurs in half.

The blizzard followed, white and raging, falling in a blinding curtain, until there were only the walls and the fire within.

The gates jumped on their hinges, pulsing with every blow.

Oscovko rattled his shield one last time and raised his sword. Too many blades to count rose with his own, Dom's greatsword included. Snow lashed the length of his steel.

"Charge!" the prince screamed, and Dom roared with him, a guttural sound exploding from his throat.

His horse shuddered and exploded into a gallop to match the rest of the war band. Their column jumped out ahead of the soldiers on foot, the first wave of the assault. The blizzard blew at their backs, as if pushing them all forward.

The immortal settled into himself as instinct and memory took over, his long years in the training yard directing his body. His grip changed on his sword, and his muscles rolled in his back, drawing the blade to strike whatever came through the gates.

He expected the corpse army. Gallish soldiers. Taristan himself.

When the gates burst open, shattering out toward them, Dom's immortal heart nearly stopped beating.

At first glance, he thought they were gigantic red wolves, but they were so big, taller than a man. Their legs were too long, black from the shoulder down, as if dipped in charcoal. Flame licked over the creatures but did not burn them. Because it *came* from them, marching down their spines like a ridge of raised fur. Snow swirled around their bodies, melting on their flaming coats. They screamed and barked, keening at the charging army, the insides of their mouths glowing like fiery coals. The dead grass sparked beneath their paws and sweeping tails, bursting into flame.

The edge of Dom's sight went black, his vision spotting, but he fought through it. His horse bucked beneath him, screaming in protest, trying to turn away from the hounds of Infyrna. But Dom kept a firm grip on the reins, forcing her back on course with the other horses. The war band surged forward, the Companions with them, their eyes filled with the flaming light.

There was no going back now.

A volley of Jydi arrows sailed over the charge, sizzling as they shot into the hounds. Most missed their mark or burned to nothing, but a few hounds screamed, pawing at the iron arrowheads deep in their flesh. The flames on their back flared white with pain. One even guttered out, the hound turning to ashes as it died.

Dom leaned forward in the saddle, eager to fight.

They could be wounded.

They could be killed.

And that was enough for Domacridhan.

30

DEAD ROSES IN BLOOM
Sorasa

Her sword slid back into its sheath with a neat click and Sorasa drew her bow, the horse still galloping beneath her. She nocked an arrow to the string, taking aim between the riders ahead of her, her eyes narrowed on the impossible monsters guarding the gate. The arrow sang from the bowstring, flitting past Sigil's ear, so close it ruffled her black hair. She didn't flinch. Sorasa put another arrow to the string and fired again. She managed to get off four shots before the main gates loomed, yawning wide. It was like riding into the mouth of a hot oven.

The Infyrna hounds keened and howled, their muscles bunching beneath their furs. They moved as one, lunging into a charge to match the army. Sorasa tried not to imagine what it would feel like to have her throat ripped out by a monster made of flame.

Such was her way, taught in the Guild so many years ago. Her mind shrank to hold only what she needed. She killed every useless emotion as soon as her brain could birth it, tossing away all thoughts of pain or fear, regret or weakness. They would only slow her down.

Oscovko kept his sword high, howling with his men, leading the entire charge. Sigil rode right behind him, alongside his lieutenants. And then the Companions charged together, knotted around Corayne. Sorasa sensed her now just behind her horse's flank, bent low over her mare's neck.

"Charge through them—don't let the horses slow," Dom shouted somewhere, his voice distant though he rode only a few feet away.

The blizzard tore at Sorasa's back, blowing hard against the oncoming wall of fur and flame. The wolves opened their jaws, the air before them wavering with the lines of heat.

Sorasa drew her faithful sword and kissed the flat of the blade.

The charge felt like riding the crest of a massive wave, with the shore rising up to meet them. The hounds were a wall of oncoming flame, their eyes glittering with menace.

Sorasa braced, gripping the reins in one hand and her blade in the other.

The fastest of the hounds gave a mighty leap, launching up over the first line of the Treckish charge. It landed hard, taking down two riders and their screaming horses. The monster tore them apart, the flesh of their bodies sizzling as it worked, cooked by its own flame.

Bile filled Sorasa's mouth but she swallowed it down.

The other monsters of Infyrna slammed into the charge head-on, their burning bodies as dangerous as their claws and teeth.

Horses and men screamed, their skin blistering with burns even as they rode through. Dom acted as a battering ram, his greatsword sweeping back and forth to cut a path through the wolves. The Companions followed, pressing together, Corayne within them. Heat blazed along Sorasa's cheek as she passed a hound, her sword slicing through the flesh at its shoulder. The blade hissed as if cutting through cooked meat. The hound screamed but she was already ahead, knowing better than to look back. Blood dripped from her steel, black and smoking in the snow. Another hound lunged and she pulled hard, the horse moving with a sharp jerk of her reins. The hound missed them by inches, colliding with a Treckish mercenary.

The two charge lines braided together, each overwhelming the other. Both sides were made of flesh, succumbing to flame and steel in equal rhythm. Howls filled the air, both human and monster. Flame, smoke, snow, and blood swirled before Sorasa's eyes until all the world was red, black, and white, burning and freezing, her body sweating and shivering at the same time. The terror she held back peeked its head over her inner walls, threatening to break through.

"Keep moving!" a voice shouted over the fray.

Sorasa spotted Sigil's head behind the line of hounds, within the splintered gates. She stood squared to the battle, boots planted. Her horse was gone, and black blood streamed down her body. Her ax hung heavy in one hand, dripping smoking blood onto the ground.

It was the push Sorasa needed.

"This way," she snarled out, urging her horse toward Sigil, with

Corayne and Andry close behind. She felt like a mother hen leading chicks through a tornado.

Dom's blond head gleamed at the edge of her vision, bringing up the rear. The immortal took a hound's head off with a single swipe of his Elder steel, its body collapsing to ashes beneath his horse's hooves.

And then the Elders reached the hound line, the immortal warriors weaving through the cavalry like lethal dancers. Dom's cousin led them, her black hair loose and streaming, splaying out behind her in an ebony cape. The Elder swords flashed, shedding smoking blood like rain. The Jydi crashed through after them, ferocious, a pack of wolves themselves, clad in fur and leather. Their axes and arrows arched, leaving ashes in their wake.

The burned earth turned to stone beneath her horse's hooves as Sorasa rode through the gate. Sigil grasped her by the elbow and leapt, swinging up into the saddle behind the assassin without so much as a grunt of exertion. The horse slowed but didn't stop, adjusting to the new weight as best he could.

"I think you're missing an eyebrow," Sigil shouted in Sorasa's ear.

Sorasa winced, touching the space above her left eye. She felt a gap in her brow, hot to the touch and stinging.

"At least I didn't lose my hair this time," Sorasa hissed back.

She looked back over her shoulder to find Corayne and the others bearing down, almost on top of them as they galloped through the gateyard onto the wide streets of Gidastern. Fire crackled all around them, as more hounds leapt from roof to roof. They barked and snapped, stalking the heights of the buildings, a pack of hunters surrounding a bowl of prey. A few jumped to the street, barking out a call, the ridge of fire jumping up on their backs. Wood splintered and stone collapsed everywhere, booms resounding through the city as flame consumed it whole. The heat was nearly unbearable, and sweat poured down Sorasa's face, filling her mouth with the taste of salt.

More of their patchwork army streamed past the gate, finding gaps in the packs of Infyrna hounds. The Elders cut through with stunning precision, so fluid and graceful Sorasa almost stopped to watch the display. Instead she pulled her focus forward, deeper into the burning city.

The hounds grew in number, collecting on the battlements and rooftops.

The others fell into line next to her, even Valtik. She held half the broken leg bone, as good as a knife in her hand. The sharp, splintered end dripped black blood. The old witch eyed the hounds above them, her teeth bared to match their fangs.

Corayne's face seemed to glow, reflecting the flickering light of a thousand flames. Like the rest of them, her skin gleamed with sweat. Her black eyes ate up the red-and-orange light.

Sorasa gritted her teeth, snapping her reins. "Let's hunt."

The Companions were the first raindrops of a storm, with the hurricane rolling behind them through the Gidastern streets. They dodged a dozen Infyrna hounds, leaving the monsters to face the war band, the Jydi, and the Elder warriors. Timber-framed walls and thatched roofs collapsed at seemingly every turn, the city turning into a monster itself. Smoke stalked through the streets, clinging in heavy dark clouds, making it difficult to breathe even as the horses galloped through.

Sorasa squinted through the spiraling black and gray, shielding her eyes from a hail of sparks. Gidastern was a trade port, built on the coast of the Watchful Sea, its walls and towers meant to defend against raider attack. There was a market close to the docks, and a church near the keep, but the rest tangled in her mind. She tried to remember the city as it was, reaching through the years since she last walked these streets. The inferno didn't help, nor did the pursuing hounds. The map in her mind faded and she let instinct take over.

People lived in patterns, their lives repeating the same rhythm. It was the same with every village and town, every city. They grew along crossroads and natural harbors, like water filling a bowl. Sorasa kept her band on the widest street, knowing it would lead them to the center of the city. Her nostrils flared, and she gasped against the smoke, her eyes stinging even as she hunted for the spire of a church among the flames.

There.

Fire wreathed the tall steeple of the church, red flames creeping up the carved stone in a hellish sight. The golden image of Syrek stood at the highest point, the god's sword raised against the smoke as if to ward it off. As Sorasa watched, the figure melted, the steeple crumbling in on itself.

She rounded the corner as the roof of the church collapsed, spitting out a cloud of dust and debris. It washed over the surrounding churchyard, painting the grounds and graveyard in flaking shades of gray. The Companions hacked and coughed, even Sorasa, who spat on the ground with a wheeze. Gasping for air, they rode into the fenced churchyard, once an island of green within the city. Now it was as gray as anything else, washed of all color, the grass and tombstones blanketed in a fine layer of ash. Dozens of statues lined the church walls and stood guard among the graves, all covered in soot, but it was otherwise empty. Beyond the churchyard, the castle keep of Gidastern held watch, stones standing firm against the flames. Its ramparts and battlements were quiet too. There were no hounds here, even as their shrieks echoed from the gates.

Fighting for air, Sorasa slowed her horse and the others matched her, looking around the yard with trepidation. The sounds of fighting and flame echoed, but silence pressed down between the church and the keep. It felt like standing in the eye of a storm.

Sorasa shivered, remembering the three girls who'd escaped Gidastern. She put a hand into her leathers, closing her fingers around Lord Mercury's jade snake. The stone was cool to the touch, grounding her against the unbearable heat.

"Where is everyone?" Corayne said in a low voice.

Next to her, Andry shuddered. "Taristan left none alive in Rouleine," he breathed. "It seems Gidastern met the same fate."

Corayne frowned and swiped at her face, brushing some of the debris away. Her cheeks flushed red beneath the dust. "But where are the bodies?"

Sorasa wondered the same. Her stomach twisted, every instinct shrieking. She met Dom's eye over Corayne's head, and saw the same alarm in him too.

"Something is wrong here," he growled. His eyes hunted among the statues and gray tombs, searing through the drifting clouds of smoke.

"What gave you that idea?" Corayne muttered.

At her back, Sorasa felt Sigil shift, her body going rigid. The Temur bounty hunter adjusted her grip on her ax.

"Ride on, Sorasa," she whispered, sounding afraid for the first time Sorasa could ever remember. "Ride on."

The assassin knew better than to argue with Sigil's intuition. She shifted in the saddle, but before she could direct the horse, Corayne thrust out a hand.

"Wait," she gasped, eyes wide as she scanned the yard. "The Spindle *is* here. I can feel it."

Dom whirled to her and took her shoulder. "Where?"

Before she could answer, the statues around the church *moved*.

As one, they lurched forward, ashes falling from their bodies, revealing flesh instead of stone. Snarls escaped their ruined throats.

Sorasa jumped in her skin and the horse jumped with her, braying in fear. The stallion toppled sideways and Sorasa leapt from its back just in time, narrowly avoiding being slammed against the ground. Sigil wasn't so lucky. She landed hard, the horse pinning her down.

While the others shouted and yelled, Sorasa slid to the grass, bracing her shoulder against the wriggling horse. All thoughts of the Spindle disappeared. Sigil breathed hard beneath her, one leg trapped under the stallion's heavy body. Her eyes shone as she fought against the pain, pushing against the horse on top of her.

Then Dom was there, squatting low to get his hands under the horse's shoulder. With a grunt, he lifted the entire horse back onto his feet.

"Go, go, go," Sigil yelped, eyes wide as she stared between Sorasa and Dom at the steps of the church. "I'll be right behind you."

"Not a chance," Sorasa growled, dragging Sigil to her feet, with Dom on her opposite side.

The three whirled to face the statues hurtling down among the graves, their jaws slack and eyes rolling. Sorasa blinked at them, her mind slow as she tried to comprehend the sight in front of her. Her knees buckled and she nearly crumpled under Sigil's weight.

Beneath the soot and debris, the lumbering figures wore normal clothing. Cloaks and skirts, tunics, boots. Some armor. The usual trappings of merchants and shopkeepers, farmers, watchmen and guards. They lunged with halted steps. Most sported burns of some kind or clutched at wounds. *Fatal wounds*, Sorasa realized, watching as a woman tripped over her own entrails.

These were the bodies, the people of Gidastern.

"Dead," she heard Corayne whisper somewhere, still astride her horse. "But—"

Dozens more burst from the keep, spitting and snapping their teeth, more animal than human. They slammed against the fence around the churchyard, reaching with curled fingers. Some began to climb while the rest lunged for the open archway. Sick realization crept through Sorasa. They moved like the corpse army, without thought, their souls gone but their bodies remaining.

"Keep going," Sorasa snarled, forcing Sigil to walk. "Find the Spindle."

After a single trembling step, Dom slung the Temur woman over his shoulder. He looked like a mountain carrying another mountain.

They ran together as Corayne and Andry slid to the ground, leaping from horseback. Their horses tossed in fear, galloping off into the burning city.

Andry drew his sword and cast his cloak aside, revealing his blue-starred tunic and mail. He looked like a knight, while Corayne steeled herself, facing down the undead horde. She kept the Spindleblade sheathed on her back and drew her long knife, the tiny spikes on her vambraces springing out. The realm's hope knew how to defend herself now. If nothing else, Sorasa Sarn had accomplished that.

The assassin moved backward, her sword drawn to fend off the first of the undead. They fell just as easily as the corpse army. She cut apart man, woman, and child, severing limbs with abandon. It felt like butchery, and even the assassin's stomach churned. *They're already dead*, she told herself. But their numbers only grew, as if summoned to the churchyard. Dozens more undead bodies shambled down the many streets of Gidastern or lurched out of doorways, some of them still on fire. They broke against the iron fence around the yard, but the barrier only bought a little time, forcing them to bottleneck through the arches. The assassin didn't bother counting, focusing only on the closest person. The next opponent.

"Follow the Spindle, Corayne," Andry called out, putting the others to his back. He dueled well, holding off a stumbling line of undead. Snow and smoke swirled around him.

Sorasa bit her own tongue. *Run!* she wanted to scream at him. Dread rose up inside her, too much to shove away. She felt like a pot on the fire, boiling over and set aflame. But she let her muscles move without her mind. They knew how to hold a sword, how to strike with a dagger or snap a whip. She danced between all three, her Amhara teachings keeping her and the others alive. But her chest tightened, her lungs straining to breathe in the smoke. Water ran from her irritated eyes and sweat slicked her palms, loosening her grip. Little by little, she slowed.

But the others are coming, Sorasa told herself. *The raiders, the Elders. Oscovko and his men.* The city echoed with the sounds of battle, steel and shrieking hounds. The roaring fires, the shattering of wood and stone. Sorasa only hoped the army lasted long enough to find them.

Sigil tried to keep her weight off her wounded leg and fight at the same time, leaning hard with her ax in one hand. Dom braced her under one arm and fought with the other, his greatsword cutting through the undead as easily as the hounds. Andry now wore a look of sorrow, his frown deepening with every body falling dead beneath his blade.

And Valtik was gone again, of course, as *always*.

Behind them all, Corayne circled, searching the graveyard and the church.

"I can feel it," she said again, her voice rasping with smoke. "This way!"

She took off and Sorasa swore, ducking under an undead guard's sword so she could follow her. The others did the same, turning tail from the oncoming horde. Corayne sprinted through the graves, leaping over tombstones, her braid trailing out behind her. She wavered back and forth, desperate in her search. The realm depended on it.

The destroyed church loomed, with more undead still crawling out of the ruins. They were slower, far more injured, moving on broken limbs or clutching lolling heads. At the sight of Corayne, they moaned as one and changed direction, aiming for her.

"All these people, they're after Corayne," Sorasa hissed, hoping Dom would hear her. Hoping he would understand what it meant.

The Elder made a strangled sound, a strange noise between a grunt and a shout.

Ahead of them, Corayne rounded the corner of the church, into a garden. She skidded to a halt, almost falling to her knees. The blood drained from her face and she puffed out a gasp of surprise.

Sorasa slid after her, agile and quick, never losing her balance. Until she looked up, and her heart quailed.

An old, giant rosebush grew over the garden like a canopy, its thorny branches twisted and gnarled. Despite the winter and the falling snow, it stood in full bloom, garishly bright against the smoke. Old limbs splintered and fell apart as the vines curled onto themselves, shedding dead limbs as they spread. The green leaves and fat, bloodred roses seemed to grow before Sorasa's own eyes, flourishing in the destruction. Thorns glinted like daggers among the vines.

And something gold glimmered in the trunk, filtering between the flowers with impossible light.

The Spindle.

But Corayne did not step forward or draw her Spindleblade. Someone guarded the way.

We knew he would be waiting, Sorasa told herself, but it didn't make him any easier to see.

Taristan of Old Cor sat beneath the roses, perched on a stone bench with his Spindleblade across his knees. He looked worse than he had in the palace, having traded his velvets for old leather and a worn cloak. His dark red hair fell about his shoulders, matching the odd sheen in his black eyes. The scarlet-robed wizard, Ronin, loomed at his side, his bone-white fingers like claws. As he twisted one hand, the undead horde sounded out a bloodcurdling scream.

Without thought, Sorasa pulled a dagger from her belt and threw the blade.

It hurtled through the air, perfectly aimed, the steel of it gleaming.

But the dagger turned to ash inches from Taristan's heart, and the wizard laughed. He broke his stare to look at Sorasa, his horrible, red-rimmed eyes roving over her body. She felt them like a cold hand and shivered.

Dom shouldered in front of her, stepping between Sorasa and the cursed two.

"Domacridhan!" Taristan crowed, as if he faced an old friend.

The Elder raised his blade in reply.

With a spin, Sorasa braced her back against Dom's, facing out into the graveyard. Hundreds of undead shadows moved through the smoke, still lunging forward, still hell-bent on killing Corayne and whoever stood in their way. Sorasa assessed the situation as she'd been taught, balancing odds. Next to her, Sigil struggled to stand but raised her ax. Andry grabbed for Corayne, but she was frozen, rooted to the spot.

There was nowhere to run anyway. Nowhere to turn.

Sorasa licked her lips and looked skyward. She wished she could see the moon or the sun, whichever hung above them now. The face of Lasreen. She prayed in her head, begging for a miracle.

None came.

"You are beaten, Immortal," Taristan growled, and Sorasa felt Dom flinch against her back.

The hands of the undead reached out, too many to cut apart, though Sorasa certainly tried.

31
FOR NOTHING
Corayne

The undead wrestled Andry, Sorasa, and Sigil to the ground, forcing them to their knees. Corayne could only watch, horrified. All three struggled in vain, arms wrenched behind their backs as the sheer number of bodies overpowered them. Their weapons fell to the ground, sword, dagger, and ax. Tears sprang to Corayne's eyes as Andry held her gaze, his breath coming hard and fast through flared nostrils. She wanted to shut her eyes, to somehow stop her own heart from breaking. *This is all a nightmare. I'm going to wake up in some cold field, with all of us still riding toward this hell.*

Corayne did not wake.

But the undead did not kill her friends.

Because they have not been commanded to, she realized with a start, looking back to Ronin. *Yet.*

The wizard clenched his fist, and the undead tightened their grasp on the others. Her fear turned to rage, both for her friends and for all beneath his thrall. Somehow the ragged red rat held sway over the corrupted bodies of Gidastern's dead. Corayne wanted to rip the smile off his horrible white face, but she kept still. She angled her body so she could see both Andry and Taristan at the same time. And to do as Sorasa had taught: give her enemies a smaller target.

Only Dom remained at her side, the last Companion left standing one more time.

Flames ran along the rooftops around the churchyard, leaping at the edge of Corayne's vision. *The hounds*, she thought, gritting her teeth. Their barking roars echoed through the graves as they gathered like vultures waiting for a kill. *Does Ronin command them too?*

Behind him, the Spindle glimmered through the branches of the cursed rosebush. The roses perfumed the air, cloying with their scent, the fragrance heavy as the smoke. They grew before her eyes, born of the Spindle, born of winter-dead seeds burned back to life. Their thorns were long as her hand, black and needle sharp.

Taristan rose slowly, without urgency, unfolding his long limbs to straighten up. He gripped the hilt of his Spindleblade, letting the sword pass in a lazy arc at his side. He did not fear the hounds or the undead, barely glancing at them. He wasn't concerned with Dom either. His eyes slid from the immortal to Corayne, delighted by their predicament. A red sheen flared in the black, and Corayne shuddered.

It felt like looking at the shadow through the Spindle, the echo of What Waits.

"How did you become this?" Corayne bit out, scowling.

Taristan was still a mortal man, Corblood or not. His heart beat the same as her own. But he was somehow so much worse. "What twisted you into this monster?"

He only grinned. Corayne half expected a burst of fangs instead of teeth.

"Is it monstrous to want what is owed you?" Taristan said, stalking toward her. "I don't think so, Corayne."

Her name in his mouth made her feel sick.

She grimaced and gripped her long knife. Her body itched, her muscles tightening all over. She shifted her weight to the balls of her feet, as Sorasa had taught, putting some bend in her legs. Taristan watched her pull into the fighting stance with a look of amusement, a smirk curling on his thin lips.

Corayne bristled. On her back, the Spindleblade hummed with magic, sensing the portal.

"No one is owed the world," she said. "Not even the greatest king, and you are certainly far from that."

The insult broke against Taristan like water on stone. He barely felt it and put out his hand instead. White veins stood out at his wrist, running beneath his sleeve. They looked like dead worms.

"Give me the blade," he said.

With a growl, Dom stepped between them, his greatsword pointed at Taristan's heart.

Taristan did not move or seem to notice the blade hovering inches from his chest. And for good reason. It would not harm him, and they all knew it.

Corayne's mind whirred, trying to formulate some sort of plan. *We are surrounded, pinned down by a dead army, fire hounds, a city burning to the ground*. She looked sidelong, meeting Sorasa's flaring eyes. The assassin's gaze burned like the rooftops around them. Behind her, more undead pressed into the churchyard, forming a thick circle around the Companions and the roses. Slowly, Sorasa tipped her head from side to side. She didn't have a plan either.

Because there was only one plan to be had.

"How many people must die for your selfish dream?" Corayne barked, whirling back to Taristan. "For *hers*?"

At the mention of his wretched queen, something sparked in Taristan. His smirk disappeared and he threw back the folds of his cloak. Corayne expected finer clothing for a prince but knew this was Taristan as he chose to be. A rogue, a murderer, a mercenary behind someone else's throne.

"I would hope you would be lucky enough to find someone to share your ambitions, as I have. But I doubt you'll survive the afternoon," he answered hotly. Then he eyed Dom's blade, still raised and ready. "Has he forgotten how to speak since I last saw him?"

Corayne glared. "No, he's just thinking of all the ways he's going to kill you."

"Well, he's failed twice before," Taristan replied, settling back into his smooth manner. He gave a nod to Ronin, and the wizard spun his hand, fingers gnarled like the branches above his head.

With a wet snarl, three undead lurched forward and seized Dom by the arms, trying to drag him down. The immortal snarled back and threw them off, their bodies slamming against the nearby graves. Stone cracked and split, spines snapped, but the undead were undeterred, pushed on by Ronin's clawed fingers.

They eventually overwhelmed the Elder, and wrestled him to his knees, his body half covered in walking corpses.

"Coward," Dom ground out, breathing hard against the arms wrapped around his neck.

Corayne could only watch, her heartbeat ramming in her ears.

Taristan raised a single brow. "Coward?" he said, crooking a finger.

Behind him, Ronin did the same, and the undead fell back, freeing Dom. The immortal wasted no time, a blur as he closed the distance between them. He hit Taristan with the force of a marauding bear, his massive hands going to his neck. Corayne tensed, eyes wide. She expected him to tear Taristan's head clean off, but her uncle snarled back, gripping Dom's wrists with long, slim fingers. Corayne watched in horror as the mortal peeled off Dom's grip, Elder that he was. Somehow, Taristan was now stronger. He wrapped a hand around Dom's throat instead and squeezed, lifting him clean off the ground.

"Call me a coward again, Domacridhan," Taristan said in a low, dangerous voice. Above him, Dom's face was unchanged, set with rage. But his skin began to purple.

He struck hard, kicking and punching at Taristan. It did nothing.

"Don't," Corayne heard herself whisper, her voice lost in the chaos.

On the ground, Sorasa strained at her captors. They only pinned her down, holding her head to the dirt and grave dust.

Suddenly, Taristan let Dom drop. The undead scrambled to hold him again, forcing him onto all fours.

"Funny, you Elders raised my brother," Taristan said as Dom wheezed, gasping for air. "But I'm more like his precious immortals than he could ever be."

At Ronin's command, the undead shoved Dom's head down, his body bent. He looked like a prisoner before the headsman's block, awaiting execution.

Taristan raised the Spindleblade in both hands.

Without hesitation, Corayne stepped sideways, planting herself between Dom and Taristan's sword. She raised her own long knife, ready to parry his blow.

Again, he laughed. "Is that supposed to be a sword?"

"You're not as strong as you think you are," she snapped, with a laugh of her own. It echoed darkly through the yard. "Not when the realm rises against you."

"The realm," Taristan spat, lowering his sword an inch. "So many splintered kingdoms and countries, all set against each other, all concerned with their own foolish endeavors. This realm is broken. It deserves to be conquered and claimed."

Corayne didn't falter. "And turned into this? Into the Ashlands?" Her brow dipped, her face going grim. Taristan's eyes bored into her own, the black orbs nearly eaten by hellish red. "I *saw* it."

To her surprise, her uncle wavered, the red flickering in his eye disappearing for an instant. He blinked at her, his jaw going tight. The white veins on his neck strained, suddenly jumping. A strange look crossed his face and Corayne knew it well. *Fear.* She delighted in it, knowing she struck a blow against a man who could not be harmed by steel or flame.

"You never have," she sneered, shaking her head. "He didn't show you what it means to be overthrown. This realm cracked with his own, consumed by Asunder. You didn't *see*."

Taristan only growled, adjusting his stance and grip, lowering the sword to Corayne's height. The blade mirrored her reflection. She looked terrible, covered in soot and dust, tear tracks running down her face. Her braid was a wild tangle, her black eyes broken.

Her uncle hissed down on her, his hot breath like smoke. "I will be an emperor like my ancestors before me. I will rule this realm as destiny demands."

Corayne held her ground. "You will be ashes beneath His feet."

"Give me the blade," he said again. "Or they die."

Behind her, she heard the undead press down on the Companions. But her friends remained silent, bent but not broken, resolute before their doom. The smoke stung Corayne's throat, making her eyes water. Hot tears gathered, threatening to fall. But she refused to weep in front of her uncle. She would not give him the satisfaction.

"If I give you the blade, we're all doomed anyway," she murmured.

Taristan only shrugged, greedy eyes moving from her face to the Spindleblade behind her shoulder. His brother's sword. The last remnant of her father upon the Ward.

She thought of What Waits, his shadow clear before her. He'd offered her a kingdom for surrender. A small piece of her wondered if it would have been smarter to take it, to barter for their lives. To live on their knees, if it meant they would still live.

Her pulse hammered in her ears, cut with the thunderous

booms of collapsing buildings. The flames ringed the churchyard, holding back like the hounds and the undead. Her chest tightened, overwhelmed by the impossibility of it all. Taristan held each and every card.

But one.

The Jydi horn sounded through the city, followed by the Treckish howl.

The noise broke his focus, just long enough. Corayne dropped her knife and rolled, catching Taristan off guard. He swung the Spindleblade but missed, misjudging her speed. In the same motion she swiped out her forearm, catching him across the face as Sorasa had taught her. The Dragonclaws dragged over his skin, the spikes of steel cutting a long gash across his cheek. He yelped and sprang back, reeling, the Spindleblade still in his grip.

Like the fire, he threw off a feverish heat. All black had gone from his eyes, replaced with a livid blood red. He gingerly touched his face, feeling the sudden well of blood from ragged flesh. His eyes widened, puzzled and afraid.

Corayne smirked, raising her Dragonclaws. The steel spikes dripped red.

"You're indestructible to most things, Taristan," she said. Overhead, the blizzard swirled. "But not all."

In her mind's eye, Corayne saw the old witch on the deck of a ship, chanting over her Dragonclaws with herbs and old bones. Whatever she did many weeks ago seemed to have stuck.

Jydi blessings. Bone magic.

Ibalet beliefs. Godly echoes.

Valtik's power. Isadere's gift.

In the corners of the churchyard, the army appeared, Elder and Jydi and Treckish together, swords and arrows and shields flashing. They cut through the scores of undead like a hot knife through butter. Corayne could not dare to hope, but relief coursed through her anyway.

The play for time worked.

"Hold them off!" Taristan snarled, clutching his bleeding face.

Behind him, the hounds leapt from the rooftops, jumping down into the yard to join the fray. Their flames spread rapidly, setting fire to the dry grass between the graves. And the undead burned too, their clothes catching light.

Ronin stumbled forward, fingers twitching. His eyes reflected the blooming fire, going red as his robes. "No—"

On the ground, Dom lurched against his undead bindings, throwing them off with a roar to rival giants. He grabbed for his sword and swung with abandon, freeing the others with a few precise cuts of the blade.

Corayne lunged for them but something grabbed her collar, throwing her deeper into the rose garden. She landed hard against the ground, her head spinning from the collision. But she forced herself up, fighting the dizziness, trying to get back to her feet. Voices called for her somewhere, but a figure blocked them out, his white hand reaching over her shoulder.

She flinched away, but it wasn't her body that Taristan grabbed for.

Her Spindleblade sang from its sheath, its steel bared to the flame and roses. Taristan's fingers wrapped around the hilt, white against the leather. Corayne saw death in the edge of the blade, thin as the Spindle. Without thought, she reached for it but fell over on the grass, her head still spinning.

Her vision cleared long enough to see Taristan's wicked smile, two blades in his hands. The Spindle burned behind him, its golden light reflected in the swords. Though identical to his own, Corayne's blade looked wrong in his grasp. Its jewels seemed to glow, pulsing with her own rage and sorrow.

"Don't—" she heard herself scream as he raised her Spindleblade high.

Will I feel it? she thought dimly, bracing for the sharp bite of steel at her neck.

Instead he brought the sword crashing down on the bench.

The stone broke in two.

And the Spindleblade shattered with it, shards of steel exploding across the garden.

Corayne felt each one pierce her living heart.

Despite the battle rolling across the graves, despite Dom and the Companions fighting their way toward her, despite the inferno, the smoke, the snowstorm—Corayne's world fell away. All went slow and silent, frozen before her eyes. She heard nothing, felt nothing. Her body dragged itself through the dirt, hands scrabbling for the fragments of her Spindleblade.

A boot stomped down on her hand and everything returned with blistering speed. Corayne cried out in pain, rolling onto her back.

"Now, where were we?" Taristan said, tossing the ruined hilt into the roses. The light of the jewels guttered and died, Cortael's sword a ruin in the dirt.

Just like my father, Corayne thought, cradling her hand. *Broken and gone.*

Taristan's shadow fell over her and she recoiled. Bleary-eyed, she raised her Dragonclaws to her uncle, the vambraces her only weapon against a man turned to monster. He batted them away with ease and seized her by the collar, using the neck of her tunic to drag her across the garden.

She tried to struggle but he was far stronger than she was. No amount of hacking could break his grip, even as her vambraces drew blood.

The Companions ran for her but Taristan pulled her upright and put his Spindleblade to her throat. Corayne swallowed against cold steel, the world spinning around her. She saw Andry in the spiral, his brown eyes rimmed with red. She tried to hold on to the sight, but Taristan dragged her away, her body flailing over dirt and then stone.

The steps of the ruined church dragged beneath her, every inch forward another inch away from the Spindle. And still she fought, limbs flailing.

Satisfied, Taristan halted and pulled her straight, forcing her flagging body to stand before the decimated churchyard and the streets beyond. Above them, the carcass of the church loomed, its columns and archways like exposed ribs, a single stained-glass window looking down like a great eye. Corayne squinted, trying to see straight, trying to find something to hold on to. Noise and color seemed to blend, inscrutable. Her heart beat too quickly in her chest, her stomach churning with sickness. The broken shards of Cortael's blade rose up before her eyes, still filled with red-and-gold light. She reached for them, but her hands touched only air.

"I am Taristan of Old Cor, blood of the Spindles!" her captor shouted, still holding the blade to her throat. Corayne could barely stand, her head swimming. "The last of my kind."

The shards remained, turning slowly before Corayne's eyes, losing their glow. They changed to mirrors, each one holding a different face. Andry, Sorasa, Dom, Charlie, Sigil, Valtik. She wanted to weep but had no more tears left to give. The faces looked back from the reflecting steel, waiting for her. Then one more face appeared, and Corayne went rigid, a sob in her throat.

I will never see my mother again, she knew, looking into Meliz's eyes. The captain of the *Tempestborn* glanced back, smiling, bronzed and bold as Corayne remembered. Again, Corayne reached out, and again felt nothing there.

The sword at her neck bit against her flesh, drawing blood. Corayne hissed and smashed back her head, trying to butt against Taristan. He laughed over her, his chest trembling against her shoulders.

"You have the Cor spirit, that much is true," he said, his voice going oddly gentle. "This death is well earned."

"And blessed are the burned," said a crowing voice, the familiar cackle of an old woman.

Out of the corner of her eye, Valtik's face wavered—and became real. The witch ascended the steps of the church, still astride her strange horse. Her blue eyes seemed to burn hotter than any flame, bright as lightning.

Then a black shadow fell over them, a hot wind bearing down, sudden and strong as a hurricane. Behind her, Taristan jolted, his grip on Corayne loosening a little.

Many things happened all at once.

The cathedral window exploded outward in a hail of colored glass as the dragon landed, its four-legged body as big as the skeletal ruins, its wings as wide as the churchyard. Its deafening roar shook everything in an earthquake. Corayne fell to her knees, clutching her ears, as Taristan whirled, the dragon's head bobbing high above him.

Valtik's hands were cold on Corayne's face, her whisper going through her like winter wind.

The spinning stopped. Her eyes sharpened. All nausea and dizziness disappeared and Corayne jumped to her feet, single-minded. Below the steps, the living army surged in all directions, some scattering from the dragon, some running right for it. Corayne could no longer tell one soldier from the other. They were all covered in blood now.

No matter their heritage, Elder or mortal, mercenary or raider, each one of them bled the same.

Without hesitation, she turned—and ran for Taristan.

Ronin in his scarlet robes flashed in the corner of her eye, scurrying toward them. His fingers curled, reaching up to the dragon. Ronin gave a yell of frustration and the creature bellowed, almost knocking Corayne off her feet. Taristan stumbled too. The dragon flapped its wings again, kicking up a windstorm over the city. The hounds roared in protest, some of them leaping at the dragon itself. They were all swatted away, landing hard in broken heaps of ash.

"Under my command—" Ronin shouted, knotting his hands in desperation.

Then Valtik leapt into his path, the old woman a wall between the dragon and the red wizard.

Her eyes flashed. "Under *my* command," she echoed, twisting her fingers.

With an explosive crack, Ronin's leg snapped beneath him and he howled, collapsing sideways, clutching at the broken bone.

"You meddling old *bitch!*" the wizard screamed, his red eyes like living fire. His shriek carried between them, forceful as a blow.

But Valtik didn't flinch, her bony fingers still clawed in the air. Her thin lips formed a devilish smirk. "Better bitch than wizard broken, the gods of the Ward have spoken."

The dragon remained free, its scales black and glistening, set with countless precious stones. Jet, ruby, onyx, garnet. No better shield existed across the realms. Its eyes were black too, but its menacing teeth were white. It stared at Taristan and Taristan stared back, terrified.

"Under my command," Taristan said, raising the Spindleblade. But he had no magic, not like Ronin. Corblood or not, he could not control the dragon as Ronin did the undead, or the corpse army of the Ashlands.

The dragon was its own monster, with no allegiance or loyalty. To anyone.

Its long, snaking throat seemed to glow, a fireball rising up from its belly. Smoke poured between its jaws as it rose up to its full menacing height, taller than the church steeple ever was.

Taristan raised his Spindleblade as Corayne ran. Her legs pumped beneath her with all speed as she aimed for her uncle.

And then an Amhara whip curled around his wrist, pulling hard.

From within the fray, Corayne heard Sorasa's piercing laughter.

Taristan buckled in surprise, his grip on the sword failing. It clattered to the steps as Corayne reached him. She closed her hands on the hilt, never breaking stride.

Flames erupted behind her as she sprinted, disappearing into the battle beneath the church. She never looked back, but she felt the fireball's heat, exploding over the spot where Taristan stood.

Sorasa was first to her side, coiling her whip as they ran, finding holes within the breaking tide of their own allies and the undead. Andry appeared next, holding off the undead with the skill of a knight. Dom ran close behind, Sigil under one arm, the pair of them spinning with greatsword and ax in some kind of hellish wheel.

"The Spindle!" Corayne shouted, but the dragon roared, spitting another burst of flame.

The garden went up before her eyes, consumed by fire, the gold of the Spindle still winking within. Even so, Corayne took a step toward it, only for Sorasa to grab her by the neck.

"It's over—leave it," she heard the assassin breathe, dragging her backward. Away from the church, away from the garden.

Away from the roses and the Spindle.

"Then this is all for nothing," Corayne screamed back, the

world spinning again. But not from injury. It was failure that clutched her now.

Andry took her other side, pushing her along. "Not if you *live*!"

Gidastern burned.

The way back to the main gates was destroyed, the streets swallowed up by fire and destruction. They could only stumble along, clutching each other, bleeding and scorched, their skin black with smoke.

What now? Corayne wanted to scream. She also wanted to lie down in the gutter, her body threatening to drop. Her fingers ached, clawed to Taristan's Spindleblade, the leather beneath her skin burning hot. But she dared not let go.

She looked back down the street, toward the churchyard. The living army ran in every direction, most on foot, with the majority of Oscovko's cavalry gone or dead. Through the buildings, the dragon screamed and tossed, fighting off the Infyrna hounds, monster against monster. With a snarl, the dragon took flight, bursting into the air with one beat of its black wings. To Corayne's dismay, it seemed to be following their path.

The hounds kept up their hunt, leaping onto the collapsing rooftops and sprinting down the streets after the dragon. The undead moved with them, giving chase like children following an older sibling.

Andry swore loudly as they gained, forgetting his manners in the face of death.

"There's another gate," Sorasa said, her breath even despite her pace. She raised a hand to point. "Near the eastern docks. It spits you out onto the coast and back along the Cor road."

"Domacridhan!" A woman's voice rang out behind them, gaining fast.

Over her shoulder, Corayne glimpsed Dom's cousin, the Elder princess, along with a contingent of immortal warriors and a few Jydi, the blond chief among them.

Dom showed a rare grin but didn't stop, none of them breaking stride. It would be their death, and the death of the Ward.

Corayne's legs burned with exertion, but she matched Andry's pace next to her, hemmed in tight among the Companions.

"Charlie was smart to sit this one out," she panted.

If only I'd done the same.

Andry only huffed. His tunic was torn and bloody, ruined almost beyond recognition. The sight turned Corayne's stomach, not because of the gore, but for what it meant for Andry Trelland.

They kept running, Sorasa in the lead with Dom and Princess Ridha fanned out behind. Sigil limped along between them, fighting to keep pace as best she could. The city burned and the hounds roared, the dragon circling overhead, the streets and alleys crumbling together. But Sorasa kept them moving, always sliding and turning, winding a serpentine path toward the dock gate. They left footprints in the falling ash, the blizzard still swirling beneath the pulse of the dragon's wings.

Finally they found a half-clear street running up close to the city walls. Corayne almost wanted to climb them, but the flames jumped and spat, giving no quarter. She found herself dreaming of the port and plunging into the icy waves.

A rider jumped out from an alley, careening around a bend at blistering speed. Corayne squinted at him as he rode, not for the sea, but directly toward them. The horse was coal black, bigger than the shaggy horses the war band rode. And the rider was all in black armor, the metal gleaming, too dark to be steel. Even at a glance, she knew he wasn't one of Oscovko's men, or anyone else's.

"Go," she heard Ridha bellow as she all but shoved Sorasa into the closest alley. The Elder princess did the same to Corayne and Andry, her immortal strength making them skid through the ash and snow.

Sorasa whirled. "What are you—"

"There's no time," Ridha barked back, drawing her sword. The green steel of her armor looked sickly in the firelight. "Dom, get her out of here—"

The black horse slammed into Ridha's body, sending her spinning out into the street. Her armor ripped sparks along the paved stones.

Dom roared out in anguish and ran to his cousin, sliding to his knees at her side.

Her warriors reacted as one, jumping at the black rider. The Jydi screamed too, led by their chief. She roared loudest of all, giving a shuddering cry before leaping onto the rider's back. He tossed her bodily against the wall, her head colliding with a sick crack.

Ridha roared a guttural sound and fought to her feet, sword still in hand. Dom rose with her, his teeth bared, his blade shining. The pair of them were the sun and moon, golden and black-haired. They faced the rider together, even as he rode over the Jydi, splitting throats with a horrible black blade.

Numbness crept over Corayne as she watched, the edges of the world turning to flame. "Dom," she murmured, trying to call for him.

But Sigil pushed her on, deeper into the alley. She limped, wincing with every step.

"He'll be right behind us," she said. "Follow Sorasa."

The assassin stood half in shadow, watching the black knight bear down on the immortals, felling them one by one. Her copper eyes followed every pass of his blade.

"Don't worry about the immortal brute," she murmured, her voice tight. She gestured for Andry and Corayne to keep going. "We're close."

Corayne wanted to scream against every step without him, the alley twisting farther and farther away. Then the street was gone entirely, the sound of hooves and steel swallowed up by flame and the dragon's pounding wings. Andry kept on beside her, his eyes forward, his brown skin beaded with sweat. His face seemed a mask, pulled down to hide the terror they all felt.

With a swoop of her stomach, Corayne looked around.

"Where's Sigil?" she bit out, half a scream.

Up ahead, Sorasa faltered. Her steps slowed but she did not turn. "Keep moving," she hissed.

Corayne ignored her, glaring back down the alley. "Sigil!"

A familiar form slumped away around the distant corner, her shadow rippling in the firelight as she made her way back to the street. Her ax dangled from her hand, the last piece of her to disappear.

"Keep moving," Sorasa said again, louder now. Her voice went raw with emotion.

Corayne could only pray Sigil's iron bones would hold against the black knight's wrath.

The next road was another ruin, choked with debris and a wave of the undead, all scrambling through the burning rubble. They broke through walls and doorways, pawing at the air, grasping for whatever skin they could reach. Corayne shrieked and stabbed one away, Andry another. But as in the churchyard, their numbers only grew. Sorasa urged the Companions on, her own daggers flashing like serpent's fangs. They fought their way along, gaining some ground, but not enough.

Dread clutched at Corayne, its grip tighter than the hands of the undead. She looked up, searching for some sliver of sky between the plumes of smoke. Even the snow was gone, the blizzard losing its resolve. She did too.

Horse's hooves nearly sent her to her knees and she whirled, expecting to see the murderous knight or Taristan himself, fresh from the dragon's fire.

Instead it was Valtik on her strange gray horse, its breath steaming in the air, as if it stood upon the tundra instead of a burning street.

"The boy I'll take," she said, jumping out of the saddle. She grasped for Andry with one hand and threw the reins with the other. Sorasa caught them deftly, her bronze face flushed red. "Corayne, you follow the snake."

The air seared from Corayne's lungs, even as the undead surrounded them, pressing in from all sides. She looked to Andry and found him staring, his mask shattered, every emotion warring on his face. Corayne felt them too, each keen and cutting as a knife.

Shame, regret, sadness. And anger, so much anger.

She opened her mouth to protest, only for Andry to seize her under the arms and throw her up into the saddle. His lips were fire on her palm, grazing the bare skin, before he wrenched himself away. It was the only farewell he gave, and Corayne's heart bled, too many words bubbling up inside her throat.

None seemed right. None would be enough.

"We'll meet you on the road," Sorasa barked, jumping up behind Corayne. She looped the reins, bracing herself against Corayne's back.

The horse reacted without command, bolting off down the street, leaving Andry Trelland and the old witch behind. To face the horde or be consumed by it. It only took a few strides of the horse for the smoke to swallow them up.

Corayne felt hollow from the inside out, as if her own heart had been carved from her chest.

Sorasa was not Sigil, born to the saddle, but she rode like a demon. The flames of Infyrna raged and she raged with them, coaxing the horse through narrower and narrower gaps in the fire. Even Corayne lost their heading, unable to tell north from south, but Sorasa never did, riding on and on, until Corayne caught a gasp of fresh salt air. The docks were close, and with them, the sea gate.

Behind them, the wave of undead rolled on. With a gasp, Corayne recognized Jydi among them, and Treckish warriors too. On the rooftops, the hounds kept up the pursuit, though the dragon was gone, disappeared into the smoky sky. Corayne hoped it had Taristan in its belly.

She bent low over the horse's mane, trying to urge it faster. But even Valtik's horse struggled to gallop under the weight of two riders.

"There," Sorasa called, and Corayne raised her eyes to see it: the side gate of Gidastern.

It was blissfully open, portcullis raised, the wood already charred to nothing. *At least the gods smiled on one thing today.*

The hounds bayed, their sharp, stuttering calls echoing all over, but Corayne ignored them. She kept her focus ahead, on the gate, on the glimpse of road beyond, the sea crashing. Empty, open land. Freedom from this hell. The others would be waiting for them, whole and safe. Dom, Andry, Sigil, Charlie, Valtik. She saw their faces in the shards again, the broken steel shimmering like a mirage in the sand dunes.

Suddenly the reins were in her own hands, and the strong, bracing presence at her back was gone. Her eyes widened as she turned to see Sorasa leaping from the saddle, her body tucking into a ball as she hit the street.

Corayne felt her mouth open, a yell loosing from her own throat, but she couldn't hear it. She tugged hard on the reins. It did nothing but make the horse faster, its hooves sending up sparks on the stone. The hounds quickened to match their pace, closing in.

Sorasa rolled to her feet and sprinted, not toward the undead wave or the hounds approaching, but to the gate, charging after the horse.

Screaming, Corayne leaned back over the mare's flank, stretching out a hand for the assassin as the archway passed overhead. But Sorasa ignored her, going instead to the gears of the portcullis.

With a kick, she loosed the mechanism and the iron bars fell into place, slamming shut inches behind the horse's tail.

Everything pulsed, flaring with the rhythm of Corayne's own heartbeat. Her mouth closed, her eyes still wide, as she watched the gate get smaller and smaller.

Sorasa's figure turned her back, blade and whip raised. Her shadow ran long against the road, guttering with the flames, twisting and dancing, all her lethal grace on display. Hounds yelped and undead moaned, but the portcullis never rose. The gate remained shut. The road guarded, the realm of Infyrna contained.

And Sorasa with it.

Corayne was alone, a mad horse beneath her, galloping with all the speed of the four winds.

The Cor road ran hard along the coast, turning to packed dirt as the horse carried them away from Gidastern. The cold blue sea crashed to her left, kicking up frigid spray. Corayne trembled, her face wet with the sea and tears. For once, saltwater brought her no comfort. Weeping, she raised her eyes to the sky and realized she was out from under the smoke, with gray light above her.

One last snowflake landed on her cheek, shivering her spine.

Her throat burned, ragged from the smoke and her own anguish.

Without warning, the horse slowed, blowing hard, its flanks dark with sweat. Up close, it seemed a common horse, a simple gray like the winter clouds. She tested the reins, trying to pull it around, but the horse held firm, stubbornly faced away. Corayne glared at it, cursing whatever Valtik had done to make the horse disobey her.

She felt sick and looked out at the empty landscape. There was only coast and dead farmland. *Another graveyard*, she thought, looking over her shoulder.

There was no one on the horizon. No one at the gates.

Not even Charlie.

She heaved a painful breath and wiped her face, her hands coming away black. Then, with a will, she unbuckled the sheath from her back, bringing it forward. Shivering, she gripped the black leather of the Spindleblade's hilt and drew an inch of the blade, the steel clean. Taristan had not drawn blood this day. Even so, the sword felt wrong in her hand. Again she mourned for the blade broken behind her, and all the people with it.

A failure, she thought, choking back a sob.

Andry's voice answered in her head, his words an echo.

Not if you live.

And that, at least, she could do.

32

THE FLAMES OF ASUNDER
Ridha

Her breath came in wet, heaving rasps. Blood bubbled up in her throat as it did from the wound in her chest, her life slowly seeping out into the street. The black knight was long gone, riding away after the dragon, but he left so much deadly evidence behind. Ridha's eyes rolled as she tried to move, her back flat against the ground. The other Vedera lay dead around her, their bodies still and quiet. The Jydi were gone too. Moaning low in her throat, Ridha saw Lenna crumpled against the city wall, her eyes open but unseeing.

The Temur woman still drew breath. She was propped up against a wall, her wounded leg stretched out in front of her. A large ax lay broken at her side; her chest rose and fell with labored breath. Ridha saw no other wounds on her. She almost laughed. A mortal lived where so many children of Glorian had died.

At least there is still Dom.

He crawled through the wreckage of the black knight, a belt lashed around his thigh to stem a bleeding wound. She tried to smile at him but only gasped, choking on another wash of blood.

"Don't speak," he said, reaching her side. With a hiss of pain, he set himself upright and pulled her head into his lap. "I'm here."

"So is she."

The white light of her mother's sending glowed to Ridha's left. If it was magic or a hallucination, Ridha could not know, but she was glad for it either way. Isibel's form wavered and then went solid, edged with a silver glow as she bent over her only child. She wept shimmering tears that disappeared before hitting Ridha's face.

"I wish I could be with you," her mother said, hands running over her face. No matter how hard she tried, Ridha could not feel them. "Sleep, my love."

She wanted to do as her mother told her, but Ridha of Iona clung to life, fading as it was. Her gray eyes wavered between Isibel and Domacridhan, trying to hold them both. He looked down at her, fresh tears coursing over his dirty cheeks.

The footsteps were faint, boots ringing on stone.

"Would you like to see what this Spindle gave me?"

Dom's face crumpled above her and he spun, trying to stand. But he collapsed on his wounded leg, dropping again, holding his body over Ridha's. Defending her from one last insult.

Taristan's cloak and clothes were burned, black all over, but his face was clean, his hair slicked back. The wizard limped at his side, leaning heavily on a makeshift crutch. Neither looked particularly pleased, in spite of their victory.

The Spindle was still open, the realm still ready to fall.

Before Dom could try to strike again, Ronin snapped his fingers, and a half-dozen undead surged forward, chains and bindings in hand. The same approached Sigil, tying her wrists and ankles before lifting her clean into the air. Both fought, but weakly, utterly spent by the battle.

Sound faded in and out, matching the beat of Ridha's slowing heart. She struggled for another second, another breath, eyes on her cousin as the undead bound him.

Then Taristan stepped between them, his leering face the only thing she could see.

"Another gift of What Waits," he said, standing over her like a tower, his eyes red as beacon fire.

Ridha cursed in Vederan. At her side, Isibel's sending flared white-hot with rage. The Monarch glared at Taristan, and Ridha dearly hoped this was truly her mother, and not some illusion born of death. *See what he is—see what must be fought*, she wept in her mind.

Taristan only shook his head. "You immortals take a long time to die," he muttered, before drawing a dagger.

Isibel wept too. "Sleep, my love," she begged.

It was the last thing Ridha heard as the blade plunged through her armor, into her heart.

But the last thing she saw was Taristan, the son of Old Cor, bent over her body, his eyes a burning blood red, yellow at the irises, like the heart of a flame. The eyes ate up the world, until she tipped forward, falling into the fire he now carried in his ruined soul. It consumed her, every inch burning, the pain like nothing she had ever felt before or would ever feel again. It was acid; it was boiling water; it was an inferno in her skin. Ridha of Iona hollowed out, her mind and soul torn away.

Her limbs moved, one hand twitching, then the other, even as her grasp on life disappeared. Ridha's soul pulled away, disappearing, leaving her body behind. And all went black.

ACKNOWLEDGMENTS

I feel so lucky I get to keep writing, and luckier still to continue this series. Realm Breaker continues to be my joy in difficult times.

As always, forever, my first thank-you goes to my parents. Without them, my words wouldn't exist. I don't know where I'd be without their support, and frankly, I don't want to think about it. I'm indebted to my brother as well, my first captive audience. Sometimes literally.

To my extended circle of friends and family, thank you for your constant support. Morgan, Jen, and Tori, my dearest ladies, you never let me fall down and you never let me slow down.

At home, my partner and my pup, Indy, are always there for every high and every low. You make the sun brighter. I love you both so much more than you'll ever understand. Mostly because one of you is a dog.

I'm just as blessed to have a wonderful circle of publishing friends who keep me honest, in check, and just sane. To the Patties, to Soman, to Sabaa, Adam, Jenny, the East Side LA Coven, Emma, thank you for your friendship and guidance.

They say it takes a village to raise a child, and it certainly takes a village to publish a book. My own village happens to be spectacular. Alice continues to be my fearless editor, ready to tackle all the wild chapters I throw at her. Thank you to Erica for your wisdom and support. And so much love to Clare for staying on top of everything. To Alexandra, Karen, and Lana, thank you for making all of it *work*. To Vanessa and Nicole in production, thank you for making all of this *real*. To Jenna and Alison in design, thank you for making this *beautiful*. To Audrey, Sabrina, and Shannon in marketing, thank you for making this *connect*. To Jenn and Anna, thank you for making this *known*. To my sensitivity readers, who made this *thoughtful*. To the Epic Reads crew, thank you for making this *fun*. I am so indebted to all of you, and know how much you've done to make the Realm Breaker series the success it's become. *And* for all your continued work on our first baby, Red Queen.

I feel overly blessed to be represented by New Leaf Literary, and especially Suzie Townsend. She has been my north star since the beginning of my career, and I hope I never lose sight of her. Thank you to Pouya, for never giving up on anything ever. To Jo, for her boundless vision. To Veronica and Victoria, for all the globetrotting, as well as my foreign agents around the world. To Hilary and Meredith, who feel like my own personal safety nets. To Kendra, Sophia, and Katherine, who never miss a beat, and keep this whole thing running. Thank you to Elena Stokes, for holding my hand down a new path. And to Steve, my legal shield and friend. On the entertainment side, thanks to Michael, Roxie, and Ali. You guys elevate me to new heights; I'm so grateful to keep working with you all!

Most of all, I must always say thank you to the readers, educators, librarians, bloggers, Instagrammers, TikTokers—thank you to everyone who picks up a book and passes it on. You are the reason our community exists, and why we continue to thrive. Writing and reading feel like a solitary endeavor, but it isn't one, because of you. Your continued support means more than I can say, because you make me who I am. I'm so grateful to keep writing stories for you, to live in your head as you live in mine.

All my love, forever,
Victoria

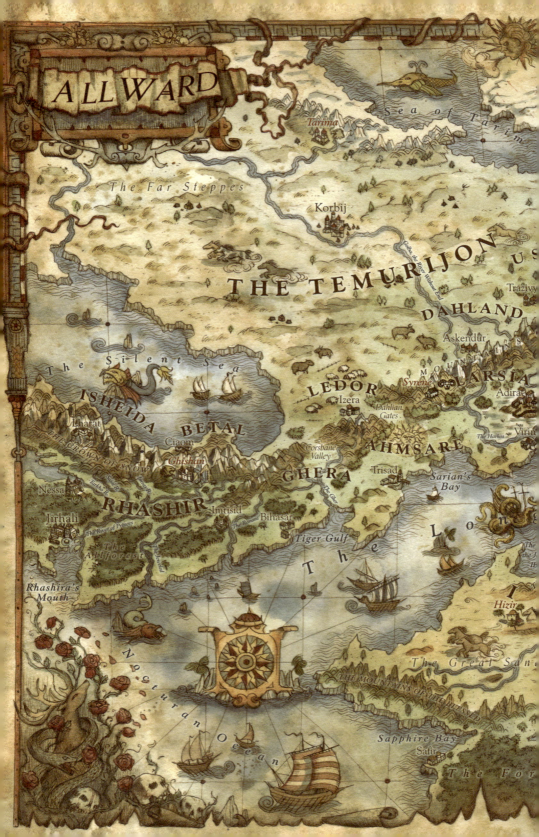